A LIFE OF SHADOWS

THE REDEMPTION SAGA

KRISTEN BANET

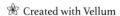 Created with Vellum

To those who walk through the dark:
There's light on the other side.
Sometimes, the journey is long.
Sometimes, the journey is lonely.
Sometimes, the journey seems hopeless.
Don't give up hope.
You are brave.
You are strong.
And you are not alone.

GLOSSARY

GENERAL TERMS

- Ability Rankings - Common, Uncommon, Rare, Mythic. A simple system created to judge how rare abilities are among the Magi.
- Burnout - When a Magi uses all their magical energy and must consume life force to continue.
- Doppelganger - Magi with the sole ability to shape-shift into other human beings. (Legend)
- Doppler – Slang for Doppelganger
- Druids - Female Magi with a plethora of natural abilities. They take over large areas of uninhabited land as caretakers. (Legend)
- Imp - Derogatory term for agents with the IMPO.
- International Magi Armed Services (IMAS) – The Magi's military in case of war against non-Magi or an uprising against the WMC.
- International Magi Police Organization (IMPO) – The Magi's organization for tracking down Magi criminals across the globe.
- Legend – A unique groupings of Magi. They are of equal power and have the same abilities per

group. Incredibly rare. Many non-Magi legends have their roots in these Magi.

- Magi - Humans with magic. They have anywhere from 1 to 5 abilities and a magical Source.
- Reading - A ceremony after a Magi comes into their magic, where a Magi who can 'read' (see Ability Glossary), discovers all the Magi's abilities. This information is then recorded for the Registrar.
- Registrar - A documentation system for recording all Magi and their powers during their teenage years. Viewing a Registrar entry requires approval by the WMC. Magi are required to submit to having a Registrar entry made via a Reading. There are lists Magi can join for public use, such as lists of healers in case of a global crisis, also kept with the Registrar.
- Source - The well of magical power inside a Magi. It's two-fold in how it can be measured—strength and depth. How powerful a Magi is versus how much magic they can do before running out of energy.
- Vampyr - Magi with the sole ability "borrow" abilities from others. They can also become immortal by "feeding" off a non-Magi's life force. (Legend)
- The World Magi Council (WMC) – The governing body over Magi. A group of 15 individuals voted into power every ten years.

1

SAWYER

JUNE 2017

S awyer stood quietly on the roof of the skyscraper, looking down to the second, lower roof. Her black domino mask was hot. Sweat already stung her eyes, and the job hadn't even started yet. Her cloth face guard was sweltering, making her neck itch. She hated needing all this shit, but protecting her face from cameras was important.

She heaved a sigh and jumped. Instead of falling between the two buildings, as no one could have made that jump, she rolled through her landing on the other roof. To any onlooker, it would have appeared she teleported from one roof to the other. She had, so they wouldn't be insane. Though they might not have believed their eyes, even knowing magic was real. Blinking wasn't the most common magical ability around, but it was one of hers.

"Get in, get out," she mumbled to herself as she dusted herself off. She needed to shake the bad feeling she had about this job before it messed her up. "Get in, grab the files, then get out. Then I just need to drop them off with the middleman and get the fuck out of Los Angeles."

She readjusted the black long sleeve shirt she was wearing. The damn thing kept sticking to her, but she was working and even in the June heat of LA, she had to wear it. The black cargo pants didn't help, either. She wasn't in any real rush to get this done. She always planned these out so that she could take her time. Rushing led to mistakes, and Sawyer didn't make mistakes.

She strolled across the roof, not worried about security. Her research had told her that they didn't have any cameras installed on the roof. Two months of back-breaking research went into this job, just like any job she took. Was it worth ten million dollars? Damn right it was.

"Nearly one a.m.," she mumbled, checking her watch. Two more minutes. "Three night-security guards in the building; since it's a quiet night, two will be going on break instead of one because they don't take their jobs seriously enough. The third will have a cigarette with the others, thinking no one cares if he slacks on the job. I'll have twenty to thirty minutes to get into the server room, download the information, and leave. Plenty of time. No one will ever know I was here."

She tapped her foot, waiting for the moment she knew it was safe to go in through the roof access. The second she knew it was safe, she knelt and pulled her lockpick set out from a cargo pocket, getting to work with a master's efficiency. Once she heard the lock click open, she grinned. She could have walked through the door, but sometimes doing it the traditional way gave her more satisfaction.

Now it was time to have some real fun, she chuckled silently. She closed her eyes, touched her Source, the magic core of her being, and pulled out just a touch of power. She focused on her cloaking talent and knew the moment she disappeared from the world. When she reopened her eyes, the world was colorless—a side-effect of being cloaked by her magic.

Sawyer was a Magi, and she excelled in her craft. Not every Magi could cloak or even had similar abilities to her. They weren't pop culture wizards and witches with spells. Magi had abilities or talents that they could do and a Source to power those, a magic well of power that was unique in power and depth for every Magi. She could cloak, which was using magic to make herself invisible. It had its draw backs, but normally it was a very useful talent. She couldn't stay cloaked all night because it would drain her Source quickly, but staying invisible for this job wouldn't be the worst thing.

She stepped into the building, holding back a happy sigh at the blast of cold air from the AC. *Thank fuck.* It was so goddamn hot outside. She trotted down the stairs silently, keeping her feet light, even in the combat boots she wore. She'd been doing this for nearly seven years, so experience and muscle memory took over for the easy shit, like not making a ton of noise.

Getting to the server room was probably the most dangerous part of the plan. She moved quickly to an office that she knew was three floors above the server room she needed to be in. She let go of her cloak and watched the world become color again, though it was too dark to really change anything. Time for her third magic trick of the night, going through solid objects.

"Let's hope no one stayed late tonight," she sighed.

She had to do three blind drops to get into the room she needed. The first drop happened instantly. One moment she was standing in an empty office, the next moment she was slipping through the floor to land in the office below it. Phasing was a Common ability, though it had its limitations.

Going through something that was too thick, not having enough energy to make it, and solidifying too early was an awful way to die or lose limbs. If she wasn't careful, she could lose body parts, and she nearly never used phasing while using another ability. There was just too much to focus on.

She made the second drop without thinking about it. Phasing down through floors was a bit easier, since gravity took over. It involved ignoring the current floor and dropping down to the next, but she had to make sure she didn't drop through several floors, so it still required her utmost attention.

"One more." She reached into her pocket and pulled out the USB she needed for the server room. It would hack in, copy the files she needed, destroy the originals, and leave a virus for the dirt bag she was working against on this job.

She dropped one last time and groaned at the heat of the server room, but that wasn't what she should have been worried about.

A shield slammed over the room seconds later and she froze. Whoever made it was smart enough to make sure it went under her. Shields, or force fields, were made by a Magi who had the talent for it.

"My Shadow," a smooth, velvet voice crooned from behind her, "it's been too long."

Sawyer clenched a fist and closed her eyes. Shadow. No one had called her that for a very long time. Four years, to be precise. She turned to the source of the voice slowly, opening her eyes as she faced him. She pulled down the cloth that was over her mouth, letting it relax around her neck, so she could speak to the memory-made-real standing in the room with her.

"Axel," she tried to keep her tone light, but it wouldn't

fool the Italian man with dark curls standing across the room. Of all the people who could be there, this was the only one she hadn't been prepared for. Nothing ever could have prepared her for a run-in with him, and the spike of fear in her sent adrenaline coursing through her system. "Why are you here?"

"Really?" He chuckled and crossed his arms. She wanted to claw those olive-green eyes full of humor out of his head. She wanted to ruin the perfect, chiseled bone structure of his face. Sawyer had to bite back on her temper, on the violent anger and fear that made her veins feel hot and icy all at once. Air and heat were swirling around him, meaning she couldn't even think to attack him. Plus, if she was going to attack Axel, she would need to kill him; and she didn't have any weapons on her. She hadn't thought she would need them for this job. "Shadow, *love*, that's all you have to say?"

"It's all I have to say to you." She grinned unkindly. She needed to get out. Fuck the job and fuck the money. She didn't need it, and now she didn't want it. "I'm going to leave, and you're going to let me."

"Sadly," Axel sighed and stepped closer to her, "I'm here to finish something. Four long years, Shadow... Did you really think you could hide?"

"I'm not sure what you're talking about." Sawyer began stepping away, moving towards the door. She knew what he wanted, but damn, she didn't want to die tonight.

"You were supposed to die four years ago," he growled with a grin. "I told you the only way you were leaving my employment was in a coffin, but it seems killing you is more difficult than I thought."

"Well," Sawyer shrugged, inching even closer to the

door, "maybe you should take that up with the ass who should have checked to make sure I was dead."

"I already have," Axel chuckled. "Now, now, love... Don't play hard to get. I've got the room shielded, so you won't be leaving. We're going to have a long chat before I end your miserable existence."

The air left her lungs, and she began to suffocate. She watched him give a deadly smile, completely calm.

"Anything you want to say?" Axel asked with a chuckle as he stepped close to her. He thought he was being funny. Arrogant piece of shit.

She narrowed her eyes on him, and decided to give up on trying to breathe—now or in the future. She focused on his face and, once he was close enough, slammed her forehead into his.

The shield dropped, and air rushed into her lungs. Most Magi couldn't keep their magic going if they were suddenly hurt. Some could, but Axel so rarely had the tables turned on him that he was inept at it.

"Fuck you," Sawyer growled at him as she ran for the door, phasing through a wall into a different room at the last moment because fire engulfed the door she had planned to use. Seconds, it only took seconds to evade Axel's hands and make it into the next room. She looked around to see where she was and hissed as the wall behind her shook. Just as she was leaving the room, the only wall between her and Axel exploded outward. A chunk of drywall slammed into her back, and she didn't spare a moment to look back.

"Sawyer!" He roared. "We didn't need to do this."

She made a sharp turn down another hallway, only to see a woman at the end grinning at her. Sawyer cursed at the sight of the woman's scar, stretching from her left ear, down her jaw, and down the side of her neck. Missy. And she was holding a damn AR, aimed for Sawyer's head. Sawyer phased into an office to keep running as the gun went off. She didn't bother trying to get back into a hallway, going straight through walls.

"Fuck me," she hissed, stopping when she could feel several other Magi near her. They were reaching out with their Sources to feel hers. This was very quickly becoming the second-ugliest night of Sawyer's life.

The door to the office she was in blew open, and Sawyer found herself looking at Talyn, who shot her a glare.

"I always did hate you," he snarled.

"Steal Colt's abilities today?" She grinned defiantly. "Those won't stop me."

She dropped through the floor as Talyn tried to grab her. She didn't wait for her feet to hit the floor below before blinking to the closest door. She phased through it and kept running.

She ducked when part of the ceiling above her collapsed and Missy dropped down with Axel. Sawyer continued to run.

"You are all useless!" Axel roared, and Sawyer was flung by a gust of wind into a wall. She didn't respond fast enough, and the drywall cracked and broke from the impact. Her mask flew off, but Sawyer had no idea where it ended up.

"I'm so fucking tired of this," Sawyer sighed, trying to pull herself out of the wall. Everything hurt. Her vision spun, making her unable to focus on the shapes moving closer. She got to her feet and staggered into the unbroken wall across the hall.

"Ready to extend your short life by talking to me?" Axel strolled over, looking furious. She chuckled and shook her head.

"There's nothing to say." She laughed, waving a hand around wildly at him and the other criminals behind him. They were all there, all the people she once worked with, all the people who had hated her and the relationship she had with their boss. Missy, Colt, Talyn, Karen, Toni, and Felix. The best of the best at being the absolute worst. "Why isn't Toni dead, though? He's the one who dumped me in the ocean without checking to see if I had a pulse."

"Shut up, bitch," Toni growled, but then he collapsed to his knees, holding his neck. His face slowly turned purple from the lack of air. Sawyer swallowed as Axel slowly choked him to death without laying a hand on him.

"Be quiet," Axel told them casually, and Sawyer saw Toni gasp, sucking in air as Axel finally released his control.

The entire scene reminded Sawyer of the first time she met these assholes. Talyn had said something, she couldn't remember what, but Axel had nearly killed him for it. Axel was possessive over his property; and in the eyes of his organization, she had been his property, not to be toyed with or insulted.

"Now," Axel smiled at her, "let's talk. I want to know where you've been hiding, who you've spoken to, and what you've been doing. I don't like having messes, and you are definitely a mess."

"Why the fuck would I tell you any of that?" She snorted, straightening, but she still needed the wall for support. She realized that Axel didn't have them shielded this time. He thought she was done for, too tired to keep running, too injured to put up a real fight. Arrogance was always Axel's downfall, and Sawyer was thankful for that tonight.

"So I make your death painless." Axel stepped up closer to her, and she rolled her eyes.

"You don't do anything painlessly, so you'll have to find a

better reason," she reminded him, spitting on the floor at his feet. He had screwed up, and she was getting the hell out of there. "Also, fuck you."

"Don't ever fucking-" He went to slap her but missed. She phased through the floor again, his hand passing over her head. This time, she let the drop take her two floors down. She didn't know much about the lower floors and she landed on a metal desk, the impact jarring her leg and buckling her knee.

She didn't waste time on the pain, as loud noises could still be heard above her. She pushed into the hallway and blinked toward the end of it. As Axel and his followers came into the hallway, she phased through the window she had found and jumped.

Free falling from a plane was a cool experience. With a parachute. Skydiving was an exhilarating pastime. Free falling from an office building onto a busy street without a parachute wasn't nearly as enjoyable. Base jumping was stupid and reckless, something only the foolhardy thought was a good idea.

She let herself fall for half the height of the building before reaching into the last of her magic to change shape. She wasn't a shape-shifter, per se. That was only because the ability to shape-shift was limited to changing into animals, and she didn't become an animal.

Doing this was going to send her into Source burnout, but she didn't have a choice. The ground was coming to meet her quickly, and she wasn't particularly interested on becoming a part of the street.

One moment, she was a solid human shape. The next, she was ethereal, airy, and light. Sublimation, an incredibly Rare ability, and her favorite. As a cloud of black smoke, she could float on the wind, making it so the concrete and asphalt below her weren't scary anymore. She couldn't do it inside with Axel because of his elemental control. He would have trapped her and torn her to shreds, since she was now part of the air itself.

She had enough energy for about two minutes in this form, since she had to force her movement against the air currents to get far enough away, but it would be enough. Axel was stuck in the building, probably unwilling to make even more of a scene than he already had, and even he couldn't stop the natural wind currents from carrying her away.

Eight blocks from the building, she lowered herself into an empty alley. She'd done this mission without a go-bag or any of her weapons, preferring to go light over hauling a bunch of crap around, so she only had the phone and wallet she kept on her. Now she just needed to find a taxi and to get the fuck out of the city. Fuck her employer. She sure as fuck wasn't calling him ever again.

She pulled off the face guard, stuffing it into her pocket. She couldn't take the long sleeve shirt off. She was pretty banged up, and people would see that if she was only wearing the tank top she had on underneath.

She had to stay calm and keep her head. She couldn't draw attention to herself now. If she freaked out, people would ask questions and she would be noticed. She had to stick to her emergency escape plan and just focus on living through the night.

She walked out onto the street, pulled some Marlboro Menthols from her pocket, and lit one as she kept moving. She rarely smoked. She knew how bad it was for her; but damn, on some nights, a good cigarette was the only thing between her and a total meltdown.

Sirens could be heard in the distance, and she took a

moment to appreciate that Axel wouldn't come looking for her tonight. He needed to get out, too, or he and his little band of merry murderers would be having a standoff with the non-Magi police. It was enough of a break that she felt some tension leave her.

She strolled quickly down the desolate street. Most people were intent on ignoring the ruckus nearby. Groups of people hung out on their steps, and one group of guys eyed her.

"Hey baby, you know that shit is bad for you, right?" A man called out as a friend of his whistled. She stopped and rolled her eyes at him.

"Probably as bad as you are in bed." She flipped him off with a smile, the cigarette hanging from the side of her mouth. She started walking again as one of the guys sputtered and his friends taunted him.

"Now wait a minute, gorgeous," another called out as she moved farther away. She didn't have the time nor the energy to stop and deal with them. She needed more distance between her and Axel, so the catcallers would need to find other prey. Fuck, normally she would stop and teach them a lesson, but her Source was depleted, and she hurt to her bones.

"Another night, boys," she called back, taking a drag off the cigarette. Her hands shook from exhaustion as she flicked the ash off the end. She stopped on a corner and sighed as she took another long drag. She waved down a cab once she was done and had stomped out the cherry, pocketing the butt so she didn't litter.

"Where are you headed?" the guy said in Arabic, and she held back a groan before responding as she slid into the car.

"This address," she mumbled back, also in Arabic,

KRISTEN BANET

handing him a card with only an address on it. She continued in English. "As fast as you can."

"Okay," he nodded and handed the card back to her once he had punched it into his GPS. She repocketed it and watched LA fly by them. Cops were everywhere, and Sawyer mentally cursed everything that had happened. Now she needed to get the fuck out of Los Angeles before the cops started putting together what had happened. She kept her fingers crossed in the hope that they were more worried about Axel than her.

"We're here," he said in heavily-accented English. "Your fare is-"

"Here. You never saw me." She pulled out her wallet, grabbed three hundred, and tossed it in his passenger's seat. He nodded. The moment she closed the door, he was spinning wheels to leave.

She took a deep breath and walked into the decrepit apartments where she had the cab leave her. She staggered up the steps, trying to ignore the pain stabbing through her knee. When she bumped into the wall, she winced because of her injured shoulder.

She got to the fourth floor and pounded on the door until she heard locks being turned. The woman who opened it looked at Sawyer wide-eyed as she pushed into the apartment. Sawyer didn't have time for civilians.

"Travis!" Sawyer called out, looking around the trashed living room. "This is fucking disgusting," she mumbled to herself as she heard Travis stumble around in a back room. "Travis, I don't have all fucking night."

"I'm coming!" She watched him spill out into the living room, pulling on sweatpants. Another woman was behind him, wrapping herself in a robe. "You weren't supposed to be here for another two days."

12

Sawyer looked him over. Ragged, brown hair and blood-shot, muddy eyes. Too thin. Sawyer knew a drug addict when she saw one, and Travis, once a rising Magi star, was definitely an addict.

"I'll double my payment if you get me out of LA in the next hour." Sawyer looked to the couch, needing to sit down and get off her bad knee, but the couch looked like she would get some unknown disease from it. No, thank you.

"Fuck." Travis glared at her. "And if I say no?"

"I hire someone else, permanently," Sawyer snapped. "And we both know I fucking fund your dumb ass."

"Fine." Travis nodded, looking away from her.

Finding a Magi who could make portals was hard, but Sawyer had connections. She didn't need Travis as much as he needed her. It was a bargaining chip she didn't like using, since Travis wasn't a bad guy. He had made some shit decisions that had ruined his life, though. Sawyer was the only person who was willing to give him a decent paycheck for the work he did. Others would just come in and threaten him or rough him up until he agreed.

"Thank you," Sawyer whispered kindly, inclining her head to him. He nodded back and waved for her to follow him. She ignored the two women watching them as she was led into the back room. "Come with me to New York? I know I promised you a few more days to enjoy the city, but we both need to get out of here tonight."

"That bad?" Travis frowned at her. "I like Los Angeles, though."

"People tried to kill me tonight, Travis," she whispered to him, closing the door for the back room. It was the cleanest room she'd ever seen, but Travis took his magic seriously. Magi who could make portals were Rare and well paid, but also highly regulated, much like pilots for non-Magi aircraft.

He took the utmost care that his portals were perfect, even when he was as high as a kite. "I've got that apartment for you, and we can get you cleaned up. I don't want to leave you here in case they find out about this and you."

"Who tried to kill you? You're just some thief with a lot of money," Travis hissed. He looked paler than before. "In the three years that I've worked for you, nothing like this has happened."

"Doesn't matter who." Sawyer shook her head. Travis, while a nice guy, wasn't the most trustworthy person when it came to secrets, especially when he wasn't on a sober streak. On top of that, he had no idea about her ties to Axel and the Ghosts, and she didn't want him to. "We've got to get out of here. Get the portal up and aim for home. Charlie is going to want to see both of us."

"I hate that guy," Travis mumbled. "I'll put us in that empty warehouse. You know the one."

"The warehouse works," Sawyer sighed. "I'll tell the girls to get the hell out of here."

"Thanks," Travis waved at her absentmindedly, already focused on his task.

Sawyer walked back out into the main room and found the women giggling on the couch with a pile of white powder on the table in front of them. A simple inspection told her that they weren't Magi. Of course, Travis would get a brunette and blonde to have fun with. Both had the largest fake tits Sawyer had ever seen, but that wasn't something she was going to fault them for. She did fault them for not putting on a single shred of clothing while she was there. That was just rude.

"You girls have to go," Sawyer announced. "Travis and I are leaving, and you are too."

"What?" The brunette frowned, and Sawyer wanted to

roll her eyes at the glazed, confused look in those brown eyes.

"You heard me." Sawyer grabbed the clear baggy the blonde was holding and the credit card on the table. "You're leaving. Now. Go get some clothes on."

"Are you stealing our coke?" The blonde hissed, and Sawyer shook her head.

"I'm putting it away. Plus, I know for a fact Travis bought it," Sawyer sighed and slowly pushed the powder back into the bag. "Go get dressed. You can have the cocaine when you leave."

The girls shuffled away quickly, and Sawyer took a moment to refocus. Her shoulder ached. Her knee pulsed. Her emotions... well, she just needed to keep those under control for a little longer. *Stay calm*, she chanted internally. She and Travis were running out of time. Axel would never follow them back to New York, but they had to get there first.

She waited near the door, gingerly holding the bag for them. She didn't enjoy just giving these women the drugs, but she didn't want to put their lives in danger by sticking around for the argument like she normally would have. She would rather them be high as kites anywhere else than in this apartment if Axel found it.

"Here," Sawyer groaned, shoving the bag into the blonde's hand when she tried to pass. "Call a cab and go anywhere else."

"Alright." The blonde shrugged with a nonchalant air. Sawyer felt a pang of jealousy, which was a strange moment for her. She didn't like being jealous of drug addicts, but Sawyer wished she could be so secure of her place in the world. She wished she felt nonchalant and easy about how her night was going.

Sawyer locked the doors and limped back into the room where Travis was nearly done. Portals took a lot of magic and time, depending on the distance crossed. If she had asked him to just go across the state, then he would have been done in a minute; but from one end of the country to the other... that took time, skill, and raw power. Travis had two of those, but Sawyer couldn't trust that they had time.

"How close?" She asked him quietly, staying away from the swirling vortex of blue magic that Travis seemed to be shaping. Touching an unfinished portal? Terrible way to die.

"Another minute," Travis grunted. She saw sweat bead on his forehead. He would be in burnout when this was over, that much was certain.

Sawyer lit another cigarette as she waited. Once Travis was done, the swirling blue magic became what looked like a blackhole. It was standard for a portal, but it freaked Sawyer out to look into what seemed like the abyss.

"Let's go." Travis reached out a hand to her, and she grabbed it. She took a long drag on her smoke as he led her into the dark.

2

SAWYER

Sawyer staggered out of the portal, shivering from the cold that had seeped into her bones during the trip. Portals were efficient, but they weren't instant. Rather, you had a seemingly endless fall in the dark, and it was *cold*. Magi scientists hadn't yet figured out how they worked, but they did work, even if they bent the laws of physics. Sawyer didn't really know why it was a big deal. She could turn to smoke and retain thought without a brain, and that didn't make much sense either.

"Call a cab, Travis," she gasped. He didn't seem bothered at all. Sawyer huffed. The ass.

"Alright," he chuckled.

Yeah, get a laugh, Sawyer growled internally.

They waited in silence for the cab. Sawyer looked up into the sun, letting the heat soak back in. Travis was twitching, something Sawyer had stopped letting get on her nerves years ago.

The only thing either of them said when the cab arrived was the address for Charlie's gym. Sawyer lived there, in an apartment with Charlie on the third floor. She needed a couple of days to get Travis resettled, but she always had an apartment in New York for him. While he hated using it, he wasn't going to get the choice this time.

She used her remaining cash to pay the driver without saying anything. She didn't give Travis a chance to ask for a ride somewhere else, either. She just grabbed his arm and dragged him out of the car with her.

"Sawyer, I really don't find this necessary," he groaned at her as she took him in through the back.

"He's going to knock you out until you sober up, then you can go to the apartment," Sawyer told him sharply. "This is serious, Travis. You need to listen to me for a few weeks until I know we're completely safe here."

"No one is going to try and kill us here in New York," Travis complained in a whiny tone. "That's why people hide here. No one causes shit with *them* nearby."

"I know that," Sawyer growled, yanking him to look her in the eyes. "But I know how bad this really is, and you are going to fucking deal with my rabidly over-protective nature for a couple of weeks. Is that clear?"

"Yeah," he whispered, going a little pale. She felt a pang of guilt at her harsh tone, but she didn't want to wake up one morning and find out that he accidentally got high and left the city for a weekend romp, only to wind up in a ditch.

"Go upstairs and lay on the couch. Charlie is probably in his office; I'll get him. We've got a guest room if you want to use it instead."

"I'll see you up there," Travis nodded, and she was glad to see some color returning to his face.

She looked around the garage and sighed at the familiarity of it. It was good to be home, but it was soured by the night she'd had. It wasn't over, either. She touched the handle of her motorcycle and wondered when she would feel comfortable with going on a long ride again. It would be months before she felt comfortable leaving the city. She ran a hand over the hood of her other baby, a blue 2016 Audi R8 V10, as she walked by it. It was a gorgeous car, and Charlie hated it, but she wouldn't give it up for the world.

She was nearly to the back stairs leading up to the residential floor when she heard the yelling. She sighed and looked over to main gym, narrowing her eyes on Charlie.

At six feet two inches and three hundred pounds, Charlie was a born-and-bred Bronx resident. He was an imposing African-American who didn't take shit from anyone, for any reason. She watched him grab a water bottle and throw it as he told someone to get the fuck out of his gym.

"Charlie?" She called out, raising an eyebrow at him. She began walking over as he turned to her, giving her a deep frown.

"Sawyer?" He picked up the water bottle he had thrown and put it on a fold-out table nearby. "You're home early. Why?"

"Later," she whispered, looking to see who he was yelling at. It wasn't someone she recognized, and who would be in the gym at this hour, anyway? It was nearly five in the morning, and Charlie looked like he hadn't slept all night.

"You might be able to help me." The guy looked her over. She stiffened her spine in response, waiting for whatever this guy had to say.

"She won't help you either," Charlie snapped. "Get the fuck out of my gym."

"What the fuck is going on?" Sawyer looked between them. Charlie looked furious, and the other guy glared at him. She saw the resemblance this guy had with someone else she knew.

"Nothing," Charlie growled at her. She raised an eyebrow at him. They stared at each other for a long time before Charlie began cursing under his breath. "He wants me to train him."

"And you won't?" Sawyer laughed as she looked to the other guy. He was young, probably around her age—early to mid-twenties—and healthy. He had the body of a fighter, and she wondered if he'd tried it before or if he just took care of himself. "What did you do?"

"I didn't do anything." He glared at her. "I was at Fight Night earlier and asked him to help me get in, but he's been turning me down."

"That sucks, but at the end of the day, this gym is choosy with its clientele." Sawyer shrugged. "You should go. There are other gyms. Though, if you keep up with the attitude, you'll find that none of them will train you, either."

"Fine," the guy huffed. She didn't bother to ask for his name as he turned and stormed out. She looked back at Charlie and frowned.

"Why did that piss you off so badly?" Sawyer narrowed her eyes on him.

"That's Liam's older brother," Charlie mumbled. Sawyer clenched her jaw and looked back to the door. She hadn't recognized him, but she also had never met him in person. She had seen some resemblance but unrelated people looked like each other all the time. He'd walked out on Liam two years before Sawyer had met Liam. "He came back into town while you were off in LA. He's trying to get back into Liam's life, but then he started showing up at Fight Night saying our gym trained his brother to fight and he wanted to learn."

"Liam doesn't fight," Sawyer whispered coldly. "He only defends himself."

"Exactly." Charlie nodded. "So, how does Carson know Liam can fight?"

"Fuck," Sawyer whispered. "I'll deal with it."

"I was waiting on you to get home. Liam is still making it to class and work, and he's keeping his grades up, so he's not really giving me a reason to talk to him. I figured you would know what to say where I am failing."

"Yeah." Sawyer nodded. She could handle it. She *would* handle it, but five am and injured wasn't the time. "Now, for why I'm home early..."

"You're burnt out, you have several minor injuries, and I need a closer look at that shoulder...and that knee, holy shit." Charlie walked toward the front of the gym and locked the door. "Let's go upstairs."

She followed him up slowly and put Liam out of her mind for the moment. She was good at compartmentalization, and it came in handy. She couldn't get riled up over the kid right now. When she had moved in four years earlier, she had agreed to help Charlie out once she was back on her feet. She dealt with kids, that was what she ended up with, and it worked really well for her.

She was also the enforcer for Fight Night, a semi-illegal fighting ring they had started to give people a chance to use their skills and have a good time. The cops ignored them because they were small time and B.Y.O.B. No illegal alcohol sales, and the gambling wasn't organized. There was also an entry fee for anyone who wanted to hang out and party. That wasn't illegal, and it was how Charlie made his money from the event. That and fighter buy-ins.

She sat down in their fairly classy apartment at the dining room table, gingerly pulling her black shirt off. She winced at the sight of the bruises on her shoulder. They looked fucking awful, and she wondered if even Charlie could do anything about them at this point. He was an exceptional healer and was once a successful doctor because of it, but this was bad. Also, he was getting up there in age.

"Go deal with Travis first," she told him softly as he eyed her shoulder. The guest room was open, and Travis wasn't on the couch. She would have bet money that the addict was already asleep, but she still wanted Charlie to keep him out for a long time before she started talking. Hearing what she was about to say would freak Travis out, and she didn't need that.

She unbuttoned her pants and slid them off next. She looked at her fucked right knee and tenderly tried to bend it. Adrenaline was a glorious thing, but it was leaving her system. The pain was really starting to set in.

"Charlie!" She called, realizing the apartment was too cold to sit in just her underwear. "Bring me some sweats!"

"Alright," he called back.

She waited silently for him, leaning back in the chair, continuing to try and use her right knee. It was the size of a softball, and she wondered if she had fractured anything.

"Well, you really fucked yourself up," he sighed, throwing his medical kit on the table and tossing her the sweatpants. He studiously ignored her in the thong as she stood up and slid them on. She rolled up the right leg, so he could see the knee, and slowly sat back down. "Sawyer, I think you need to retire."

"I can't bring myself to," she mumbled. "We've had this talk. The money goes to mostly helping these kids, and, let's be real, this gym doesn't make a profit, Charlie."

"Yes, but you've never come back looking like this, and you can't say it wouldn't be safer just to stay here in New

York. What you do here isn't nearly as bad as what you do outside of the city."

"Charlie..." she groaned and shook her head. "It's worse than you think."

"You aren't killing anyone, are you?" Charlie glared at her, and she shook her head again. That was their deal. He was one of two people on the planet who knew everything about her: who she was and what she used to be. The only other person was Axel, who had kept her far away from the rest of his organization, the Ghosts, so his underlings wouldn't learn too much about her. Didn't stop most of them from hating her though.

"No. Axel showed up during my job tonight." She winced when Charlie put his hands on both her shoulders. She felt the heat from his palms, but it was unnaturally hot, meaning he was healing her as best he could. She knew he probably couldn't remove all the bruising and soreness, but she had hope that he could bring it down to something manageable.

"Explain everything," Charlie whispered.

She did, walking him through the mission and what Axel had said. She told him about her escape to help explain the injuries. The entire time, Charlie got more and more tense.

"You need to find *help*," he told her when she was done. "But, yeah, you should lay low while you heal. Stay here in New York, live your life. We'll get through this. We both knew it was coming."

"I can leave, Charlie," she told him, but he shook his head.

"I've sheltered you for four years since you 'died'. Even if you left now, they would still come after me if they figure it out." Charlie smiled at her. "I accepted that when I took you

23

in, Sawyer. The only deal we have is that you never go back to being..."

"Yeah," she sighed. He was all she had, the old fart. He had opened up her world of death and pain into something half decent. "So, *retirement*." The word sounded a little distasteful, but what did she have to lose? If Axel did this again, remaining active was going to get her killed. She'd gotten lucky twice now, when it came to him, and she damn well knew that luck would run out eventually.

"Yeah. You've got something like forty million dollars in off-shore accounts; live off it and walk away. If things get hot, turn yourself into the IMPO or something to get protection. You made a deal with them once, you can do it again. But the Ghosts haven't found you here, yet, so if you don't go off causing trouble..."

"The Ghosts never will be able to trace me back here," Sawyer grinned at him. "He won't come here, even if he did. The IMAS and IMPO are both run from this city by the World Magi Council. It's just too hot for him, especially after he went to number one on the Most-Wanted list. No Magi criminal plays around in this city except me, and I get away with it because I don't work in the city."

"You were number seven on that list, at one point, if I remember correctly. I still think you could get away with joining the IMAS," Charlie chuckled. "They would give anything to have someone with talents like yours."

"I'm not joining the International Magi Armed Services," Sawyer groaned, shaking her head. "I'm not going within a hundred yards of the Police Organization, either, so don't ask."

Charlie laughed, pulling his hands away.

"This could get ugly, Sawyer." He touched her chin, and she nodded.

"Yeah, like your face, old man." She laughed, and he whacked her on the side of her head. "Charlie, I love you! I'm sorry!" She kept laughing as he threw a few more playful swings at her.

"People are trying to kill you, and here you are making fun of my damn face," Charlie huffed, but she could hear the laughter in his voice, too. Charlie threw a hand towel at her. "Look, you'll have a week or so with a sore shoulder and some minor bruising. Two weeks off the knee. I repaired the ACL tear you had. Everything else is taken care of, so if you give it a few weeks, let your Source recharge, then you'll be fine."

"A couple of weeks?" Sawyer sighed happily. "I thought it would be worse."

"I might be slipping in my old age, but I'm still a strong Magi," Charlie reminded her.

She snorted. Slipping? He was an accomplished doctor and fighter with years of experience. He was in the IMAS for a decade and only left to settle down with his wife, who had passed away a year before Sawyer met him. He'd sold off everything when she left this life and had opened the gym, a lifetime dream of his. And he could still kick the ass of any punk who walked in the doors.

Charlie wasn't 'slipping', he was getting *lazy*. There was a difference.

"Thanks for talking to that guy," Charlie finally told her. "I know you don't like dealing with them when they come in on occasion, but I appreciate it. You prefer the kids who genuinely need help, not the punks."

"That one really pissed me off," Sawyer chuckled. "But it's not a problem, really. I'll figure out what's going on with him and Liam."

"Get some rest." Charlie smiled at her. "I've got to get a

nap in before the gym opens. And Fight Night is on Friday. You won't be one-hundred percent, but I'd like to have you around again, so hurry up and get healthy. I can't have an enforcer that limps around."

"Alright, I'm going," Sawyer stood up slowly, testing her shoulder and knee. A little physical therapy and rest and she would be as good as new. She had gotten lucky when she met Charlie, that was for damn sure.

She walked out as Charlie went to his own room. She moved quietly to her room and sighed happily at the vanilla scent that filled it. She lit her favorite candles and moved into her bathroom.

The apartment used to be shabby and cheap, but when Sawyer moved in, she convinced Charlie to let her bring it up-to-date. She paid for millions in renovations, doing a lot of the work by herself. She liked living in nice places, and she didn't see any reason that Charlie shouldn't enjoy a nice place when he was helping her out by letting her stay.

She put her candle down on the edge of the large jacuzzi tub that she called her own. Once she got the water running, she stripped down and looked at herself in the mirror.

She was sure every person had a moment when they didn't recognize the person in the mirror, but with Sawyer, it was becoming a daily occurrence. Her eyes were a dark brown that looked like obsidian in the dim light. Her face wasn't soft, but it was feminine. Defined cheekbones and thinner lips that would be beautiful if she could ignore the scar on her bottom one. Her hair was coffee-colored. It was thick and textured, and a mess when she didn't use the right products. It curled wildly, and she stupidly kept it longer then she should. It fell to the middle of her back. She liked straightening it on occasion, especially for Fight

Night, when she couldn't be bothered to deal with the curls.

When her eyes left her face, they moved over her body. That was more recognizable than the face. An even, golden, dark tan skin tone that reminded her of a light caramel or topaz. She was proud of the body she had: defined arms, a solid six pack, and toned legs. She had broad shoulders for a woman, though that was due to the strength she built into them. Squats had given her a *great* ass. There was only one thing she had a problem with: the few scars she had were hard to miss. One down her breastbone, courtesy of Axel. Another along the right side of her rib cage, courtesy of Axel. A third on her left hip bone, thin and long, and guess what? Courtesy of Axel. The two bullet holes weren't from Axel, though. Missy had given her those, the bitch.

She had smaller scars on her knuckles from fighting and work. Those didn't piss her off as much. They were hers, and she owned them. The missing finger did bother her to the point of irrational anger though. She knew why Axel chopped it off, and that reason was still enough to piss her off.

She sighed and shook her head, trying to dispel the face that popped up in her mind. Suave, Italian, with olive-green eyes and a *beautiful* face. Not handsome. He looked too refined for handsome.

"Fuck me," she hissed as she sank into the tub. She didn't need to be thinking about him. She needed him to stay the fuck out of her life. Four years, and she'd never made a mistake. How did he learn she was even alive? And if he knew... who else did?

That guilt welled up in her chest from earlier, finally breaking past all the barriers she had built around it.

Sawyer was once the rising star in a world of darkness

and death. She would have done anything for him. She *did* do anything for him, for a variety of reasons, from fucked up hero worship to just plain fear. By twenty, she had a reputation for silent and bloody death. Five kills in two years was all it took for her to gain such a dangerous reputation that she had found herself on the IMPO's Top Ten Most-Wanted list. She'd started out as just his thief; by the end, she was so much more. So much worse.

Until she was declared dead four years ago. Four years and three months. The events that led to her 'death' were both a nightmare and a blessing, but nothing she did, from helping abused kids and Charlie to retiring from that work, could clean the black stain on her soul. Nothing would bring back the people she had killed or the ones she got killed with her failures.

She leaned back in the hot water, angling her back into a jet and sighing as it worked the tight muscle.

"I need a fight," she mumbled. "A clean fight. A couple weeks to heal up? I'm going to go mad with cabin fever."

She closed her eyes. She didn't know how long she was soaking in the tub when Charlie knocked on her bathroom door.

"Sawyer?"

"Yes, Charlie?" She called back, refusing to open her eyes.

"The boys and I are going out for breakfast," he told her sheepishly.

"And I'm your mother, old man?" She chuckled. They always told each other when they were leaving. It was a safety thing, but they also gave each other hard times over it. His laugh told her that everything was fine between them, for now. "Have a good breakfast."

"Well, you know the rules. Keep the door locked and

don't accept any injured, fevered, dying people in to use the bathroom. You know how that ended last time. Just send them to the hospital."

She heard him walk off and chuckled to herself for a long time. She did know how it ended last time. She was still living in his apartment. She owed him everything, and he never expected more from her then she was willing to give. It took nearly a year for them to even talk regularly, but she never regretted meeting him. He had saved her life, in every way.

She rose out of the tub since the water had cooled down. She blew out her candle and left it at the side of the tub as she dried off. Blow dry the hair; towel off the rest. She strolled into her room and grabbed her favorite pair of over-sized gray sweats and a black tank top. By the time she was settled onto the couch in the living room, she was half asleep and didn't even make it through a single episode of Grace and Frankie.

∾

BLOOD SEEPED ONTO THE TILE. *Her eyes locked on the cracked and dented plaster where his body had hit the wall. Her vision doubled, and she swayed. She couldn't look down at the figure that was laying there. She couldn't. This was her fault. He was dead, and it was her fault.*

A whimper filled the room.
It was hers.

∾

SAWYER GASPED and jumped off the couch, wincing as her

knee buckled from the sudden weight. Fucking nightmare. She hadn't had it in months. *Fuck.*

She staggered into her room, wiping her face. Tears drenched her cheeks and slid onto her lips, salty and bitter. She collapsed onto the bed and pulled a pillow over her face. Of course, seeing Axel would bring back the nightmares. She sobbed into the pillow, letting it muffle the noise.

"I fucking hate you," she cried, not sure if she was talking about Axel or herself.

3

VINCENT

Vincent and Elijah landed in LA only hours after the Axel incident. They got on the first plane out of Atlanta to get to the scene as quickly as possible. They had tried getting a Magi to make them a portal, but no one had been available, so Delta had been their only option.

"I hate Delta," Elijah groaned, kicking a cowboy boot out onto the rental's dashboard. Vincent resisted the urge to knock the foot down. Seven years as friends and they still had problems. "I mean, it was a six-hour flight, and I only got two drinks? What the fuck?"

"Calm down, Cowboy," Vincent sighed. "We've got a lot to do, and we'll be flying Delta back, so just get over it."

"You wound me, Vincent," Elijah placed a hand over his heart, feigning a chest pain. "But you're right. What did our contact say?"

"Axel set up a high-end, reclusive thief," Vincent mumbled. "But no one really knows why. She's not a high priority for us, since she's not really a danger to the public.

Axel has never hired her before or shown any interest in her. I was told that the security footage is fairly interesting."

"Maybe he's just losing it?" Elijah tried to shrug. In the compact rental car, Vincent equated it to a giant squeezed into a tuna can. How he got his foot on the dashboard was a mystery to Vincent. At six feet five and a wall of muscle, Elijah wasn't exactly a contortionist. "I mean, Axel's been slowly slipping for years now, ever since he lost that little pet of his."

"Yeah," Vincent mumbled. "I remember that. He's always been a little mad." Vincent shook his head. "I think that incident just brought it to the surface."

"Yeah, well, now he's going after fairly innocent thieves and blowing holes into office buildings. Messy for him. I think it's a pattern." Elijah pointed to a building, and Vincent turned into the building's parking lot.

There were only 3 black Range Rovers there, all IMPO. They had realized it was a Magi incident and had taken over, kicking the LAPD off the scene entirely. Vincent would feel guilty over it, but the non-Magi law enforcement services really didn't have the talent or the resources to handle Magi criminals known for torture, mass murder, and a variety of other things.

"*You know,*" Elijah continued as Vincent parked them. "Maybe there is a pattern."

"Excuse me?" Vincent frowned and narrowed his eyes on his second in command.

"Think about it," Elijah chuckled. "These things only really happen when it's Axel and a woman."

Good lord. Elijah would assume they were fucking. There was no evidence of Axel ever taking a long-term lover before in his life, and Vincent was the world's leading expert on Axel. Vincent rolled his eyes as he shook his head.

"Come on." Elijah laughed when Vincent didn't even bother giving a response. "You can't tell me that it doesn't work! Hot woman turns him down or breaks off the relationship. He's a control freak with a complex. It would make him furious in a way that nothing else could."

"You make a lot of assumptions about him by entertaining that," Vincent sighed. "He's never had a girlfriend. He doesn't care enough. And if he did take a lover and they left he would..."

"Kill them." Elijah pointed at Vincent and walked past him.

Damn it all to hell, the cowboy was probably right. Vincent shoved the theory out of his mind and followed Elijah onto the elevator. It was a stupid theory. Axel was well known for keeping clean prostitutes and slaves for those types of relationships. He didn't do lovers.

When they stepped off the elevator on the third floor, they moved quietly and as a unit to the room that security and the IMPO had taken over for their investigation.

"Special Agent Castello, Special Agent Grant." An agent held out his hand for Vincent. "Detective Robins."

"Nice to meet you, Detective." Vincent shook his hand and then did the same introduction with other agents around the room. When it was all over, he looked back to Detective Robins and pointed at the computers they had set up. "What do you have?"

"Well, we called you in since your team is point on the Ghosts." Robins grabbed a remote and started up a projector, so they wouldn't be huddled around a laptop. "He was here, Castello. Right in this building, raging at her when she got away. Tore up several floors."

Good Lord, Axel was slipping. This was personal, but how? He had no evidence that these two had been in contact before. He was missing something important, and it sat on the edges of his mind where he was unable to reach it.

"Play the tapes," he mumbled. Robins nodded and got the security tape started. The fact that there was no sound bothered Vincent, but he'd have to deal. This was the first time they had gotten Axel on camera in a year, and that was a blessing on its own.

They watched the tall thief run out of the server room. They saw her mask get knocked off, and Vincent heard Elijah mumble, "What the fuck?" as the scene continued to play out. Vincent quickly realized that this thief knew exactly how to get away from Axel. Axel was losing his temper the entire recording, and she had to know what he could do. She had to know what any of the Ghosts could do, since she outplayed all of them at every turn.

When the tape ended, Vincent held up a hand at Robins to stop him from playing the next video.

"Elijah, you got something?" He turned to his second. Elijah was frowning.

"Call Jasper or Zander. Have them send a picture of that girl they grew up with," Elijah mumbled.

"They're on vacation," Vincent reminded him. "I can't bring them in. They are required by law to take the next month to themselves."

"A phone call won't get anyone in trouble, Vin." Elijah crossed his arms and waited. Vincent sighed, pulled out his phone, and made the call.

Zander answered on the second ring, sounding pissed.

"What the fuck, Vincent?" He was cranky, but Vincent would be too if his vacation was interrupted for even a second by a call from the boss. Zander had two moods. Reckless or cranky. There was no in-between for him.

"Elijah would like one of you two to send a picture to him of that missing person case you've been secretly, not-so-secretly, working on for the past six years." Vincent looked over to the projection and frowned. The woman was beautiful, but since he never got involved in the weird manhunt the guys had been up to, he didn't recognize her. He had never seen a picture of her, and his team knew they had other shit going on, so their personal missions needed to stay personal and off the company dime.

"Why?"

"Just send it," Vincent groaned, rubbing a temple. Vincent waited for Elijah's phone to go off, ignoring Zander's grumbling. "Thank you."

"I'll see you in a month, Vincent. Not a day sooner," Zander growled, hanging up on him.

"He was cranky," Vincent commented mildly, putting his phone away as Elijah compared whatever photo he had to the woman Axel had tried to grab.

"You probably ruined some pick-up line he was trying out," Elijah chuckled, but the chuckle was dark, and Vincent frowned. "Call him back."

"Why?" Vincent crossed his arms. "Do any of you remember that I'm in charge of this team and I outrank you, therefore I don't take orders?"

Elijah held up his phone, and Vincent noticed his hand was shaking. Vincent looked at the picture. Younger versions of his team members, Jasper and Zander with a younger woman between them. They must have all been teens.

"How old is this picture?" Vincent whispered.

"Nine years. The guys are seventeen and eighteen, and she was fifteen. They grew up together," Elijah informed him. Vincent remembered, wondering how he had forgotten the story. Zander and Jasper were both orphans for different reasons. Magi had a small population and had very few kids who didn't have anyone looking out for them. They didn't allow Magi children in foster care, instead, putting them all into one of two orphanages in North America. A friend who was there since her birth, Sawyer Matthews, was adopted and then went missing about eight months after the guys joined the IMAS. When Vincent recruited them into the IMPO, they started looking for her.

He looked from the photo to the woman on the screen. They had found her. Staring at Axel in what Vincent could only describe as unadulterated disgust, was Sawyer Cambrie Matthews. He hit play, watched her spit at Axel's feet and then drop through the floor. Ballsy and reckless. He was astounded that her body wasn't in the building somewhere.

His team members' long-lost friend was being hunted by *Axel* of all fucking people. It was already a small world for Magi, and Vincent felt it become a lot smaller.

"I'll call him back," Vincent whispered. "Shut this down. I want all the tapes in our possession. No copies. We're taking over. We aren't going to be able to catch Axel from here, but," he pointed at Sawyer on the screen, "I have a feeling we can catch him with her."

"Find her, find him." Elijah nodded slowly. "Good call, boss."

"You know her?" Robins finally spoke up. "And what about what happened here? We need resolutions."

"No. *You* don't," Vincent told the Detective. "Like every other Magi incident, there's a payout system. The damages will be taken care of. When you called me in, didn't you think I was going to completely take over this case?"

"I…" Robins trailed off, and Vincent gave him a wry smile.

"Thought so," Vincent sighed and hit call for Zander. Vincent rarely felt nervous, but this phone call made him more anxious than he had felt in years. "Elijah, handle all of this while I figure out what we're going to do about Jasper and Zander's vacation."

4

___

SAWYER

"Liam," Sawyer called out as her ragged band of kids wandered around the training room. She watched them as Liam walked over to her. She saw a couple joke around, the teenagers. One young woman was helping the youngest ones with their pads. Sawyer had them all here, ages nine to eighteen.

"Sawyer," Liam greeted her tentatively.

"I've heard things, and I've only been back for two days. Care to elaborate on the rumors, or do I need to go digging myself?" She met his eyes and watched him look down at the floor after only a couple of seconds. "We've known each other for four years this month, Liam, and we've been through a lot together. Now isn't the time to start keeping secrets from me."

"My brother showed up." Liam shrugged. "He's a dick."

"He knows you can fight," Sawyer whispered. She looked back to the group and sighed. "You all can take some time to warm and stretch together. Jessie, you're in charge!"

"Aye, aye, Sawyer!" The teenage girl helping the younger

kids gave Sawyer a mock salute. Jessie, a seventeen-year-old from the same neighborhood that Charlie grew up in, was a sweet girl with a bite. She was easy to get along with if you didn't step on her toes, which made her one of Sawyer's favorite people to leave in charge of the class. No one could push her around, and that kept the peace while Sawyer was dealing with other things.

"Come with me, Liam." Sawyer waved him to follow her. When they were alone in Charlie's office on the second floor, she locked him in with her and glared at him. "What the fuck, Liam?"

"He's back, and it's okay!" Liam scrambled to tell her. "He's a prick, and he's got a few friends that like to mess with me, but I can handle it. I'm still going to school and getting here for work. I'm not letting him impact my life."

"Where's he staying?" Sawyer asked softly.

"On my couch," Liam mumbled, playing with his hand wraps. Sawyer crossed her arms and waited. "So are a few of his friends. They've taken to partying at my place and smoking a fuck load of weed because I have a nice place."

"I know you have a nice place," Sawyer reminded him. "I fucking pay for it."

"I know," Liam whispered, nodding his head. "I've tried to kick them out, but there's like five of them. Carson knows I can fight because one got really drunk and tried to start some shit. I ended it. I told him about the gym since I work here. He put it all together and started bothering Charlie."

"God damn it." Sawyer shook her head. "Pull up your shirt."

"What?" Liam frowned at her, but she also saw the fear in his eyes. The shame.

She knew why.

39

"Liam. You heard me."

He closed his eyes and pulled up his tee. He normally worked out shirtless so him even having a shirt on in the gym was a dead giveaway.

Sure enough, Sawyer wanted to rage at the amount of bruising he had.

"How many?" she asked in the flattest tone she could summon.

"All of them," Liam whispered. "A week ago, when I tried to throw them out."

"Including your brother?"

"Yeah," he sighed, swallowing. His voice was tight, and she took a long breath to remain calm. "He told them not to mess with my face like..."

"Like your dad used to say," Sawyer finished for him. "Well, that apple didn't fall far from the tree."

"No, I guess not," Liam whispered. "Sawyer, Charlie said you-"

"I'm injured, but I'm not an invalid," Sawyer snarled at him. "I'm not letting you live in that place until I clear those mother fuckers out. I just got a friend out of the guest room; it's yours again. I'll get you back in your place by tomorrow."

"Sawyer," Liam tried to argue with her.

"No," she snapped. "Damn it, Liam!" She slammed a hand on the wall in frustration. "You don't go it alone. You don't put on the tough face and pretend it's okay. It's not."

"It's what you do!" Liam yelled at her. "What happened in LA, Sawyer? I know you're a thief, but Charlie said this has never happened before. In the four years I've known you, you've never gotten hurt like this. But there you are, putting on a tough face and trying to protect the rest of us."

"You have no idea what you're talking about," Sawyer

growled. "You're a kid, and I'm not letting you turn this back on me."

"Two years ago, I would have bought that." Liam glared at her. "But I'm nineteen, Sawyer. I'm not the fifteen-year-old you dragged here when I had nowhere else to go. I've got four years of training from *you*. To not only protect myself, but them." He pointed towards the door, and she knew he meant the other teens and children in the class. "I'm going to college, so I have the education to *take your place*. Remember?"

She winced. Damn him.

"What do you want?" she asked him, looking away from him this time.

"I want to be there when you clear them out. I'm not a Magi like you, but I want to be there."

"It's assault," Sawyer reminded him. "As a Magi, that low-level crime is generally ignored, but it wouldn't be for you."

"I don't care." Liam's jaw clenched, and Sawyer sighed. Two days ago, she had nearly died, and now Liam was getting older and more independent. She could feel the shift in her life, and it bothered her on a deep level. She had a foreboding feeling in the pit of her stomach from the swift change storming through her life.

But swift change meant she needed to prepare herself for anything. She didn't know if she was going to live through the year, now that Axel knew she was alive. Liam needed to know why only she could do what she did, and that he was only taking over the legal parts and the gym one day. Nothing more.

"Stay in the guest room," she whispered. "I need to talk to Charlie about something... I'll see you at dinner."

"That's it?" Liam looked shocked.

She only nodded, opening the door and letting him leave. She closed the door behind him, knowing he would run the class in her absence.

Three months after she and Charlie met, she found a teenager getting the shit kicked out of him by his dad. She'd lost it. Liam was left an orphan because she couldn't stop herself from killing his dad. He was the last man she'd killed. The last. Liam's father was also the one she felt the least guilty about.

She got rid of the body with a terrified, lanky kid following her around. He'd been smart enough to not ask questions that night. The questions surfaced later. How did she know where to hide the body? How could she kill him without blinking an eye? Where did she learn to fight? She'd always told him she would explain when he was older. She would tell him why she did it when he was older.

He was older now, and he wasn't a terrified kid anymore.

She stewed for a long time, waiting for Charlie. Jessie told her when class let out, and Liam let her know he would make dinner in the apartment. She just waited.

"Sawyer," Charlie greeted her as he finally walked in. Three hours. He had been avoiding her, she knew that.

"I don't want to do it," she told him without preamble. "I don't want to ruin the way he looks at me."

"He's done nothing but love you like a sister, even after seeing you kill his dad," Charlie sighed. "I don't think that will change now."

"Axel tried to kill me, and now this." Sawyer covered her face with her hands, leaning on the desk. "He's my 'heir apparent' in some fucked up way. We all know it. I don't want him to..."

"I know." Charlie sat down on the desk and rubbed her shoulder. "You want him to know, just in case you don't survive the next encounter."

"Yeah." She didn't uncover her face. "I'm going to fill his life with my shadows and secrets, and damn it, I don't want to."

"I'll tell him," Charlie whispered, continuing to rub her uninjured shoulder. "He needs to know. Not only so he can decide if he really wants it, but also for his own safety. People may come asking questions one day, and he needs to know why."

"I know," Sawyer moaned desperately. "You'll tell him?"

"I'll tell him. Tonight, after dinner. Go for a run after dinner, and I'll get it taken care of."

"I hate this." Sawyer stood up and shook her head. "I hate that he needs to know. I hate that I did it. I hate that, after all this time, I thought it was over, and now it's blowing up in my fucking face. Why did Axel have to show up after all this time? How the fuck did he find out I was alive?"

"It's the life you have," Charlie reminded her gently.

"Dick." Sawyer told him with a bit of snark. "You think he'll stick around?"

"You think anything will ever convince him to *leave*? Because I didn't sign up to become a father for every pup you bring home." Charlie smiled at her, and some little weight lifted off her shoulders. "He going to help you deal with his brother?"

"Yeah," Sawyer sighed with a nod, giving Charlie a smirk. "He won't be as helpful as he thinks he will be, but it might be time to show him why I can get away with it and he can't."

"It is definitely time for that," Charlie chuckled. "None

of them have any idea what your magic is, and that astounds me. I'm not sure how you've done it."

"Easy." Sawyer shrugged as she spoke. "I just don't use my powers in front of them. Not hard, and they know better than to ask."

"You'll be a great mom one day." Charlie kept chuckling. "You keep them all in line so well."

"Ew." Sawyer felt a lip curl. "Much too young for that. I'm only five years older than Liam. That sounds awful."

"Yeah, and you would need to find someone who can put up with your ass." Charlie began to fully laugh, and she glared at him.

"My ass is just fine." Sawyer pointed at it as she spoke.

"That's right," Charlie howled with laughter. "It's your attitude they'll need to get over."

She couldn't stop the smile that broke out on her face. It was that easy for Charlie and her to lighten the mood. He had taught her that a laugh eases the soul and to never feel guilty for a smile.

"Get up there and help the poor kid with dinner." Charlie waved her away. "And Travis called. He's agreed to sober up for a little while and stay in the apartment without causing any problems, but I recommend you check on him every couple of days."

"God," Sawyer groaned. Travis. Her list of problems never seemed to end. "Sometimes I wish I cared less about these people."

"I wouldn't go that far," Charlie shrugged, "but I do think you should stop bringing them home. To *my* home, I'll remind you."

"You can't deny I've turned into New York's fucking resident babysitter," Sawyer mumbled a little petulantly. She didn't mind it as much as she pretended. She loved it. She loved helping all of them, but sometimes it was nice to complain a little.

"*I've* turned into New York's babysitter. *You* are their damn vigilante," Charlie told her in an even tone that impressed her. "Now get the fuck out of my office and stop moping."

"I'm going." Sawyer raised her hands and retreated.

SHE DIDN'T EAT DINNER. She helped Liam prepare it and then decided to go on her walk. She didn't want to sit there and pretend everything was fine when Charlie was about to dump her life story on his head. It was cowardly of her, but Charlie had a way with words that she didn't.

She strolled at a leisurely pace for nearly two hours. She didn't do this often. She didn't like wandering around the city with nowhere to go, and it seemed to always get her into something. It was how she met Liam and a few of the other kids in her class. She stopped a mugging once, and then there was the time she found Travis coked out in an alley.

It was late, nearly nine, when she decided to start heading back to the gym. She hadn't run into anything yet, but Sawyer knew something was going to happen soon.

She passed an apartment building and heard the yelling. She heaved a sigh and looked up at the window it was coming from. Second floor. Yup, there it was. She was getting into trouble tonight.

"This is why I don't wander around the city," she murmured to herself. "I just can't catch a single break. Just one night, New York. That's all I want."

She pondered her next move and saw a teenager

running down the street. He was panting and cursed when he got close enough to hear the yelling.

"What are you looking at?" he asked her as he got even closer.

"Nothing." Sawyer shrugged. "You know what's going on up there?" She pointed to the window, and the teenage boy glared at her.

"Yeah, you got something to say about it?"

"Who?"

"Who what?" He wrinkled his nose at her, confused.

"Who's yelling?" Sawyer rolled her eyes.

"My step-dad," he told her tentatively. "Look, stop being fucking weird and get off my front step. I need to get inside."

"Wait." Sawyer stopped him from running inside for a moment. She pulled out her wallet and removed a card. When she handed it to him, she added, "Call me or show up if the arguments get violent. I can help. I teach teenagers and kids self-defense, so they protect themselves and their loved ones."

"Serious?" He took the card from her slowly, and she shrugged.

"Yeah." Sawyer stayed nonchalant about it, but she wanted him to show up. She didn't want to have to go up there and deal with it if she didn't have to. If they were just arguing, it wasn't her business. "I need to head out. You have a good night, kid."

"You too," he mumbled back. She left him on his front step holding the door knob. She really did need to get going. It was time to face Liam, and she couldn't wander around the city picking up strays all night.

She was a block away when she realized she had forgotten to ask for the kid's name.

"Damn," she sighed. She shook her head and kept walking. Her knee was starting to ache in a way that worried her. Charlie was going to be cranky that she walked on it for so long.

She crept into the apartment and instantly found both of the guys on the couch in the living room. Liam's eyes were big as he stared at Charlie, who was still whispering.

"She is what she is," Charlie sighed. "And she's not... she's not bad. She's dark. She helps you kids because of..."

"Henry," Liam mumbled.

Sawyer swallowed and hid in the shadows of the apartment to listen. *Henry.* Charlie hadn't skipped any details, she realized. There were a couple things that Charlie didn't know, but he knew most of it. Damn, he had told Liam everything he knew, if Henry was being brought up.

"Yeah." Charlie nodded.

She stepped out and coughed softly. They looked at her, and she blinked back a flood of tears. Liam looked horrified.

"Sawyer," he whispered.

"You can go if you want," she whispered kindly, gesturing towards the door.

"No." Liam shook his head and stood up. He crossed the living room, and she took a moment to realize he was taller than her now. When had he passed her five-foot eleven?

She found herself holding him in a tight hug.

"You and Charlie are the only family I have," he whispered. "I won't leave you."

"Told you," Charlie said gruffly from the couch. Sawyer could only choke out a laugh for a moment, pushing Liam away.

"We might have a new kid showing up," she told them.

"Nice change of topic." Liam smiled at her. "Charlie told me everything... I take it you won't want me asking more questions about it."

"I definitely don't want you asking questions about it," Sawyer confirmed with a tight smile. "Better if you don't."

"Tell us about this new kid, then." Charlie waved them back to sit down, and she grinned.

"Well, I was out on the walk, and I heard arguing," she began as she sat down.

"Every fucking time," Charlie groaned.

5

ELIJAH

Elijah sat in the office and ran a hand through his hair. Zander looked like he was about to blow a gasket, and Jasper was pacing on the far side, looking uncomfortable with the revelations they had uncovered. Vincent was watching them patiently.

In the two weeks since the LA incident, the team had picked apart Sawyer's life as much as they could. Fake identities so she didn't put her real name on anything, corporate espionage jobs, millions in offshore accounts. The mask she left behind in LA had been enchanted so a Magi Tracker couldn't use it, and it didn't have any residual Source from her at all. She had been thorough and careful.

Only a few photos ended up giving her away. The security footage in LA and one single photo that had found itself on Facebook, posted by a non-Magi who must not have realized she was protecting her identity. It had been tagged with the location, and that had been the break they needed to completely invade her life.

They didn't know what she was up to in New York,

though, only that it was her home base where she always settled between jobs.

"Why?" he snapped. Elijah looked at Zander for a long moment as they all considered the question none of them could help him with. The tall, lean redhead was covered in freckles and had somewhat of a boyish look, but Elijah didn't let that fool him. Zander tended to have a red-hot temper that matched his hair. "Why the hell would she become this?"

"Considering it's been nine years since you've seen her, who knows?" Vincent reminded him. Elijah sighed and nodded in agreement.

"She's not even the worst, Zander. Sure, she's good at what she does and gets paid a lot of money, but she's not evil. I think she's more... chaotic neutral. We can work with that." Elijah put his cowboy hat back on.

"We're still missing over three years of information on her," Jasper said, stopping his pacing to look over to them. "Sixteen to twenty-one. We have no idea where she was or what she was doing during that time. We know she got adopted after we joined the IMAS, but what happened after that? Where was she? She didn't go to college."

"We can ask her when we go get her," Vincent told him. "There's no reason to sit here pondering over it."

"So, how do we want to do this?" Elijah asked, grabbing a bag of sunflower seeds off his desk and kicking his feet up. He admired his cowboy boots for a moment as he threw a few seeds in his mouth.

"We need to watch her closely and figure out her schedule." Jasper walked over and grabbed a chair to sit. Elijah frowned at the sight. Jasper's limp got worse the more he moved around, and it was pretty pronounced now. Elijah would need to tell Zander to look it over before Jasper screwed up his left knee and hip any more than he already had. "Then we need to decide who goes to speak with her."

"What do you mean by decide, Jasper? You and I grew up with her, we should talk to her." Zander glowered at Jasper, and Elijah shook his head.

"No," he chuckled. "That's exactly why you two shouldn't approach her."

"Elijah is right," Vincent nodded, "and Quinn is a no-go. He's staying here. New York isn't the place for him, even if you ignore the fact that he would probably just scare the shit out of her. We need to keep her from bolting. She's skittish; most thieves are, and she's incredibly reclusive. None of her employers even know what she looks like. We're lucky we got the break we did. If Axel hadn't knocked her mask off, we'd have no idea who to look for to keep safe from him."

"Anything that might give away we're looking for Sawyer the thief, and she's going to disappear," Jasper sighed. "Vincent, why do you even want to go get her? I know why Zander and I are going to pursue this but…"

"She's got a connection to Axel, and this team was built to catch him and the other most dangerous Magi on the planet." Vincent lifted a photo from his desk and handed it to Jasper. Elijah knew the photo. Axel and Sawyer in the hallway with all the Ghosts around them, right before she dropped through the floor and made her escape.

"Fine. We go to New York, stalk her for a couple of weeks, and then figure out how to get her to stay still long enough to talk to us." Elijah grinned. Easy enough.

"Not just talk to us." Vincent looked at Elijah, and Elijah frowned, "I want to get her in protective custody."

Oh, fuck. Elijah wasn't so sure that was going to fly with anyone outside the team. The IMPO and the WMC would be furious if they harbored a criminal. Their handler would lose his mind, that was for sure. James hated dealing with the big wigs on the Council, and bringing her into protective custody would mean he'd have to go sit in meetings and shit.

It's not that it was a bad thing to do. It happened all the time, but they were talking about taking in a criminal that another criminal wanted dead. This was rife with complications, but Elijah knew better then to bring all those up to Vincent, the strategic master. He still needed to ask though.

"Vin." Elijah raised an eyebrow. "Have you thought this through?"

"If they want me to catch Axel one day, they will give me whatever I want." Vincent gave him a tight smile, and Elijah sighed.

Wasn't that the truth?

"We also don't want her to die," Zander huffed. "Right Vin?"

"Yeah, sure." Vincent shrugged, and Elijah winced. Sometimes the similarities between Vincent and his brother were just too much.

Two days later, they were on a plane to New York to hunt down a woman, and they had permission to take her into custody.

"This is going to be so easy," Zander mumbled gleefully. Elijah laughed, nodding as he slapped Zander on the back.

"Won't it? Once we figure out what she gets up to in New York." Elijah shrugged. "Should only take a week to figure out how to grab her."

"Both of you need to not get overconfident," Jasper cut

between them and found his own seat. Sure enough, Elijah learned that the blonde-haired, blue-eyed, pretty boy had overworked his left hip and knee again as they were trying to get to the airport. It was an old childhood injury, and Elijah knew there was really nothing they could do, even if they hired the best healer on the planet.

"And you need to take better care of yourself," Elijah reminded him. Vincent might have been the team leader, but Elijah had to play mother hen for all the guys. He took care of them on a personal level while Vincent took care of them on a professional level.

"He's right, Jasper," Vincent remarked as he walked down the aisle of the plane. He sat next to Elijah and stretched his legs out like the rest of them. They were all too tall for planes, even the private jet the IMPO was letting them use. The shortest of them, Jasper, was still sitting at six feet even. He and Zander were around six and a half feet tall, the tallest in their group. They stood out, that was for sure. Zander's flaming red hair, gauged ears that had inch-sized holes, and his obsession with body art made him even more obvious.

"I've been a bit stressed out," Jasper mumbled. "Sorry."

"Just makes sure you keep up with the physical therapy, bud." Zander grinned at Jasper, and Elijah chuckled a little sadly. Seeing those two always made him miss Quinn when they didn't have him. Vincent must have noticed his mood change because he elbowed Elijah.

"Quinn would hate New York, you know that," Vincent whispered. "He can barely go into town, and it's three streets."

"Yeah, and we need someone watching the house when Shade and Scout can't go on a mission," Elijah sighed.

"You talk to him about us bringing a woman around, if

we can catch her?" Vincent leaned over to rest his forearms on his knees, watching Elijah.

"Yup, and he took it about as well as anyone can expect from him." Elijah gave a dry chuckle. "You know him. I was lucky to convince him to get everything set up."

"Who on this plane doesn't know Quinn?" Vincent smiled. Quinn was their most precious teammate, and most peculiar, as well. "He can handle it though, right?"

"Yeah." Elijah nodded, just once. "He was fairly adamant that he would be *fine*." Elijah started laughing as he said it. Quinn hadn't been truthful, but Elijah could still appreciate the effort Quinn gave to making Elijah believe him. "What do you think we're going to find in New York, Vincent?"

"Hopefully, the key to catching Axel. At the least, Zander and Jasper's long-lost friend so they can stop wasting resources on that." Vincent shrugged. "We'll see which when we get our hands on her. Let's review what we have so far. We tracked her to the city, but we don't know what she's up to there. While it's the main headquarters for the entire Magi world, information about the underworld there is scarce because there's barely an underworld at all."

"You know." Jasper looked up at them from his book as he spoke. Advanced particle physics. Elijah felt a headache coming on just looking at the title. "If you had let us use the facial recognition software years ago, we might have already been able to catch her before Axel tried to kill her."

"Yeah." Zander waved a hand around, glaring at Vincent. "This would have never happened."

"You've said this already," Vincent mumbled darkly. It had been an ongoing argument since LA, and Elijah kept his nose out of it.

Elijah watched Vincent pull out the massive manila folder they had. Vincent kept files on fucking everything, from their groceries to any case they would ever possibly work on. His organized, control freak nature made Elijah itch sometimes.

"We know that she's pretty hot," Elijah mumbled, grabbing a recent photo of Sawyer from the top. It didn't have the grainy, low quality of the security camera from LA. Someone had been able to snap a picture of her standing in a gym, then shared it on Facebook. They had run every piece of facial recognition software they could get their hands on to find it. She was so hard to find, if they hadn't gotten a look at her from the LA incident, they would have had no idea that the toned, gorgeous fighter was also the thief Axel was trying to kill.

"Of all the things you notice." Vincent rolled his eyes. Elijah only offered him a grin in return. He knew Vincent had noticed, too, or there would have been a discussion about why Elijah thought she was good looking.

"I hope she doesn't let you within ten feet of her," Zander called from his spot next to Jasper, who ignored them all for his book.

"I'll make you a bet," Elijah taunted. "A hundred dollars says I'm the one who captures her."

"Deal." Zander grinned back. Vincent groaned and pushed the file away. They weren't supposed to bet on missions, but Elijah couldn't resist trying to get close to a beautiful woman. "She's not going to fall for your shit, I promise. She's never fallen for your type."

"And what is *my type*, fuck head?" Elijah laughed. "Attractive and wonderful?"

"Southern and arrogant." Zander threw a balled-up napkin at him. Elijah lit it on fire and let it burn away before it got close to him. Zander narrowed his eyes at him. "Damn cowboy."

"You grew up in Georgia, and you call me a cowboy?" Elijah raised an eyebrow, still grinning. "Redneck."

"Jasper and I don't run around in boots with *actual spurs*. If you don't like cowboy, how about Texas boy?" Zander looked Elijah over. Elijah looked down at his feet. Well, Zander had him there. He was wearing cowboy boots and spurs. "And I'm not a fucking redneck."

"Doesn't matter what you call me, as long as you remember that women *love* a good, down-to-earth, country boy. So, we got a deal?" Elijah pulled out his wallet and showed Zander the cash he had as Zander nodded. "Let's see it, you know the rules."

Zander did the same, proving he had the money to back up his mouth. Elijah was going to have a lot of fun trying to take the poor guy's cash.

"That's if you are needed, Elijah," Vincent finally told him blandly. "We don't even have a plan, yet, so both of you put your money away."

Elijah and Zander both sighed but maintained eye contact, trying to hold back smiles. The bet was still on, but they needed to keep Vincent from strangling them. Not like the six-two Italian could, but he was their boss, so they had to keep up appearances.

"She's not going to fall for you. Maybe Vincent, but not you. I hope you keep that cash ready."

Elijah snorted at Zander's telepathic thought. He didn't have the ability, so he couldn't respond, but he was going to have a good fucking time proving Zander wrong. Nine years changed people, and Elijah figured that the Sawyer in New York wasn't going to be the same Sawyer they drank cheap moonshine with as teenagers.

6

SAWYER

Two weeks went by slowly, and, by the end, Sawyer was in the gym pushing herself to make sure she didn't grow complacent. She kept a strict workout routine and no injury was going to keep her from pushing her body to the limit.

Two hours of weight training every day. One hour of cardio every day. Three days a week, she went to judo classes. Two days a week, she trained alone with Charlie. Then she taught two self-defense classes every week for minors, though Liam had been slowly taking over that for nearly a year.

"Sawyer," Charlie called her from the ring in the middle of the gym. She put down the barbell she was using and walked over, eyeing the quiet teen from a week before. "You were right."

"I always am." She smiled at the young man. "What's your name?" She wasn't going to forget again.

"Trevor," he mumbled, looking at the ground.

"Anyone know you're here?" she asked him plainly.

"No," he continued to mumble. She was used to the kids

she trained being quiet. They were either terrified of her or defiant and ready to fight the world. They were all full of the same two things, though: anger and shame.

"Good." She patted his shoulder. She had nearly eight inches on the small kid. It reminded her of when she had first met Liam. He looked up at her and frowned.

"You said you trained minors self-defense?" He looked from her to Charlie, and they nodded. "I want to learn."

"Who?" She asked softly.

"Step-dad," he mumbled. "Not me, though. He goes after my mom, and I want to protect her."

Sawyer tensed and looked up at Charlie. Their eyes met, and she knew he would be okay with it. If it had been another teenager, she wouldn't get involved, but if an adult beat up on kids or defenseless people, she stepped in when she found out. She couldn't stop herself. She refused to see people beaten on like that for nothing more than existing, and that was really the only reason some abusers needed.

"Good thinking, young man." Charlie waved him closer. "Let me get your information and give you the schedule. If you want private lessons so you can advance quickly, we allow anyone over fourteen to work around the gym to earn hours of training. Ten hours of work for one hour of private training. You're allowed to work twenty hours a week in exchange for time with me or Sawyer."

She watched them walk off and clenched her fists. He was a good kid. Defending his mom? That was some noble shit right there. She and Charlie would make sure Trevor knew everything he needed to achieve that goal.

But Trevor wouldn't be dealing with the step-dad. She would be.

"Liam," she called him over. "Remember what I had you do the night we dealt with your brother and his friends?"

"Yeah." Sawyer could hear how uncomfortable he was. She had handled all five of the guys with ease right in front of him. He'd gotten the full show on how her powers worked and how she used them to fight. It was efficient. His entire job was to help her throw them into the truck they drove and get them to a hospital.

"Want to do it again?" She raised an eyebrow. She knew his answer. She had purposefully roughed up Carson more than necessary to put some fear into Liam at the idea of initiating violence. He was a non-Magi, and he would have no idea when he was in over his head if he accidentally picked a fight a Magi. She had shown him that.

"Not really," he mumbled.

"Good," she chuckled and slapped his shoulder. "Go help Charlie with Trevor. I'll handle the rest."

"Alright." Liam nodded. "You won't be around for the rest of the day?"

"Nope," she said softly, giving him a deadly smile. He only kept nodding before walking off. He knew what she was planning, but she figured it looked different now that he knew she was once an infamous and proficient assassin.

SAWYER WAITED PATIENTLY. She knew he would show up. A few easy questions around the neighborhood had told her what she needed to know in order to corner this guy on his way home.

It was nearly midnight when the asshole got home, drunk as fuck, trying to stumble up the stairs to his apartment where Trevor and his mother were. This dick wasn't going to make it up there, though. In fact, if he knew what was good for him, he was never going to see them again.

Charlie had gotten the boy's home address and his mother's name for paperwork. It was standard. Then Sawyer would use that information to fix the youth's problem. All the teenagers she trained knew it was her, but none of them ever confronted her, and they didn't tell anyone else.

She walked across the street to the man leaning against his building's door.

"Mr. Green?" she asked quietly. She didn't wear a mask, she didn't hide who she was when she showed up for these...meetings. She wanted these assholes to know exactly who was sending them on their way.

A little more side research during the day had told her that Trevor's mother was a hard worker, but her husband kept screwing things up for them. He was spending all their money on alcohol, then beating on her when there were no groceries. He refused to work, making her handle everything. Instead of the one steady job that could have covered her and Trevor, she was working three to keep up with his demands.

"Yeah?" He eyed her and then grinned. "What's a hot thing like you doing out here?"

"Fixing a problem." She smiled. "I'm only going to say this once. Listen closely." She pointed to the door. "I had the locks changed today, so your key won't work. All the other tenants have been taken care of, but I'm here to inform you that you won't be getting a key."

"Why the fuck won't I be getting a key? I fucking live here." He glared at her.

"Your name isn't on any lease for this building." She shrugged. "Therefore, you don't need a copy of the key. Now, on to part two. Find a new place to live. You don't live here anymore."

"Why?" he growled at her. "My fucking wife lives here, and I'm going to live with my wife and good for nothing step-son. He needs a father-figure in the home."

"He doesn't need one who beats his mother." She stepped closer. "We can do this the easy way, Mr. Green. You can leave and never turn back. When divorce papers show up, you'll sign them and pretend that Alicia and Trevor never existed. You will never hit another woman or her kid again. Trevor said you didn't hit him, but I have a feeling that it wasn't truthful."

"And if I say, 'Fuck the easy way'?"

"Then I send you to the hospital."

"Try me, bitch. No girl can-"

She didn't wait for him to finish. They never chose the easy way, but she always offered the choice just to see if they were even a tiny bit redeemable. She felt bone crunch under her right fist. She had hit him hard enough to give him an orbital fracture. She didn't wait for him to recover, grabbing his shoulder with her left hand and sending three solid upper cuts in his gut, making him vomit on to the stairs. She kneed his face, sending him flying back into a bush. He tried to stand up, and she let him wobble around, bringing his hands up. She gave a dark laugh and sent a left hook into his jaw. He staggered, and she stepped in close, leaning until her lips nearly touched his temple.

"You want to fight with a woman?" she snarled in his ear. "Then find one who can fight back, coward."

His groaning reply was satisfying, but not enough for her. She stepped back and landed a kick into his knee, buckling it backwards and sending him to the concrete, screaming in agony. Now *that* was the response she wanted.

She knelt and whispered to him, "You are never coming back here. Is that clear?"

KRISTEN BANET

"Yes, please! I beg you, stop. I'll never come back. I'll leave them alone. I'm sorry!"

She'd heard the same thing one hundred times at this point. She would keep his information on hand and check in every now and then, just to make sure he did what she asked. So far, none of the people she went after ever repeated their offenses. It wasn't just men, either. She'd taken out a couple of women who thought that they could treat their kids badly.

She and Charlie would let the kids stay with them until other family arrived. If there was no other family, they had a list of trusted and respected foster homes to put them in. They didn't let anyone get lost in the system. Trevor was lucky to have his mother. Most of the kids she helped had no one. Liam had only been the first, but he wasn't close to the last.

She hauled the man up and dragged him to the pickup truck she used only for this. No plates, all black, beat-up. If the cops got onto them for this, it was hard to identify and harder to find. She pushed him into the passenger seat and drove them to the hospital. She didn't bother getting out to send him in. She kicked him out his side once he opened the door, speeding off the moment she knew she wasn't going to run him over.

She couldn't leave them bleeding on sidewalks—it drew unwanted attention if they accidentally died—so she dropped them off at hospitals all over the city.

She slammed the truck door closed when she got back to the gym. She didn't bother checking to see if Charlie was around or out with his friends. Liam was tucked away in his apartment, now that they had run his brother back out of the city.

She hit the kitchen and began scrubbing. Blood covered

her hands, and she bit back the revulsion at the sight. Blood didn't really bother her, but the sight of it on her hands brought back memories.

She was looking down on an old man, choking on his own blood. Her hands were covered in it; her shoes were soaked. She reached to pull the dagger out of his chest, causing another pulse of blood to pour out and cover her shoes. A hand touched her shoulder, and she shook, fighting the urge to vomit at the scene as the hand led her away, telling her how well she did.

She swallowed and felt a cold sweat break out on her forehead. A door opened and closed as she scrubbed. The water was scalding hot. She never really felt good at the end of these things, but, in her mind, it was a necessary evil. She would deal with the nightmares of blood if she could help people make a step toward rebuilding their lives in safety, away from those who would force them to live in fear.

"Sawyer..." Charlie whispered, stepping to her side. "Your hands are clean, Sawyer." He reached out and turned off the water. She kept trying to scrub, her eyes still closed. She felt him grab her wrists, and she opened her eyes. Her hands had gotten red and would have started blistering if she had kept them in the water. She didn't feel the heat from Charlie's hands when he healed her this time, indicating she had probably screwed up the nerves in her hands.

"You normally don't do this," he said after releasing her. "It's never this bad."

"I think it's because I ran into Axel. Everything has been fucked up since then," she mumbled. "Will they be alright, old man?"

"Yeah, I stopped you before you did any real damage to yourself." He rubbed her shoulder. "And that problem you dealt with?"

She met his eyes, showing no emotion.

"Trevor and his mother will be fine," she whispered. She never told him more. If anyone ever found out what she was doing, her story was that she was breaking into his records without his knowledge. She wasn't going to tell him details. Details got people arrested instead of just questioned.

"Good." He nodded. "Friday Fight Night is in three days. Work out whatever is riding you there."

"I will, have no fear." She stepped past him and went to her room. The moment the door closed, she turned off all her lights, stripped, and climbed into her bed. Sleep wasn't going to come but she wasn't going to do this on the floor.

She curled into the fetal position and shook. At some point, Charlie walked in and put a blanket over her, but neither said anything. She didn't move until dawn.

"HENRY! NO!"

She thought she screamed it, but nothing came out of her open mouth.

A thud.

Blood on the tiles.

Cracks in the wall.

7

SAWYER

Fight Night, Fight Club, illegal fighting ring that shouldn't exist. Whatever anyone called it, they all meant the same thing. A good time.

Sawyer walked in, waving to the two guys who had volunteered for door-duty that night. She never did door-duty personally, but that was because she ran security for the entire thing. On Fight Night, the gym was hers and no one else's. Charlie even asked for her advice on matters.

Tonight though, she was also another fighter. She didn't participate very often, but she needed it tonight.

She wore a standard pair of low-rider jeans, torn thanks to actual work, and a black tank. She purposefully stepped heavier, so people didn't realize how silently she really moved. She nodded to Charlie as she passed him, not stopping to tell anyone hello on her way to the locker room. She could have just used the apartment, but she liked getting into the locker room and meeting the other fighters, or at least getting eyes on them.

She dropped her bag onto a bench and looked over at the other fighters. Sawyer was the only woman who showed up regularly to fight. She hadn't seen another female fighter in months, actually. The other women were girlfriends, ring girls, and patrons. So, when she looked over to the other fighters, she only saw a ton of dudes and nearly half were staring back at her.

"Can I help you?" She raised an eyebrow and began to untie her boots. Most of these guys knew who she was, but she saw more than a few new faces as well.

"You here to get with someone?" A new guy asked, causing a few of the other regulars to start coughing. A couple chuckles rang out, including one from her. "Because I'm single." He said it with a tiny smile and a suave voice.

"No." She grinned, kicking off her boots. New guys always thought they were cute. This one seriously was. Not her type, though. Too Italian. Not that she had anything against sexy Italians, they just reminded her of Axel and that made them... not her type anymore. She also wasn't sure she would ever want to get involved with a guy with a scar like his. Nearly two-inches wide and cutting his pec in half diagonally, it was a nasty piece of work. "I'm here to fight."

She pulled her tank off to reveal the black sports bra she wore to fight. She didn't have large breasts, so it wasn't like she was showing off anything. She saw the guys appreciate her abs.

"Well," the newbie continued, looking her over. "If you're interested, I'm game."

"I'm not, but thanks for the offer." She shook her head, still smiling. She got into her shorts quickly, ignoring the guys all talking shit before their own fights. No one knew who was fighting whom until they were called to the ring. There were rare occasions that they would know, but those fights were planned well ahead of time—rivalries and rematches, drama fights.

The locker room emptied, and she was still taking her sweet time getting ready. They wouldn't start until she got out there. Charlie found her as she was wrapping her hands. He pointed to her left hand and she sighed.

"What, Charlie?"

"Someone was asking how you lost it," he told her. She nodded slowly. "One of the new fighters, probably too scared to ask you himself. That Italian."

Of course, the one that hit on her. Cute.

"What did you tell him?"

"Same thing I tell everyone," Charlie chuckled. "If you wanted people to know, you would tell them. I wasn't going to offer the information."

"Thanks." She grinned at him. "Who am I fighting?"

"You know I'm not telling you that." Charlie patted her shoulder. "But you're in the prime spot tonight. People missed you while you were in LA."

"Well, I'm here now." She stood up and looked herself over one last time. When she was satisfied that she was ready, she gave him a cocky grin. "Let's get this show on the road."

They walked out together, and Sawyer waved to the crowd. The prime spot was the first fight, the show-stopping opener that everyone spent most of their gambling money on. People cheered, and ring girls riled the crowd up further, strutting around and showing off. One helped her into the ring, and Sawyer planted a kiss on her lips, making the crowd holler wildly. Sawyer wasn't the type to sleep with other women, but even she could appreciate some of the gorgeous ring girls that showed up.

Plus, it was good for her image to be involved like that.

Something sexy, fierce, and completely out of the viewers' leagues.

Being a fighter was as much show as it was fighting. A fighter developed a reputation as a hero or villain, a player or reserved character. She liked the limelight from fighting. She lived in the shadows for so much of her time, that when she got in the ring, she reveled in the lights and the crowd. It made her a fun fighter to watch, and people recognized her. No one in this group was going to give her up, either. They were all hiding from something outside of the gym. This was sanctuary.

"Tonight, we have a treat for you!" Charlie stood in center ring. "My very own Dark Darling is back in town, and tonight, we'll be seeing her bring out all the stops in a Magi fight against the up-and-coming star, Brick!"

People screamed, and Sawyer bounced on her feet, trying to get a little more limber before the punches started flying. She rolled her eyes at what Charlie called her, making him laugh as he continued.

"Now, we all know the rules, and there are very few!" Charlie pointed at them both. "No leaving the ring, and no letting your magic leave the ring. We don't call rounds here; you fight until you drop. Once someone is on the ground, you back off. If they get back up, go for it. If they don't, you've won the match. Finally, keep it short of killing each other. Fighters, ready to get started?"

She nodded and looked towards her opponent, Brick. He was short, maybe five and a half feet tall, but he was built like a truck. She made a quick judgement based on how he was carrying himself. Slow but he was probably a knockout champion. She couldn't afford to take too many hits from him.

"Fight!" Charlie stepped out of the way, and she moved

towards the center of the ring. Brick met her and took the first swing. She jumped back from it and grinned.

"Brick, huh?" She dodged another swing, and he glared at her.

"You going to dance around all night?" he asked, and she chuckled.

"I normally get to talk to all the fighters before getting in the ring, but I didn't see you in the locker room." She shrugged and looked out to the crowd. They were pressing to the side of ring, and she noticed they were nearly all cheering for her. "And you don't want me to stop dancing around."

She got hit with a blast of wind and raised an eyebrow at him. Wind manipulation. Well, if he had any finesse, he may cause her a problem.

"Why's that?" He grinned viciously at her. He was definitely going for the villain persona. Even if he wasn't trying for it, he was going to gain a reputation of being rude to the other fighters, and people would talk about it.

She sighed and blinked behind him. She no longer bounced on her feet as he turned around, wide-eyed, to face her. When he took another swing, she ended up behind him again. Blinking was instant, and there was nothing anyone could do to stop her from doing it. She couldn't blink through shields, though, and if someone got their hands on her, they would go with her for the ride until she could end the contact. She also needed line of sight. Cool ability, lots of stipulations to stop her from killing herself using it.

This time, she didn't wait for him to turn around. She put a punch into his kidney and kicked out the back of his knee, making him stagger.

"My fights are always a bit longer," she told him as he turned to face her after regaining his balance, "since I try my best not to use my powers too much. They seem a little much, don't they? But you want to rush things, so let's just get this over with."

He swung at her, roaring in anger. She didn't blink and let the hand pass through her. She had a lot of control over her sublimation ability, and when he was about to make contact, she had started the change into smoke. She solidified as she made her move. Two right jabs into the gut. Left hook into the jaw, and his head snapped to the side, blood and spit flying away from them.

She didn't wait for him to recover, pulling his head to her and sending her knee into his gut twice, making him grunt in pain. Hitting him was like hitting a brick wall, and she laughed at her realization. *Brick.*

She threw him back and blinked behind him before he could hit the side of the ring. Her elbow connected with the side of his head, and that was it. He fell to the mat and the crowd cheered, but Sawyer felt deeply unsatisfied with the win. The fight just didn't work it out for her. It was too short, too easy. This guy had wanted to rush it and she wanted more time in the ring.

She let Charlie raise her arm in victory, but her mind was elsewhere as she smiled out to the crowd. She didn't know where she was mentally or what was eating at her, but the distraction was there, taunting her.

She got out of the ring and sank into her seat, letting people come over and welcome her back. She laughed and tried to shake off her bad mood, but nothing seemed to help until Charlie sat down next to her and let another guy handle the ring.

"You need to have a drink and loosen up," Charlie chuckled. "I know you don't like Italians, but I hear there's one who thought you were pretty hot in the locker room. The one that asked about your hand."

"Wow," she snorted. "Really, Charlie?"

"Seriously," Charlie elbowed her. "Think about it."

"No." She shook her head with a grin, her eyes finding the new guy. He had a small fight and won. He hadn't used his magic, but he was obviously a Magi. She met his eyes, and even she could admit he was handsome. His voice might have been suave, but he had a ruggedness to him. A five o'clock shadow accented dark green eyes that seemed to bore into her. She looked over his cut abs and finally just shrugged at him. She saw his eyes go a little wide before she looked back to Charlie.

"Well?" Charlie started laughing softly.

"Still a no." Sawyer grinned. "I don't sleep with the fighters."

"I've never understood that rule of yours. I sleep with the ring girls when they offer."

"You old pervert," Sawyer laughed, slapping Charlie's arm. He only shrugged with a cheesy grin.

"My wife wouldn't want me to stop living life just because she was gone," Charlie reminded her. Sawyer knew that since she was the one who had convinced Charlie to live his life in the first place. He'd been a wreck when she showed up, at least emotionally. If he was going to force her to continue in this world, she had decided she would do the same to him.

"But a ring girl? Those girls are my age." Sawyer continued to laugh until tears rolled down her cheeks.

"I ignore that part," Charlie huffed. "Don't make it weird."

"Oh, I'm going to make it weird." Sawyer elbowed him. It

was actually a little gross, but Sawyer was going to make fun anyway. "Which one?"

"I'm not telling you that." Charlie narrowed his eyes on her. She didn't back down and broke out in a triumphant laugh when he relented. "Susan."

"Seriously? She's *twenty-one*, Charlie," Sawyer howled, delighted with the news.

"Deal with it," Charlie grumbled.

After that, the night moved along quickly. Fights were intense, everyone trying to give their best show. She cheered and even got in on the gambling, going from a hundred dollars in her wallet to a thousand. She poured everyone shots at one point because of her good fortune. Everyone except Charlie, who had just lost a bet to her and was pouting over it.

When they got inside the apartment after cleaning up, she and Charlie were laughing about a fight where some noodle-armed guy decided he had what it took and won. He had ten to one odds against him, but he got in a lucky hit. It was the clumsiest shit Sawyer had ever seen, but he'd done it. She and Charlie hadn't bet on that fight, since they thought it was too one-sided, but they were already making plans to bet on the kid's next fight.

"Good night, Charlie," she called to him as she staggered, a little drunk, to her own room.

"Good night, kid," he laughed, waving her along.

She collapsed into her bed and drifted into a deep sleep. For the first time in weeks, it was dreamless.

8

SAWYER

Sawyer straightened her hair slowly, preparing for another Fight Night. Three weeks of day-in and day-out life had done a lot to ease her concerns over what had happened in LA a month before. Once she was done, she went downstairs to find Trevor and his mother waiting in the main area. The gym would be closed in twenty minutes, so she frowned and walked over. It was late, and the teens were normally out of there around seven; it was nearly nine.

"Can I help you?" She stopped near them, careful not to get too close and in their space. Alicia smiled at her and nodded, extending a hand. Sawyer shook it and was pleased to notice that Alicia gave her a real handshake and not some dainty, weak-wristed one.

"Yes, actually. My son takes classes here, and I was hoping to join, myself." She elbowed her son, and Sawyer grinned.

"We have adult classes on every night of the week for those parents with busy schedules. You can pick any days you want to come, and your first five classes are free of charge."

Sawyer ran over to the desk and grabbed a flyer. She handed it to Alicia when she got back. "Any reason you want to learn?"

"I'm recently single and thought that it would be a good idea to learn to protect myself, since I don't want Trevor to feel that he needs to do it all." She pulled her son closer into a hug. "We're a team, he and I."

Sawyer eyed Trevor and gave a knowing smile. He nodded a little. He was telling her that the step-dad was officially out of the picture. She had contacts with a few divorce lawyers and tried to help them expedite the process. Alicia had no idea, but Trevor did.

He'd been the first kid to call her out about his missing step-dad, and she had chosen to be honest with him. Yeah, she beat the shit out of him and chased him off. Since then, they had been as thick as thieves about getting his mother free of her now-ex. Sure, the other teens she trained knew what she did, but there was a general rule that it wasn't talked about. Trevor had confronted her after his first day in her class, right in front of everyone, the little shit.

"I'm glad. He's a good kid around here, we've been happy to have him." Sawyer heard Charlie come in and looked over to him. "Right, Charlie?"

"Huh? Trevor? Yeah, good kid, but needs work on his right hook. He's a leftie so it's to be expected." He shrugged, and Sawyer rolled her eyes to Alicia, who was laughing.

"We won't keep you any longer. I just wanted to grab some information, and we were passing by and saw you were still open." She waved to them, and Sawyer waved back. She fist-bumped with Trevor and watched them walk out.

"Feels good, doesn't it?" Charlie walked up to stand next to her, and she nodded.

"Yeah, it does."

"There's no money in it..."

"I have enough money," she laughed. "You said it yourself. Retire with what I have and just live life. I'm following *your* advice."

"You have a bug though, Sawyer," Charlie chuckled. "I give it another month, and you'll be itching to go back out and get a job, break into something, or cause some level of general mayhem in someone's life."

"So much faith." She rolled her eyes, but the smile didn't leave her face. He was probably right. Sawyer didn't have it in her to settle down and never had. Once she got out of Georgia, she started traveling the world. New York was her home base in a sense, but she loved picking up sometimes to see a new place. Jobs did that for her.

"Let's get this all set up." He thumped her arm and began to walk off. She started pulling out chairs and prepping for Fight Night. Tonight was special. Liam was coming in for the first time. He was old enough, and it was going to be fun. This would be the first time she did a fight with him in the building.

A chime from the front door told her Liam was there.

"I'm here!" He called, and Sawyer grinned at him.

"Get over here and help me set up!" She laughed, pulling him in for a hug. "You excited?"

"Yeah, and you sure seem to be," Liam laughed. "It's not like I haven't been asking for a year."

"Well, I figured, since you know all of the rest, why not let you in on this, now?" Sawyer shrugged. "I also think you're the only one interested in this."

"Well, I did spend four years listening to it from the stairs," Liam chuckled.

"Yeah, I know." Sawyer elbowed him. "I remember Charlie and me chasing you off every time, too."

"What about me?" Charlie walked by and frowned at them. She just grinned until he narrowed his eyes and shook his head before leaving.

"People are going to get here in like, ten minutes," she whispered to Liam. "Let's get this done."

They worked for nearly an hour to set up, even as people started filing into the gym. Tables were set up for the makeshift bar where people could put their alcohol for anyone to drink. Sawyer nearly couldn't finish her work when the ring girls started hitting on Liam, who had never had a girlfriend, as far as she knew. Liam kept his secrets when it came to those relationships, and she didn't blame him. She and Charlie were nosy.

"I need to get ready." She could barely speak without cackling, and Liam tried to hide his face as a girl sat on his lap. "Behave."

By the time she made it to the locker room, the first fight was being called into the ring, and most of the fighters were out in the main area to watch. A couple girls hung around outside the locker room door, trying to get some private time with any of the men left, and she only nodded to them. She didn't hold it against them for looking for a night with a hot fighter, and she never would. A girl had needs, and those needs had to be met, which only reminded Sawyer that she hadn't gotten laid in two long months. Between the job in LA and getting back into the groove in New York, she hadn't gone out hunting for her own night of fun in quite some time.

When she got inside, she stopped at the scene in front of her. She quietly recited the most important rule to herself.

What happened in the locker room, stayed in the locker room.

"Baby," a woman whispered, tears running down her face. "Please! I ain't cheating on you!"

"Yet, you seemed real interested in Carlos," the fighter snapped at the woman, who must have been his girlfriend. Sawyer quietly put her bag down and watched. She wouldn't get involved in a break up, which this obviously was, until she felt it went too far. She had a line where she decided to step in, and she couldn't do it earlier.

"He's an old friend from high school!" She cried, and the fighter pinned her to a set of lockers between his arms. Sawyer narrowed her eyes. He wasn't touching her, yet.

"One you used to fuck," he snarled. "Don't fucking lie to me. You've been seeing him behind my back."

Sawyer wished she could say she rarely saw scenes like this one, but when someone was involved in more... criminal activities, they didn't exactly see the shiny gold stars of society. This was all too familiar to her.

"We just met for dinner before coming here! He's an old friend, that's all. I promise," she begged, and the fighter lost his patience at that. Sawyer didn't wince at the sound of his hand connecting to the girl's cheek. It was Sawyer's sign to step in.

"Girl, get the fuck out," she growled. Both looked over to her. "Girl, *leave*. Find Charlie. Tell him to come back here in ten minutes."

"You don't get to order my woman around." The fighter turned to Sawyer fully, and Sawyer slowly pulled off her tank top. "If I think this whore needs some di-"

Sawyer didn't wait for him to finish. She blinked forward and connected a swing to his jaw, causing him to recoil back. Sawyer had a lot of patience for a lot of things, but this had never been one of them. It was why she went after abusive parents and spouses. People didn't deserve to get beat on by people who were supposed to love them.

The girl screamed and started running out. The fighter wasn't a Magi, but Sawyer didn't care about that as she used her powers to get behind him and kick his legs out from under him. When he hit his knees, she kicked him square in the face. Sawyer was brutally efficient and efficiently brutal, and she never pulled a punch.

He fell on his back. She straddled him and grabbed his shirt, pulling him up just a little to get close to his face.

"You must be fucking new here," she snarled. "No one fucks around like that when I'm in town, asshole. I don't give a damn what you think or feel. I don't give a damn if the other guys here don't care. What happens in the locker room, stays in the locker room, right? Well, you better start praying to whatever god you believe in that I decide to leave you breathing, because no one is going to stop me while we're in here."

She kept hold of his shirt and punched him. Bone crunched. Once. Twice. Three times. She lost count at four, but always made sure he was still breathing. She couldn't kill him, no matter how much she wanted too. Her temper was cold. Her magic had the room frigid. Her face gave away nothing. She went to the place that had once made her the best assassin on the planet. The place that desperation had created in her mind, so she could handle the violence that her life had been soaked in at the time.

When she felt it was over, she stood up and threw a towel on him.

"Now clean the fuck up like a good boy and get the fuck out of *my* locker room," she told him, her voice matching the chilly temperature of her temper. He groaned and tried to stand. Instead, he just sat up. He tried to stand again, but fell back over into a bench.

She waited patiently, looking at her watch. Her right hand was covered in blood, but she was able to hold herself together as Charlie walked in slowly.

"What happened?" He asked quietly, pointing to the groaning man on the floor.

"He slapped her," she whispered. "I saw it, and I handled it."

"Okay. Go clean up. Remember, once you walk out there, this didn't happen. Carly was taken home by one of the regulars."

Carly. That was her name, huh? She should have asked before sending her out.

Sawyer turned away and went to the small bathroom. She stared blankly at the woman in the mirror. Blood had spattered over her right cheek. Well. She washed it off quickly. This wasn't the place for her to go into total freak mode over the sight of blood.

When she stepped out of the bathroom, the guy was no longer on the floor. Charlie was still waiting for her though, watching her carefully.

"This can't keep happening," Charlie whispered to her. "Since LA, you've been different. You're trying to hide it, but you are failing miserably. I've never seen you behave this... cold before."

"I'm fine, Charlie. This guy just... scratched an old memory that had been a little close to the surface." She met his eyes, and he shook his head.

"They all scratch old memories for you, but you never-"

"I always do this to them, Charlie." She smiled ruefully. "It's why I don't tell you about it. Not the gory details. Liam's dad was a one-off."

She stepped around him as he put a hand on his chest and rubbed his heart. She grabbed her bag and changed as he just watched her.

"One of them is going to call the cops on you one day," he told her, quiet and stern.

"Why do you think we have the truck without a license plate?" She wrapped her hands without a care. She'd cut one of her knuckles on the guy's face and she relished in the sting of it for a moment. "Drop it, Charlie. It's worked for us for years and there's no reason for that to change now."

"Of course," Charlie huffed. She knew he wasn't mad at her. He was worried. Some part of her still craved the hunt and thrill of being an assassin, even if she didn't kill people anymore. She had diverted that part to the dregs of humanity, those who deserved to be taught her brutal lesson.

"Let's get out there before people start to notice that something is going down," she told him shortly, pointing toward the door out to the main area. She left him standing there as he mumbled that it was too late. She grabbed a ring girl as she made her way into the crowd. With her arm over the woman's shoulder, she bummed a smoke and let the little Magi woman light it for her.

She took a long drag as she sat down, pulling her new friend onto her lap. She still had appearances to keep, so she reclined back her seat, and the ring girl laughed about something with someone who passed by.

"What's your name?" Sawyer asked as another fight got started.

"Stacie." She smiled at Sawyer. "You don't need to tell me yours. I hear you are pretty secretive."

"Really?" Sawyer grinned. "Well, you can call me Cambrie." It was her middle name and one she gave to her hook ups, since it was easy to remember. She wouldn't be hooking up with Stacie, not Sawyer's type, but she could at least give the ring girl a name.

"Well, Cambrie," Stacie leaned into her and kissed Sawyer's cheek. "Do you want me to get you anything to drink?"

"I'll take a whiskey on the rocks, but only one. I've got a fight later." Sawyer chuckled as Stacie left her lap and walked away. When Stacie brought the drink back, she didn't stay with Sawyer. *At least I got a drink out of it*, Sawyer thought to herself.

She sipped on the whiskey and watched the girls flirt with Liam. He was going to avoid her for the rest of the night now, and she couldn't blame him.

Charlie never did show up and sit with her, but they didn't always hang out at these things. At one point, she saw that handsome Italian wandering around. He wasn't dressed the same as he'd been the previous times she'd seen him. Tonight, it was black cargo pants and a tight black shirt. She wasn't sure which was better. Him in a well-fitted shirt or him shirtless. Sawyer was mildly impressed that he made a simple black tee look that good.

She slipped between the ropes and looked over at her opponent. She grinned, ready to get in another fight. She hadn't expected to get two fights in one night, but then again, what happened in the locker room was hardly a fight.

It was a magicless fight, and it was exactly what she needed. She even took a couple hits.

9

ZANDER

Zander leaned against the wall when she walked in at the start of the night with the large black guy, Charlie, trailing behind her. He remained in the thickest part of the crowd, invisible to her as he observed. She had such a swagger to her walk that he wanted to grin. Some things, he thought, never changed.

They had been watching her for weeks, with Elijah or Vincent closer while Zander and Jasper backed them up. They learned about her work at Charlie's gym, and, one night around midnight, they found her leaving and tailed her. She was so confident in her privacy in New York, she hadn't noticed them.

They didn't intervene when he and Vincent saw her put a man in the hospital that night. What had been said and their own plans to get her into custody deterred them from trying to stop the brutal, back-alley justice Sawyer had a reputation for dispensing. They had only heard the whispers of rumors until that moment. That night, they had a front row seat to the woman Sawyer had grown into.

He remembered the rush of pride and utter terror he felt

at the look on her face when she was done. She had blood splattered all over herself. It dripped from her knuckles and was starting to create a pool in the dark summer night, though carefully out of range of the streetlight.

He waited impatiently for her to leave the locker room, wondering why she hadn't come out within minutes, like she had on other nights. When a young woman ran out with a red, bruising mark on her, Zander tensed. Vincent met his eyes from across the room and gave a tiny shake of his head. They couldn't reveal themselves. No one else even paid the girl any attention, and Zander curled his hand into a fist. Sawyer hung around some real pieces of shit at these things. She didn't interact with them much, but she was in their world and they were in hers.

What had led the feisty young teen he'd known to live like this? Zander was confused and a little irked, but Jasper was having a hard time with it. The lack of knowledge on *why* was eating away at him. She had been so awesome when he and Jasper left for the IMAS, to make a better life for all of them, but then she got adopted and promptly disappeared, never contacting them again. When they got into the IMPO, they started to search. After six years, they had found nothing—until Axel nearly killed her.

He watched Charlie stroll back to the locker room and repositioned himself to get comfortable. People around him had gone a little quiet, except for a few whispers.

"She's done it, don't you think?" A guy whispered to another attendee. The other one slowly nodded.

"Yeah," he mumbled. "She's why I don't bring my girl to these things. She jumped out of the ring once and took a guy outside for a beat down when he slapped his girl around a little. She's got a gnarly temper and doesn't know how to mind her own business. She's just scary as fuck."

Zander raised an eyebrow. So, even the people here knew about her. She'd always been the type to go from zero to one-hundred with her temper, but somewhere along her road to this place in her life, something had changed. Zander knew that much.

"Shit, look at that guy," another person in the crowd gasped. Zander flicked a look back over to the locker room. Holy hell. She had made him unrecognizable. Why weren't people freaking out more? Why was she allowed here to fight, if she could do that to a guy in the locker room? Surely there had to be some rules.

"I'd fuck her, if I didn't think she'd eat my head like one of those bugs do," the first one chuckled. Zander wanted to grab him by his long brown hair and slam his face into the wall. "Maybe that's what she needs, a strong man to put her in her place."

Zander's own temper flared at the conversation happening only feet from him.

"Nah, she's too muscular for me," the second snorted. "I mean look at her," he jerked his head toward the locker room.

Sure enough, Zander had been distracted by their conversation and missed her coming out. She had a fake smile plastered on her face, one he'd seen years before. She was never very good at pretending and had always worn her emotions on her sleeve. He watched her flirt with one of the ring girls and smirked. The Sawyer he grew up with really was still there. Darker, more dangerous, but still there.

He kind of liked the dangerous feel to her now. The toned body, the sharp edge of barely contained violence, and the swagger to her walk. He had been infatuated as a teenager, but something about Sawyer all grown up really got him going. Zander always was a risk taker, and toying with a woman like her seemed incredibly risky.

"Why isn't she in trouble?" he asked a ring girl who passed by. "For that guy?"

The girl looked him over and smiled. Zander gave a smile back to the blonde, hoping to coax the information he wanted out of her.

"You must be new," she chuckled. "What happens in the locker room stays in the locker room. If she caught him hitting his girl, then he deserved what he got. Some of the guys here might not like her for it, but she's got a fan club with the women." Then she shrugged. "Plus, she's Charlie's roommate and business partner. Those two own this gym, so if people don't like how things are done, they can stop showing up."

"Makes sense." He grinned, showing a pearly white set of teeth. She blinked and blushed a little. "I'm glad someone is looking out for you gorgeous women, here. Seems like a rough place."

She stuttered a little bit, then wandered off, still blushing. Zander smiled to himself as he looked back to Vincent. He was talking to Charlie. Zander wondered how mad Sawyer was going to be when she found out that their contact for getting close to her was the old man she trusted the most. He was cagey with them, but he wanted to get her out of the criminal world and knew only the team could do that. Charlie had been thoroughly freaked by her and Axel running into each other.

When Sawyer got called to the ring, Charlie left Vin and headed towards Zander. Zander shook his hand when he got close.

"Charlie," Zander smiled pleasantly.

"Z," Charlie said curtly. "You aren't going to get her on assault charges, right?"

"We already caught her on a midnight... escapade and didn't arrest her. We haven't shut this place down. Why would we drag her off in handcuffs now?" Zander shrugged. "Doesn't do us any good."

"Sure. So, Vincent said you all had a plan, but he didn't elaborate. He told me to come talk to you, away from the ring." Charlie seemed uncomfortable, but Zander could forgive him for it. Zander was impressed with the guy. He'd been great about not letting Sawyer in on anything going on behind her back.

"Get her to go out tonight," Zander whispered. "Then, you should stay with a friend for the night."

"That's all?" Charlie frowned. Zander nodded, dismissing him. Charlie's eyes turned hard, and Zander rolled his own.

"We're not telling you the entire plan. I'm telling you what you need to do," he growled softly. "Take it or leave it."

"You are lucky as hell I recognized you from her old photos. It's the only reason I trust you or your friends in this building. You're my only option for getting her out of all of this," Charlie growled, turning to stomp off. Zander ran a hand through his hair, sighing to himself.

They had wasted so much time setting this up that they had no idea if Axel was close to finding her. He didn't have access to the things they got from the IMPO, but Zander knew that nothing stopped Axel for long. New York might be considered a safe zone for Magi, but that probably wouldn't stop Axel from trying to get what he wanted.

He heard a cheer rise from the crowd and looked back to the ring. Sawyer was fighting without magic tonight, and she was killing it. She was as quick as lightening, determined, and intelligent. She got a focused look in her eyes, but she always kept a taunting smirk on her face unless her opponent pissed her off. She was popular among the crowd, too. She was made for the ring.

But Zander still was haunted by the most important unanswered question. How the actual fuck did she end up as a thief and fighter hiding in New York after nearly getting killed by Axel?

If their plan worked, he and Jasper would be getting the answers they wanted very soon. If their plan worked, he was also going to be out one hundred dollars.

10

SAWYER

Sawyer changed and showered in the apartment after the fight. She was about to sit down when Charlie stomped in.

"Get up. We're going out," he told her, grabbing her elbow and pulling her from the half squat she was in.

"Excuse me?" She jerked away, confused. "I didn't agree to go out tonight."

"You need it." Charlie grinned at her. "And I want you to come out with me and all the guys and other fighters. Come on, you haven't been out with us since before LA."

She groaned and leaned on him. The night had been interesting enough, and now the old fart wanted to drag her out? *It's one in the morning*, she thought, a little cranky.

"Charlie, why?" She considered pouting, but she was too old and much too tough for that. He wouldn't buy it, anyway.

"Because no matter what I've done over the last few weeks, you haven't gotten out of your slump." Charlie dragged her to her room. "Get changed. Wear something hot, get laid, and out of my hair for a couple of days. Shit, I'll stay with a lady friend so you can have the apartment."

That had her laughing hysterically, even with her aching and tired bones. This wasn't the first time Charlie demanded that she relax and cut loose for an evening. She was already clean and just needed to change.

"Charlie, are you taking your own truck?" she called out.

"Yeah, no worries!" he called back.

She changed into her favorite pair of leather pants. She didn't get to wear them enough, sticking to jeans when she was running around on errands. She grabbed a few shredded tank tops and layered them, then spent a moment frowning. Should she cover up the scar between her breasts or not? It wasn't like she could hide the missing finger, and if the night went well, some guy would be seeing her scars anyway...

She decided not to cover it and grabbed a light leather jacket. She knew Charlie was waiting on her to get moving, so she couldn't just hide out. She slipped into her favorite boots. She didn't own any heels. She would probably look good in them, but she didn't want to be over six feet tall. The boots added an inch, and that put her at six feet even; she had no need or desire to be much taller. It was hard enough to get laid, since she really liked men taller than her; she didn't need to make it impossible.

"Let's go, old man," she laughed, walking back into the living room. Charlie looked her over and nodded, satisfied. She was sliding a ring on her right middle finger when he finally started moving again.

"Come on," he chuckled. She was quiet as they walked into the garage. She got into her own car, and Charlie led them to their favorite biker bar in his truck. She slid out of her car and followed him inside. She saw the ring girls having beers in a booth and the more regular fighters scattered around the bar, talking to women. She left Charlie as he walked to the booth and immediately hit the bar. Him and those ring girls. Sawyer shuddered at the thought. She should have never asked.

"Whiskey." She wasn't in the mood for anything else. She found that the one she had earlier in the night had hit the spot. When she got her drink, she turned and looked over the bar. Some new faces that she wanted to pay attention to, but no one she found interesting *enough*. Damn.

She turned back to the bartender and sighed. He chuckled at her, took her glass, and topped it off, even though she had only taken three swallows. She and Jeffery had a connection, though they never spoke to each other beyond drink orders.

She sat on a stool, placing her elbows on the bar as she drank. By the end of her drink, the bar was getting more crowded, not less. By two a.m., all the seats in the bar were taken, and she knew that Fight Night had followed the fighters to the bar.

"Another, Jeffery," she sighed, sliding her empty glass to the bartender. He nodded and began pouring her a new one, leaving his other orders waiting.

"Let me pay for that," a deep, country-accented voice said over her right shoulder. It was friendly and masculine. This guy was out looking for a good time. She slid off her stool and turned slowly so she could see this new option for her night. He was obviously making the first move, and that seriously impressed her.

She didn't believe in the gods, from any pantheon, but she knew one when she saw one. Not really, he was just another Magi like her, but *holy shit*. She thought the Italian was handsome? Ha. Ha. Ha.

He towered over her by more than a few inches, and his hazel eyes danced brightly under the shadow of his black cowboy hat. It hid the color of his hair, but that didn't matter. Hell, he could have been balding, and she wouldn't have cared. He had a warm face and an easy-going smile that had more than a touch of cockiness to it. He knew he looked good with a couple days scruff on his jaw. She looked down his body slowly, taking her sweet time. She was in no rush as she took in the man's physique. Thick neck, broad shoulders and chest, trim waist, arms bigger than *her* thighs, and his legs, in blue jeans, promised to be just as defined as the rest of him.

"Having a good time there, gorgeous? Going to take me out to dinner before you undress me in your head?" He chuckled. His southern accent brought out her own, something she worked hard to hide, but she couldn't stop herself.

"We're past that point," she laughed, giving him a smirk. "I'll take your name, though, before I fuck you in my imagination." She waited a long time for that piece of information as he looked her over just as slowly as she had done to him. At least she and Mr. Cowboy were on the same page. She saw the heat in his eyes as he looked over her toned legs wrapped in leather. "What, I don't get even a name before *you* undress *me*, big fella? Like what you see?"

"Evan. I hate bars, but I would love to see more nearly anywhere else. You?"

Well, he was forward. So was she, but she had just gotten a fresh drink. She needed to slow them right on down. She was here to get laid, but she was far too sober.

"My name is Cambrie," she chuckled. *Time to bring out the middle name for hookups*, she thought. "I'll make you a deal. You stand there, look good for an hour, let me wear the hat, and I'll follow you anywhere. Also, keep the drinks coming, Cowboy."

His laugh was booming. He immediately dropped the cowboy hat on her head and leaned down to her.

"Just promise me that you know how to ride." He winked. She tipped the hat's brim, a dare for him to try and find out later.

"Riding is the easy part, Cowboy," she told him confidently.

"Ride a lot, do you?" He leaned on the bar, looking down on her. The cowboy hat was just a little too big, and she had to push it up to keep her eyes on his.

"I've never ridden a horse in my life." She shook her head with a laugh at the face he gave her. She knew where his mind had taken that comment. "Motorcycles are more my thing."

"Find yourself on the back of a lot of motorcycles then?" He raised an eyebrow back at her, and she shook her head again.

"No, Sugar." She poked his chest. Sugar. God, sometimes the Georgia just fell right out of her mouth and she couldn't stop it. It might have been the cowboy in front of her and his own accent bringing hers on. "I ride my own. Got a problem with it?"

"Not at all." He raised his hands. "I *love* the idea that you can handle something big and powerful. That's a good skill to have. What do you ride?"

Did everything he said have to sound like he wanted her to ride *him* into the sunset? This guy was gloriously good at making a woman feel wanted. Shivers ran up her spine at the thought. Very good shivers.

"My BMW R 1200 R is my favorite, but I've owned a few over the years." She shrugged. "You ride?"

"I don't have any motorcycles, but I have a few things I like to race. Don't get to go out with them as much as I want." He sighed and shrugged back at her.

"I feel you." She nodded. "Never enough time, and the nice days just go too fast."

"Amen." He ordered himself a Jack Daniels and sipped on it. "Where you from?"

"Georgia." She smiled out to the bar, a little wistful for a moment. She missed the simplicity of it sometimes. Only sometimes.

"Long way from home, then," he said as he stepped closer to her. "I'm from Texas, but currently live in Georgia, myself. Miss the hell out of it while I'm away."

They talked about everything and nothing after that. Work (she kind of lied), family (she definitely lied), what hobbies they had (she didn't lie on this one).

"You like working on engines?" He sounded a bit shocked. "You're a hobby mechanic?"

"Yeah, give me a tool kit and a little fixer-upper and I'll stay in the garage for days. I like doing things with my hands." She grinned, raising one of her eyebrows. She hadn't been able to work on anything in months, too wrapped up with everything else going on in her life. Bringing it up reminded her how much she missed toying around with mechanics.

"You want to do something with those hands tonight?" he asked her seductively, leaning in close, his broad chest close to her own. Her hour was up, and this guy had a one-track mind she could appreciate.

She put down the empty glass that had been her third drink and ran her right hand across his chest. She was a little tipsy at this point, so her sex kitten was coming out to play.

"Damn right, I do." She stepped back and beckoned him to follow with a finger. "My place?"

"I think your place is perfect," he growled softly, a smile on those full lips. She would be enjoying those soon enough. "I've got a rental for my trip up here, so if you're okay riding with me..."

"We'll take my car. It's nicer than a rental." She smiled and continued moving toward the door. She also wasn't leaving it in a parking lot all night.

They rode in relative silence, Sawyer enjoying the buzz she had going and the anticipation of a nice night with this gorgeous man. When they got to her place, he helped her out of the car and pulled her close to him. Finally, a chance to get an idea of what he was packing.

And he was packing. It pressed into her stomach, and she swallowed at the prospective size of it. *Well.* Her inner sex kitten was going to climb trees tonight.

He kissed her, pushing her into the side of the Audi in the garage, and she gasped from the rough, sensual nature of it. His hands roamed her sides, pushing her tanks up and exploring the bare skin of her hips. He kissed her jawline down to her neck, then back up to her ear. He nibbled her ear lobe, making her moan from want.

"We should go to my room," she mumbled, distracted by what he was doing.

"We should. Tell me how to get there," he growled softly, grinding his hips against her own. He picked her up and led her legs to wrap around his waist. Now this was something she could get used to. "You got protection, sweet thing?"

"I'm protected," she whispered. She had magical protection, actually. It cost a pretty penny, but the enchanted ring on her right hand kept her from getting pregnant while she wore it.

"Thank fuck," he chuckled, wrapping a hand in her hair and kissing her before she was finally able to give him directions up to the apartment over the gym.

The moment the apartment door was locked behind them, they were all over each other again. Her hands were under his shirt, and she let her nails trail over his exceptional abs, making him groan and squeeze her ass roughly. She thrilled at the strength in him.

Once they were in her room, he dropped her on the bed and moved her hands over her head, kissing her as he held her down with one hand. She wasn't paying attention to his second arm as it went above her head as well. She was focused on his mouth on her neck, on her jawline, on her ears, and finally her lips. Fuck, Evan knew what he was doing.

She was, however, paying attention to the handcuffs she heard click into place.

"Well, Evan, I'm just not into that." She leveled a stare at him and tried to go into her smoke form to get out of the cuffs. She couldn't. Oh, fuck. The heavy sensation of her magic being locked away from her suddenly became very apparent. *No.*

"Well, my name is Elijah," he growled, lifting off her. His tone was still playful, but she was definitely *not* feeling this hookup anymore. "And those are enchanted, so they block your abilities. Specifically, yours, Sawyer. So, let's not beat around the bush." He pulled something out of his back pocket, and she felt the cold rush of realization at the badge he flashed and his use of her real name. "I'm actually Special Agent Elijah Grant with the International Magi Police Organization, and you are now in the custody of the World Magi Council and the IMPO."

"You fucking *imp*," she growled, sitting up and bringing

her hands in front of her. Imp was a derogatory term for agents of the International Magi Police Organization, or the IMPO for short. They hated getting called that most of the time, but this ass seemed completely unfazed.

She couldn't blink or phase. She couldn't do fucking anything. She kicked out at him and he grabbed her leg and flipped her over, so she was on her stomach.

"Fuck you, asshole!"

"Calm down," Elijah chuckled. "The rest of my team will be here soon enough, and then you are going to have a long talk with us."

"You can go rot," she hissed, looking over her shoulder at him. He had her legs pinned to the bed, and she couldn't kick at him anymore.

"Sawyer, calm the fuck down. You're only cuffed so you won't run." He groaned, and she was mildly disturbed by the fact that he still had a hard on while he held her pinned for his team to get there.

She heard the front door open and close minutes later. Footsteps of several people could be heard, and she bucked wildly.

She was fucking arrested. Of all the ways her Friday night could go, she went and found the one guy in the bar who would fucking arrest her.

No, she didn't find him. He had *targeted* her, and the fact that he knew she was there... That had implications she didn't want to consider.

When had she gotten sloppy?

The fucked job when Axel had set her up. She'd been so worried about Axel that she'd forgotten to cover her tracks better. Holy fuck. She'd been so worried he would show up, she didn't consider the fucking IMPO. Of all the fucking things.

"Hmmm," Elijah mumbled to himself. "I'll have to remind Z that he owes me a hundred bucks when he gets here. He said this wouldn't work..."

"I'm right here," another voice said. It tugged at a memory, but Sawyer couldn't place it. "I'll pay you later, asshole." Elijah finally got off her, and she took the chance to throw a kick at him, hitting his thigh.

"Holy shit, mother fucker, goddamn it," he groaned louder, obviously in pain this time. Someone grabbed her leg, so she kicked with the other, rolling over to see who was stupid enough to touch her.

The red hair left her stunned. The brilliant green eyes left her speechless. The freckles she could still count to the very last one made the blood leave her head, making her a little faint.

The face from her past was staring down at her, trying to hold back a grin. Z. Zander Wade. Her best friend and the guy she gave her virginity. Standing in her bedroom wearing black combat gear and holding her leg to keep her from kicking again.

"Nice to see you, Sawyer." He grinned and kept his tone friendly. "It's been a long time."

A long time. Nine years. She didn't respond, but she knew her mouth was open. He didn't have gauged ears when she last saw him. He hadn't been inked so much that even his neck was covered. But even with those superficial changes, he hadn't changed at all. Well, he was taller. He looked to be about Elijah's height.

"Jasper's here too, in the living room. We were recruited into the IMPO after a couple of years with IMAS. How have you been?" Zander didn't move, only kept talking. Elijah was rubbing his thigh, looking between them, as if he expected a bomb to go off.

"What the fuck?" was the first thing out of her mouth.

"Should have figured that would be what you had to say," Zander sighed, looking at Elijah. "Help me get her out there?"

"If she promises not to try and send my balls back into my body." Elijah looked at her, and she hissed, baring her teeth. "I think that's a no."

"Don't be a coward," Zander chuckled. "You won a Benjamin from me, dick, but now you get to deal with the pissed off woman it cost you."

They both reached for her at the same time, and she finally snapped back into action. She didn't care if it was Zander. He was IMPO, and she wasn't going to fucking jail. She kicked out with both legs; but the guys were ready for her, each grabbing one leg and yanking her off the bed. Her back hit the floor with a thump, and the air got knocked out of her.

"Fuck," she groaned. "What the hell?"

"We wouldn't have done that, if you hadn't tried to fight," Zander sighed. "Now let us get you into the living room without any more stupid shit, Sawyer."

"Was she like this growing up?" Elijah reached down and hauled her up with one arm. She shook him off the moment she was on her feet, glaring at the gorgeous trap they had set. *Gorgeous. Fucking. Trap.*

"Yeah." Zander nodded, watching her. "Come on, Sawyer. Living room."

"I'm not seven, asshole," she growled. "I can go where I damn well please."

"Actually, you're in the custody of several IMPO Special Agents, so you can't." Elijah laughed, grabbing her elbow and hauling her out of the bedroom. Zander stayed next to her until she was nearly tossed into one of her dining room chairs.

She looked around the room and frowned. Yeah, there was Jasper, still looking like the star of some football team, even though he had never played the sport a day in his life. Maybe he picked it up, but she didn't think so, not with his old knee injury. She also recognized the other one. That fucking *Italian*.

"Sawyer," Jasper whispered, staring at her. She couldn't identify the emotion on his face, but whatever it was, he wasn't very good at hiding it. "You look..."

"Let's not go there," she mumbled, looking away from him. "So, where am I going to prison?"

11

SAWYER

"Y ou're not," the Italian told her blandly. "You're being forcefully brought into protective custody. For your own safety."

She snapped her head over to him and frowned, bringing her eyebrows together. What? She focused on the darks curls, refined face, and... olive-green eyes. Darker than Axel's, but she instantly hated this guy because of them. He really looked nothing like Axel, even with the similar eyes. She hadn't gotten this close of a look before, but she knew he irked her for a reason. He reminded her of Axel.

"Can you elaborate?" She didn't trust him, and it wasn't just his looks. Something about the way he spoke and the way he behaved, disinterested and reserved, set off warning bells in her head. It was completely different than his attitude in the locker room had been.

"Sawyer, our team was called in to investigate the LA incident with Axel." Jasper leaned forward in his seat, closer to her. "We saw what happened there and tracked you down to keep you alive."

"Well," the Italian kept his reserved tone and his nearly

cold and calculating look, "they did. I'm here because I want you to tell me everything you know about him."

"Vincent." Elijah swatted his arm. "Can you... just not with that for one night?"

She still hadn't found the right words to say, watching the men around her. They were here only because of LA? *Only* LA?

"How did you know I would be at the bar tonight?" she asked evenly, leveling her eyes on Elijah. Stupid *sexy-as-fuck* cowboy. She nearly hated herself for still considering that jackass attractive. She did hate herself for falling for the ruse.

"We've been following you around for a little while, now." He met her eyes, unfazed by her stare. "And before you get even more upset, we didn't want to just storm your home. We planned this, so I could get those on you. That way, you couldn't run when we tried to have a conversation with you. I wasn't out to take advantage of you."

"How kind," she snarled, and the aggression in her tone shocked the cowboy, who swallowed and shifted a little uncomfortably, "especially since you were betting on it."

Silence met her. She turned her glare to Zander, who had the courtesy to become a wonderful, dark shade of red from embarrassment, and, she hoped, a fair amount of shame. She looked back at the Italian after that. He watched her with no interest, which told her that it was very much the opposite. She knew the technique. Feign a lack of interest so the target doesn't know you are clearly following everything they did or said. Cute. Amateur.

"I don't know anything about him. He tried to kill me." She shrugged. "I've been wondering if maybe I did a job that interfered with something of his, but I don't know."

"Assuming that's not a lie," he whispered, "and I very

much believe it is, then please explain why he brought out his entire inner circle. He never does that. Or why you thought you needed to spit at him."

"He's a fucking creep." She raised an eyebrow at him. She wasn't going to give him a real answer. He had to know that. "There's not a female criminal on this planet that doesn't know that Axel loves women and will do whatever he wants to them, whenever he wants. A bit weird, really, since it's not exactly *loving*, but what can ya do? He said some shit, and I thought it was disgusting. So, I spit at him."

She watched Vincent's jaw tighten and wondered what she had said that would have pissed him off. Except lie to him, but, while he might believe she was lying, he had no evidence of it. She wasn't completely untruthful, either. Axel loved women and had zero respect for them. If he wanted one in his bed, whomever he targeted normally found herself there. Sawyer knew that from experience.

"You always talk about him like that?" Elijah chuckled softly.

"Everyone does when he's not looking." She grinned at the cowboy. "We're also not stupid enough to say it to anyone who will tell him. You know, the entire criminal world *doesn't* revolve around his crazy. He's just another fucking crime lord. He's got enemies."

"They die fairly quickly though." Jasper was frowning at her. She only shrugged.

She needed to tread a fine line between knowing about Axel but not really *knowing* him. At this point, it was obvious to her that they had no idea just how close she and Axel had once been. They had no idea they had handcuffs on Shadow. Shadow was dead, and it was better for everyone if she stayed that way.

"Either way," Zander interjected, "you are being taken

into our custody as a person of interest in the ongoing investigation into Axel and his organization, the Ghosts." Zander stopped and looked over to Vincent. "Who came up with that name? Really?"

"It wasn't something they chose," Sawyer answered without thinking. "They got it because their enemies tended to end up shells of themselves, losing everything; only ghosts of what they were before they toyed with Axel. And they're freaks who love to wear white."

"That's right," Vincent confirmed. He eyed her from head to toe, and she kicked her long-ass legs out, letting him enjoy the sight. When he made it back up to her face, she gave a smirk. He didn't react to her and just looked back the other agents. "Let's get her on a plane and get out of here. I don't want to stay in this city any longer than necessary."

"Wait!" She looked between them. "You can't just drag me off in the middle of the night! I need to make arrangements, plans."

"Arrangements and plans for what?" Vincent stood up and turned back to her. "Who's going to pay the hospital bills of the guy you sent to the ICU tonight?"

"No, dickhead," she snapped. "Who's going to teach my classes here at the gym? Charlie will need someone helping him out. I normally make a schedule for my students to work around the gym so Charlie doesn't get too overworked when I'm gone."

"Charlie can take of that." He was stern, and she shook her head.

"I'm not fucking leaving this city without a fight until I can tell my students that I'm headed out." She lifted her chin and glared at him.

"Sawyer, why are you fighting with us?" Zander glared at her in turn. "Axel could be here any fucking day looking for you. We've wasted enough time. You need to come with us, now."

"I'm not leaving without telling the kids and Charlie goodbye," she said with steel, her back straight. She stood up and jingled the inhibiting handcuffs around. "And they can't see me in these."

"Why?" Vincent asked her with just as much steel.

"Why the fuck do you need to know?" she growled. Finally, Elijah walked over and put his hands up between them.

"We can take the handcuffs off, but you need to put this on first," he told her, placing a thick bracelet on the table. She grabbed it and held it out to him.

"I can't do it myself," she hissed. He took it and slid it over her left hand. It resized itself to fit her snugly, and she knew she wouldn't be pulling it off. Damn thing was probably enchanted to make sure she couldn't remove it. She saw the way he eyed the mostly missing ring finger before he released her wrist. It had been removed at the second knuckle, leaving her a bit of a moving stub that couldn't hold anything. "Don't ask."

"I wasn't going to," he murmured. Once the bracelet was on, he pulled keys from his pocket and started unlocking the handcuffs. "Don't attack us or these go back on."

"Fine," she told him, watching the handcuffs unlock. Finally, she would get her magic back at least. She was so excited she could taste it.

But when Elijah was pocketing the handcuffs, Sawyer realized that she didn't have her magic back. The stupid fucking bracelet. It had multiple enchantments on it. It sized to her perfectly, so she couldn't slip it off, and it was an inhibitor. She raised her wrist to eye level and looked it over. It was just a silver bracelet, nothing special. There were no designs etched in the metal or anything. Enchanting was just another of long list of Magi abilities, and it was Common, though only the more powerful Magi with the ability could make an inhibitor. Whoever made this was very powerful, if they could layer on different enchantments. She sensed three total and wondered what the third was.

"Figure it out yet?" Elijah was watching her closely, a grin spread over his face. "You really think we're going to let you have your magic, especially since we've seen your Registrar entry?"

"What?" She looked up at him and felt the air leave her lungs. They had seen her Registrar entry?

"Sublimation, blinking, cloaking, phasing, and animal bonding," Vincent rattled off all her abilities. Her fifth ability was a secret to everyone, except her and the Reader who made her Registrar entry. Readers were Magi with the Rare ability to learn the abilities of other Magi through touch. They recorded the name of a person and all that person's abilities in the Registrar, something the WMC had created nearly a thousand years before. They also gave the person an idea of how strong their Source was. The Registrar was only viewed under times of emergency, and the WMC had to grant someone access to view another person's entry. "Speaking of that last one, where is your animal?"

"I don't have one," she snorted, gesturing to the rest of the apartment. They wouldn't find an animal, she knew that. "You've been watching me for weeks, that should have been fairly obvious."

"You haven't gotten an animal to bond with you at twenty-four years old?" Vincent frowned. "We figured you hid it, to keep it safe."

"Nope." She stepped away from them and moved

towards her kitchen. She wasn't telling them about her animal bond. No fucking way. She didn't even tell Charlie that, since he didn't even know it was her fifth ability. It was one of the few things even her old roommate didn't know.

"Where are you going?" Zander stood up quickly to try and stop her. She turned and gave a heavy sigh.

"I'm getting a bite to eat so we can continue arguing about whether I'm allowed to say goodbye to my class." She pointed into the kitchen. "Now, if you'll excuse me."

She went and opened the fridge, listening to the guys talk while she was out of the room. She noticed they didn't give a damn if she heard them.

"Well," Vincent sounded a bit short of patience, "your old friend is... difficult."

"Yeah, she's always been that way." Zander sounded amused. "Right, Jasper?"

"She punched one of the people who ran the orphanage for telling her she couldn't hang out with us after dark," Jasper responded blandly.

"Probably because they thought you were fucking," Elijah laughed. "Were you?'

"No," Zander mumbled.

Ha! They didn't know she and Zander had done that. Looked like she wasn't the only one with secrets in the room. It gave her some leverage over Zander, at least. Of course, it had only happened about a week before Zander and Jasper had left. It wasn't like they had been in a relationship or anything. They had been best friends and very drunk that night, celebrating his and Jasper's future in the IMAS and the exciting adventures they would have once she aged out of the orphanage. Life had stepped in and changed those plans.

She paused for a moment as she pulled out a salad she

had prepared earlier in the week. Did Jasper know? Surely, Zander would have told him after all these years. Those two had never let secrets sit between them.

"Look, we need to get out of New York as fast as possible," Vincent was saying as she slowly grabbed her dressing and a drink. "We can't sit around waiting for her to talk to some kids."

"If we took a vote, Vincent," Elijah chuckled, "you would lose. I also don't want her to try and kick my testicles across the room for the entire duration of this."

"Yeah." Sawyer felt a flare of Zander's passionate temper in the word. "I mean, if she's going to come willingly afterward and be a bit easier on us, why not?"

"I concur," Jasper sighed. "She will make your life hell, if you force her to leave before she's ready, Vincent."

"You know what," Vincent snapped, "why didn't you give me a run down on her *before* we had handcuffs on her?"

"We didn't know how similar she was to who we used to know." Jasper was trying to be diplomatic, and Sawyer hopped up on the counter. She opened her drink, drizzled dressing on to her salad, and began eating. She could sit here all night and listen to this. It was telling her more than anything else they had said.

"Fuck," one of them mumbled. It was low enough that Sawyer couldn't identify which. "Quinn is going to hate her."

She took another of her salad and tried to hold back a smile. This Quinn person could hate her as much as they fucking wanted.

"Too late to worry about that. We gave him a heads up before we left." Vincent was nearly groaning. She raised an eyebrow. Who was Quinn to elicit a warning that she was being caught? "I need to call James and let him know we have her in custody. Keep an eye on her, she's too quiet in there."

"Hey, tell James we're going to do that thing she wants. Saying goodbye to her students, or class, or whatever." Elijah sounded easy going, and Vincent only gave him a growling okay. Jasper walked into the kitchen and met her eyes.

"You trying to hide from us?" He was quiet, but she saw that he was a little hurt. Jasper always was the sweet one out of their little gang of delinquents.

"No." She shook her head. She really hadn't been. "Just decided to eat in here while you all had a *very important conversation.*"

"Of course," he whispered. When he walked closer, she frowned. He was limping.

"I knew your knee was fucked up, but what gave you the limp?" She pointed with her fork. She had never been very tactful, and Jasper winced in embarrassment, which hadn't been her intention.

"The knee injury caused a problem with the hip while we were in the IMAS. Nothing can really be done, unless someone figures out how to fix the knee." He leaned onto the counter next to her, and she watched him carefully, finally giving him her full attention.

He hadn't changed much. He was more filled-out than he had been at eighteen, but that was something she had expected. He was still a golden blonde with blue eyes that reminded her of a storm on the coast, churning with emotions he didn't talk about and refused to confront. He sported a decent tan, making him look like a cover model. He'd always been pretty, beautiful. There wasn't much about Jasper that was rugged or rough. He was *definitely* more man then he'd been the last time she saw him, though.

Sawyer swallowed. *Wow, what the fuck is wrong with me*? Of all the places her mind could go, that one needed a big red stop sign. Thinking like that got her in with Axel. Now it had gotten her caught. She didn't want to know where else it was going to send her. And of all the times she could be thinking about it. She had too much to drink, that was surely the reason.

"You know, you're handling this better than I expected," Jasper whispered, grabbing her drink. "Anything in this I should know about?" He held up the water bottle, and she shook her head. He took a couple swallows and put it back where she had set it.

"Grab a few more from the fridge," she sighed, "and, Jasper, I'm a criminal. I knew someone would track my ass down one day. I just wasn't expecting it to be so soon. I'm a bit peeved, but things could be worse."

"You make it sound like you are resigned to that fate." He was keeping it light, friendly with her. "You're just some over-paid thief. It's not like you've killed anyone."

Well. That was the confirmation she needed. They had no idea who she was. It helped that her identity as Shadow had a very public death, and no one dared to question it since Axel had already killed several IMPO agents in the event.

"If the IMPO didn't arrest me, someone I stole from would have killed me, eventually." She shrugged.

"What about the people here in New York? The ones you…" Jasper put several waters on the counter next to her. "You aren't worried about them?"

"Fuck, no," she snorted. "Should I be?"

"No," Jasper sighed softly. "Probably not. You know… we saw one of those… meet ups a little while ago."

"Which one? I've had a few since coming back from LA."

She took a couple swallows of a fresh water, instead of using the one Jasper put his mouth on.

"Make that two, then," he told her. "We saw the one where you jumped the guy in a back alley. We also had eyes at the fight tonight and saw the aftermath of the guy you must have caught in the locker room."

"Ah," she nodded. "Yeah. I do that…"

"You've always hated injustice in the world," he reminded her. "You fought with bullies growing up, you stood up for littler kids in the orphanage. It's just who you are."

"Except now I put them in the hospital." She took another sip of her water. "You all aren't going to lock me away for that, are you? Because I'm willing to go down for the thefts, but not for *that*. Someone has to take care of these people, show them that their shit isn't tolerated in the twenty-first century."

"We're *not* sending you to prison, Sawyer." Jasper shook his head. "Not for any of it. Catching Axel and keeping you alive is more important. You're the first person we've seen escape him like that. Normally, we only find the body."

"No one ever gets away," she whispered, looking away from him.

"Exactly." He pointed at her. "But you are sitting here, living and breathing, after a run-in with him. We're going to keep it that way. You are the one-in-a-million."

"Fine, and I'm not fighting into protective custody." She put her salad down as she spoke. "But I'm not just going to disappear into the night when people here count on me."

"That's fine, and we'll even set something up, so you can stay in contact with them if you want to." Jasper nodded.

"You know, I'm disappointed in you becoming a criminal, but, Sawyer?"

"What?" She already knew he was disappointed. That much had been obvious. There was no way her golden boy wouldn't be. Not *hers*, she realized. She couldn't call him that, not after so long.

"I'm proud of what you do for this area." He swatted her arm and turned to leave. He stopped at the door and snapped his fingers before turning back to her. "Eventually, you'll need to tell us how you ended up here."

She snorted. Nope. That wasn't going to happen. Considering that story was saturated in Axel, and she needed to pretend that she wasn't Shadow, she wasn't going to tell them fucking anything.

"Sure, whatever." She nearly laughed. "Look, I'm going to get a nap in before people start showing up to the gym. Can I trust you all not to whisk me away to a plane in my sleep?"

"Yeah, you can trust us on that. Vincent's been overruled on this." Jasper gave her a gentle smile. "He might be our team leader and boss, but he's expected to listen to the majority on some things."

Well, that was an important piece of information. The cold and calculating Italian, *Vincent*, was the leader, but he wasn't allowed to be a dictator. Good, she could play that to get this over with more quickly. She would play along for a month or so, maybe even a couple, and then she would find a way to sneak out the back door, claiming she had nothing to tell them.

"Alright then. Goodnight, Jasper." She slid off the counter top and walked past him into the dining room. Elijah and Zander were playing a silent game of cards while

Vincent must have stepped out to make a phone call. "Can I get my car and motorcycle sent to wherever we're going?"

"Not a good idea," Elijah told her without looking up. "Someone might recognize it and connect it to you. We don't want them having any idea where we're hiding you."

"Of course," she groaned. "I'm going to catch a couple hours. "

"Want me to come finish what we started?" Elijah did look up at her this time, grinning. He was still wearing his cowboy hat, and she couldn't resist the urge to walk over and flip it off his big head. She didn't need to, however, since Zander looked up from his cards, glaring at the cowboy. The next moment, a thump was heard, and Elijah was grimacing in pain. "No reason to kick me, asshole. Shit, everyone is so violent tonight, and now my poor hat has touched the floor. It didn't deserve that."

She didn't say anything, turning towards her bedroom. Sleep. She might get a couple of hours, and there was no reason to stress over the IMPO agents all over her apartment. What was done was done. Now, she just needed to figure out how to keep her secrets while forced into their care.

At least it wasn't Axel in her apartment? That was some sort of fucked-up silver lining.

12

JASPER

Jasper watched her move into her bedroom and couldn't ignore how their lanky Sawyer had grown up into a stunning and confident woman. He swallowed the lump in his throat and turned to Zander, noticing that he was also watching her walk out. Shit, so was Elijah.

"She's barely changed," he said, sitting down at the table. "Still the same Sawyer."

"She's darker," Zander whispered, voicing something that was obvious to him and Jasper. "You can see it in her eyes. Life hasn't been easy, even if the money she's sitting on says something else."

"Y'all are a weird bunch, you orphans," Elijah chuckled. "You had her, and you left for the IMAS? Lost your fucking minds."

"You joined the IMPO at eighteen." Jasper frowned at him, but Elijah just shrugged.

"I wasn't leaving behind a gorgeous woman like that." He grinned. "There was nothing at home for me."

"Other than her, there was nothing for us," Zander

growled. "You know that. It's not like you've never seen pictures of her. Elijah, we've been on this team together for six years."

"She was supposed to stick close to the orphanage until she aged out, then come to us." Jasper was dealt into the hand and sighed. They played in silence for nearly ten minutes, only tapping the table to send messages, until Vincent walked back in.

"James is fine with us spending one more day here in New York. He's also got the backup team waiting in Atlanta, so they can get eyes on her when we land. They've been told not to engage to avoid spooking her."

"Shit, we need to deal with Jon?" Elijah sighed, and Jasper brought his eyebrows together. "He's a fucking prick."

"He's Old Guard, and yeah, he's an asshole." Vincent nodded, "but he's the leader of the only other team we can count on if shit goes sideways on the East Coast."

Old Guard was a term used for those who were agents before the IMPO did a massive restructuring, nearly two decades ago. They lived by a different code, one that Jasper and the guys didn't. The IMPO's leaders had decided they wanted to entice more people to join, since there weren't many Magi who wanted to lose what freedom they had to work for their government. So, new rules were brought in while several, including those on physical standards, were thrown out.

It led to people like Zander joining, with his ears gauged out an inch wide and tattoos covering his body while always getting more. It led to Elijah joining, an openly bisexual Texan who didn't believe in pretending to be anything he wasn't. Then Jasper considered himself, the permanently injured one. They were a team of misfits, and all of them would have been found unfit for a number of reasons before the rule changes.

Jon Aguirre hated their team, but both teams were based in Georgia, making it convenient to get help from each other.

"If he gives you shit, let me know. I'll talk to him as best I can," Vincent told them. "I wish I could do more, but he hates me, too, so it's not like he'll listen. James isn't their handler either, so they have no reason to pay him any mind."

"Just as long as he keeps his *pet names* for us to himself," Zander growled. "IRA, Brokeback, Cripple, and all of that fucking shit. We would be fine if he kept his fucking mouth shut."

"He calls me Vinny," Vincent sighed. Jasper winced. That was fucking cold. "His names for Quinn don't need to be repeated under any circumstance."

"Yeah," Elijah sighed. "So, we let her say good-bye, then we hop on the jet, get her past Jon and his team. Then what?"

"James wants us to train her." Vincent held up his phone. "Once things with Axel have settled down, he wants us to recruit her into the IMPO. She's got the talent, the sense of justice, and it would keep her out of trouble. She wouldn't be the first criminal brought to our side, and he's made it clear that while we have her, we still need to work. So, she'll be getting on the job training with us, as well."

"Maybe we should ask her if being an IMPO agent is a job she wants," Jasper whispered, worried they were going to chase her off if they pushed her to join the very thing she had tried to hide from.

"She'll have a choice, but while she's with us, she'll need

to follow us around." Vincent gave Jasper a tiny smile. "Afraid she's going to betray us and help the bad guys?"

"No," Jasper told him quickly. "But-"

"Good, because Jon is apparently already raising hell in Atlanta, and we need to be a unit on this. We can't have him trying to find weakness in the team."

"You are so fucking weird." Zander shook his head at their boss. "One minute you are cold as shit to her, and now, you want her on the team."

"Not our team, but we would be recruiting her into the IMPO." Vincent shrugged. "James had some solid points about the situation."

"If she joins the IMPO, she can use her old ties from being a criminal to help cases, create set ups, helping bring down big names all over the world." Jasper nodded. It was a smart move, but he felt uncomfortable talking about her future without her in the room. They hadn't even had her in custody for an hour, and now they were whispering about making her train to become an agent? She was going to blow a gasket.

"I knew someone else would see James' side." Vincent nodded. "So, we need to kill time until we can get her on a plane. While she's dealing with the gym, we'll pack up all her stuff and get it ready to go. No reason to buy her new clothes in Georgia. She's got plenty here, it seems."

"Look at you," Elijah grinned, "worried about her stuff."

"Fuck off." Vincent glared at him. "I don't want us wasting our money. And it would be our money. James had the tech guys lock out her accounts when I called him. She's completely dependent on us now."

"Oh, that's going to piss her off," Zander chuckled. "I'm looking forward to this. What about you, Jasper?"

"I'm wondering if everybody will still be among the

living when we fly out of here." Jasper gave Zander a knowing look. They had intended to let her keep her money because growing up semi-poor and dependent on others had always made Sawyer very protective of her resources. She might not have realized it, but Jasper knew she liked having money ready just in case shit went down.

"Blame James." Vincent rubbed his temples in a circular motion. "He made that call. His reasoning was that, if she was poor, she would be more likely to take paying work that wouldn't get her arrested. He also reminded me that her money was gained from illegal activities. Charlie doesn't pay her for anything she does in New York. She doesn't even take winnings from the fighting ring they are a part of. Charlie gets all of that, as well."

"Why don't we give Charlie everything?" Elijah asked. "He could use it, since we're taking away his employee and his friend."

Vincent turned back to look at Sawyer's bedroom door, and shook his head a little. Jasper knew where this was going, so he just spat it out.

"Sawyer has no idea Charlie was in on this," he told Elijah. "It's obvious. And she'll be furious when she finds out, so giving him her money could possibly make this worse."

"Really? I mean, we're leaving her car and motorcycle here," Elijah chuckled. "Surely-"

"We're actually not leaving those here," Vincent shook his head again. "They are going to be sent to our place and locked away in the garage with their keys in my safe."

Jasper looked at Zander, who was frowning. What was Vincent trying to do, wipe her from existence?

"Why?" Jasper asked, turning back to Vincent.

"Because we need to leave no evidence of her here to

keep Axel from killing Charlie or any other bystanders who won't know where she is." Vincent's mouth was a hard line. "And that sucks for her, I know, but she can't come back to New York. Not until Axel is no longer hunting her, which means not until Axel is in prison or dead."

"You really think he's going to hunt her to the ends of the earth?" Zander snorted. "We figured maybe six months tops, and then she could walk away."

"Axel always gets what he wants. He won't stop until he has her or whatever he wants from her," Elijah mumbled. "Come on, we've been chasing that SOB across the globe for five years. This team was built for the express purpose of catching him. She's not going to be able to walk away until we have him."

Jasper chewed on that. He knew that already. He hadn't wanted to admit it, but he knew it.

"Let's just play some cards." Vincent pointed to the deck they always had with them. "Nothing we can do right now with her getting some sleep, and we're stuck here until we deal with her requests."

"At least she's not still trying to kick our balls through the wall," Elijah mumbled petulantly. They all chuckled softly at him and his plight.

"She was only trying to do that to you," Zander rolled his eyes.

~

JASPER WAITED for her at breakfast while the other guys were down in the gym with Charlie. He had shown up early, expecting them to already be gone. Luckily, the old man hadn't given anything away when he saw them. Jasper wasn't sure how Sawyer would take the betrayal, and it wasn't something he wanted to confront that early in the morning.

"Good morning," she told him brightly, sitting down with a bowl of yogurt.

"It's nearly noon," he reminded her, taking a sip of his coffee. They hadn't expected her to sleep in like this.

"I don't teach anything in the morning." She shrugged, "so, this is my morning. I have too many late nights to be waking up any earlier."

"I know," he sighed. "So, your class will be here in an hour?"

"Yeah, enough time for me to eat and get stuff set up for Charlie to take over." She took a couple bites of her yogurt. "Tell me, did you contact him or the other way around?"

He couldn't stop his flicker of worry.

"How did you figure it out?" He was looked away from her. "And we cornered him."

"He would have been more concerned about you all being here if he didn't already know," she told him quietly. "I'm not mad. Charlie just wants me safe, and if he felt the need to help you, then I'm not going to hold it against him. It's just how he shows he cares. He's seen me go through a lot."

He didn't know how to take this from her. He thought she would have stormed out and confronted Charlie, but here she was, sitting with her breakfast, shadows and secrets filling her eyes.

"He didn't tell us much," he offered her, hoping to relieve any sense of betrayal she might not be showing him. "He just said you showed up a few years ago, needing help. He brought you in, taught you how to fight, protect yourself. Within a few months, you were out in the streets helping other people. He offered a little more in terms of your work, just so we had a better idea of how you pulled off the secrecy."

"Layers," she chuckled. "I look at life in layers, compartmentalize different sections so they don't bleed together. The fact that you are sitting here though, proves I didn't work hard enough."

"We have all sorts of technology and Magi who helped, that Axel doesn't." He shrugged. "You were smart to keep your face covered for everything. Not your mistake to have the mask knocked off."

"I could have gotten into the security and wiped the tapes from existence." She pointed her spoon at him. "I screwed up, and now I've got IMPO agents dragging me out of my house. Don't play with me, Jasper."

"I'm not playing with you." He smiled gently at her, hoping to ease her a little. "If it weren't criminal, I would be incredibly impressed by what you've done."

"You are too nice," she groaned. "Where's Zander? He'll give me the argument I want."

"Let's not start that again," Jasper sighed, taking her bowl from her. At their best, Zander and Sawyer were perfect together; Jasper had always known it. At their worst, he was needed to step in and fix things before they killed each other. They were explosive, temperamental, and passionate people which made it necessary for Jasper to stay between them. "Go get ready. Wear something you can travel in. Elijah and Zander will be packing your things while you and I see your students. Vincent is handling some other details."

"You think I'm going to let two strangers pack my shit?" She stood up slowly. "You've lost your damn mind, Jasper."

"Fine, then make a bag of stuff you don't want them messing with, and they will make sure it gets on the plane."

He didn't want to know what that bag could possibly have in it.

"Fine." She suddenly sounded cranky. With her, there was no telling what would set her off. Jasper rolled his eyes up to the ceiling and prayed for a moment of strength. Having her back in his life was going to be wonderful, stressful, and, sometimes, downright terrifying. He shouldn't have expected anything less.

It took the entire hour before her class started for Sawyer to have the bag ready. Jasper tapped his foot, waiting for her. Elijah and Vincent were waiting with even less patience to get in and pack her things.

"Good lord, little lady," Elijah grumbled when she finally walked out. "Took you long enough."

"Fuck you," she growled, shoving the bag into his arms. "Don't look through it. It's my fucking underwear. Unless you're into being a fucking pervert, in which case, I hope you don't mind losing fingers."

Jasper coughed, reaching out to grab her arm so he could drag her away before anything else could come out of her mouth. He didn't make it in time, as Elijah gave a pithy response before Jasper could separate them.

"Considering I could see your underwear by just asking, I'm not sure why I would *need* to go through your panty drawer," he teased. Jasper knew it was innocent flirtation, but he also knew Sawyer wasn't going to take it that way.

"Like you have a chance," she snarled. What had pissed her off since she had woken up? Jasper groaned, and started dragging her away. "He's a fucking prick."

"Elijah is harmless," he told her on the stairs. "He flirts with everybody, it's nothing personal."

"Like that makes it any better," she huffed.

"Sawyer, I need you to calm down," Jasper finally sighed.

"I get it. This fucking sucks for you. You've built up a life and a place for yourself here, but we don't really have another option. We need to keep you alive. We can't let Axel continue to leave bodies all over the planet, and we need to bring him down."

"That's not why I am upset," she growled. "You're about to see why."

She left him confused on the stairs. He raced after her, wincing at the ache in his knee and the shooting pain up his thigh and into his hip. It was getting worse, and he already wasn't allowed to do anything too physically active during assignments. He was a geek anyway, so that was okay, but damn, working out was hard when one entire leg didn't want to cooperate. Keeping up with her was going to be a nightmare.

He found her in a room connected to the main gym and put it together. Nearly twenty kids, almost all of them under the age of sixteen, were waiting on her. They looked at her like a goddess descended to teach them, a big sister that would always love them. Hero worship was an understatement.

And the smile on her face was glorious. Radiant. She hugged the smaller ones, one or two looking like they were probably only seven or eight. She exchanged goofy secret handshakes with the older ones, and laughed when a couple tried to trip her up.

He had known, but he had never witnessed it. Charlie hadn't allowed them in the gym when it wasn't Fight Night, and he didn't have cameras for Zander to break into. Jasper stood awkwardly at the door, watching it play out. These kids loved her, and she loved them. She was relaxed, and the cocky swagger she usually kept was missing. She was at ease in a way he'd never seen her, even when they were young.

"Alright, so I have some bad news for all of you," she called to them. "Everyone gather around."

Jasper swallowed a lump in his throat. Tiny hearts were about to be broken. Jasper didn't like to witness this level of emotion. It made him itchy and uncomfortable, but someone had to keep eyes on her at all times.

"Last night, I learned some bad news, and I'm going to need to leave for a little while." She knelt to the smaller children's eye level. "I don't know when I'll be able to come back, if I can, but I was told that I'm in danger, so they need to hide me away."

She was being honest with them, and he frowned at it. Did she really think they needed the gory details? Couldn't she just say she was going on a business trip?

"But," a teen interrupted, looking upset, and Jasper knew the boy was a newer one of the group. "What are we going to do?"

"What you do every time I leave." She smiled sadly at him. "You are going to listen to Charlie, Liam, and Jessie and never miss class. They will take over until I can come back. If anything happens at home, you need to tell Charlie, and he will help with that too."

"My daddy isn't scared of Charlie like he is of you," a tiny one whispered. Jasper rocked back with shock. These kids *knew*. They knew what Sawyer did for them.

"Your daddy is never coming back." Sawyer pulled the small one to her as she spoke. Her eyes flicked up to him and back to the minors around her. "He's not going to do that."

"Promise?"

"I don't make promises, but I'll make you a deal." She held the little girl's head to her own. "If he comes back, you tell Charlie. Charlie will tell me, and I will do whatever is necessary to come back and help you." She looked up from the kids and met Jasper's eyes again. "Whatever is necessary."

He gave a small nod, acknowledging her warning. He knew what she was telling him. She would risk her life and freedom to help these kids, and it was something he would need to tell the team. She didn't give a damn about her own life, not when it came to them. These non-Magi kids from the roughest neighborhoods of New York meant everything to her.

She was mad because she was breaking their hearts and leaving them without her for a length of time that she couldn't confirm would ever end. They could fail, she could wind up dead, and these kids would never see her again after this.

"This is Special Agent Jasper Williams. He and his friends are the ones who want to protect me," she told them, pointing over to him. "I grew up with him, if you can believe that. So, if you want to know all my dirty, embarrassing childhood stories, now is the time to ask."

He froze and broke out into a cold sweat as all the eyes turned on him. The teens were glaring, angry at his intrusion into their lives. The small ones were curious. He didn't know how to deal with children, and when a couple of the young ones started walking over, he backed away.

"This really isn't..." he started, looking at Sawyer. She grinned and waved, turning to the teens and beginning a quiet conversation he couldn't follow.

"Sir." one of the little ones was tugging on his shirt. He looked down to find the young girl staring up at him. "Are you going to keep Ms. Matthews safe? Are you?"

"I'm going to do my best." He looked away from her and out the doorway, hoping to call for help. He didn't appreciate this, and he knew Sawyer did it to him on purpose. She had always been better with the younger kids at the orphanage.

"Will you tell us a story about Miss Matthews?" A young boy asked, and Jasper groaned. He looked around and finally decided to just sit on the floor. He stretched his legs out and glared over to Sawyer, who watched him as a teenage girl said something. "She said you would!"

"She once fell out of a tree," he told the young boy. The kids were sitting all around him now, and standing in the doorway was Zander, grinning at Jasper's misfortune. "Not really much to it."

"Now, don't do that to them," Zander chuckled. "She was trying to throw rocks at some high school bullies, and then she fell out of the tree."

"Into a bush, right?" Jasper felt more comfortable with Zander there. Thank God for small miracles.

"Yeah." Zander launched into the story so that Jasper was saved from having to tell it. Jasper liked books, quiet, and a good video game on occasion. Children terrified him. He stood back up, extracted himself from the crowd of kids, and walked towards Sawyer whispering with the teenagers.

"So, you can watch Jonas when school gets out?" She pointed to an older young man, probably the oldest in the room.

"Yeah, he and Izzy can hang out together with me." He nodded. "Jonas' mom causing trouble?"

"Yes, but you aren't to engage." Sawyer was stern. "You know the rules- bring them here, and Charlie will keep anyone away and give you all my room in the apartment."

"I've been training with you since the beginning," he whispered back hotly. "Let me do this."

"Remember your brother, Liam?" she whispered darkly

at him. Jasper saw the young man pale. Liam, Jasper knew, was the oldest. Sawyer paid for his apartment and his education. "Could you do that? Day in and day out? You hated driving the truck, Liam. Don't think you can be me. I've made it clear to all of you how this works. That's not up for discussion." She turned and saw Jasper. He crossed his arms. "Well, you might as well come on over, Jasper. I see Zander saved you from my trap."

"Yeah, he must have gotten the flight scheduled faster than expected." He looked between them. "What is this?"

"When I leave town, the teens and I make plans on what do in case anyone gives them trouble." She lifted her chin and met his eye. He only had an inch, maybe two, on her. She was intimidating when she needed to be. "Most of them are in the same foster homes or live close to each other. The plans are given to parents and foster parents so they don't need to worry about babysitters and things like that."

"No one takes up *your* job?" He had to ask.

"Fuck, no. Did you not just hear me tell him that?" she snapped, pointing at the young man she called Liam. "Are you crazy? *They are kids*. Plus, we don't talk about that here. Don't bring it up again."

He frowned. They were just talking about it... Oh, they weren't supposed to talk about it in front of him. A stranger.

"Yeah, we're supposed to pretend not to know," a young woman commented. She had blonde curls, cut short, and a scar on her left cheekbone. These kids were just as tough and beaten up as Sawyer. "I mean, we all do know but..."

"I'm an IMPO agent, please stop." Jasper held up a hand to silence them. They were all non-Magi, but with Sawyer involved, the IMPO could very well find this a problem. The team could be implicated in, what amounted to, a conspiracy. This was becoming an actual criminal conspiracy. He hadn't expected it. "I'm going to pretend I've heard none of this." He pointed to Sawyer after that. "You have fifteen minutes to meet us out front."

"Fine, we'll be done by then," Sawyer growled, turning away from him. He took that as the dismissal it was and left her to it.

Jesus. He shook his head as he passed Zander who was telling the kids that it was time for him to leave. When he got out of the room, Zander was hot on his heels.

"These kids worship her," Zander mumbled. "Like they are head over heels in love. It's awe-inspiring and a bit terrifying."

"Yeah," Jasper hissed. "And all the older ones are in on it. They fucking *know* what she does. They know, even if they don't talk about it. This shit is straight up a criminal conspiracy involving minors."

"She's done good things for those kids." Charlie walked over to them, hearing them talking about Sawyer and her little 'class'. "No one paid them any mind, but Sawyer saw what was happening and started putting an end to it."

Jasper turned to Charlie and frowned. Jasper liked the law, the rigid expectations that society was held up to. He was willing to bend a little, unlike Vincent, but he wasn't sure he could bend as far as Sawyer did. Zander could but not Jasper.

"It's not legal," he reminded Charlie, "and you are an accomplice."

"She breaks into my files, and I have no idea what she does with the information." Charlie grinned for a second. "When the 'good guys' forget about them, who else do they have? She gets them part-time jobs, finds them homes if they need them. She teaches them self-defense, so they can protect themselves from bullies and their own families, if necessary. You're taking her out of here anyway, get over it."

"You'll keep those kids out of trouble?" Jasper pointed to the door leading to their training room as Charlie nodded.

"You make it sound like it's hard," Charlie grunted. "Those kids don't get into trouble. You need to understand —Sawyer does the dirty work, so they'll never have to. She gives them the protector they need and cheers them on to making better lives for themselves. All of those teenagers are straight A students now, and the oldest is in college. He just won't move on from this. Liam is getting a physical therapy degree and becoming a personal trainer, so I'll have to hire him."

Jasper felt like he had just been reprimanded, and Zander cleared his throat. She was their hero. That much was clear.

"You all need to hurry up and get her out of here," Charlie sighed. "I'm starting to feel guilty."

"She's got you figured out, by the way," Jasper told him. "She guessed on her own."

"Wonderful." Charlie turned and walked away, grunting in annoyance at the situation. "I didn't want her to..." He walked away without finishing, and Jasper rubbed his eyes.

This was becoming a bit messier than any of them had intended. They hadn't really considered that Sawyer had things she needed to take care of before she left. They just assumed that she was a criminal, always ready to run, so it wouldn't be a big deal if she disappeared into the night. Sure, they looked into her life, but they hadn't *really* considered it.

Jasper started reciting facts he knew about New York's non-Magi crime problem. He was getting stressed, and that would calm him down. It didn't help as much as he wanted, since he remembered she was a part of the crime problem in New York.

After two minutes of trying that, he switched to random Magi facts. He recited the rarity rankings for abilities in his head. *Common. Uncommon. Rare. Mythic.*

He had two Common-ranked abilities and two Uncommon abilities. Phasing, air manipulation, dream walking, and illusions. Phasing and air manipulation were Common, while dream walking, and illusions were Uncommon. He had a strong and deep Source, so he could create powerful illusions that could fool a mind that wasn't strong enough to fight back. He could delve into someone's subconscious with dream walking and find out their most hidden secrets. He never used that skill, since it was an invasion of privacy.

He moved on to Zander, who was standing next to him. He had three Common abilities, and one Uncommon. His Common abilities were water manipulation, shielding, and healing. His Uncommon ability was telepathic communication. Zander could touch his Source to someone's mind and send them messages through that connection. It was a one-way street, though, unless the other person also had the ability.

As Sawyer walked out, he sighed. Animal bonding was Common like phasing. Blinking, that annoying short-range teleport was Uncommon, but her sublimation and cloaking were Rare. He was seriously impressed with that. She had two Rare abilities, and her evident control over her powers meant she was a force to reckoned with.

"Are you doing that weird thing where you recite facts to yourself?" she asked him, stepping in front of him. He snapped out of his thoughts and frowned at her.

"How did you...?" He ignored Zander's laughter.

"You always get a spaced out look when you do it. That much, it seems, hasn't changed." She rolled her eyes. "Geek."

"Brute," he mumbled.

"You're both weird," Zander chuckled. Jasper watched him look over Sawyer casually. "Ready to go?"

"Yeah..." she sighed, looking around the gym. Her gaze landed on Charlie, and Jasper took that as his sign to get out.

Jasper left the gym quietly and made his way to the loaned Range Rovers they got from the IMPO's New York headquarters. New York was the permanent home to the IMPO's leaders, along with the World Magi Council. He hated being in this city because it put their odd team too close to those who *really* didn't like them.

He leaned against the Range Rover and tapped his foot. He was ready to get the hell out and see home again. A good book, some quiet classical music. Maybe he could start another online class, teach himself another new skill. He already had four bachelor's degrees. What was one more, at this point?

"She's still beautiful."

Jasper nodded aimlessly at Zander's communication. He looked through the front windows of the gym and saw Zander smirking at him.

"Brazen. Tough. Not much has changed, except now I think she could actually kick my ass instead of just trying. It's hot. I am excited about this. You?"

Jasper gave an exaggerated eye roll. Zander was right, but Jasper wasn't ready go down that path again. She might not have changed much, but Jasper didn't know this new Sawyer. She took the law into her own hands. Not only did violence not scare her, but she wasn't afraid of blood, either.

Zander found it interesting and sexy. Very Zander.

"*It could be like old times again once we get this Axel shit settled.*"

Jasper narrowed his eyes at Zander. *Damn him.* Jasper couldn't respond without alerting everyone in the parking lot and building to what was going on. He also didn't have a response. He just didn't know where this was all going to go. He *did* know that Zander was getting ahead of himself, but Zander always did.

"*She's done with Charlie and I see Vin and Elijah on their way. It's time to go.*"

"Thank fuck," Jasper mumbled to himself, pulling open the door he was leaning on.

13

SAWYER

Sawyer was loaded into a Range Rover and sat in the back by herself. Elijah drove while Vincent read over her file again. He carried it everywhere, the fat thing that apparently held most of her life.

"Where were you from sixteen to twenty?" He looked back at her, and she shrugged.

"Just roaming around, really. Didn't put down roots, pickpocketed. That sort of thing." She gave him a tight smile. She had practiced this story a long time ago, and everyone who knew her after Shadow 'died' would only know this version of her life. Except Charlie, and he'd been nice enough to keep her secrets tucked in the shadows where they belonged. "Tried to find my place in the world."

"You were adopted though, what happened with that?" Vincent pressed. She was going to lose her patience if he didn't step-the-fuck-back on this line of questioning.

"He was an asshole, and I hated him." She shrugged nonchalantly. Not a lie in the slightest. Her 'adoptive' father was a prick, and he'd been a recruiter for Axel. He looked out for any potential strong, young

Magi that could be easily swayed to crime. A lonely young woman whose friends were off traveling the world and hard to reach? No family whatsoever? An easy mark.

"You are going to make this difficult, aren't you?" Vincent gave a small frown. He was quiet like Jasper, she'd noticed, but it was colder and more stand-offish. He only had small expressions, tiny movements of his lips and eyebrows, that meant she had to pay attention to him when they spoke. His voice gave away nothing. "I thought we had an agreement. You get to tie up loose ends, and we get a cooperative protectee."

"I agreed to come willingly," she grinned, "not give you all of my deepest secrets. Or even, really, talk to you at all. So be thankful I've told you as much as I have."

"She's got you there, Vin," Elijah chuckled. "Also, can this wait until we get home, or at least on the plane?"

Vincent continued to frown at her, so she flipped him off. That, oddly, made him turn the frown into a small smile. He was a weird man, this Italian Magi.

"Yeah, wait for the plane, Vincent," she mumbled in Italian to see if he would respond.

"You don't give the orders here, little thief," he responded, also in Italian, his smile growing.

"If both of you could speak English, that would be fantastic," Elijah muttered under his breath. She watched Vincent give a small eye roll, and she started getting increasingly more curious about the guy.

"Learn Italian," Vincent told him, back to the straight face and bland voice.

"You keep saying that," Elijah groaned. "But I learned German for you. I don't think I've got the mind for any more."

"A pity." Vincent turned back to her. "How many languages do you speak?"

"Six." She smiled at him. "I've been trying to learn German and Japanese as well."

"Well, Elijah can help with your German." Vincent looked thoughtful. "Jasper is our Japanese speaker."

"Is it common to know multiple languages as an imp?" She leaned back in her seat, and Vincent gave a small shrug.

"It's preferred, but many don't learn multiple languages; so, they can't get sent out around the world. Only Zander doesn't speak any second languages on our team, which is fine." Vincent pulled a notepad and pen of out his pocket. "Write your languages down. I wouldn't mind having a translator for anything if none of us speak it."

She took the notepad and pen slowly as Elijah turned them into the airport. She didn't write anything, wondering if this was really something she could give up. She considered it for a long moment, wondering what future repercussions could come from them knowing. She made her decision quickly when she noticed Vincent was still watching her with quiet intensity.

"I tried to get a variety of languages, so no matter where in the world I end up, I can find someone to talk to." She wrote them down as she spoke. She tore off the page and held it out to him.

"My notepad and pen." He looked over the list and then folded it. She watched it go into a pocket of the black cargos. They were all wearing the exact same thing: black cargos, black tees, black boots. She rolled her eyes as she gave him the notepad and pen she had tried to keep. "Thank you."

"Yup," she sighed.

"You didn't really think that was going to work, did you?" He frowned.

"It's actually surprisingly easy to steal from people. Take smokers and the endless lighter conundrum. Hand someone your lighter to borrow, and suddenly, they're walking off with it while you completely forget about it." She shrugged. "Speaking of a smoke, can I get one before getting on the plane?"

"Yeah." Vincent pulled out a pack. "I'm also a smoker."

"You are both gross," Elijah cut in. "But I dipped as a teen, so I really can't say anything. I'll take one of those if you're willing to bum me one."

"Yeah, I can bum you one, hypocrite." Vincent stepped out the moment Elijah got the SUV parked near a stylish little jet. Sawyer had to be released by Elijah. Someone had decided child locks were necessary.

"So, when do I get my magic back?" She held up her left wrist, and Elijah shrugged.

"When we can be sure you won't run for it." Elijah smiled as he said it, even throwing in a little wink. "You can start trying to convince me any time, now."

"Pervert." She rolled her eyes, but he had made a solid point of excluding the implication she needed to have sex with him. The faster she had her abilities back, the faster she could jump ship on this. Without her magic, she wasn't stupid enough to even consider running for it. She needed them to get comfortable with her and think she was cool with them, then they would relax the leash, and she could run. Not back to New York, though. That burned. She would probably never be coming back to this city. If she ran, this would be the first place they looked.

"Always," Elijah chuckled. "Let's get a smoke in before we're stuck on the plane."

She followed him to where Vincent had already lit one up. He held out the pack, so they could each grab one of their own. She was happy to see they were menthols, at least, though they were Camel and not her own Marlboros.

As she lit it up, she looked around. She saw Zander and Jasper headed their way. She took a long drag and flicked the ashes as she exhaled. She looked over to Elijah, the unlit cigarette in his mouth. Then, it had a small flame on the end, and he started smoking slowly.

"You can create fire," she pointed out, and he grinned at her.

"Fire manipulation is a Common ability," he reminded her. "Just like any single element manipulation."

"Yeah." she nodded toward his cigarette, "but you've got to be fairly strong to create fire from nothing. You didn't even steal it from one of our cherries."

Elijah only shrugged his massive shoulders in response, taking another drag. She went back to her own smoke as Zander got close enough for them to hear.

"Everything is ready to go," he said, stopping near her. Jasper was right next to him, waiting patiently on them to get moving.

"Great." Vincent took one last drag and then dropped his smoke and stomped on it. Elijah groaned, which caused Vincent to reach down and pick up the butt. Sawyer finished her own cigarette quickly, anxious to get started so she could get this over with. "Let's get out of here."

She put her own smoke out, and kept the butt without Elijah needing to say anything. She didn't just toss litter around, she wasn't that much of an asshole. She followed Vincent onto the plane. Elijah tailed behind her, as close to her ass as if he had been glued there.

"Can I get some space, dickhead?" She looked over her shoulder at him, and he shook his head.

"Until we get back to our place, you won't be allowed

much personal space. That's something you're going to have to deal with."

"Damn it," she growled. "I'm starting to think I'm more of a prisoner than a protectee."

"And she figures it out," Elijah chuckled, pushing her slowly onto the plane so the rest of them could get on.

"So where are we headed?" She looked at Vincent as she sat where he pointed.

"You'll find out when we get there," he told her, opening a bag he had with him. "As we travel, I want to go over some of the rules."

"What type of rules?" She inquired as the plane started moving.

"You can't leave our property without someone with you." He pulled a file from his bag and flipped it open. Yeah, she figured that would come. No going out alone. "You are required to go through training to know how best to protect yourself in case someone tries to take you." She snorted at that one, but he ignored it and continued. "You will be required to travel with us. We still have jobs and work to do. Once we're satisfied you won't get killed on one of our assignments, we'll start taking them up again. We think it'll only take a month to get you up to speed."

"What about getting my magic back?" She kicked her feet up on the table between the sections of seats they had. Private jets were always fancy. This one was all black leather and dark woods with small sections of seats and tables that made groups. She looked around to find Elijah stretched out, his feet kicked up on a seat in front of him. Jasper and Zander took an entire section at the back of the plane, both hunkered down for a nap.

"Eventually, you will be able to use your abilities at home, but we're still in debates over whether you can have them off the property. Elijah said it earlier, it's really up to you to prove to us we can trust you with them."

"Anything else?" she sighed and pointed to the file.

"No." Vincent gave a small shrug. "Sawyer, this can be easy. Think of it as a job or mission. Just do the simple training so we can trust you, and you'll be fine. You might even like the work."

"Of course." She rolled her eyes. "Let's just forget that you four decided that I needed to go with you, regardless of my personal rights as an American citizen."

"You're a Magi, first and foremost," Vincent reminded her. "The WMC doesn't recognize individual county rights and laws concerning Magi citizens. You go by the WMC's rules."

She curled her top lip in disgust, remembering that. Magi didn't have Miranda rights, or the First Amendment, or anything like that. Well, they did have their own version of the First Amendment, but the point was that they were treated differently, regardless of where they were born. She was an American citizen, but she was also a Magi.

The Magi part was the one that mattered. If they had known she was Shadow, she would have been captured, collared, and thrown into a cell where the sun doesn't shine. No one would have spoken out for her, and there would have been no trial, no mandatory state provided attorney, no chance to plead her case. Magi weren't given such luxuries. The WMC claimed it was because Magi were held to higher standards. She thought it was because they liked absolute control.

"Criminals," he muttered, watching her expression. "Deal with it. We could have thrown you in jail and said it was to protect you. Instead, we are keeping you alive and free."

"You are putting me in a bigger cage," she told him with a glare. "That's not free." She stood up once the seat belt light turned off. "Now, if that's everything, I'm going to go sit somewhere else."

"Fine." He watched her carefully, and she walked away without another word. She found an empty section and hunkered down for the trip. She didn't know how long it was going to be, so she did her best to stay awake. This was going to be a long few months. *Well*, she thought, *it had better be only a few months.*

SHE KEPT track of how long the flight lasted. Between two and three hours could put her in a thousand places. She felt the wheels touch down and the jet slow. She could have looked out the window, she knew that, but she wanted her feet on the ground and to breathe the air.

"Let's go," Vincent called to them once the jet crawled to a stop. The door popped open, and a staircase was brought over as she walked to rest of the group.

"Welcome back to Atlanta, Sawyer." Zander grinned at her before pushing her out into the hot, humid air. *Damn it all to hell.*

She felt the July heat seep into her bones, but all she noticed was a chill run down her spine. Whatever tiny shred of good mood she had was leaving quickly. She stomped down the steps and was immediately stopped by another agent, one she didn't recognize.

"Sawyer Matthews?" he asked her, chewing on something as he took in her face. His tone was rude and condescending.

"Yeah, what of it?" she snapped back.

"I'm Special Agent Jon Aguirre." He held out a hand, but she only looked down at it. Was he stupid? She wasn't shaking hands with a Magi until she knew all their abilities. Even then, she probably still wouldn't have shaken it.

"Nice to meet you." She looked back up and met his eyes. She took a moment to take in the scene. This Jon and the agents around him were older, probably in their forties or fifties. IMPO teams tended to stick together for decades, that much she knew, so this group must have been around the block a few times.

"I'm here to tell you that if you screw up with Vinny's team, you will be coming to us. We wanted to get eyes on you, and for you to get eyes on us." He smiled but there wasn't much kindness in it. She raised an eyebrow as Vincent stepped up to her side. "Right, Vinny? Are you excited to finally have a chance at-"

"Jon is an experienced IMPO agent," Vincent cut in. Sawyer frowned and looked at him. He was glaring at the older man, who looked pleased with himself. There was some bad blood here. "If we can't handle keeping you safe or out of trouble, you will need to go into his care."

"Sawyer," Jasper walked to her other side. "You are better off with us. Let's go so Vincent and Elijah can deal with them."

"What is his problem?" she asked him as they walked away. Jon was watching her leave, and she flipped him off, making him go beet-red with anger. He started ranting to Vincent, who just stood there and took it.

"He's a prick, and we're a young team with a bit of a reputation. We're the only two teams in the Southeast with Special Agent classification. The closest other team to us is by New York. Normally, it takes nearly a decade for an

IMPO team to rise high enough to start taking the hard jobs, but we got it about 3 years ago."

"What's so important about that?" She frowned. "And how did you get it so young, if it's so hard?"

"Special Agents work globally. We're tasked with taking on the most dangerous Magi on the planet, whereas regular agents and detectives handle smaller crimes in their designated areas. We also get paid a pretty penny due to the danger of job," Jasper was talking with his hands, and Sawyer put some distance between them to avoid getting smacked on accident. Wouldn't be the first time Jasper had whacked her while he rambled. "I'm talking Legends, and serial killers that work through multiple countries. Crime lords like Axel."

"And-" She tried to cut in, but failed. Jasper was explaining something, and nothing would stop him now. Sawyer remembered the important rule of never asking him for an explanation.

"We got the promotion when another team on the East Coast was completely wiped out. The team tried to make a deal with Shadow to take down Axel. We were brought up because the IMPO and the WMC realized that the only person who has any chance of taking down Axel is Vincent. He put this entire team together for that purpose." Jasper took a breath. "You haven't met him yet, but Quinn is our final member. With him, we have someone with control over each element. Most teams don't take the time to round out their members like Vincent did. It helps that we all get along but-"

"Okay, Jasper." She held up her right hand. She didn't need to hear anymore. "I get it."

Jesus. No wonder Vincent wanted her around so bad. He clearly was obsessed with Axel, which was the last thing she wanted. He was going to be on her ass constantly until she could truly convince him that she didn't know anything. If Axel found her giving secrets over to an IMPO team again, they would all die. Again.

With Jasper and Zander involved... she couldn't let that happen. She hadn't run to them years earlier so they wouldn't get caught in her mess. And now here she was, wondering how to keep them out of it, even though they had to go and join a team *dedicated* to taking Axel down.

It didn't help that they got the job because of her last fuck up. She had contacted the team to strike the deal that would get her out of Axel's control. She had so desperately needed to get out. Axel had found out, and, not only did he kill the team, but he had also nearly killed her. He thought he actually had.

Trying a second time would only lead to even more of a nightmare.

She shook her head slowly, closing her eyes as she tried to push back the memories. No, she couldn't let them get killed. Fuck her freedom. No one else was dying for her like that again, especially not Jasper and Zander. She needed to fall in line and keep her mouth shut if she wanted to keep them alive.

"You okay?" Jasper asked quietly. She reopened her eyes and nodded.

"Yeah, just not used to this heat anymore." She smiled at him, hoping he bought the lie.

In the twelve or so hours she had been in their 'custody', she had lied more than she had told the truth. She didn't need them in her shadows, and she was going to do her damn best to keep them out.

"Sure," he mumbled, opening the door of the truck they

had arrived at. "You're riding back with Elijah. The rest of us are taking a Range Rover."

"Why?" She frowned.

"Because none of us like being in the same vehicle with Elijah for nearly four hours. That's why he gets to bring his truck. But we don't let anyone travel alone, so you are riding with him."

"Why doesn't anyone like riding with Elijah?" she asked cautiously.

"You'll see." Jasper smiled and turned away from her. "There he is now. See you back at the house."

He left her as Elijah climbed into the driver's seat. She didn't like the grin he wore.

"My baby, I missed you," he purred to the steering wheel. "Ready to head to your new home?"

"Sure." She watched him warily. He started it up, and she immediately realized why no one drove with him. His foot hit the gas and he released the clutch, forcing the manual truck into second without it stalling. Holy shit, he drove like a mad man.

"Hold on," he grinned at her. "Awesome thing about being in the IMPO? No one is going to pull me over."

"Oh, fuck." She grabbed the 'oh, shit' bar and began praying. She didn't know who she was praying to, but surely there had to be one god keeping an eye on her, right?

He had them on good old Interstate 285 in a minute, where she watched cars get lost in the dust behind them.

"How fucking fast are you going?" She screamed, seeing her life pass before her eyes. It wasn't that she hated speed. She loved going fast in her car or on her bike, but she had no control here. She didn't trust other drivers, and now Elijah was going to give her a damn heart attack as he wove through traffic.

"About a hundred and forty," he laughed. "This baby has nitrous too, if you want-"

"No!" she yelled. "Are you fucking mad? Look at this traffic!" He grinned at her as she yelled. "Keep your fucking eyes on the road!"

Four hours? Hell, they would be where ever they are going in three tops with how fast he was going. She felt her hand cramp on the bar after ten minutes, and looked up at it. Her knuckles were white, and her palm was sweaty.

"Can you not kill me today? I've worked really hard to stay among the living for several years." She was getting clammy.

"You ride a motorcycle." Elijah continued to laugh. "I don't see why this such a problem for you."

"I'm in control of my motorcycle," she growled. "I also keep it under a hundred and twenty. I feel like your truck it about to take to the fucking air."

"It has never left the road, and I've gotten it to about two hundred." Elijah chuckled, but she noticed he slowed down. "Turn on the radio and take a nap."

She wasn't going to be able to sleep while he was behind the wheel.

"You didn't drive like this in New York," she mumbled.

"Well, I don't know the roads there well enough. And it wasn't my truck."

"Do you race this thing?" She clicked through the stations. She caught a glimpse of his speedometer and sighed happily. He was back down to one hundred miles an hour. That shouldn't have pleased her, but it really did.

"Yeah." Elijah grinned at her. "Once a month, if I can pull it off. All legal, of course."

"Of course," she muttered under her breath.

They spent the rest of the ride in silence, and she

wondered what she would find at their home. She also wanted to know who this mysterious Quinn was. She heard them reference him more than a few times, but only Jasper really told her anything. Earth manipulation, the final of the four elements that Vincent had stacked onto the team.

∾

"WE'RE HERE," Elijah whispered to her. She blinked and wondered when she had fallen asleep. "Take a look."

She blinked several more times, clearing her eyes. When she could focus, she took in the large, white, old home. It was an old plantation house, or something based on that style. Large pillars held up a balcony coming from the second floor, which provided shade for the wrap around porch on the first. Large windows in the front gave her a view of the dining room, kitchen, and living room. She didn't need to step inside to realize that while the outside looked old, the inside had been modernized. A new addition had obviously been built, as well: a garage that was connected on the side with the dining room and kitchen. It had, not one or two doors, but four.

"Do you use the garage?" She asked since he had parked right in front of the... *house.*

"Yeah, but I wanted you to see the house before I pulled it in." He grinned at her, and she nodded.

"Thanks, it is impressive." It was, and it probably cost a fortune. "How did you guys end up here?"

"Special Agents get a pick of stuff before auctions happen. This was owned by a real dick-head who was smuggling drugs into the country. When he was arrested, we asked for the house and renovated it to suit our needs. We've been in it for two years now." Elijah passed the garage doors, and Sawyer frowned as he went around to the back. On the other side of the garage, four more doors.

"An eight-car garage? Are you fucking serious?" She chuckled at it as Elijah hit the garage door opener and pulled in.

"Yeah, we haven't filled it yet. Vincent and I are the only two with personal vehicles. Jasper and Zander share a Range Rover, which was given to us for work. Quinn doesn't drive. We have two Range Rovers, actually, because we technically aren't allowed to use personal vehicles for work."

"And that thing." She pointed at a car that was in pieces, and he nodded, shutting off the truck.

"Yeah. So... five vehicles. Oh, and our beat up little property truck and the two four wheelers."

"Jasper said you get paid really well..." she sighed to herself.

"About five-hundred thousand a year, without bonuses." Elijah nodded. "Teams normally have four to eight members, who normally live together in the early years, unless one gets married or something."

"Bonuses?" Who had any idea that IMPO agents made so much fucking money? If that was public knowledge, they wouldn't be suffering from a shortage of recruits.

"We get anywhere from a hundred grand to a million for finishing cases." Elijah got out of the truck and she followed him. "We, on average, have two to three shorter cases a year, and this team does a couple longer term things, like trying to catch Axel. There's only ten Special Agent teams on the planet, so the IMPO can afford to throw a lot of money at us."

"So, this team is rich, and made to catch Axel." She trailed behind him into the house, ending up in the dining room that she had seen from the front. "What will you do if you catch him?"

"Go after the next one." Elijah grinned at her. "What else?"

Huh.

"The others are probably an hour behind us, which should give you time to see your room and get a little settled." Elijah waved her on to keep following him. "You know Sawyer, I am sorry we had to rip you from your life. I promise we'll make this as easy as possible for you."

"Thanks," she responded. "Truthfully, I should feel grateful. I could be in prison..."

Though, at this point she would rather be. Her fears about Axel realizing where she was hiding were amplified, now that she had been dragged out of New York, her haven. Add in a few nice guys who were just trying to make the world a better place...

"So, we only have four real bedrooms on the second floor. We had Quinn setting up an old apartment that was hiding in the attic while we were getting you. It doesn't have its own bathroom, so you'll have to share with us on the second floor." He was trying to sound friendly and optimistic.

They made their way up the central staircase by the front door. The second floor was divided into halves, with three doors on one side and three doors on the other. Right in front of the staircase, though, was a narrow door.

"Quinn's bedroom is on the first floor," he told her as she went to jiggle the handle to the mysterious, out-of-place door. "And that's the door to the attic, let me unlock it for you."

Once it was open, he led her up. A second door at the

top of the stairs also needed to be unlocked, and they both stepped into the attic.

"Almost there," he sighed, leading her to a door about ten feet away. That last one wasn't locked, and he swung it open for her.

Lush, navy-blue carpet was the first thing she noticed—that and gray walls. A queen size bed had somehow been brought up, and it had a padded dark gray headboard, dark blue blankets, and a mix of gray and blue pillows. They had set up a desk for her, black and modern. A black dresser and a black end table finished off the room.

"He did well," Elijah nodded. "Zander and I ordered it all, but Quinn had to get it all set up. I wasn't sure he could get it done."

"It's nice." She looked around more, and then kicked off her tennis shoes. "Thank you."

"Of course." Elijah grinned at her. "If you ever want help breaking in the new mattress-"

"Get out." She rolled her eyes and pointed to the door as he laughed. When he reopened the bedroom door, Sawyer nearly jumped at the person standing there. *This must be Quinn.* He was not what she had been expecting. Like every person she met, she analyzed him before saying anything.

He stepped in, looking at Elijah for a moment, and then at her. She noticed he had walked quietly as he moved towards her. He was obviously part Native American. His dark brown hair was long and pulled back into a ponytail that he had over his shoulder, letting her really see the length of it. It was longer than her own, but straight. Like the rest of the guys, he was over six feet tall, but she could see he was shorter than Elijah. He was leaner, like Zander; and, thanks to his shirtless state, she could tell he maintained an excellent form and a full, intricate tribal sleeve that covered his right arm and pectoral muscle.

What was throwing her off when looking at the gorgeous man were the cold, ice-blue eyes that looked like they could cut into her. He had a sharp brow, sharp cheekbones, and a full bottom lip. But those eyes were captivating and terrifying.

"You must be Sawyer," he said in a harsh, gravelly voice when he stopped a few feet from her, and she nodded slowly.

"You must be Quinn." She tried her best to keep her voice even.

If there was ever a person she could describe as feral, it was him. He was barely restrained violence. She watched his muscles tense and relax, as if he was trying to keep himself relaxed, but failing. Something about the way he looked at her reminded her of a beast ready to pounce on unsuspecting prey.

He turned away from her, a complete dismissal of her existence. When his back faced her, she bit her lip in sympathy. Scars covered his back from the top of his shoulder blades to the arch of his lower back.

"Did I do this right?" Quinn's tone remained harsh.

"Yeah." Elijah grinned at him, and she watched Quinn's shoulders relax completely. Every muscle relaxed, really. She hadn't realized just how tense he was. "Now we just need to test the internet and electricity."

"I let all those people in to handle it," Quinn growled.

"We'll get it figured out." Elijah reached out and patted Quinn's shoulder. After a moment, Quinn closed the distance between them, and Sawyer only watched the two of them quietly. "I think we should get a TV in here, a couple of couches. What do you think?"

"You say that like I am going to be up here," Quinn huffed out. "You are here now, you do it."

"Yeah, I'll stop bothering you with this." Elijah was still grinning, but Sawyer felt like she was missing whatever he found so humorous. He looked over to her. "But seriously, Sawyer, you want a TV in here?"

"I don't really care... I can just buy one of my own, if I want one."

"Well..." Elijah nodded slowly and looked back to Quinn, who held his hands up and left the room before anything more could be said. Elijah pulled his cowboy hat off, frowning at her. "We locked you out of your accounts."

She finally blew a gasket. The lid on her temper popped off as if it had been pressurizing since the moment Elijah put the handcuffs on her.

"I'm going to fucking kill all of you," she growled.

"Now, wait a minute," Elijah pleaded. "Our handler, James, made the decision. Even Vincent had thought to leave you with your money, but our handler made the final call."

"I have accepted being dragged out of my house, away from my life, and being sold out by my only friend," Sawyer growled. "And you tell me now that I'm also poor?!" She ended in roar. "Who the fuck is James?!"

"Yeah." Elijah gave a small but sympathetic shrug. "Sawyer, look, we'll take care of everything-"

"Just. Get. Out." She snarled, pointing back to the door. *Holy shit, I'm poor.* She pulled out her wallet as Elijah closed the door behind him. She opened it and counted her cash. A thousand in Benjamins. She always kept a steady amount on her in case of emergencies. She also had thrown a few grand into the bag she had packed, but now she was increasingly paranoid that money would be gone when she got the bag back.

"Fuck me," she growled to herself. "I can't believe this." She sank on the edge of the bed, opening and closing her hands. She needed to resist the urge to break the cute furniture around the room. She reminded herself that they didn't need to do this for her. They didn't need to make a cute little room in their home. They didn't need to keep her out of prison.

It was a sticky situation. Prison wasn't safe from Axel. He was well known for staging breakouts or murders within prison walls. Being here might be safer, but it also put another IMPO team in danger, and she had too many dead bodies littering her past. She didn't want to add Jasper and Zander to that trail of corpses. She didn't want to add any of them to it.

But damn, here they were, dedicated to taking down one of the craziest men on the planet. Sawyer looked down at her left hand and felt a kernel of hope. A crazy feeling that maybe the IMPO could actually do it this time.

She was going to get her fucking money back, though. That shit was just unacceptable.

"Sawyer?"

She looked up to her door at the sound of Zander's voice.

"Come in," she called out, trying to leave her thoughts. He stepped in with two bags, neither being the one she packed.

"I figured you would want to help bring up all your stuff." He grinned at her. "We have all your clothing from

Charlie's before we left, so there's a lot of bags waiting to get brought up."

"Yeah, I'll go down." She stood up and frowned at her stiffness. How long had she been sitting there? She waited for him to put the two he had down on her new bed and left with him. They waited for Elijah and Vincent to come up the narrow stairs, each holding two more. "Damn, I do have a lot of stuff."

"Yeah, and you lied to me," Elijah laughed. "You didn't pack all of your panties."

She groaned and punched his shoulder, making him grunt in pain.

"Alright," Vincent hissed. "Both of you quit this."

"Yes sir, Boss man," Elijah laughed. "Tell her to stop hitting me."

"Stop being a pervert and I might," she growled.

"Seriously, Elijah," Zander snarled. "Keep your fucking thoughts to yourself." She turned to Zander and shoved him, making his green eyes widen with shock.

"I don't need you backing me up," Sawyer snapped. "Mind your own fucking business."

"Are you serious?" Zander glared at her. "After everything, you are going to tell me to mind my business? Sawyer-"

She turned and jogged down the stairs, ignoring whatever he had to say. She didn't need him playing protector with Elijah. She didn't need him to do it when they were teens, she damn sure didn't need it at twenty-four. She could handle Elijah.

She made it to the garage before Zander was able to catch up.

"Fine," he grumbled angrily at her. "It's not my place. I won't get involved like that, happy?"

"Yes," she said curtly. She grabbed two bags from the open trunk of the Range Rover. Only three left, so she grabbed an extra, thinking Zander could get the last two. One of the bags she carried was her personal bag, and she didn't want their hands on it anymore.

"Can I at least carry the extra bag?" he asked her, his face tight. There was the Zander she remembered. Trying to be helpful and angry all at the same time.

"No," she grinned, walking away from him. Jasper was sitting in the dining room as she passed by. She had missed him the first time. "How was the drive?"

"Good. You like the room?" He looked up from the book he was nose-deep in.

"Yeah. I met Quinn too."

"Good." He nodded as she looked back to Zander, who was stuck in the door to the garage, waiting for her to move. She did, ignoring him and making the long climb back up to her new room. Vincent and Elijah were still there, opening bags and putting stuff away for her.

"I would thank you for that, but I would also like you to stop touching my stuff," she told them with a polite sweetness. She could have sworn Elijah paled a little.

"Forgive me." Vincent raised his hands. "My mother just raised me to be helpful to guests, and I figured since we packed it, we could help unpack it."

"Thanks, but no thanks." She smiled. That was actually nice. Strangely, it made her a little uncomfortable. "I appreciate that though."

"Alright, we'll be out of your way." Vincent grabbed Elijah and led him out, taking Zander with them, as well. She dropped the bags she was holding and closed the door. She noticed there was no lock. That was going to have to change, and fast.

She opened her personal bag and took inventory. Only half of it was underwear, she knew that. Her two vibrators were wrapped exactly as she had placed them, so that was good. A small set of black throwing knives were untouched, and now she wondered why she had even brought them.

Because if I had left them out, she thought, *they would have found them. And then I would have probably gone to prison.*

She ran a hand over them and left them in the bag, so she could find a hiding place for them last. The next item she looked for was also there, her small box of photos. She took that out and put it on the desk. That box also had tons of secrets, but they were more personal in nature. She would rather they learn those secrets than find the knives. She really preferred that none of her secrets came out, but she needed something easy for them to find if they snooped. If she was too secretive, they would look for other hiding places.

Her laptop was next. She didn't know if she was allowed to have it, but she hadn't been willing to leave it behind. She placed it on the desk next to the box of photos.

Last but not least, her money. It was all there, and she knew she would hide it with the daggers, wherever that would be. She looked around the bedroom a little more and then rolled her eyes upwards.

Beams. She was in the *attic*. Oh, this was perfect.

She grabbed the case holding the throwing knives and climbed onto her bed. She took a deep breath and remembered she was going to have to get up there without her powers. It wasn't the highest vertical jump she had ever done, but the bed made it harder, not easier; and she didn't want to make too much noise by jumping on it.

She got it on the second try, her hands latching onto the lowest beam. It left her feet nearly three feet from the bed, and she pulled herself up. She was thankful for all the upper body training Charlie had recommended for her.

Once she was up, she straddled the beam and opened the folding case again. Five throwing knives were all she kept of her old weapon set. The rest was hiding... in Atlanta. *Holy shit*. She closed the case and put her face in her hands. She had chosen this city because she refused to work here. Because she was never active in the city, they had never thought to look there for her or for her things.

She had buried all of her past in Atlanta. The last place she'd seen Jasper and Zander, the last place people would look for her stuff as Shadow.

She laid the daggers carefully on another beam and then crept on the balls of her feet to another section of the tall ceiling and stashed her cash.

She swung down carefully over her new dresser and tried her best to keep her controlled fall silent. This would have been such a simple task with her magic.

She groaned when she got off the dresser and looked to her other bags. She turned to the second door in her attic bedroom and opened it. A closet. Perfect. She at least had a place to throw most of this without worrying who saw it.

14

SAWYER

Sawyer lay in bed long after dinner, frowning to herself. She couldn't sleep at all. She hated trying to sleep in new places. She also needed a shower and forgot to ask where the bathroom was on the second floor. The only bathroom she had found in the house had been on the first floor, near the living room, and it didn't have a bath or shower in it.

She pulled on her gray sweats and a tank top. She usually slept in the nude, so getting a lock on her door was becoming a major priority.

She quietly crept out of her room and down to the second floor. She heard voices from a couple of the rooms, but further listening told her it was televisions, not talking. She didn't know where to go, and that made this awkward. She would need to knock on a door and ask.

She picked the one closest to her staircase that had noises coming from it. She rapped on it three times, crossed her arms, and waited.

The door opened to reveal a shirtless Zander. He wore

low-slung black sweats, and she looked him over in shock and appreciation. He'd been fit when he left, but now? He was ripped. She had a decent six pack, but she wanted to know how he had fucking *eight*. He had two revolvers tattooed pointing down that V men got from working out. Sure, he was covered in ink, but those guns were pointing to a place Sawyer suddenly wanted to visit.

When she finally looked up at his face, away from the V that led beneath the sweats, Zander was smirking at her, leaning in the door frame. That V had been doing awful things to her—things Zander was not allowed to do to her anymore.

"Sawyer," he stated simply. She could hear the small hint of amusement and arrogance. Zander had always been a bit of a ladies' man.

"Where's the bathroom I can use?" She tapped her foot as he looked her over slowly. "I want to get a bath or shower in before bed."

She looked down at herself and groaned. She'd pushed her breasts up, making her lack of a bra obvious. She placed her arms over her tits and waited for an answer.

"Zander. Bathroom."

He looked lazily back to her face and nodded.

"Follow me," he stepped past her and went across the hall. He pushed the door directly across from his open and revealed a fairly decent bathroom with a shower and a tub. "There you go. "

"Thanks." She waved him away, so she could get everything she needed. She needed towels and a change of clothes. She wasn't going to walk around in a towel in this house.

He stayed in the bathroom's door, not letting her pass.

They were nearly chest to chest. She took a moment to really let it sink in that he wasn't a teenager anymore. Neither of them were dumb teenagers anymore.

"Sawyer," he mumbled. He was too close, much too close. "I missed you and-"

"Leave it, Zander. I'm not doing this right now." She didn't look up at him. He was practically talking into her hair, so looking up would put their faces inches apart. "I just want to get clean, not talk about teenage hormones."

"Alright, but we will." He stepped away and went back to his room. She heard the click of a lock and sighed heavily.

"No, we won't," she whispered to herself.

She got everything ready as hot water filled the tub. She sank in and moaned happily. It wasn't her tub with the jets, but damn, it felt good. A few candles that smelled nice and she would be in heaven.

She kept thinking about Zander, what he had looked like, and felt the itch that needed to be scratched. *Oh, no.* That was not okay. Elijah was one thing. She didn't know him, and even that had ended up with her getting *arrested*.

Well, not arrested, but she was still a criminal stuck in a house full of IMPO agents.

She tried to think of anything or anyone else, but as she soaked in the tub, she only came to one realization.

They were all hot as fuck. She at least had *fantastic* eye candy for the remaining short existence she was going to have until Axel found her. She might even have a good time before it happened, as stupid of an idea as *that* was.

She did the only thing she could—she laughed until she cried.

She was so fucked.

She dipped her thick hair into the water and sighed as she surfaced. Twenty-four hours ago, she had been getting ready for another standard Friday Fight Night. She should have known LA and what happened wouldn't just disappear, but she hadn't been expecting this.

When she was done, she rose and grabbed a towel that she had waiting. She wrapped her hair first, deciding that it was too late in the evening to give it a blow dry. She dried the rest of herself and put on her clean clothes.

By the time she was back in her new room, it was nearly midnight. A howl rang out, and she looked out her window to see the woods beyond the house. When a second wolf joined, she raised an eyebrow. At the sound of a third, she realized that magic was involved in this. Wolves didn't live in this part of the country, only coyotes, but those were definitely wolves out there.

The midnight serenade continued as she set her laptop up. She didn't use the Wi-Fi for the house, instead she plugged in a USB with a program that allowed her to use the internet without being charged. She didn't have a Facebook or anything like that, but she did have some things she needed to check out.

She typed in the address to the Dark Web site that she normally got her jobs from. She had avoided looking at it for a couple of weeks, but now it was time to see what was waiting for her out in the world, since she was no longer sheltered in New York.

She clicked through the chats, keeping an eye out for any names she knew. Then she stumbled on it. Talyn had been active in the last... twenty-four hours. Talyn was one of Axel's closest... friends? She snorted softly at the thought. Axel didn't really consider any of them friends, but the top, most trusted members did get special privileges and freedoms that Axel didn't allow others.

She didn't find anything interesting about his activity or

posts. She ended up finding three other Ghosts from Axel's inner circle as well, but none of them had much to their activity either. She closed her laptop and leaned back.

She grabbed the box of photos and immediately put it back down. She didn't need to go through those tonight; there was no reason to see those memories.

She gave up on trying to be even remotely productive and moved to her bed. She didn't know when she fell asleep, but eventually, the darkness claimed her. Like normal, it wasn't peaceful.

$\approx$

SHE WOKE to something else in her bed. She could feel the weight of it, but she couldn't identify the what... or who. She opened her eyes slowly and focused on what she could hear. Even breathing. A who, then. Which one of these assholes decided it was okay for them to get in her bed? How had she not woken up and noticed?

She rose slowly and went still when she saw her bedmate. *Oh fuck.* The dark gray wolf was obscenely large, and behind it was a smaller, lighter gray one. The smaller one lifted its head and watched her while the darker one just bared its teeth.

The intelligence in those eyes told her something important.

"Shade! Scout!" Quinn's harsh voice yelled. Both wolves were up in a beat and ran for her door, leaving her in shock. She woke up to wolves in her bed. How did they get into the room?!

She started shaking a little as she got out of her bed. What. The. Fuck. She walked slowly to close her door, and took a long, shaky breath as she found clothes to wear. It was Sunday, so unless they had plans, she would be staying in sweats and a tank. She frowned. No, not sweats. It was too hot for that. She found some gym shorts and pulled those on instead, making sure to wear a bra this time before leaving the room.

She made her way downstairs, keeping a wary eye on the halls in case the wolves were back. The intelligence in the wolves' eyes made it obvious they were bonded to a Magi, but she didn't know the magic signature of the guys around her well enough to identify which one it was. Her first guess was Quinn since he had called them.

The guys were all sitting in the dining room, and sure enough, both wolves flanked Quinn with their own bowls on the floor.

"Good morning," she said cautiously, her eyes on the huge wolves. "They were in my room when I woke up..." Quinn looked up to her and his ice-blue eyes narrowed.

"They sleep wherever they want," he told her coarsely. "But I'll make sure they know you didn't appreciate it."

"I just wasn't expecting it," she mumbled, sitting down in an empty chair. The guys all looked at her, and she looked around at all of them. Elijah's brown hair was a tousled mess. Zander's was even worse. Jasper and Vincent were the only two who looked put together in any way. Quinn looked the exact same as he had the day before, and she hadn't seen him at dinner the night before. He was also still shirtless. So yeah, there was that. "No one told me there were wolves here."

"They are Quinn's bonded animals," Vincent told her, holding a newspaper and looking at her over the top. "I have a raven, named Kaar. Oh, Quinn, remember how we were trying to guess her bonded animal?"

"Yeah," Quinn mumbled, and Sawyer was beginning to

wonder if his voice was just permanently that hoarse and harsh.

"She doesn't have one." Vincent put his magazine down. "Think there's anything to that?"

"Odd," Quinn whispered, continuing his sharp stare at her. She frowned at him, wondering what the fuck was going on between him and Vincent.

Animal bonding was such a Common ability. You also had no choice in the bond and the type of animal was completely random. An animal would see you and say, 'that's my Magi'. After that, there was nothing that could be done. The moment the animal made the decision, the Magi would feel the bond complete itself. Sometimes, exceptionally strong Magi would have more than one animal make the bond, which made her even more wary of Quinn with his two wolves. Strong predators were rarer as bonded animals. Most Magi had a bird, domesticated pet, or something small and common.

The real magic came in what Magi and their animals could do together. A Magi could feel the emotional currents of the animal or, when the Magi focused, he or she could look through the animal's eyes. The animal's life span lengthened to that of the Magi, and it would pass away when the Magi did. A bonded animal could get killed, though, and the Magi would be fine. If the bonded animal died, then a Magi could get chosen by another animal, though it might never happen.

She never got a second chance.

"I can imagine a few reasons." He huffed, keeping her pinned with his stare.

She didn't appreciate how much his eyes seemed to look into her, and she saw the moment he made his judgment of her. He didn't elaborate on what he'd said. Vincent seemed to accept it, and she just kept frowning.

"Speaking of powers," Elijah yawned. "We need to tell you ours since we'll be hanging around together and training you. You should know what you've got around in case you need anything. I'll start. I've got four Common ranked abilities; enchanting, fire manipulation, animation, and telekinesis."

"Cool." She nodded slowly. "So, you can enchant an item and animate it? I bet you're fun at parties." Animating was exactly what it sounded like. Dancing brooms from that Disney flick? It was that.

"I am fun at parties but not because of my magic, darlin'." He winked as he said it, making her roll her eyes. "Vin?"

"Hm." Vincent took a drink of coffee, and Sawyer took the chance to fix herself a plate from the assortment on the table. "2 Common abilities, telekinesis and my animal bond. 2 Rare, petrification and sublimation."

She stopped what she was doing, buttering a piece of toast, and met Vincent's eyes. They both had sublimation and a second Rare ability. Her cloaking could stop him from petrifying her if push came to shove but he was the one she would need to be wary of when she tried to escape—after she convinced them to give her magic back to her.

The heavy mental weight of the bracelet became more apparent at the thought, reminding her of the missing, full connection to her Source. Damn inhibitors. It felt like an entire piece of her was missing, just out of reach, her fingers barely able to graze it, but not truly grasp it.

"I know Jasper's and Zander's," she told them as Vincent started to point to Zander, who was blinking, half-awake for the conversation. "I was there for their Readings."

"Good to know." Vincent nodded and looked to Quinn, who glowered. He didn't seem to like the idea of telling her what his magic was. "Quinn."

Quinn bared his teeth at Vincent, and Sawyer felt a shiver of fear at the presence of the feral man. He behaved more like the wolves around him then the other people in the room.

"Earth manipulation, my animal bonds, naturalism, shape-shifting, and *tracking*." Quinn gave her a grin, but there was nothing happy about it. It was threatening. She swallowed and realized her throat was suddenly very dry. She took a sip of water and hoped that Quinn wouldn't be looking at her when she turned back.

"Tracking," she muttered after two large gulps of water. Damn, he had a full set. Five abilities. No Magi ever had more than that, as far as anyone knew, except the Legends, who were a breed of their own.

"Tracking," Vincent affirmed. He knew exactly where her mind had gone. They probably all knew what she was thinking.

Tracking was the Rare ranked ability. That made Quinn the *worst* person in the room in her opinion. He beat out Vincent by leaps and bounds. If he got his hands on any of her personal items, something that she touched regularly or held onto because of sentimental value, then he could literally find her anywhere on the planet. That was bad news for her, since it would be easy for him to get his hands on something sentimental to her.

It would be so easy for Quinn to make sure she never got free of them, magic or not. That meant she only had one plan left, and who knew how long *that* would take to pull off. She had to convince them that she didn't need their protection.

"You see, Sawyer." Vincent gave her a small smile, "I didn't just build a team for capturing Axel. I built a team with very few weaknesses at all. All four elements, tracking, stealth, spying through our animal bonds. Jasper's dream walking. Zander's healing and shielding. Elijah's enchanting." He pointed to her bracelet. She looked down at it and then to Elijah, who shrugged.

"Yeah, I made it," he told her, giving her a sympathetic smile. "I also enchanted the handcuffs, so they would work on you and only you. That way you couldn't sleight of hand them onto one of us."

"Well," she tried to sound neutral, "fantastic."

"You could just stop thinking about escaping," Vincent offered, taking another sip of his coffee. "I mean, I know it's a criminal's natural instinct to run, but we're doing you the favor here."

"A favor would be letting me have my magic to protect *myself*," she pointed out to him with a smile.

"We'll think about it." He went back to reading his newspaper after that. She looked to her old friends and Jasper gave her a nod. Zander only shrugged.

"So helpful, guys," she muttered to them.

"Yeah." Zander grinned at her. "Aren't we just the best? Personally, I like the idea of you being stuck here for an indefinite amount of time. Jasper and I can now figure out why you dropped us out of your life."

"Fuck you," she told him plainly and started eating her breakfast. She didn't drop them. Shit happened, and it hadn't been a good idea to find them. They would never forgive her for any of it. "So, what's the routine around here like?"

"We figured every day you'll be with someone on the team, so we can get an accurate judge of your skills without your magic. We know what you can do with it, but we want to make sure you can hold your own without it. Weapons, firearms, and more hand-to-hand training." Vincent told her without looking up from his reading.

Firearms? Disgust curled in her stomach for a moment. She detested them. If she wanted to kill someone, she would do it in their space, not from across the room like a coward. She opened her mouth to say something about Vincent forcing her to train in firearms, but Zander cut her off.

"Real martial arts, none of that nonsense, bar fighting you do," Zander joked, and she raised an eyebrow at him, realizing he probably thought she was going to complain about more hand-to-hand training.

"I kick the shit out of wannabe MMA fighters all the time, Zander. Who here do you think is so good that I can't win?"

"Me," he told her, still smiling. She noticed that the idea of a fight brought him to life just like it did for her. His green eyes were blazing with the possibility of a little violence, and she could get down with that. There was something seriously wrong with them.

"Bring it," she taunted, grinning and motioning for him to come closer with a finger. "Want to know why I'm going to win?"

"Why, little girl?" Zander leaned closer to her like she had wanted.

"Because I don't need fancy-ass moves to put bodies on the floor." She flicked his nose and he jerked back. "And I'm not afraid to fight a little dirty when it's needed."

Elijah was chuckling, and Jasper had a smile hidden behind his book. She kept her taunting grin, ready for anything Zander might have up his sleeve, but the fun was cut off.

"No fighting at the table," Vincent commented, looking between them. Sawyer leaned back in her seat, distancing herself from the redhead.

"Yes, sir, Boss man," she said with more sarcasm then she probably should have used. Vincent paid her no mind, but Elijah snorted milk through his nose.

"Is this going to be every morning with you?" he finally asked, wiping his face clean.

"Probably," Zander chuckled.

She looked over at Jasper, still hiding behind his book and saw his shoulders shaking a little. He was holding back his laughter as well as he could.

"What are normal days like here?" She looked to Elijah and tried to ignore the quiet Quinn next to him.

"On weekends, we take time to ourselves." Elijah ate a piece of bacon as he spoke. "During the week though, we all work out every morning together, starting with a five-a.m. run followed by two hours in the gym together. After that, we'll separate to work on our own projects. We always meet for breakfast, but after that you can do whatever you want for meals."

"Anything you want to do?" Jasper finally closed his book and put it on the table, watching her.

"I think I'm going to wander the property and see what you've got here." She shrugged and began to push away from the table. "Also, Vincent, I'm not touching a gun, so you can free that time up for something else."

He frowned at her as she picked up her plate. She met his eyes and began to walk out of the dining room. They could drag her here, they could remove her ability to escape, but they would never make her budge on the guns. She wouldn't use one, even in training.

She rinsed her plate as a chair scraped against the floor and footsteps came up to her.

"Why not?" Vincent asked, putting a hand on the counter next to the sink. He kept his chest to her. She took a moment to admire that chest. He was a good-looking man, even if he did reek of the same control-freak nature as Axel.

"Because I don't fucking like them," she snapped. Because she'd been shot before.

"That's too bad for you," Vincent snapped back. She bared her teeth. "Make this fucking easy on both of us and suffer through it."

"No," she told him with finality. With a curse, he slammed a fist on the counter top in frustration. Something about the gesture startled the hell out her, making her jump nearly out of her skin.

It was something Axel would do.

She closed her eyes and tried to fight the flashback creeping up on her. She tried to remember where she was and who she was with.

"Sawyer..." Vincent sounded concerned, and his voice was different from Axel's. Deeper. It brought her back from a moment. "Sawyer, are you okay?"

"Just... go the fuck away," she mumbled. "Even better, I'll go."

She turned and left, her blood cold. Adrenaline pumped through her system, and she took a deep breath as she pushed out onto the back porch and into the yard.

PTSD was a wicked thing, she knew that. With so much going on, she should have realized it would be easy for things to set her off—especially Vincent. He had reminded her so much of Axel in that moment.

She had been having a fairly decent morning. She

rubbed her face for a moment, standing in the sun, hoping the heat would sink to her core.

"Sawyer?" Jasper's voice reached out to her. She turned and sighed to see him standing on the back porch. She curled her toes in the grass and wondered when she had decided being barefoot was a bad thing. She used to love being barefoot in the grass as a kid, and somewhere along the way, she had stopped searching for the beautiful feeling of it.

"Jasper," she said when he didn't continue.

"Want to have a tour of the place?" He shuffled uncomfortably, and her heart squeezed a little. Jasper had always been uncomfortable with emotion, but this was his way of offering help.

"Yeah, I'd like that." She gave him a weak smile, and he beckoned her to follow him. "How's the IMPO treating you?" she asked as they made their way back into the house.

"Better than the IMAS." Jasper gave her a small smile back. "They're willing to work around the knee, and now hip, problems."

"That's good," she followed him towards the stairs. "Where are we going?"

"I heard your run in with Zander last night, so I figured you should know whose room is whose, first." He smiled at her and she groaned.

"You know, don't you?" She side-eyed him and he nodded.

"He told me during boot camp." He shot her an apologetic smile. "I don't care. You know that, right?"

"I didn't think you did," she said nonchalantly. She did think he cared, at least when he first found out, even if he didn't now. Things had been different that last six months before they left. Teenage hormones and tempers. Her own weird teenage girl feelings about the guys she grew up with, and their apparent weirdness about those feelings.

Jasper had been a virgin, and she had stupidly hit on him, trying to lose her own v-card while she was drunk and he was sober. Then she had rolled into bed with an even drunker Zander, like an idiot, because Jasper had turned her down. She had been so conflicted about her feelings for them both. She was almost a little thankful that they left when they did, because it had been getting to the point of nonsense.

"Well, here on the right, you know where Zander's room is, and the bathroom," he pointed to the third door as he spoke. They both studiously ignored the previous topic. "That one is me. Zander and I share the bathroom on this side." He turned to the left and she followed. "The first door here is Vincent, then it's Elijah. They share the bathroom on this side. Quinn's bedroom is on the first floor, and he has a private bathroom, so you don't need to worry about running into him up here, for the most part."

"For the most part?" She didn't miss that tacked on at the end of Jasper's little second-floor tour.

"He does come up here to hang out." Jasper shrugged. "Let's go back down, and I'll show you everything on the first floor, then the basement."

"Basement?" She frowned. "You have a basement?"

"Yeah, we put a gym down there with all of our training equipment. Keeps it from prying eyes. Also, the entertainment room is down there." Jasper led her down and began pointing out things she had already seen. Living room, rarely used unless there was company. Dining room and kitchen, check. A drawing room, never used and wasn't even furnished. Quinn's bedroom door, in the hallway that led to the backdoor.

She stayed quiet as he led them to the basement, through a small door near the kitchen that she had somehow missed. A narrow staircase led to a narrow hallway with three doors.

"Come on," Jasper led her to the single door on the left and pushed it open. She nearly dropped her jaw.

"This is some state of the art shit," she whispered in appreciation. They had it all from treadmills that hooked up to the runner and monitored vitals to every piece of weight-training equipment she could think of. He pointed towards the back of the room and she saw an entire training area set up with a mat and mirrors.

"We are required to stay in the best shape we can be," Jasper told her. "Hence, our schedule."

"Damn, this is nice," she chuckled. "Elijah told me you guys were paid well, but I wasn't expecting this."

"Actually, the gym stuff is from the IMPO, itself." Jasper shrugged. "They give this equipment to all their top teams."

"And I get to use this stuff?" She gestured around and resisted the urge to go touch all of it.

"You'll be following our workout schedule, so yes." Jasper nodded slowly. "Sawyer, about what happened in the kitchen with Vincent."

She froze, and whatever shred of relaxation she found evaporated.

"Want to tell me about it?" he asked her softly.

"Not really," she mumbled, still looking over the gym. She wasn't officially diagnosed with PTSD, but she knew the signs. She wasn't stupid. Charlie had tried to get her into therapy once, but she'd resisted. She could handle it on her own, and most of the time it didn't affect her life. "Any more cool facts you got about it?"

"You aren't the only person in the house who deals with that kind of stuff." Jasper watched her carefully. "You could talk to Quinn. He would understand better than the rest of us."

"He's..." She tried to find words that didn't make her sound rude or assumptive.

"He's different," Jasper nodded, "but don't change the subject. You know, you can talk to me or Zander while you're here, too. We would listen. I know I'm a stickler for rules, but I wouldn't hold anything against you."

"Thanks." she gave him an indulgent smile. He would hold all of it against her. He might have turned a blind eye to her business in New York, but she didn't think it would extend to murder. "I'll consider it."

She wanted to try, though. She wanted to open her soul and let the shadows pour out. She wanted to peel back the layers and find some peace with knowing the secrets were gone. She was accustomed to secrets and shadows, but she didn't like them. If she could get rid of all of them, she would, but lives were on the line, and they were all safer if she kept her silence. She couldn't forget that... But maybe he was right. Maybe there were a few things she could tell them just to get them off her chest without putting them in danger.

"Please, do." Jasper ran a hand through his hair, looking away from her. He was turning an adorable shade of pink, her golden boy. "You'll be here for a little while, so..."

"I get you." She nodded. "I missed you, Jasper. And Zander."

"We looked for you." He swallowed. "We started searching the moment we joined the IMPO. We weren't allowed to put company hours into it, but we tried to find you."

"I'm sorry to say," she sighed, "that I didn't look for you. I felt it was better that you stayed a pleasant memory for me, and I stayed a hopefully pleasant memory for you."

"You were always more than just a pleasant memory, Sawyer," Jasper whispered. Sawyer swallowed on a lump in her throat, trying to ignore the amount of emotion loaded in that sentence. After a minute of silence, Jasper cleared his own throat. "Zander wants to take you into town, if you're willing to go."

"I would rather get a feel for this place, first." She went up the stairs first while he trailed behind her. "Anything else you want to tell or show me?"

"No." Jasper shrugged. "Vincent wants to see you again later today. And if you want to go wander in the woods, you're allowed, but stick to the trails and *don't* go down the second east trail at all. There's a marker, you'll know it if you see it."

She stopped in the hallway at that. That was a weird rule.

"Why?" She tilted her head a little.

"Quinn runs the woods here; there's no local Druid since we're only twenty minutes from a town. His garden is down that trail." Jasper snapped his fingers as he remembered something. "Our offices. Quinn doesn't have one, but the rest of us do. Come on."

"Alright..." She followed him slowly to another hallway on the first floor, past the living room. Two doors, alone in this hallway, and Jasper opened the one on their right.

Inside were two desks with computers and stacks of paperwork. Pictures slid out of files, showing her faces of criminals she both knew and had worked for. She had even worked against some of them. One of them was dead and had been for years. She was amazed no one had found that body. She didn't kill him, but she knew where the body was. She had been there when it was buried. He had discovered one of the Ghosts' secrets, and they had dealt with him. Axel had dragged her along to see it. She'd been eighteen, and it was the first dead body she had ever seen. It obviously wasn't the last.

"This is my office with Zander." He waved around at it. "It's a bit of a mess. He and I were on vacation when LA happened, and when we got back, we sank neck deep into finding you."

"And, let me guess." She pointed to the other door. "Elijah and Vincent share that one."

"That's right." He nodded to her, closing the office door again. "You aren't allowed in the offices without us. You'll find us here during most of the working day, though, if you need anything."

"Cool." She bit her bottom lip and saw Jasper's eyes fall to it. She rolled her eyes. "That scar is fairly obvious, Jasper. I'm a fighter, and lips tend to get busted easily."

"I wasn't going to ask." He raised his hands slightly, and she narrowed her eyes on him. "Today. I wasn't planning on asking today."

"Thought so," she huffed. "I'm going to go relax in my room all day. Is there anything you all want from me, or am I allowed to do that?"

"You can do that." He smiled, and she left him there.

"When Charlie said retire, I was thinking something totally different," she sighed, collapsing onto her bed. "Something with beaches and cabana boys for a few weeks. Sexy and plentiful cabana boys who would massage me and cover me in lotion. Drinks with umbrellas that taste like fruit punch and come in obscenely large pitchers. The cabana boys would serve them to me, so my glass would never be empty."

She didn't even like drinks with umbrellas, but that wasn't the point of her little fantasy.

"Fuck," she pulled a pillow over her face.

15

SAWYER

Five in the morning on Monday, and Sawyer was sleepless from the day before. It would take weeks for her to get comfortable sleeping here, and that meant she was going to start getting cranky quickly. She gave it another two or three days before sleep deprivation finally allowed her a single full night of sleep.

She stood in the backyard and stared at the stars above. Just a tiny bit of sun was peeking over the horizon, not quite bright enough to ruin the night sky yet.

"Good morning," Quinn's rough voice called out to her. She turned to him and reveled in the shirtless sight of his sweaty chest. For a mystery wrapped in an enigma with more than a bit of danger topping it off, he was an insanely attractive man. One that she felt would probably bite the hand that tried to touch him. A shame, really, because she had the feeling that touching him would also be fantastic. Him touching her? Now *that* was a fantasy she could get behind.

"Good morning," she answered brightly. "Am I late for the run?"

"No, I go out early with Shade and Scout." He stepped a little closer and her instincts told her to step back, but she didn't allow her feet to move. She realized what it was about him that really set her off. It was his magic, which seemed to fill the air around him, vibrating with barely restrained wildness—like a rabid wolf on a leash held by a toddler. She snorted internally at the mental image she'd conjured for herself.

"How long have you had them?" She looked around for the wolves and finally spotted them, close to the woods, lying in the open grass.

"Eleven years," he told her, his voice dropping to a whisper.

"What do you shift into?" She needed a piece of duct tape for her mouth. This was the guy who made a smile seem like a threat, and the strength of his magic outpaced hers by miles—and she was strong.

"A wolf," he told her with a curtness that made her look away from him. Three howls. That made sense.

"Cool." She swallowed.

"Yup," he said, and she took another quick look at him. He was watching her like she was a hare, and he was hungry for a snack. She wondered if she could make some sort of animal metaphor for everything he did and decided to make a game out of it for herself. She figured it would help her get more comfortable with him. Comfortable? With him? She snorted out loud this time. She had a feeling she would find cuddling a rabid dog easier.

"Am I early?" She looked around, and he shook his head.

"No, they are all a little late." He pointed to the back door. "They always are."

She looked to where he was pointing, and, not ten seconds later, only three of them walked out. Vincent,

Zander, and Elijah all jogged down to where she and Quinn stood on the grass.

"Where's Jasper?" She frowned.

"He does low-impact cardio inside," Zander told her, moving to stand next to her. "I love your running outfit. Are we going to be blessed with this every day?"

She was confused for a moment and looked down at herself. A black tank top with a black sports bra, then her black spandex running shorts that went about a third down her thigh. They were supposed to reach halfway but her legs were just too damn long for that to work.

"Real mature, Zander." She looked back up at him and he shrugged.

"I won't lie to you and say I won't be enjoying the view. You've got a killer body." He grinned and threw a playful look down her long legs.

"Amen," Elijah chuckled. "She also looks like she's going to take those killer legs and use them to pop your head open like a grape."

"I'm seriously considering it," she agreed, and Zander stopped checking her out.

"It wouldn't be the worst way to die, though," Elijah continued, elbowing Zander. "I mean, your head would need to be between her thighs for that to work."

"You made this very perverted, very quickly," Zander laughed. "Elijah, does your mind go anywhere else?"

"No." Elijah grinned, and Sawyer didn't like the naughtiness in it. Scratch that. She didn't like how much she enjoyed the naughtiness in it. "My official street address is Plantation House, Middle of Nowhere, Georgia. Room number, The Gutter."

She snorted and covered her face. Holy shit, their jokes were bad. How did she get caught by Elijah and his awful lines at the bar? She looked up a moment and took in the fact that none of the guys were wearing shirts. Elijah's massive frame was only five feet from her, and then she remembered. He had been just fucking too damn good looking to pass up, and she'd been a little drunk.

"Are all of you done, or will we be standing here for this all morning?" Vincent was stretching farther away from the group.

"I'm ready when you are," she told him, hopping on the balls of her feet.

"Let Zander and me stretch," Elijah said and got to it. She looked at Quinn, who was glowering at her, now. His hungry stare had turned into one that bordered on hostile. She wasn't sure what changed, but she didn't like it. She met his eyes and watched his nostrils flare a little before he turned away. She looked back to Vincent, who wasn't paying attention to any of them. These guys were going to drive her insane from confusion within a week.

"Well," she mumbled to herself, "at least they all look pretty."

"What was that, Sawyer?" Vincent asked, looking up from his stretching.

"Nothing," she called to him. *Fuck, how had he heard her?*

"Let's get going," he called out after another couple of minutes. He led the group and she was pushed in right behind him, with Elijah and Zander behind her.

Only a minute into the run, her eyes began to wander, and she looked down to Vincent's ass. Even in his basketball shorts, she had a good idea of how nice that ass was. She shook her head and looked back up. They weren't going a very hard pace, and even the wolves were running with the group.

"Stop," Vincent called after another few minutes. "Twenty pushups."

She dropped with the rest of the group and began. None of them were keeping count out loud, so she kept track on her own.

This pattern repeated until they were nearly forty-five minutes into the run. 100 pushups and 100 sit ups total, she counted. The house came back into view and they slowed down. Even the wolves were panting softly as they made it to the back porch.

"Gym in ten minutes for upper body today." Vincent looked at her as she leaned down on her knees.

"Can do," she told him with a nod. "Every morning like this?"

"Yeah," he said as he walked away to go inside. She looked around and saw Zander stretching with Elijah and Quinn following his lead.

She ignored them and went to the gym without stretching. She would get her stretching in down there; it was time for her to get out of the heat.

She found Jasper in the gym getting off the cardio bike. He had a towel wrapped around his neck, and she wanted to groan in agony at the sight of his chiseled form. Did they all have to look like this? Was this what she would have to see every morning of her captivity? She wasn't sure if it was a blessing or a curse.

"Hey Jasper," she called to him, and he looked her way.

"Morning." He smiled at her. "How was the run?"

"Vincent tried to kill me but failed," she laughed softly as Jasper nodded.

"Did he do the intervals with you?"

"Yeah; is that not what he normally does?"

"No." Jasper shook his head, opening a minifridge she

hadn't noticed the day before. He pulled two waters out and tossed one to her. They both took a drink before he continued. "That's a once- or twice-a-week thing when he needs to work himself harder."

"Good to know." She found a basket of clean towels and grabbed one. "Who maintains all of this for you guys?"

"We hire a nice old Magi lady who lives in town to come out twice a week. She's supposedly retired, but don't tell her that. She wouldn't let five adult men live alone without a 'woman keeping us out of trouble.'"

She snorted. Good for that old lady. Keep the guys honest.

"You and Zander are only twenty-six and twenty-seven. That is hardly an adult for a man." She pointed her water bottle at him and watched him try to hold back a laugh and fail. She grinned at the clear, masculine sound of it. Jasper had always had a beautiful laugh, and she was happy that hadn't changed. Her heart thudded a couple of times in reaction.

"Don't say that to Vincent," he finally got out. "He's only twenty-seven and prides himself on his maturity."

"Elijah and Quinn?" she asked, wondering if all the guys were roughly same age. They seemed like it.

"Twenty-seven and twenty-five respectively."

"Elijah is one of the oldest?" she asked incredulously. "Have you met him?" That earned another laugh from Jasper as he nodded.

"Yeah, and Quinn never seems like the youngest here, either." He began stretching and she joined him, tossing her bottle to the side of the mat. "How do you feel about him?"

"Quinn? He scares the shit out of me," she sighed. "His magic is wild."

"He's the strongest Magi in North America," Jasper

grunted. "Well, except for any Legends."

"Holy shit," she huffed. "That's impressive."

"He was completely unknown to the IMAS and the IMPO until Vincent found him and recruited him to the team," Jasper continued. "It'll take a little while to get used to him, and for him to get used to you, but he's not mean or anything. He's careful and wary."

Like a wild animal, Sawyer thought to herself.

"Are you telling her how to make Quinn like her?" Zander's voice filled the mostly quiet gym.

"Yes," Jasper responded. She looked over and narrowed her eyes on the redhead.

"Is there some trick to it?"

"Of course." Zander grinned at her. "Get Shade and Scout to like you and there's nothing he can do. They're friendlier than him, and he trusts their judgment."

"Stop talking about me," Quinn growled as he walked in after Zander. Zander spun to him and Sawyer edged a little closer to Jasper. She wasn't normally so wary of someone, but goddamn, Quinn terrified her.

Vincent and Elijah were close behind him, and they were called to get to work. Sawyer kept a mental list of the workouts they were doing, in case she needed to add anything for herself. Jasper spotted her for the workout, while Zander paired up with Vincent and Elijah with Quinn.

Bench press, pull ups, the overhead press, lateral raises. The list went on and on. Sawyer quickly realized that these guys were going to make sure every single muscle in her upper body screamed for forgiveness. Now she knew why they were all fucking ripped, and this was coming from a woman who knew how to work out.

"Holy fuck," she groaned, sitting down after Vincent

made sure everyone completed their two-hour rotation around the gym. "It's not like this every day, right?"

"We only work this hard three times a week," Zander panted to her, collapsing next to her on the floor.

"You get the rest of the morning to shower and eat. Meet me in my office at ten," Vincent told her before leaving. She groaned and leaned on the wall.

"What does he want?" She asked Zander, who sighed.

"He wants to know why he should take firearms off your training. They were the morning training session we had planned, but..."

"But I lashed out yesterday," she grunted as she stretched her legs out in front of her. "It wasn't about the guns, but yeah, I'm not touching them."

"What do you have against guns?" Zander swatted her sore upper arm, and she rubbed it slowly.

"I think they are too easy, too cheap," she snapped. "If someone is going to kill me, they owe it to me and themselves to have the balls to get in my face when they try it."

"Wow." Zander went wide-eyed after she was done. She stood up and looked down at him. "Everything about crime and death to you?"

"Yeah." She offered a hand to him, and he took it, standing up. "It's all I've known for eight years, Zander."

"You could lighten up," he pressed. "Just for a minute. Like, I bet those kids and their parents would have been better off with a gun for self-defense. Assholes wouldn't hit them if they had a gun to protect themselves."

"That goes both ways, Zander." She rolled her eyes. "Drunk, mean pricks get guns and threaten lives. Sometimes, the trigger gets pulled and innocent people die. And, you know what? I just don't like them. That should be enough."

"A bit hypocritical," Zander said as they left the gym. "A woman beats the shit out of people in back alleys, but god forbid someone own a firearm to keep themselves safe."

"Anyone can learn to defend themselves from a beat down," she hissed. "Not even I'm a good enough Magi to dodge a bullet, unless it's from a distance and I can fucking blink and sublimate."

"Fine." Zander stepped back. "I'll let him know, but he's still going to expect you to talk to him."

"Fine." She stomped up the stairs and was able to claim the shower after Jasper stepped out.

SHE KNOCKED on the office door as hard as she could. She heard the opera coming from the office and knew it had to be Vincent's music choice, not Elijah's. Italian opera, at that.

"Come in," he called out to her, and she pushed the door open and stepped in. This office was classier and more organized then Jasper and Zander's. It had a full wall of books, and Sawyer eyed them as she walked in. The Art of War stood out to her, along with several books on chess. His book choices told her more about Vincent than she felt he ever would.

"You wanted to see me," she said as she took a seat in a chair he was gesturing to. He turned down the music as he nodded.

"Firearms freak you out?" he asked softly. "With your life-style, I'm actually a little surprised."

"No, I just don't like them." She stretched her legs out. Sometimes she wished they weren't so long. They felt like they got in the way on occasion.

"I don't care if you don't like them." Vincent narrowed his eyes on her. "In the kitchen yesterday-"

"What happened in the kitchen had nothing to do with the idea of learning to use firearms," Sawyer told him with chilly voice.

"Well, since the guns don't cause the... reaction, then you are still going to learn about them. I don't care if you never carry one," he told her, holding a hand up when she opened her mouth. "I'll never make you carry one, and I'll never test your proficiency. But you will learn, Sawyer. One day, getting someone else's gun could be the only thing between you and the grave. Everyone here knows that, including you."

"And who's teaching me?" she asked bitterly. "Who's going to drag me out there and force a gun in my hands?"

"I am," he said, standing up. "Let's go."

She curled a lip in disgust as she followed him. He had a solid point, but fuck, she didn't like this. Even the idea that she may one day need a gun made her angry.

"With my magic-"

"But you don't have your magic," he turned and snapped at her once they were out of the house. "You can be angry about this. Fine. You can have a death wish. Fine. But I'll see you trained so you don't get my team killed while you are here. We've got more important shit to worry about."

"More important than the imminent threat of death? That's impressive," she growled. "You think *I* have a death wish?"

"That's not what I meant." Vincent glared at her. "And you know it. I'm going to catch that son-of-a-bitch if it's the last thing I do. You can help me willingly, or you can help the hard way. The choice is yours, but you are helping."

"Why do you fucking want to catch him so bad?" She

shook her head. "Remember the last IMPO team that got close? They're all *dead*. You think *I'm* going to get your team killed? Have you lost *your fucking mind*? I'm the only one smart enough to realize that the best way to deal with him is to stay the fuck out of his way."

"My team is vastly more prepared for the task than the last team." His jaw was rigid like the rest of his posture. "And I know more about Axel than anyone on this planet."

She snorted and kept shaking her head, stomping past him. No, he didn't. He had no idea what Axel was capable of past the stories.

"You live in a delusion," she said, stopping to wave her arm around at him.

"If you have all of this figured out, then please, enlighten me," Vincent hissed, looking her over. "You are probably the most arrogant person I've met in my life, and that includes Axel."

"You've met him?" Sawyer felt like cold water hit her.

"Yes." He didn't elaborate for her.

"Me too," she whispered, not giving him anymore either.

"I think you and I have more in common than you might be willing to believe," he sighed. "He's an awful human being. I just want him behind bars."

"He is," she bit her bottom lip, her tongue feeling the scar, reminding her.

"Help me," Vincent pressed, stepping closer to her. She eyed him warily and sighed before looking off into the woods. "I'll make you a deal. Help me catch him and I'll never pry into whatever you're hiding. Let us protect you, and I'll let you walk away when this all over."

He was seriously obsessed with this. From building this team, to tracking her down and taking her into custody. Three days in, and she could see it from a mile away. She didn't know what drove him to this, but damn, some part of her wanted to believe it was possible again. He exuded confidence that he had it all figured out and knew exactly how to hit Axel where it hurt. If he was this driven, she wanted to think he actually had a chance, to be a little optimistic that they might not all be dead at the end of it.

She was always a bit of an optimist, but every time she indulged it, people got hurt. Did she risk indulging the hope again? She wanted to, she really did. And then that tiny fire grew brighter in her and whispered that this could be it. This could be the revenge on Axel that she had wanted for years, but never had the power to grasp.

"Are you going to listen to me?" he asked when she was a few feet away, and she sighed, throwing her hands up. She had to make a decision on this, and she needed to make it now. Her life shifted again, and Sawyer resigned herself to a brutal death.

"Sure, Vincent, I'll listen to you," she turned back to him as she spoke, "but don't expect me to die for you."

"I don't," he whispered. "I don't expect anyone to die for me."

"Then let's train," she muttered. He started walking again, taking her to a building deep in the woods, nearly a fifteen-minute walk from the house. "What is this?"

"You'll see," he said quietly, punching in a code to open the door and letting a finger print reader verify him. He swung the door open and ushered her in ahead of him.

She was more stunned by the sight than she had been by the gym. Weapons were everywhere.

"Quinn makes sure hikers and people who live on the neighboring properties don't stumble upon it," Vincent told her as he closed the door. "Full indoor shooting range and then an entire area for Elijah's work. Elijah! You in here?"

"Back here!" Elijah's voice came from the far corner of the main room. Sawyer looked towards it and found Elijah in a leather apron, goggles, and with gloves that went to his elbows. He held tongs with a red-hot piece of metal on the end.

"He crafts our weapons," Vincent informed her as she stared at the cowboy who went back to work as soon as he laid eyes on them. "We still follow the Old Ways as well."

"The Old Ways are the best," she told him.

Even with magic and modern technology, many Magi still practiced the Old Ways. Combat with real swords, daggers, hammers, axes, and the like. There were rules of combat that were strictly followed, and even she respected them most of the time. Well, she tried. Kind of.

"You practice?" Vincent frowned at her and she shrugged. Not truly, not for a few years, but she liked the ring fighting for the same reason. The ring had rules that were followed, no matter the circumstances.

"I learned them about seven years ago," she mumbled, looking away from the massive wall of weapons and the racks of gear that surrounded Elijah's area. "When do I get to do that?"

"After firearms." He led her away and she sighed, a little wistfully. How long had it been since she practiced with her own blades? Three years? Four? She only kept those throwing knives in case of emergency, but damn, she suddenly wanted to see her twelve-inch daggers, or her kukri. Maybe even her stilettos.

She watched him pull out several firearms, and she felt her upper lip curl in distaste. .44 Magnum, 9x19mm Walther P99, M&P9 Shield from Smith and Wesson. There were several others after those.

"You okay?" Vincent looked at her with concern. "You

seem a little pale."

"Really? I just don't like using firearms," she waved him off. She had been serious when she told Zander that not even she could outrun a bullet. "It's not a big deal."

"Would you tell me if it were anything else?" He set out magazines and ammunition.

"Probably not." She gave him a smirk, her hand over the scar that was the exit wound. She had been shot in the back, and the bullet had left after passing through her liver. Charlie had saved her life, he truly had.

"Figured," he sighed.

"Oh, good. You have an indoor range, but we're going outside into the heat. How nice." She followed him out after a few more minutes. They had covered a shooting area with a couple partitions to give shooters their own space. Vincent put her in the middle lane and picked the first gun for her to use. The Glock 17, simple, a bit weak, but reliable depending on whom one talked to.

"You know how to do this?" Vincent stood at her back and she nodded.

"I've done it before, but it's been years." She hadn't shot a gun since she was fifteen. She and Zander had been playing around with one like idiots. An older friend of Zander's had let them borrow it and shoot a few rounds off. She didn't hate them then, but she was a different person now.

"I'll walk you through it." His arms came around her, and he walked her through loading. She had to resist the urge to just lean back into him. His chin sat above her right shoulder, and he spoke softly in her ear. He smelled like the city, and his voice was professional and disconnected from the physical closeness. She couldn't ignore it nearly as well. She didn't like this guy, but he was attractive and intense.

Her body wasn't agreeing with her mind. Her body liked him more than a little.

"Take it and I'll make sure you're holding it properly," he mumbled. She did and realized something quickly. Holding a gun wasn't much different when you were missing a finger. His hands adjusted hers to the perfect spots, though she had been fairly close. "Aim and take a shot."

His hands stayed on hers as she took aim. After she fired it, she grinned at her decent aim. She'd hit the guy on the paper in the second ring on his chest.

"Now, do it again," Vincent chuckled in her ear, staying right where he was.

She did, emptying the clip. He set her up with a different gun, something with more kick to it, and she didn't do as well. The recoil had screwed up her aim.

By the end, she was used to him right there behind her, his chest on her back. He was only a few inches taller than her, and he never raised his voice in her ear.

"We're done for today." He turned the safety on for the handgun she was holding and took it from her. Once he had it out of her hands, he put it on the table and turned her around by her hips. "Go back to the building; Elijah is waiting on you. We'll work indoors on Wednesday."

She nodded mutely, but couldn't get around him. He was also still holding her hips. They weren't touching anywhere else, but she could feel the space vibrate between them.

"You're in the way," she whispered.

"Yeah." He shook his head like he didn't realize what he was doing until that moment. He released her hips and stepped out of the way. She walked away quickly, leaving him packing up everything.

The entire thing had been weird. She didn't like the feeling curling in her chest, the one that said maybe Vincent wasn't so bad. She had a weak spot for wanting to help the lost causes, and this was definitely one of them.

She found Elijah waiting for her in the building. He was pulling out several blades of different sizes. He looked up at her, a level of concentration on his face that she hadn't expected, and then he pulled out several more blades, frowning.

"I like daggers or short swords, even though I'm strong enough to use bigger," she told him, and he sighed.

"I should have known," he grunted, putting half of what he had away. "Experienced with handheld weaponry?"

"Very, though I might be out of practice," she said as she walked closer. "No jokes?"

"I don't joke about weapons." He smiled at her. "No, these beauties deserve respect and care. Plus, joking is normally relaxing, and being relaxed will lead to injuries."

"Of course." She nodded and looked at the large wall. He had a little of everything. His collection had every style and region from daggers to long swords. Pikes, halberds, nets, and a couple whips tipped with sharp blades. "You make all these or buy some?"

"I would say about a third, I made." He looked up with her. "The rest I bought, except for three. Those I got on the job and are my most prized possessions."

"Care to share?" She smiled at him. She loved weaponry like this and wanted to see what he considered the best of this immense selection.

"Sure." He grinned at her. He walked away and unlocked a safe he had set up near his work table. She followed but respected his space. She was a known thief and she didn't want him to think she was going to steal his stuff. He pulled out one katana, one kukri, and one simple black twelve-inch dagger.

"The longsword," he began, "belonged to everyone's least favorite serial killer, Logan Harris. The IMPO didn't know what to do with it, and since we were the team that caught him, I took it for my own collection."

She swallowed and nodded. Logan Harris was served the death penalty last year. He had been the murderer of nearly ten Magi children and their mothers. He never killed the father, and he never told anyone why, even on his last day. He had magnetic manipulation, his only power, which helped him strike true with every swing. That sword was probably the one he used to cut up their bodies.

This was with the team that had caught him. That was impressive. They had stopping him from killing a five-year-old girl and her mother.

"The katana was in the property of Layla Doe." He pointed to it next, and she looked it over. She could still feel the rage of the Magi who used it regularly. "The one who-"

"Yeah, I know about Layla Doe," Sawyer whispered, cutting him off from finishing. Layla Doe's crimes didn't need repeating. She laid her eyes on the last dagger, and cold ran through her veins. No matter where she went, she was realizing, the world had a reminder for her, waiting to pounce.

"And that dagger is the only weapon on the planet that had been tied to Shadow." He picked it up and testing its weight on a finger, letting it balance precariously. "Suited her, really. All black steel, black pommel and hilt. Even black leather wrapping the hilt. Not a trace of her magic on it though. It's obvious she cleansed her weapons regularly, and there's no craftsman's mark on it so tracing it back to its maker is impossible."

"How did you get it?" she asked softly, watching her blade as he set it back down. She lost several them over the years when she was active, but none had ever been linked to her like he so confidently just did. That must have been the only one she lost on an assassination, though, since the others were just misplaced around the world. Nearly half of her collection was still in Axel's possession, for example.

"The Paris murder," he told her pleasantly. "We were training with a team in Germany when it happened. We were offered the chance to look over the scene, and I found the blade. It didn't amount to anything, and once we were given free rein on the Axel investigation, the IMPO placed it in my care, knowing I liked to keep my hands on these types of things."

"A little morbid, isn't it?" She raised an eyebrow at him, forcing herself to look away from the dagger. "You know what these weapons have done."

"Not to me." He waved a hand at all the weapons around them. "Everything here is meant to kill, to end a life, in war or self-defense, it doesn't matter. These weapons were just used by people who were very good at what they did. They were used for their purpose, even if those purposes were with evil intention."

"Can't fault you there." She sighed as he put the treasures of his collection away.

"Ready to get started?" He pointed to the selection he had out. "Pick one or two. I want to see what you can do. We won't be sparring until Zander can shield us, and I'm confident you won't slice your own fingers off."

She took two short swords and twirled them in her hands. They felt good. She didn't want to take a dagger, which she was much more proficient with, because she felt too exposed. Seeing her own weapon like that, in the hands of Elijah, had freaked her out.

It was a solid training session. Elijah knew the fighting

style of every weapon he crafted, as if he was born with the knowledge. She had problems with her form, so he stopped her and corrected her. She was used to dirty fights: quick, fast, and going for the kill or incapacitation. This was different. He wanted her to really nail the technique, so she could avoid mistakes with and without her magic. With her abilities, technique normally got thrown out the window, but without them, it was necessary.

They were sweating and panting at the end of the session, and he grinned at her as he patted her back roughly.

"We'll make a real fighter out of you yet," he laughed as he put away the weapons.

"Look here, cowboy, I *am* a real fighter." She shoved him away playfully. "You've seen me in the ring." She tossed her arms out, cocky and having a good time. He took a playful swing at her, and they were off.

For his six-foot, five-inch, massive build, he was fast. She spent the entire session getting used to his speed, but dodging his quick strikes was still difficult. They were pulling their punches, but when he nailed her in the ribs, she knew it would bruise. She got him once in the gut right after, hooking his head with one of her arms.

In the end, they were just shoving at each other like fools. It was easy to hang out with the cowboy. He was easy-going, and, once they were training, the pickup lines and compliments ended for something more relaxed and friendly. It was also easy to let her guard down and talk to him. She should have noticed that in the bar. His smile was infectious.

"Alright, you got skills, don't hurt me," he laughed hysterically. "Damn, woman. I never thought it would be hot to get the shit kicked out of me."

"Men are gluttons for punishment, hot stuff." She was laughing as well, and he grabbed her, pulling her closer while she was distracted. She found herself against his chest and her internal body temperature sky-rocketed.

"You think I'm hot, huh?" he asked playfully.

"You and every other guy here." She rolled her eyes, pulling away from him. "You're nothing special with all the competition around."

"True," he chuckled. "I do live with prime examples of good looking men."

"What is that I'm hearing?" She held a hand up to her ear. "You aren't jealous that I get all this eye candy and you only get me?"

"I get the exact same amount of eye candy as you do." He pointed a finger at her and then pointed it up and down her body, his eyes following. "You're just the only woman I now get to stare at, day in and day out. For which, I am *very* thankful."

"What?" She tilted her head to the side, and wondered where he was going with this.

"I'm bi." He threw an arm over her shoulder and forced her to walk out the door with him. He locked up the building without releasing her. "And yeah, the entire team knows."

"Well, this must be heaven for you." She shook her head, a smile toying on her lips.

"Well," he leaned down close to her ear, "I think we could make some heaven together if you want to try."

"You already know that answer." She rolled her eyes, letting him be a seductive flirt. She enjoyed it, even though she was still a bit peeved that he had captured her with it.

"I would love a reminder." He pulled her even closer and

stepped in front of her, giving her a naughty grin. "Even though Vincent told me not to try."

"I'm suddenly very thankful for Vincent," she laughed, pushing him away. "You always like this?"

"Yes, but not because I want to sleep with everyone." He shook his head, still grinning. "I like sex, like every other guy in that house. But, I like to play around and have a good time, because that's how I show my affection for people. Let me know if I make you uncomfortable."

"I'm feeling a lot of things." She kept chuckling, shaking her head. "But none of them are uncomfortable right now, though."

"I'm happy to hear that." Elijah threw his arm back over her shoulder. "Even if you won't ease my seemingly-endless suffering and sleep with me one day, I would like you as a friend, Sawyer. I don't want you thinking that everybody here just wants to use you for something. Jasper and Zander don't need to be your only allies here."

"That means a lot to me." Her throat was suddenly thick with emotion. They walked in silence for a long time until she needed to ask. "Why? You've known me for only three and a half days."

"Because I know another lost soul when I see one," he said quietly, "like the rest of this team."

She wanted to say that Jasper and Zander had never been lost souls, but she would have been lying. That's what had made the three of them friends when they were younger. Jasper's parents passed away when he was eight, and he had nowhere else to go except the orphanage. Zander's mother gave him up at six, leaving with nothing except a life of thinking his mother didn't love him. She had never had a family at all, completely raised in the orphanage.

"Jasper said everyone here was a misfit," she whispered.

"We are." He nodded. "And I think, even with all the darkness in your eyes and the horrors you think will happen, you belong here. You like protecting people and saving them. You like sticking up a middle finger at the system; and, while it might not seem like it, we do, too. Yeah... Give it time and you'll fit right in. Just give us a chance."

"I'm worried you'll all get killed," she admitted to him. "I'm worried that helping you go after Axel will get Zander and Jasper killed and that..." She shook her head, wondering why she felt the need to make that admission to this open, playful cowboy.

"You trust us to stay alive." He pulled her to him as they walked so that she was pressed into his side completely. "We know what we're doing. Vincent knows what he's doing, but I'll tell him to back off you a little. I don't want him completely scaring you off."

"Thanks," she huffed. "He's pushy."

"Yeah," Elijah chuckled softly. "I'm his second in command, so if he'll listen to anyone, it's me."

They were nearly at the house when he let her go.

"Think about what I said, Sawyer." He smiled at her. "We're just trying to keep you safe and take down the bad guy, just like you did for those kids."

She nodded and let him go inside without her. It was nearly three in the afternoon, and they hadn't said she needed to do anything after Elijah's training. The day had given her a lot to think about—a lot to consider about her future and being there.

She quietly went to her room. She took a shower after she got some clean clothes ready, then took a small nap. She missed the fact that her box of photos had been moved.

16

SAWYER

awyer wrapped her hands slowly as all the guys watched her prepare for hand-to-hand training. They were all waiting on her, but she had a ritual that she wasn't going to change for them.

"Any day, little lady," Elijah called out, laughing.

She rolled her eyes and finished the last go around her left hand. She stood up and bounced on her feet as she looked over to him.

"Don't rush me unless you are really excited to get beat on." She grinned.

Day two of training was hand-to-hand and martial arts. That was it. She looked to Zander and nodded, remembering their conversation from Sunday.

"You ready?" she taunted.

"Whenever you are." Zander grinned. "Unless you want to paint your nails first. I can wait."

"Asshole," she laughed. "Tell me, who had pink toenails for half of his junior year?"

"Casey did that," Zander growled, "and you promised never to bring that shit up again after she and I broke up."

"I forgot that she did that," Jasper chuckled softly.

"What amazing teenage Zander story are we missing?" Elijah asked, grinning between them. "Someone, please enlighten me."

"Casey Morgan," Sawyer chuckled, "was Zander's girlfriend for six months while we were in high school. She liked to practice her pedis on him. He wouldn't go barefoot for their entire relationship. Jasper and I caught on really quick that something was up. Took us like, a week, to catch him sleeping and get his socks off before he woke up. I don't think I've ever laughed so hard."

After giving them that bit of information, even Vincent was chuckling. Quinn looked a little confused, but not angry, so she thought she must have been doing something right.

She had done a lot of thinking through the night. She would train and eventually help them, even if it was only so she could keep them from getting themselves killed. She might even try to be a friend, though that one was still up in the air.

If they pressed her too hard for the secrets she hid in the shadows, they would learn a new meaning to 'cold shoulder'. She had a mental check list of what they could and couldn't know. They could know the generalities—like she had a bad relationship, which was the source of most of her scars, but they couldn't know who that ex was. They could know that the ex-boyfriend taught her how to thieve and some fighting, but they couldn't know exactly why. It was the best she could think of. Give them enough information for them to understand and feel like she was opening up, but not enough that they could connect the dots.

She knew that giving them even those half-truths would

make her feel a little better. That was an appealing thought in and of itself.

"What's a pedi?" Quinn asked, looking around the group.

"A pedicure. When women do shit like paint their toenails. A manicure is for their fingernails," Elijah whispered to him. "Well, some men do it too, but it's considered really feminine so it's embarrassing to Zander that he let a woman do it to him."

"Thank you." Quinn nodded to Elijah and looked at her. "Do you get... pedicures or manicures?"

"No," Sawyer laughed. "Manis and pedis are not my thing. I barely do my hair."

"Ah." Quinn continued to nod, rubbing the scruff on his jaw. "So it's not a mandatory ritual. What's the purpose of it?"

"To look better?" Sawyer shrugged. How had Quinn never heard of manicures or pedicures? Seriously? She wished she knew his story, she really did. Seeing him get all curious was probably the least scary thing she had ever witnessed. It was actually really cute.

"Alright," Zander coughed, and she grinned at how red he was. She was going to get Cranky Zander for training. "Let's just get to fucking training. Fuck."

"Aw, poor Zander. Don't want Sawyer trotting out embarrassing stories?" Elijah laughed, holding his sides as he bent over, howling.

"Fuck you." Zander glared at him and then turned to her. She held her arms open, basically saying 'Come at me, bro' to him. "You are so eating mat."

"Try me, bitch." She bounced around, excitement making her heart race. She loved this kind of banter before fighting. It was playful and easy, showing all the fighters involved that friendships weren't hurt outside the ring by what happened in it.

"I'll show you-" Zander pointed at her.

"Both of you," Vincent was still chuckling, "let's just get through this, please."

"Sawyer, get over here." Zander pointed to the mat in front of him, glaring. She sauntered over but stayed nearly five feet from him. She wasn't stupid enough to get in arm's reach. "Jasper, call time?"

"Can do." Jasper pulled out his phone and looked down at it. "Ten minutes. Go."

Shields formed around her and Zander, and she could recognize the feel of his magic. They weren't the strongest shields, but they would keep bones from breaking. She stayed relaxed as Zander carefully moved towards her.

The moment she was in his range, he swung out a high, test kick toward her head, and she rolled away. Fighting a trained martial artist was a different beast than fighting a boxer. She had more practice with boxers, but she always knew her most dangerous opponents were the MMA nuts who could do more than a bit of everything.

"Running scared, Sawyer?" Zander taunted, grinning at her. She stayed silent and just watched him and how he moved. He favored his right side, and, if he didn't realize it, she could exploit his left. He was heavy on his feet, lacking some of the bounce required to give a fighter the fastest reaction time possible.

He was pretending. There was no way Zander thought he could beat her fighting like he was, which meant he was fucking with her. Well, she was going to need to fix that real quick. She wasn't going to be toyed with. She was really annoyed with him now.

He entered her reach again, and she grabbed his kick

this time as it made contact. She watched his eyes go wide at how she took the kick to her ribs without a complaint. She twisted his ankle and watched him fall as he winced in pain. She kicked with her right foot, connecting to the left side of his head. She didn't hit hard, but the point was made.

"Don't be a show-off," she told him blandly.

"Fuck," Elijah mumbled. "What was that? A minute?"

"Yeah," Jasper whispered back to him.

She let go of Zander's leg and held a hand out to him. He took it slowly and stood up.

"Also, don't go easy on me," she growled, pulling him close to say it quietly to him. "I don't fucking need it or appreciate it." She pushed him away with a glare and noticed that being caught embarrassed him further. And Zander hated being embarrassed.

"Time," he snapped to Jasper.

"Nine minutes left. Go," Jasper called.

Zander didn't approach her slowly this time, and she had to move quickly to stay out of his reach. He had longer limbs than her, so she was going to need to get in behind him to avoid getting grabbed, punched, or kicked. The problem was, he was quicker than lightning this round.

She barely dodged a kick that flew toward her head, feeling the air get cut by it when she dropped down. Without a moment's rest, Zander sent a second kick with his left leg, lower to hit her ribs.

She grunted at the impact, realizing that playing the evasive game just wasn't going to work. She let him step closer to her and rolled in as he took another kick. He had long, strong legs, and she realized that was his weakness. He loved to kick, knowing he could do the most damage with that.

She came up right in his face and did something she had

learned from judo. She grabbed his shirt with her right hand, pulling him down to force his body weight on his left leg, and positioned her right leg between his. She swung the leg behind his left, making his knee buckle and then dropped him to the floor on his back.

"Judo." She grinned at him. Zander narrowed his eyes on her but didn't say anything as she helped him up. "Don't limit yourself to using one technique, even if you are just training. Practicing bringing them all together will make it seem natural if you need to use this in the real world."

"I thought Zander was leading training," Quinn whispered, and she looked over. He was giving Vincent a confused look.

"I think this training is quickly becoming a technicality that we shouldn't waste our time on," Vincent told him, sighing with a real smile. He turned back to her, the smile fading. "But firearms, you still need to work on those."

"And I want to get her sparring with shields on us," Elijah added. "Though, yeah, I think we can get back to work faster than we planned."

Sawyer only shrugged at the conversation, watching Zander who looked thoroughly displeased with something. Probably himself.

"You okay?" she asked his quietly, and he turned his hard, green eyes on her.

"Where did you learn this?" he asked her in return.

"I don't think the question you should ask is *where*," Vincent spoke up, and she flicked her eyes to him. "I think it's *why* did she learn this?"

She narrowed her eyes on Vincent before turning back to Zander. They had a deal, that ass. But Vincent had promised *he* wouldn't pry, not that he wouldn't lead others to do it for him. She should have made sure there were no loop holes.

"I learned boxing and kickboxing from Charlie," she began slowly. "Judo was something I was working on until you dragged me out of New York. Krav Maga is another I've studied, also with a trainer in New York."

"Why?" Zander pressed. She bit back a hiss that he had latched on to the question posed by Vincent.

"Protection," she bit out. "Why else?"

"Alright." Zander turned away from her, and she turned a glare on Vincent, who had the balls to give her a tiny, arrogant smile.

"How often are we doing this, and what am I allowed to do in my free time?" She needed to direct them away from this line of questioning. She learned nonlethal takedowns and fighting styles because she didn't want to kill anyone. Axel had only trained her to take life, not preserve it. They couldn't know that.

"Well, after that performance..." Elijah grinned and looked between her and Vincent, "I think we should cut this down to mornings. Oh, Vincent, you can teach her the ropes of being an IMPO consultant in the afternoons instead! Can we get her certified?"

"I'll need to check the regulations." Vincent frowned thoughtfully.

"I don't want to get certified as an IMPO consultant. Thanks, but no thanks," she huffed. She didn't need her name being officially attached to the IMPO like that. "I'll just tag along. Once this is all over, I'm going back to New York and going back to my life."

They were all silent at what she had said, looking around at each other. She was missing something here, and she didn't know what.

"I'll check the regulations," Vincent said again, quietly, his impassive stare directed at Elijah.

"I should teach her survival techniques," Quinn blurted out suddenly, breaking the strange, heavy silence around them. "Our assignments can go to dangerous places, and she will need to be able to survive."

What? Quinn, the intense wild man, was suddenly interested in her well-being? Well, she didn't really know how he felt. The others were obvious with their intentions, whatever those were, but Quinn barely even looked at her. She frowned at him, confused by the strangely talkative version of him she was witnessing this morning. After a few days of brooding, strange silence, she was growing increasingly uncomfortable with this version of him.

"Good idea." Vincent nodded to him. "I didn't schedule it because I wasn't sure how you would feel about it."

Quinn only shrugged in response, and his face returned to its usual impassive expression.

"Like what?" Sawyer began unwrapping and rewrapping her hands in boredom. "Like building fires and stuff?"

Quinn gave a jerky nod but remained silent. Sawyer figured that must mean that the conversation was over, and it seemed the others were on the same page as her.

"Let's run through some more sparring." Zander waved a hand around. "No reason to waste the fact that we're here for it."

She put him on the mat four out of five times after that. They had all paired off. Elijah and Quinn. Vincent and Jasper. Zander was definitely the best in the group, but he wasn't going to beat her consistently, she knew that. There was one difference between them. She had learned to fight in order to stay alive, then applied that knowledge to the task. He had learned to fight to do the same, but it was obvious he had never used it to do so. He didn't have the same unerring focus she had noticed in fighters who knew the cost of losing. That cost, in some fights, meant you didn't get a second chance.

By lunch, Zander and Vincent dismissed them all.

"Sawyer, remember the schedule. Morning workout, firearms, weaponry with Elijah," Vincent told her as she unwrapped her hands. She nodded. Wonderful. "I'll work with Quinn about when he wants you with him for survival training. And I'm going to work on seeing what I can do about getting you filed as a consultant for IMPO and the team."

"Alright." She shrugged. She had agreed to listen to him, she reminded herself even as she wanted to rail against the professional and authoritative tone he took. "But I don't want to be a consultant."

"See you at dinner." He ignored her, and she ground her teeth as he walked away.

She finished putting her hand wraps away as Zander snuck up close to her. She flicked a look at him and raised an eyebrow. He was still shirtless, and, while she could ignore that while she prepped for a fight, she couldn't ignore it now.

He was lean, toned, pale as the moon, covered in freckles, and damn that V he sported with those stupid revolvers... She mentally cursed her attraction to him. He'd always been too good looking, too much of a playboy. While she and Jasper had stuck close, hanging out only in their group, Zander had left a trail of broken hearts behind himself in high school—the casualties being every woman silly enough to think she could tame him.

Sawyer had never held the belief that she could do so, and she wouldn't entertain the thought, even if her life depended on it. What had happened between them had been stupid, wonderful, and probably the best first time a girl could have asked for. She wasn't up for a repeat performance, though, no matter how good he looked. That had complicated written all over it.

"Can I help you?" she asked when he just kept watching her. She looked around the gym and sighed. They were alone. The last thing she wanted was to be alone with Zander.

"I wanted to talk about your fighting," he told her, stepping a little closer. She stepped back, keeping a few feet between them. "Why did you learn to fight like that, Sawyer?"

"To protect myself, like I said." She shrugged. "It's not hard to comprehend."

"From what?"

She took a long, shuddering breath as she stood and leaned against the wall. She had made her choice to open up a little to them, and if there was a person to tell first, it was Zander.

"From getting hurt by someone again." Sawyer waved over her body. "Look at me, Zander. Scarred and maimed. By someone I thought I could..." She trailed off, looking for the right words.

"Sawyer," Zander swallowed and moved closer to her, "tell me, please."

"I'm trying," she sighed. "I was in a relationship with the guy who got me into all this. I was lonely and thought he cared for me. He was teaching me how to take care of myself and said he was giving me a bigger purpose. When I tried to get out, he tried to kill me."

Zander stayed silent, watching her intently. She

shrugged and rubbed the scar on her chest with her right hand.

"So, I met Charlie," she continued softly. "He took me in, listened to me. He taught me how to really fight and defend myself. I learned to protect myself, but one day I realized I could be doing more. I started helping others out of their problems. Thieving just kept us afloat, and I still liked the mental work of it."

He reached out and rubbed her arm. She looked up to his green eyes and gave a weary smile.

"It was a long time ago, Zander." She patted his arm. "Sometimes it's closer to the surface, and sometimes things set me off, like in the kitchen with Vincent. So, there you go, the reason I learned to fight like this."

"Sawyer, I'm so sorry for leaving you," he whispered, his arm wrapping around her and she accepted the hug from him. She held his back for a moment, and a piece of her relished in the feeling of a hug from Zander again. A large piece. "I'm sorry you went through that."

"He found me with my new adoptive *father* and offered me a sanctuary; then he took advantage of the trust I gave him. I learned my lesson," she whispered and pulled away slowly. "Tell Jasper? He won't want to hear it from me and-"

"He'll want to hear it from you, but I'll tell him if that's really what you want," Zander cut her off softly.

She honestly didn't want to repeat the story again, so having Zander tell Jasper was fine with her. She nodded and picked up her small bag of gym gear.

"Thank you, Zander, for listening," she mumbled. "And I'm done talking about it for today. Tune in next time for 'Sawyer's Fucked-Up Life' showing nearly every goddamn day on Daytime. I need a shower before doing anything else today."

She walked away, leaving Zander to chuckle. She grinned to herself. A good joke was needed to lighten the mood, and she needed the mood to lighten. He was on her heels on the steps, still laughing softly.

"I shouldn't be laughing," he snorted. "I shouldn't. I'm sorry."

"I wanted you to laugh, stupid," she chuckled, "or I wouldn't have made a joke. Seriously, don't let all of this," she waved over herself and looked back at him, "get you down. It's life and it happened. I got out."

"Alright." Zander nodded. "I'll keep from bringing it up too much with you. But, if you need anyone to talk to..."

"I can talk to you or Jasper, and even Elijah offered," she chuckled. "I know. I'm going to take a shower. Tell Vincent I don't want to be a consultant for the IMPO."

"Have a good shower. There should still be some hot water left." He grinned at her, and she narrowed her eyes at his complete disregard for the topic of being a consultant. Dick.

BEFORE HER SHOWER, Sawyer noted, her bedroom had been devoid of intruders. Now, she frowned, there were a few guests she didn't remember inviting in.

"Quinn? Would you like to tell me why you and your wolves are in my space?" she asked politely, smiling tightly.

Quinn was stretched out in her desk chair while Shade and Scout lay on her bed watching her intently. He was looking at her box of photos intently, and she was happy to see it was closed. When he looked at her, his ice-blue eyes were devoid of emotion.

"I'm taking you into the woods for some training," he told her, curt and rough. "Meet me on the back porch."

She was still standing by her door when he and his wolves silently left.

"Why is he such a weird fucking man?" she muttered to herself, closing her door. The woods. The city girl in Sawyer raged at the idea of playing in the dirt and trying to camp, but Sawyer's practical side was telling her that it was about time she learned something about survival in rural or uncivilized areas. She scoffed. Her practical side could go suck a dick. She hated the dirt.

She grabbed some tennis shoes and an old pair of jeans. He hadn't said that she might need anything and that worried her.

When she met him on the back porch, he was brushing Shade, who panted in the afternoon heat. It was sweltering, so she couldn't blame the poor wolf for having a hard time. Scout was hiding in the darkest shade on the porch and didn't seem to be doing much better.

"Are they okay in this heat?" she asked, watching the wolves and their Magi carefully.

"They stay inside a lot during the day in the summer, but for training, I want them around." Quinn put the brush down on a small table and left it there. He began to walk off, leaving her. Shade followed him, and Scout bumped into her legs. Sawyer realized he was telling her to follow. Bonded animals had a higher intelligence level then unbonded animals. No one really knew why, but it was another fact of their life.

She jogged to catch up and followed Quinn to the trail she had been told not to use. The marker was really obvious, but she remained silent as Quinn brought them to his...

garden. They walked for nearly fifteen minutes until the trail ended in a clearing.

In the center was a large fire pit that had stones circling it and a few big logs placed around it as seats. Toward the opposite side of the clearing was a log lean-to like one someone would find at a campsite. Inside the lean-to was a sleeping bag, a fold-out chair, and a camping bag. Shade and Scout were both heading over to sleep at the front of it, and she watched them both collapse in the shade. To her right, a legitimate garden was growing, organized and clean. She couldn't identify any of the plants, but it was pretty. The left side of the clearing had a drop-off, and she could hear the stream below in the silence.

"I don't have an office at the house," he mumbled. "Don't come out here unless I give you permission.

"Okay." She nodded. "Jasper already let me know."

"Today, we're going to start simply. Building a fire from scratch. Once you figure that out, we'll talk about what's next." Quinn went into the lean-to and grabbed the bag.

It was an interesting lesson. She quickly realized that Quinn did not care whatsoever about her city girl sensibilities.

"My hands are getting blisters," she groaned. She already had some calluses, but even they couldn't save her from what this was doing to her hands.

"Blisters? That's what you're worried about?" Quinn frowned at her. "Work harder and you won't get them anymore."

She did get a fire going, even if it took the entire first hour. Quinn made her do it again, and it went faster the second time.

"Water, fire, shelter, food," Quinn recited. "The most important things you need to survive. Once you can get a

fire going consistently and quickly, you'll need to learn how
to get fresh water. Every step is an extension of the previous.
At the end of these six weeks, you should know everything I
have to teach you about the basic."

"Did the guys learn that quickly?" She looked down at
her ragged palms, wincing at the sight. If she didn't want it
to happen every day, she would need to let them heal on
their own without magical assistance. Her callouses would
need to get thicker, so Zander wasn't allowed near
her hands.

"Vincent figured it all out in four," he told her, grabbing one of her wrists and frowning. "Elijah was even
faster, but he grew up in a rural area and camped a lot
growing up. Jasper and Zander both took the full
six weeks."

"Good for them," she sighed, trying to pull her wrist
away but Quinn didn't release it. "I told you I was getting
blisters. It's no big deal."

"I have an ointment, non-magical. It should help with
the pain and speed up the healing process," he murmured
quietly as he released her.

"You know," she said as she she kicked some dirt around
and looked about his camp, "some really stereotypical
things could be said about this."

He looked at her, and his eyes narrowed. He might have
heard some of those things.

"If you have any sense of self-preservation," he whispered, "you'll never say any of those things."

"I wasn't going to," she assured him, "but since I've been
dragged into all of this, I was just wondering what your
story is."

"My mother and her kind taught me all of this when my
abilities were similar to their own." He walked into his lean-

to, grabbed something, and brought it over. A mason jar of green, pasty stuff was inside. "This will help."

"Kind?" She narrowed her eyes this time as she took the jar. "Not people?"

"My mother was a Druid." He gave her a vicious smile, and she stepped back, her eyes going wide. She nearly dropped the glass. "I don't know where she originated because Druids only interact with their own, regardless of where they come from. So, she and her *kind*."

Druids were Legends, a type of Magi that inspired non-magical legends, hence the designation. There were several kinds of Legends, but the most common were Druids. A Druid was always immensely powerful, having several nature abilities. They could bond with hundreds of animals in their region, grow portions of forests over a matter of weeks, remove traces of pollution, and so much more.

No wonder Quinn was so powerful. Having a Druid for a mother, the only parent that could be a Druid since all Druids were female, would have given him a predisposition for an exceptionally strong magical Source. It made him exceptionally dangerous.

"When I was considered as trained as I could be," he gestured to the massive sleeve and chest tattoo he had, "my mother gave me this. It's considered a Druid's mark to other Druids that I know their ways and that one of them has a claim on me."

"I didn't know they did that," she whispered, eyeing his ink. "It's very beautiful."

"I hate it," he growled, "and I hate all of them."

She swallowed and nodded.

"You should go," he growled softer this time. She just nodded again, remembering that Quinn scared the shit out of her and she should have never opened her mouth.

She turned and forced herself to walk instead of run. Her fight or flight response was very clear in what it wanted. Quinn didn't threaten her overtly, as much as he made all her instincts scream to get the fuck away from him.

"Wait," he called before she got too far away. She stopped and, in a jerky motion, turned to see him jogging to her. When he stopped in front of her, she tried to edge away. "Tomorrow, bring a bag with you. I'm going to start helping you build a mission bag for this kind of stuff. The entire team has one, and it could help you when you leave."

"You seem to be the only person okay with me leaving." She was wary of this guy, and his gorgeous eyes were hard.

"Because I don't want you here," he said bluntly, "but I see no reason why you should die out there either, criminal or not. People have to do whatever it takes to survive."

"Okay." She nodded and began to walk off again. "If it helps, I don't want to really be here, and I'm doing all this against my better judgment."

She didn't wait for a response as she strolled away. At least one of them was kind of on her side and, yet, also not. She was equally happy and upset by knowing where Quinn stood. He straight up didn't want her there, and that was fine, but damn he could have told her in a nicer way.

By the time she made it back to her room, she wasn't sure if this had been a good day or an incredibly bad one.

17

SAWYER

S he was on her hands and knees, trying to crawl away.

A kick to the gut knocked the wind out of her. She gasped for air and turned blindly away from the blow, trying to escape. Why was he doing this to her?

A hand in her hair prevented her from making it very far, dragging her back to the light she wanted to avoid. She needed the dark. If he was going to do this, she wanted it to be in the dark.

She was tossed into the shining brightness and winced. She was completely drained and couldn't get away from the kick that fractured her ribs.

"Are you done?" A masculine voice growled. "I told you to get rid of him and you didn't."

"He was innocent," she sobbed. "He didn't do anything to you!"

"He was a target that I gave you," Axel roared. "Instead, I had to go in and get my hands dirty. I thought you trusted me, but this proves otherwise."

"I didn't agree to this." She shook her head, tears still falling from her eyes. He lifted her by her hair, and she tried to pull away, only to have him to shake her roughly.

"I needed him out of the way, so he didn't become a threat," Axel snapped. "I can't keep us all safe if you don't do what you're told."

She tried to shake her head again. She had only killed the first guy because he tried to kill Axel. She loved him, but she didn't want to do this. She didn't want to kill people who didn't hurt people. She never wanted this. Being a thief was one thing. Material things didn't hurt people.

"My friends keep telling me I need a heavier hand with you," he growled. "I told them that you would do anything for me."

His friends. Monsters. He promised they wouldn't be doing this forever, that it was temporary until they had enough money to settle down in a safe place. But those friends kept talking about things she didn't know about. Prostitutes. Weapons. Drugs.

When another blow fell, she realized she was the one who was wrong. They weren't the monsters—he was.

"I own you, Sawyer," Axel growled. "You can either fall into line, or I'll make your life a living hell. The choice is yours. If hurting you doesn't get me what I want, then I'll hurt someone you care about. If hurting them doesn't help, I'll start killing them."

Ringing began in the background, but Sawyer didn't know where it was coming from.

SAWYER GROANED as her eyes opened to stare at the ceiling as her alarm went off. Two weeks she had been in this house, and nearly every night was a different trip down memory lane. Another nightmare. None of them were accurate. They were blended memories, different pieces of time smashed into one nightmarish experience. Axel had never expressly told her that he would kill someone she cared about, he just did it and that was that.

She brought her hands up to her face and felt the warm wetness. She had cried. She always did. Her room was frigid but not frozen, so that was a good sign at least.

She pushed the memories away. She wasn't going to dwell on them, since she couldn't change any of it. She hadn't had this many nightmares in years, but she was also certain of the reason for them, so she didn't let it bother her. She knew eventually they would pass and become less common. For now, she just needed to suffer through it. She wondered if they would stop completely once he was dead or behind bars.

Oh yeah, Sawyer was in now. She found herself roped in by Vincent's idealism and the trust the others had for him. She still thought they were all going to die, but... this was her chance. This was her chance to pay Axel back for all the nightmares she had to suffer through.

The sun wasn't up yet as she sat up in the bed. *Two weeks*. Time passed so fast outside of her nightmares. She trained with Vincent every other day, always tense and awkward like it had been the first time. She was with Elijah on those same days, now with Zander joining them for safety reasons. Both were friendly, and Zander didn't ask any more questions about why she knew something. She and Quinn fell into a silence truce. He was cold and brutally honest, but a good teacher, although she hated every minute of her time playing in the dirt with him.

Jasper avoided her like the plague. She bit her bottom lip, knowing it was probably her fault. Starting only the day after she and Zander had talked, he had just shut down on her, refusing to be alone with her. Today, she planned on cornering him. It was Saturday, and she was done playing this stupid game with him. She would walk into a room, and he would find a reason to leave. He would come into a room, see her, and leave, saying he would come back. It was driving her bat-shit crazy and it was childish.

But first, she had something to do. She rolled out of the bed and pulled on a tank and some sweats before falling into her desk chair. She logged in and grabbed her headset.

It took a few minutes, but soon the video call was live. She was muted on her end, but she could hear him.

"Hey, Sawyer." Charlie grinned at her. "How are things?"

She typed her response. They had planned this all week, and she wasn't going to risk it by being heard.

Good. I'm having frequent nightmares, but I half-expected that. The agents aren't so bad, though one definitely hates me. His wolves adore me, but he despises me.

"I'm sure it's not that bad," Charlie laughed. "Though... Sawyer, you aren't the most likable person on the planet."

You think I don't know that, old man? Haha. How's everything up there?

"Same old, same old." He shrugged. "Let's talk about what I'm sure is bugging you, though—why I ratted you out."

She didn't respond to that, looking away from the camera. She didn't want to ask. She knew why he did it. He had wanted her out of the game, and, in the scheme of things, he could have done worse.

"Kid, you mean the world to me, and when they approached me, I saw an opportunity to get you a real chance at a good life," Charlie began quietly. "I don't have kids. My love and I didn't get the chance, but you became one for me, and then you filled my life with so many more. If I could do one good thing for you, I figured this was it."

Damn it, Charlie. I get it alright? I'm not mad. You

didn't tell them about me, so it's fine. Why them, though? Why didn't you just turn me in as a thief years ago, if this was what you wanted?

"Because turning you in would have put you in jail, which I don't think you deserve," Charlie sighed. "And I recognized those two from your old pictures and figured they would do anything to keep you safe from Axel and his crew. Those two being there was really the deciding factor."

They want me to help them catch Axel and to become a consultant for the IMPO.

"Oh," Charlie frowned, "that's not safe for you. If you help them go after ..."

Yeah, it'll get me killed. I figure though, he already wants me dead, right? Why not try one more time to take him down?

"You always did want to try one more time." Charlie nodded. "You just never acted on it before. The time was never right."

Exactly. I'm here now. There's no better time. I just need to keep myself out of prison. Catching Axel comes with the risk of exposing myself.

"I don't think you deserve prison, and I know everything." Charlie shrugged again as he placed his arms on his desk. "Once I heard your full story, I didn't think you deserved the sentence laid out for you. I considered it but... it never seemed fair to me. You didn't ask for any of that and maybe they will understand."

I don't want to rehash all of this with you. Tell me about the gym instead.

"Ha, alright." Charlie smiled at her, nodding. "Well, I've got someone here to see you and he can tell you." He moved from the camera, and she waited, wondering which kid he had roped into joining the call.

She grinned at Liam.

"Sawyer." Liam grinned at her.

Liam!!!! How's college?!?!

"It's been good," he laughed. "I'm wondering something, though. Why did my school tell me that the next two years were paid? I thought they took all your money. I had a nest egg and was going to cover it, but then they called me and said it was fine."

She leaned back, grinning madly. She had convinced Zander to get some of her money to his college. It took a few days of convincing, but he eventually relented and got it done. The money she had stashed away was for her students, anyway.

"You aren't going to tell me, are you?" Liam laughed. "Come on, Sawyer!"

You know the answer already, stop playing stupid. Though, there is something else we need to talk about.

"Everyone is fine," he confirmed for her. "No one has had any trouble since you left. We had a bunch of your cards made, though, and we're keeping them on us, so we can get more people into the class if they need it."

I can't tell you how happy I am to hear that. Put Charlie back on for me. I have something to ask him really quickly, then I need to go.

"I'm here," Charlie grumbled, leaning back into the screen for a moment. "I can read what you're saying."

How's Travis?

"You wouldn't believe it," Charlie chuckled. "He's sober and the IMPO hired him to portal them around."

Are you fucking serious?

"Yeah, and they took him out of the apartment you put him in. I think your guys had something to do with it," Charlie continued, grinning at her.

They aren't my guys. I'll ask them about it though. It's good to hear he's got a legit job now, though.

"Yeah." Charlie nodded, "I can't think of anything else."

I should let you both go. I don't know how long I have until one of them bothers me. My alarm was telling me it was time to go. **Charlie, tell Liam who Travis is.**

"I miss you, Sawyer," Liam told her.

"Me too," Charlie huffed off screen. "Be good, kid."

"I will," she whispered, unmuting so they would hear her. "Love you both."

She disconnected after that, shutting her laptop. She dropped the headphones and sighed. She had no idea how often she could call them before it became dangerous, but she was aiming for once every few weeks. She couldn't let them drift away, not like she had with Jasper and Zander as a teen.

She looked at the box of photos and flipped it open. Inside were little tied-together groups of photos, each a different day or different group of people. Her oldest stack was everything with Jasper and Zander.

Her second oldest stack were photos she took of anything while she was with Axel. Never him, she had burned those, but others, like a little boy, a prostitute's four-year-old son. He had been such a sweet boy. Then there were the places. Rome, London, Venice and all the other places she had traveled with him. He never let her leave a city without him, not until the very end of their relationship. No one knew it, but Axel had been close by for every single one of her kills. Some of the photos in this stack also included a cat, a sweet, yellow-eyed runt. Midnight was buried in a tiny yard in Rome. The little boy... she had no idea.

That brought another wave of tears to her eyes.

Her most recent stack was her, Charlie, and all the kids from New York. She flipped through those. She was lucky enough, she even got a picture of Trevor on his first day in the class, unsure and wary of everyone around him. It only took that one day for him to become a part of the group, though. Once he realized that everyone was there for the same reason, he was more at ease.

She blinked back more tears as she looked through the photos. So many of them. So many small battered children that she had been watching grow up into exceptional people. She made it to the first picture. One of Charlie and her about three weeks after she had healed from what Axel did to her. She hadn't taken the photo, but she did have the only copy. Charlie was teaching her to fight, and while she had knife skills, she wasn't any good at hand-to-hand at the time.

She held the set of photos to her chest and cried. She was never seeing them again; she knew it. She knew she couldn't keep up with her lies and secrets forever. She was either getting out of this by going to prison or getting killed. It was a truth she hadn't wanted to confront for two weeks, but now, seeing them, she knew it.

She just needed to choose which was the better option. Dying with her secrets, or being free of them and going to prison. Her stay would be short because Axel wouldn't let her live long after exposing all of his secrets with her own.

18

JASPER

Jasper groaned and threw down the book he was reading. He couldn't focus. Particle physics just weren't cutting it for him today.

"You should talk to her," Zander told him for the tenth time. Jasper was counting.

"About what?" Jasper growled. "What on earth do I possibly need to say to her?"

"How you feel." Zander smiled at him. "I know that's really hard for you, but I think it would help with... well, how you feel."

"She..." Jasper shut his mouth before he said more. No. He wasn't going there. Not with Zander or her.

"Alright." Zander shrugged. "You continue trying to be an emotionless rock. You'll crack eventually. You aren't as good at it as Quinn and Vincent are."

"Like those two could possibly be feeling what I am right now."

"Who knows what they're feeling? That's the point— they are better at covering things up than you," Zander chuckled. "Seriously, this 'bottle it up and it will go away' nonsense has never worked for you. I'm not sure why you're still trying."

"I'm not talking about this." Jasper glared at him and grabbed his book from the desk. He stood up and shoved it on the shelf. "You have no idea-"

"Don't even think I don't get how you're feeling," Zander's tone turned hard, and Jasper looked back at him. Zander's neck was turning red. "I know *exactly* how you feel, but the difference is that I'm able to deal with it. I don't stand rigidly in my own point of view and refuse to see it from her side."

"She didn't even look for us," Jasper mumbled angrily. And there was no way Zander had no idea what he was feeling. None of them could even begin to understand, which made this so much harder on him.

"She was already a criminal, and, as far as she knew, we were still in the IMAS. We were people dedicated to taking the bad guys down. We still *are* dedicated to it," Zander reminded him. "She made a decision to keep herself safe and out of prison. I can't blame her for that."

"*I can!*" Jasper snapped. "That's part of the problem!"

He stormed out of the office and went straight for the garage. He wasn't thinking, but he knew he wanted to get out of the house for a little while. He felt cooped up, suffocated, with emotions and memories, some that weren't his own.

His dreams had taken a dark turn. Her nightmares were bleeding into his nights, and he couldn't stop them. He knew more than he wanted to, more than she figured, more than the entire team could even dream.

Axel.

While most of the nightmares were just flashes and images to him, every now and then he got a word or two.

Axel was one that stood out. In her nightmares, Axel and blood were prevalent. Abuse. Fear. Pain. He caught the emotions that flavored every piece that he accidentally picked up.

Dream walking directly into her nightmares would give him the full picture, but he refused to cross that line. It would give him every piece of the puzzle, but damn, that scared the hell out him.

He didn't want to know the things he already did.

"Jasper?"

He jerked to a stop, holding his keys. He turned slowly at his name and saw her covered in grease and oil, under the hood of their work truck. It was an old thing that was used for work on the property. It never ran right. He couldn't ignore the sweat that made her tank top stick to her, outlining the hard lines of her body. Did she really need to be wearing white?

"Sawyer."

"How have you been?" She seemed wary of him, and he was wary of her. He didn't like knowing why there were dark circles under her eyes. They had grown worse over the last two weeks, and he wondered how she dealt with the nightmares that haunted her.

"Good," he said curtly with a shrug.

"Really?" She raised an eyebrow and stepped closer to him.

"Yeah." He gave a short nod and pointed to the Range Rover he was about to take. "I'm going into town. Tell them for me?"

"Can I come?" she asked him, tentative. He ground his teeth at the idea. It would leave him stuck with her, and he wasn't ready to talk to her. He didn't know how to deal with this.

"Why?"

"Maybe because I just want to hang out with you?" She threw her hands up. "Plus, I need to grab a few tools for this truck. I don't have everything I need."

"Fine," he sighed, unlocking the vehicle. "Go put on... something clean, please."

"Sure, give me ten minutes." The smile she gave him made his heart ache. The fact that she could smile like that killed him a little inside. How could she go through what he saw in her nightmares and still smile like hanging out with him was the best thing that ever happened?

And the most fucked up thing about it all was that he was mad at her. For all of it or none of it, he didn't know which. He was mad that she became a criminal, mad that she took the law into her own hands, mad that she never looked for them to help her when it got bad.

He wasn't mad that Zander had to tell him about it, though. He was *jealous* that she told Zander and not him.

He got into the Range Rover and waited for her. He leaned his head on the steering wheel and closed his eyes.

"Axel." He mumbled to himself. That was the who... maybe. He was missing something very important, and that was also driving him mad. Maybe it was Axel in her dreams because he recently tried to kill her. Dreams were fickle things, wreaking havoc on memories and confusing the truth.

"I'm here." She jumped in, and he sighed. "Let's go."

Jasper opened the garage door and started the Range Rover without saying anything. He knew he was cornered. He could have told her no, but he hadn't been able to bring himself to.

It took her two minutes to begin nailing his ass to the wall over avoiding her, and she did it in true Sawyer style.

"What the fuck has been your problem?" Her excited and happy outlook over going into town with him was dropped in favor for a glare. He shook his head.

"Nothing." He was going to fight this with every fiber of his being.

"Liar," she growled.

"You don't get to call me a liar," he bit back. "Not after the life you've led."

"So that's where we're at? I tell you and Zander something important about myself and then you avoid me? That doesn't make a lot of sense, even for you, Jasper."

"You didn't tell me anything," he snarled, pointing a finger at her. "You told Zander, and he had to tell me. The only thing you've told me was that you didn't look for us when we searched for you for years."

"Is that what this is about?" She looked to be feeling some blend of anger and confusion. "I... didn't want to tell the same story twice. Sorry for not wanting to... I thought you would like hearing from Zander more anyways since you two..."

"It doesn't matter," Jasper sighed, clenching his fists on the steering wheel until his knuckles were white.

"It does," she insisted. "Jasper, I didn't do it like that to hurt you."

"It. Doesn't. Matter."

"Well, if that's not the problem, then what is?" She was back to glaring holes into the side of his head.

He flatly ignored her and continued driving them to town. He wasn't even sure he could put it into words. His rigid sense of morality was furious at her life of crime. His old feelings for her were being pulled back to the surface by her gorgeous body, sense of humor, and tough spirit. He was upset for her because of what happened to her. He was haunted by *her* nightmares. He wasn't sure which one was worse. He was positive there were more emotions hiding underneath those. It was all just too much for him.

He refused to say a word until he parked them at the small hardware store in town.

"Let's get this stuff you need," he mumbled, cutting the engine and getting out. He waited for her at the door. She wasn't allowed to be more than ten feet away from a member of the team while they were in town. She couldn't be out of their line of sight, either.

She didn't say anything to him this time, just stomped around him and inside the store. He followed as she filled a small cart. He had no idea with what, not paying attention to what she was grabbing.

When they reached the check out, he paid for it. She could have, if she knew she was rich again, but she didn't. They had unlocked her accounts, convincing James that the money should be given to her students and Charlie. They hadn't told her that all the money was slowly being funneled to them, but they would eventually. They didn't want her knowing that the money was accessible.

They loaded the car in silence until Jasper decided to try a different approach to the problem.

"I'm hungry," he said, trying to sound friendly. "Want to grab a bite to eat?"

"Sure," she responded brusquely. He winced at it. She was furious with him.

"I'm sorry," he said suddenly. "I'm sorry, but I just don't know how to do this."

"Do what?" She snapped, slamming the back gate closed. "Be a friend? A human being? What, Jasper? Act like an adult about your problems?"

"Damn it," Jasper snarled, hurt by what she was saying.

"I've *never* been the one you argue with. I don't know how to fix it. I don't know how to fix how I feel. I'm sorry for that but I don't need your bad attitude."

"You don't *fix* feelings," she hissed. "You confront them, and you talk about them. It's fucking hard, I know, but it's not a math equation that you just solve and there's a definitive answer at the end."

"You want to talk?" Jasper glared at her. "I am fucking furious with you. You became everything I hate in this world. You have a complete disregard for order and the law. You think that just because the law isn't doing something, that means that you can. You're arrogant, secretive, and have only given me half-truths since the moment we saw each other again." He took a deep breath before continuing. "And I hate myself for being angry at you."

"Jasper." She looked stunned. "You are allowed to be angry over that, I get that."

"You got hurt," he growled, sounding like an animal in pain. "Someone hurt you when you could have been with Zander and me. We should have protected you. And I have *no right* to be mad at you after what you went through, but I am. Being mad at you is the last thing I want. You getting hurt was the last thing I imagined when Zander and I left. I had wanted so much, but never that." The anger left him and he grabbed her arm and pulled her to him, slowly, knowing that if he forced her around, he could trigger something. Once he had her close enough, he took her chin. "I'm no good at this."

He swooped down and cautiously kissed her. He'd been wanting to kiss that tiny scar. He'd been wanting to devour her. If she wanted him to confront his feelings, then fine, but he was going to confront all of them, including the ones that he'd avoided as a teenager. The ones that made all of this so much more complicated. The ones that never seemed to go away.

Her lips parted against his, and he growled softly, deepening the kiss. He felt her nails bite into his shoulders, and she pushed him back gently.

"Jasper," she gasped when he pulled back reluctantly.

"I have always wanted to do that," he whispered against her lips. They were swollen now. "Sawyer..."

"I liked that but... I'm sorry," she whispered back. He narrowed his eyes on hers at the guilt that laced those words. "I can't. Between you and Zander and... shit."

"And Elijah?" Jasper pried, knowing where this was going. He'd seen those two flirt with each other now, more times than he could count. It made him jealous as hell in ways he never felt when it was her and Zander. She always was a bit of a wild spirit. He could totally see her falling into Elijah's bed without thinking about the consequences. Hell, it was what got her caught. "We'll deal with this after Axel."

"Good idea," she mumbled. "I am sorry, Jasper. I don't know where my head is at; I can only imagine how twisted this is for you."

"We've got a lot of unresolved shit," Jasper sighed, leaning against the Range Rover.

"Yeah." He watched her bite her bottom lip. "I didn't realize how much. Sorry for being a bitch."

"I needed you to be a bitch about it, or I never would have told you." He chuckled, feeling a little lighter.

"Anything else you want to talk about?" she asked him quietly.

He stopped chuckling as the weight immediately dropped back on his chest. He couldn't tell her that he knew about her nightmares. She would think he was violating her privacy, and he didn't want her to think he was prying into her mind.

"No." He gave her a weak smile. "Let's go get something to eat."

"Maybe we should just head back," Sawyer mumbled. "I need some time to myself."

That hurt, but he knew better than to think she would still want to hang out after he kissed her. He shouldn't have done that, but he didn't regret it either. And she had *liked* it.

"Yeah," he said, walking to the driver's side. He watched her get in silently, and didn't miss the way she touched her lips while they rode home. He wanted to do it again, and that was a feeling he was more than okay with.

He watched her disappear into the house when they got back and leaned back in his seat. He felt better from having spoken to her. He just needed to figure out what to do about her nightmares without her figuring out that he knew about them. He also needed to apologize to Zander. Jasper had been an ass and he knew it.

He readjusted his pants and slid out of the Range Rover out, heading for his office. He thought the hard on would pass on the drive home, but that hadn't happened.

"Zander." Jasper pushed into the office, and he groaned at Zander who was nearly nude for some reason. "Why are you wearing less clothing now than earlier?"

"The AC broke in here and it's fucking hot," Zander growled. "You'll be just like me in about ten minutes, I promise." Jasper closed the office door and sighed. It was hotter than sin in the office.

"I'll tell Elijah later," Jasper said as he walked to his seat. He stripped his shirt off as he went, throwing it on the back of his chair. "I did something really fucking stupid."

"Oh?" Zander was suddenly curious, and Jasper nodded.

"I kissed Sawyer," Jasper informed him, hoping he didn't piss off his best friend. The response wasn't the one expected.

"Fucking finally," Zander laughed. "Thank god."

"What?" Jasper frowned at the redhead.

"Golden boy," Zander continued to laugh as he tried to talk. "Oh, golden boy."

"I hate that nickname," Jasper reminded him. It came from his blonde hair, but Zander also used it because Jasper was the good one of the group. He didn't break the rules, he didn't sleep with random women, none of the stuff his team-mates had a good time doing. Hell, he didn't drink.

"Too bad," Zander chuckled, falling back into his chair. He kicked his feet up on his desk and grinned at Jasper. "You going to kiss her again?"

"What the fuck?" Jasper was confused as hell.

"No," Zander looked away as he spoke. "You'll probably want to wait until the Axel stuff is taken care of. It's the best idea, really."

Jasper suddenly figured it out.

"We were dumb teenagers when we made that plan, Zander."

"Could still work now." Zander shrugged. Jasper didn't like the devilish smirk that curved across that handsome face. Zander, in that moment, looked every bit the playboy he was known for being. "I'll do the heavy lifting, promise." He winked at Jasper.

Jasper looked to the ceiling and prayed to the gods for mercy. Zander was going to get him killed.

"Oh shit, one more thing happened while you were out." Zander sat up straight. "Vincent let me know that Jon escalated his complaint about us yesterday. We might get stuck in mediation with his team.

"For fuck's sake," Jasper sighed. "Why can't he let this go?"

"Because he's jealous that Vincent gets special treatment from the higher ups. He hates that a young team like ours gets kept on an assignment like catching Axel." Zander grabbed a thin file and showed it to Jasper. "He also had his team look into us and Sawyer, so they're looking into our personal relationship with her and trying to make sure we aren't using our jobs to protect her from justice as a criminal. Shielding her from repercussions."

"Of course," Jasper groaned. They were doing exactly that. "What's Vin say on it?"

"He wants us to step back from her, so they don't think we're favoring her in anyway. We need to treat her like any other protectee. Maybe kissing her is a bad idea..." Zander looked thoughtful for a moment, and Jasper glared.

"Kissing her is a bad idea, no matter the circumstances, right now."

"Says the guy who's kissed her." Zander sent a grin to Jasper.

Jasper didn't have anything to say to that.

19

SAWYER

Damn. Damn it all to hell. Sawyer was so mad at herself. Of all the guys she locked lips with, it was Jasper. Just when she didn't need another layer of confusion, she had to let those feelings get stirred up.

It was a fantastic kiss, though.

"I'm so stupid," she mumbled. She knew what he'd been doing when he pulled her close. She couldn't be kissing a guy like that when she was also living with him. And lying to him. Lying through her teeth, every damn day, about all of it.

Does Sawyer know anything about Axel? No, she would tell them. She had 'no idea' why he wanted her dead. Every time she said it in some bid to protect herself from their condemnation, she felt the guilt eat away at her. It was bad enough when she could pretend her feelings for Jasper and Zander were platonic. Now, Jasper had to go and reawaken the rest: ones she never got over, but instead had buried away. She was crushing on Elijah something fierce, and she blatantly ignored the awkward sexual tension between her and

Vincent during training. She wasn't touching *that* situation with a ten-foot pole.

There was no 'after Axel' for her.

A knock on her door startled her out of her thoughts. She'd been pacing around the room, lost in her anger at herself and not paying attention. Normally she heard someone coming up the stairs...

"Come in," she called. The door still didn't have a lock, and that was still a problem. She found Shade and Scout in her room every couple of days, just covering all of her stuff in their fur.

"It's me." Vincent stuck his head in the room. "We need to talk about something. Come to my office?"

"Yeah, I'll be right down." She nodded and watched him leave. Her body betrayed her at the mere sight of him now. Any of them really. She hadn't gotten laid in months and was now locked in a house with five sexy men. She still wanted to dislike Vincent. He was still controlling, intelligent, and a bit manipulative. He was gorgeous and did terrible things to her libido though.

She gave it ten minutes before heading down into his office on the first floor. She met his dark green eyes as she entered the room. Those eyes were stunning in his face. Maybe she just really liked Italians, no matter what Axel had done to her.

"Have a seat," he told her quietly, gesturing to a seat on the other side of his chess set. She had eyed it several times since she was forcibly moved into their home, but hadn't played yet.

She was decent at the game, but not great. It helped her learn to plan ahead and make strategies. It was game for those who knew how to get into their opponents' heads.

"You play a lot?" she asked, sitting down slowly. She was

on the white side. She was always black side when playing before, so this was a new experience for her.

"I do." Vincent was focused on the board, and she was starting to wonder why he wanted to see her. It couldn't just be for a chess match. "You?"

"I was taught a long time ago," she said, toying with the pawn she knew she wanted to move. She pushed it up to d4 and Vincent gave a small smile.

"Really?" Vincent gave a soft chuckle. He pushed up his d-pawn into d5.

"I don't play white side, but I do know the Queen's Gambit." She smiled at him.

"I should have expected it from you." He met her eyes as he said it. She moved her c-pawn to c4, completing the opening. Now it was his turn to accept the gambit or not. "Choices, choices," he mumbled. He took her c-pawn with his d-pawn and accepted.

The game was on.

"Who taught you how to play?" he asked as they continued to play slowly.

"My ex," she whispered, thoughtful over her next move. "You?"

"My older brother," he told her. "He always played white side. He liked having the first move, as older brothers normally do."

"My ex normally played white side, as well," she sighed. "I wonder what would happen if we introduced them."

"My brother would find a way to get his side of the table." Vincent moved another piece, but she wasn't paying attention. She watched the way his eyes lit up when he stumbled on the opening she had left.

"I don't know." She shook her head and completed her move, letting him fall into the trap she'd set. His eyes narrowed on her. Axel had used the same trap on her multiple times. "Check."

"I haven't seen…" He trailed off, staring at the board. He blinked a few times, and she watched his face. It was stupid of her to use the trap, but she wanted to see how well he knew Axel. She wanted to test his intelligence. She wanted to know if he was as smart as he thought he was. "Huh."

She was a little irked when he correctly got out of check and backed her into a corner through the next two turns.

"Check," he whispered.

"Wasn't there something you wanted to talk to me about?" she finally asked, knowing that it going to be check mate for her in two more turns.

"Yes." He looked up from the board. "Sorry. Only Jasper normally plays with me, and he isn't as good as you."

"That surprises me," Sawyer chuckled. "What's going on?"

"In about a week, we're going to be needed in Atlanta for a meeting with Jon's team. He's discovered your prior friendship with Jasper and Zander. He's using it to get back at the team for some nonsense. I wanted to give you a heads up, so you can remain on your best behavior. You'll have to come with us."

"Oh goodie." She rolled her eyes. "That asshole."

"Yes, that asshole," Vincent grinned at her and she melted. That was stunning.

"What day?"

"It's not official yet; I just know it's coming." Vincent leaned back in his seat and looked out the window, thoughtful again. "He likes to think he can outplay me."

"Well, maybe he's smarter than me." She shrugged.

"Definitely not." Vincent flicked a look at her. "This was

the best game of chess I've had in years. Thank you. I wasn't expecting you to put up a real fight. Cute trap."

"Yeah, well, I'm useless on white side. You take it next time." She grinned at him. This was the only game of chess she had ever enjoyed. Axel used to stomp her into the dirt and call her stupid.

"I know why you're good at it, just so you know," Vincent commented as she stood up. Her blood ran cold. Did he? "Living the life you did, you had to think several steps ahead to stay safe. Chess probably feels like second nature to you."

"Sure," she mumbled, shrugging again. He was partially right. It wasn't to survive in general, it was to survive Axel. "Thanks for letting me know about the thing."

"Of course," he said quietly, standing up. "Again, thank you for the game."

She left him there and rubbed her forehead. She was playing with fire in all ways possible today. Calling Charlie, kissing Jasper, and whatever the fuck just happened during that chess game with Vincent.

THE NEXT DAY, Sawyer hoped, would fare better, not worse. Before the sun came up though, it was off to a rocky start.

"Get up, we're going out for training," a growl echoed in her room. She groaned and pulled a pillow over her face.

"It's fucking Sunday, Quinn. A day off," she yelled, muffled by the pillow. "Piss off."

"Get up," Quinn snarled. "Five minutes to get on the back porch, or I'll drag you out there."

She wanted to strangle him. Fucking asshole. She threw the pillow at the door and heard it thump against the door as Quinn slammed it closed. The noise gave her an immediate headache.

She rolled out of the bed, shoving the wolf that was there gently away from her.

"Scout, what the hell?" she growled, as the damn thing tried to crawl in her lap for a pet. She was fine with them now, but this was too early on her day off. Why did Quinn leave him in the room?

She only took a couple minutes to grab clothing and her bag. When she got to the back porch with Scout on her heels, she glared at Quinn.

"You better have coffee, mother fucker," she snarled.

"There's no coffee in survival situations," he told her blandly.

"Fuck you and your survival situations," she snapped, dropping her bag on the porch and going back inside. She headed straight for the kitchen, Scout still bouncing around her legs. She put coffee on and jumped up to sit on the counter as Quinn stomped in behind her.

"You don't need coffee every morning," Quinn growled as he walked over to her.

"Yeah, I definitely do," she hissed. She didn't get much more out, as Quinn yanked her off the counter and threw her over his shoulder. She growled but didn't fight.

This wasn't the first time. The last time had just been on Wednesday, when he got her up at two in the morning for a run-through of the things she'd learned already. She knew better than to fight him, this time. The last time, she hadn't been able to escape no matter how much she fought. He had carried her until he dropped her into the stream that ran through the property. It was like he didn't feel pain, the prick.

He placed her on the porch and waited for her to grab

her bag before walking off. She followed him, mumbling obscenities to herself. She hated playing in the dirt. She hated every damn minute of it. She would rather be tarred and feathered than rough it in the woods.

She was incredibly cranky this morning.

"Get started," Quinn told her as they made it into a clearing. She dropped her bag and began work on a fire.

Once the fire was started—it only took ten minutes—she began work on securing potable water. She moved through the process smoothly. Repetition had made the entire thing muscle memory for her.

With water secured after an hour, she wiped sweat off her forehead and moved to making a shelter. A simple branch lean-to would have to be enough for him. She broke fallen branches to the sizes she needed and continued on her task.

He just watched her silently as she finished the shelter. She looked around at the vegetation. She could identify several now. Most were inedible but the ones that weren't, she collected quickly, to make a small stash of food.

Finally, she collapsed next to her fire and glared at him.

"What's next?"

"How do you know you did it all correctly?" he asked, looking down at her. Shade was lying next to his feet while Scout trotted over to sniff her. She pushed the wet nose away from her stomach gently.

"What did I mess up?" Last time, she had screwed up on which plants she could eat. A pretty bad fuck up.

"Nothing, just wanted to know why you were so confident." He shrugged.

She kept glaring at him, mad that he had questioned her when she had gotten it all right.

"What's next?" she growled.

"Hunting and traveling," Quinn sighed, "but I'm not teaching you those."

"Excuse me?" She sat up and raised an eyebrow.

"I want you to hunt with your abilities, but you don't have those. As for traveling, it's not hard. You know the sun rises in the east and sets in the west, follow that."

"You aren't going to teach me star charts and shit?" She narrowed her eyes on him, and he shook his head.

"No," he chuckled, and she clenched her jaw at the sound. Fucking god damn it. He just had to be slightly attractive after torturing her. "I think you're fine."

"So, two weeks," Sawyer sighed. "I finished in two weeks. Thank fuck."

"For now." Quinn walked over and used his magic to have the earth devour her fire. She sighed and watched her hard work disappear. She didn't like the 'for now,' but she wasn't going to let that dampen her happiness that she wouldn't be playing in the dirt for a little while.

"Can I go back to the house?" She asked, looking at the sun that had come up.

"Actually, I wanted to show you something," he said, holding a hand out to her. She grabbed it and let him pull her up. "Follow me."

"Where are we going?" she asked as they walked on a trail she had never used.

"You'll see," was all he told her.

They walked for nearly thirty minutes before she heard the water. The property had a stream running through it, that much she knew, but what she saw wasn't what she'd expected.

"This is our swimming hole." He waved to it and then started pulling off his shirt. "You can come out here whenever you want. I figured you would like to know about it."

She eyed the area with barely restrained happiness. A couple of streams fed a clear, deep-water pond. One of the streams went over a rock face, making small waterfalls. The same rock face looked like the perfect place to jump in from and had several dry rocks that were probably amazing to lay out on.

"Is this where the guys disappear to sometimes?" she asked as Quinn unbuttoned his pants.

"Yeah." Then he dropped his pants and she let out a strangled noise. He wasn't wearing underwear. Of course, he wasn't. "I'm going swimming, but you can keep standing there like a weirdo if you want."

With that, the beautiful nude ass of Quinn's dove into the water. Fuck. She watched him surface, his long hair out of its ponytail. He stopped paying attention to her as his wolves jumped in after him. She turned back to the woods and wondered if maybe she should just make a run for it. Life was officially just too much. Screw it all, she was going to combust if she didn't figure out what to do with her... needs.

She looked back to the water, where Quinn was wrestling with Shade in a shallower portion. His head came up from the activity, and he met her eyes. His hair cascaded around his face, slick and perfectly straight from the water. He was just stunning, and her heart tried to stop when he smiled.

"You can head back if you want, but I thought you might like a day being lazy." He straightened his spine, and she took a deep breath at the sight of water dripping down his chest. He would probably kill her if he knew she found him attractive. The fact that he was being nice to her today was already throwing her for a loop, and then he got naked.

"I, uh, don't have a swimsuit," she called back, shrugging. "I'll just go lay in the sun on one of the rocks."

"Whatever works." Quinn watched her walk over to the rocks. She turned her back to him when she got there. She didn't want a farmer's tan, so she pulled off her shirt and looked down at her pants. Did she dare? She considered it and finally undid them and slid them off. She was fine with a tan in her underwear, she could even it out later in the summer.

When she turned back around, Quinn was still watching her, his eyes more intense than before. She ignored that and laid back on one of the large, smooth rocks next to the small waterfalls. She let the sun warm her, and, soon enough, her eyes were closing a little. Now this definitely made up for the shitty morning of being dragged out of bed.

She didn't pay attention to the time, rolling over when she felt like she was getting too warm. She frowned when something blocked her sun.

"Well, ain't this a sight?"

She sighed heavily at Elijah's voice.

"Drink it in," she said quickly. "It's the closest to naked you'll ever see me."

"I highly doubt that, but we all have our delusions," Elijah chuckled, and she rolled her eyes behind her eyelids. "Why aren't you swimming?"

"No bathing suit," she told him, wiggling her butt for him to notice the simple grey boy shorts she had on. Stupid thing to do.

"Shake it a little more, I need material for my spank bank," Elijah joked, toeing her butt. She turned her head and looked up at him out of the corner of her eye.

"That's disgusting."

"You should be happy I'm being honest about it." Elijah

grinned down at her and she eyed him. He was only wearing boxer briefs and his fucking black cowboy hat. She filed that image away into her own 'spank bank'. She put it right next to the image of Quinn's nude ass.

"Forgive me if I don't give you the same curtesy," she laughed, rolling over onto her back again. She put her arms behind her head and blatantly checked him out. He lifted his arms away from his body and let her. He even did a turn for her. How kind of him.

"How's that?" He winked at her, and she gave him a thumbs-up.

"Perfect, all filed away." She grinned at him, and he bowed to her.

"Now about this bathing suit problem." His grin turned devious, and she narrowed her eyes. "I think you are sorely mistaken, if you think you need one."

She tried to scramble away from him, but was too slow. She screamed as she soared through the air and fell into the cold water.

"Ass!" She roared when she surfaced, glaring at the now hysterical Elijah. He turned and shook his own and she glared at it. That fucking bubble-butt mother fucker.

She was climbing back onto her rock when she was hit in the face with the last shred of clothing he had on. He laughed as she pulled them off her head and tossed them into the pond.

"No!" He tried to sound dismayed, but the laughter in his voice was obvious. She stood up and stole his cowboy hat next, while he wasn't paying attention. He turned to her and she kept her eyes on his face. Had to keep looking at the face. "Now, you wait a damn minute."

She grinned at his more serious tone now that she had the hat. She took off, climbing farther up the rocks as he tried to grab her. She put it on her wet hair and listened to him fire off a string of curses that would have made a sailor blush.

"You ruin my hat, and I'll end you, little lady," he growled.

"Try me, tough guy," she taunted, leaving the cowboy hat on her wet head.

She'd forgotten about Quinn during the exchange with Elijah, so she was surprised when the hat was stolen from her head while Elijah grabbed her ankles. She was pulled down from her spot into his arms. She caught a glimpse of Quinn jumping down next to them as Elijah threw her back into the pond.

"Damn it!" She gasped for air when she got back to the surface. "Cheaters!"

She stopped talking the moment her eyes cleared though, eyeing the man meat on the rocks. Elijah was grinning, and she inadvertently got a look at the cock that screwed her when they met—and not the way she had wanted to be screwed. Quinn brushed dirt off the hat and handed it back to Elijah, who hung it carefully on a low hanging branch.

Both were just as great from the front as they had been from the back.

"What's wrong, Sawyer? Cat got your tongue?" Elijah dove into the water after that and Quinn followed.

Fuck, now she was stuck with them between her and the sunning rock she'd claimed. She was thirsty as fuck, and that wasn't helping her. She needed about three hours of alone time, if she wanted to make it through the day without losing her mind. She also needed to get the fuck out of the water, she realized, as Elijah swam over to her.

She dove down and let her feet touch the bottom. She

pushed off, going underneath Elijah before he could grab her. She stayed under until she reached the rock and climbed out as quickly as possible.

"Running scared, darling?" Elijah called over to her. She looked over her shoulder at him and raised an eyebrow.

"I'm going to sun-dry, and you are going to leave me alone. How's that?"

"Whatever you say, little lady," he chuckled, splashing water at Scout, who jumped in to play some more.

Sawyer laid back out on the rock, letting Shade lay next to her. He must have been out of the water for a little while, because he was already dry. She ran a hand over his fur absentmindedly.

"May I?" Quinn's voice cut into her peace, and she opened one eye to look at him. He was pointing at the rock. "Lie up here and dry off?"

"Go for it," she yawned. Shade was between them, so she didn't much care anymore. And if he was lying down, she wouldn't have to see the erection he was sporting. Hopefully.

She stopped thinking for a moment. What? Why the fuck was Quinn hard?!

She groaned and put an arm over her eyes, trying to banish the image and the thought. Thirsty. She was a woman living in an oasis, dying of thirst.

"Got room for one more?" Elijah chuckled. He didn't wait for her to respond, only collapsed onto the rock directly to her left. She gave him a look, trying to figure out why the hell he was laying buck-ass naked right fucking next to her.

Then Shade got up and moved away, and she groaned. She turned to the left and saw Elijah grinning at her. She rolled onto her right side, only to find Quinn on his back with his eyes closed.

"You guys are killing me," she mumbled angrily, sitting up to leave.

"I have no idea what you are talking about," Elijah laughed. She turned towards him and got another eyeful of the nude cowboy.

"You know exactly what I'm talking about," she hissed.

"I don't." Quinn sounded confused and she looked over to him. He had one eye open.

"She's having a hard time with us being nude," Elijah continued to laugh. "She doesn't want to see it."

"Why not?" Quinn frowned, and Sawyer closed her eyes and massaged her forehead. "It's not like you haven't seen a nude male before."

"Oh hell," she groaned. "It's not that."

"No," Elijah chuckled. "It's that she's got an itch to scratch and won't accept the open invitation I've given her to have it scratched."

"Huh." Quinn didn't say much after that, and they all remained silent for a moment. "Why not?"

"It's complicated," she sighed, slapping Elijah on his abs for bringing it up. "I've got other things to worry about."

"Well." Elijah grabbed her hand and pulled her down slowly. She playfully glared at him, but couldn't bring herself to fight him. The idea of being nearly on top of him was just too good to pass up. It was just too easy to flirt with Elijah, it really was. "When you're done worrying about those other things..."

"Like Axel trying kill me?" she reminded him, raising an eyebrow. "You mean after that?"

"Sure." Elijah let her go, still smiling. "After that."

"Fuck between you and..." She stood up, shaking her head.

"Jasper? I heard him talking to Zander yesterday," Elijah chuckled. "When do I get a kiss, darling?"

"Oh, for fuck's sake," she mumbled with a small smile. "You've already gotten one. You know. The night you put handcuffs on me?"

"Yeah but no one got a happy ending that night and..." He gestured to himself, but she didn't let her eyes follow the hand. "I could use one. You probably could, too."

"I'm going back to the house. I'll find my happy ending there, alone."

"Have a good walk," Elijah called out to her as she grabbed her clothing and threw it on.

"Walk?" She grinned at him. "The walk is going to suck, but masturbating while you're stuck out here saving your hat is going to be amazing." She grabbed his hat from the branch and tossed it into the pond.

"You are a witch," he snarled, diving into the pond. Quinn was actually grinning at her when she looked over at him and winked.

"You should run," he said as she pulled on her shoes.

"I know."

And she did, laughing as she heard Elijah cursing over his wet cowboy hat. It was easy in moments like these to forget she was a prisoner in their home, waiting to be found and killed by a man who thought he'd already done it once before.

20

VINCENT

Movie night. Vincent narrowed his eyes on Elijah, wondering where this was going.

"You think we should have a movie night?" Vincent sat up in his chair, eyeing the grinning cowboy. Zander was snickering next him, and that didn't bode well for Vincent. When these two decided something, he knew he was in for trouble.

"Yeah, to relax." Elijah sounded like it was all set. Simple as that.

"Tonight, in the next hour or so," Vincent continued, as if Elijah hadn't said anything, "when we should be preparing to go to Atlanta in two days."

Vincent rubbed his temples at the thought. They would be in Atlanta fighting with Jon over their assignment with Sawyer and Axel. He needed to focus, not... watch movies.

Jasper would understand Vincent's concerns; but considering Jasper wasn't in the room and Zander was, Vincent felt like he was missing an ally in this argument. Jasper was probably already setting everything up for *movie night*, the traitor.

"There's nothing we can do except go." Elijah laughed while Zander sat down across from Vincent and kicked his feet up on Vincent's desk. Vincent glared at the mud-covered boots on his desk. Zander was purposefully pissing him off. "You look like you're about to have a hernia, *you* need to relax. We used to do them all the time. It's been months! Come on!"

"Zander." Vincent tried to remain calm. "Get. Your. Fucking. Dirty. Boots. Off. My. Desk."

"Approve movie night and come relax." Zander grinned at him, tapping one heel on the desk and causing a clump of dirt to fall onto Vincent's pristine, organized desk. "I'll clean that the moment you say okay."

"Fine!" Vincent snapped, standing up to push Zander's boots off his desk. Zander had them down before Vincent could reach them. That was probably for the best, as Vincent had the urge to break the shithead's ankle.

"Temper, temper." Elijah wagged a finger at him, and Vincent turned his glare on the man who was supposed to be his closest friend.

"Get the fuck out. I'll be down in one hour."

"Roger that!" Elijah gave a mock salute and grabbed his enforcer, Zander, dragging him out of the office.

Vincent looked at the dirt and growled. He opened the bottom drawer of his desk and pulled out bleach and a roll of paper towels. He used a paper towel to grab most of the dirt and threw it away. Then he wiped off the rest carefully, so that none fell on the floor. He liberally applied bleach and scrubbed, making sure nothing was left.

He hated dirt on his things. His things were expensive, and he believed that his property should be treated with a certain level of common decency. If there was nothing there to ruin it through normal use, then why go out of one's way to do so? Zander could wreck his own shit, that was fine, but he and Elijah loved screwing with Vincent. He was going to strangle both of the trouble makers one day.

"Oh, boss man?" Elijah's head popped back through the door, and Vincent released a sigh, wondering when his suffering would end.

"What?"

"Can you get Sawyer? She's been in her room for like, an hour, and no one else wants to bother her."

"I can't imagine why," Vincent said dryly. Only the day before, Elijah had walked into her room without knocking. Vincent could hear the scream in the garage. He didn't want to know what Elijah had walked in on, but it hadn't been good. Zander had to heal Elijah's black eye later.

"Please?" Elijah gave him a look that Vincent could only describe as a sad and half-assed attempt at puppy dog eyes.

"Sure," Vincent answered, secretly hoping he didn't get the black eye this time. He wasn't stupid enough not to knock though.

He shuffled through papers to kill time. Elijah was right. He did need to relax, and there wasn't much they could do about Jon except convince the mediator that everything was fine. He wished he knew why Jon was being such an ass, though. He put precious resources into investigating other IMPO agents, which just wasn't done. He had no legal authority to look into Jasper and Zander without real cause, and that abuse of power pissed Vincent off.

He finally gave up on trying to delay his requested duty. He sighed, walked out of his office, and headed toward the attic. It wasn't that he was scared of Sawyer or didn't like her. He was rather surprised with her. She was a quick study, with a sharp mind and an even sharper tongue wrapped up in a body that was made to kick ass and take names. He was enamored, and he could completely see why Axel had been as well.

He sighed again; there was the problem. Her little trick during their chess match gave him everything he needed to know. Axel was most likely the ex she'd mentioned who taught her to play, and that was probably why he wanted to kill her. Leaving him would be a death sentence. Vincent only needed to think about what had happened to Shadow to know that.

As he reached the attic, he pondered the unanswered questions. He had no evidence that Sawyer and Axel had ever run into each other before the LA incident, which was why he didn't bring up his suspicions. He wanted to know, but a deal was a deal. He wasn't going to pry... himself. He had intended on manipulating all the guys into getting her to talk, but after a week, he'd given up. He'd felt guilty as hell for even thinking about manipulating his team like that.

"Sawyer?" He rapped twice on the door and frowned when he heard a thump, but nothing else. "Sawyer?"

It was only eight pm. He narrowed his eyes on the door. There was no way she was asleep. He grabbed the doorknob and began to turn it.

"Open that door and I will murder you." Sawyer's snarled and strangled voice startled him into letting go. "I'll be out in a minute."

"Okay..." he mumbled, backing away from the door. He thought it was funny that she was scared of Quinn when, in his mind, she was the scariest thing in the house.

He waited for much longer than a minute and raised his eyebrows when she opened the door. She was disheveled, her dark hair going everywhere even though she had it up in a ponytail. Her ebony eyes were a little glazed; and her chest, that gorgeous chest, was rapidly moving up and down.

He had two guesses for what she had been doing—drugs or masturbating. He was smart enough not to say either out loud.

"Can I help you?" She was curt with him, and he actually liked it a little. In some perverse, fucked up way, he wanted to know just how sharp that tongue could be. But this wasn't the time for it, and there were more secrets between the two of them than she knew. After Axel, he promised himself. He would delve into this charming woman after they dealt with Axel.

"The team wants to do a movie night down in the entertainment room," he responded, matching her terse tone. He loved the verbal sparring, loved seeing her eyes narrow at his lack of response. She wanted to figure him out, and he wanted to... well, he wasn't going to let his mind go there right now.

"Am I required to be there?" She raised an eyebrow and looked back into her room. Vincent resisted the urge to lean in and see what she was looking at. He had a strong guess.

"Yes." He gave her a smile and turned to leave. She wasn't, but he loved the idea that he was keeping her from dealing with *that* particular problem when he couldn't do the same for himself.

21

QUINN

Quinn sank into his seat, sighing in happiness. Elijah sat on his left, in his own chair, grinning.

"Like the new chairs?" Elijah elbowed him, and Quinn nodded.

"I'm happy we are finally coming down to use them," Quinn murmured to him, not wanting to get loud. "Though, I think you're more interested in... her coming down here than the chairs." Quinn almost said 'the female' but corrected himself. Before they had brought her to the house, he and Elijah had a long discussion about how to properly address her.

"I am excited about that," Elijah chuckled. "Can you blame me?"

"No." Quinn smiled at him. He trusted his friend's judgment on humans, especially of the female variety. Quinn was naturally distrustful of them.

"I'm happy to hear that," Elijah's voice dropped to a whisper. He grabbed Quinn's hand and placed his lips to his palm. Quinn cupped Elijah's cheek for a moment.

They weren't lovers, not often anyway, but Quinn and Elijah had found a physical friendship together, each getting the physical affection they needed and couldn't find elsewhere. Was there love there? Quinn thought there probably was, but they weren't soulmates. Even together, he and Elijah still found something... missing.

Quinn looked over to Jasper and Zander, lost in their own conversation. The other side of the coin: true brothers through everything except blood, those two. Quinn pulled his hand away and looked back to Elijah.

"I was worried for a couple of weeks," Elijah sighed, "but I knew you and she would figure it out when I saw you took her to the swimming hole."

"My brothers were getting angry with me," Quinn groaned. Shade and Scout had been riding his ass, upset that he wasn't nicer to the female. "They are totally in love with her."

"Of course," Elijah grinned deviously, "I think all *three* of the wolves like her more than they let on."

Quinn snorted, leaning back in his seat again. To anyone else, Elijah was referencing Quinn's wolf form, but Quinn knew better. Elijah was the only person on the team who knew the name his mother had given him when his abilities had manifested. Rogue Wolf. Quinn didn't use it and he'd only shared it with Elijah once. They had been drinking a little too much wine. He'd made his mother's recipe. It was strong wine.

They sat in companionable silence for a long time, waiting for the last two of their group to show up. Quinn heard footsteps on the stairs and perked up a little. It had to be Vincent. He would never hear Sawyer at that distance.

"We only have five recliners," Vincent told Elijah, who was nursing a beer. They had leather theater-style recliners.

They were extra wide with cup holders and seat warmers. And they only had five of them when they needed six, if Sawyer was going to watch movies with them. Quinn looked around and realized Vincent was right.

"Well, you better claim yours before I steal it," her voice drifted in from behind Vincent, and Quinn saw her stroll around him. Quinn let her vanilla scent hit his nose and nearly growled in pleasure at it. It was light, barely there, but he always knew when she walked into the room because of it. He'd noticed early on that she walked silently, so he'd learned to focus on her scent. He was happy to do so, since she smelled wonderful. His senses were above average compared to other humans. Thanks to his multiple animal bonds and his own shapeshifting, he could rely on more than his eyes and ears. "Oh, there's a bar in here! What kind of liquor do you boys keep? I haven't had a drink in ages."

Vincent sighed wistfully at her. He probably thought no one noticed. Quinn did, though. Quinn knew all the other guys were attracted to her on a primal level, and he knew she was attracted to all of them. He found the entire dance of living with her fascinating. He'd never experienced something quite like it during his time in modern society. In the wild, they would have fought against each other to claim the strong female as a mate. As far as he knew, humans were normally very similar, but it wasn't happening here. He knew from experience that males who wished to mate with a Druid were expected to do similar—fight for the privilege.

So, going against everything he knew, he watched her dance between five healthy and strong males without them all killing each other. Even Jasper, who Quinn knew was permanently injured, was a contender to be reckoned with. Yet, he saw no hostilities between any of them.

"What are you making?" Quinn asked with a frown as the strong scent of alcohol and pure vanilla slammed into his nose. It wasn't unpleasant, but it was very strong—stronger than the beer Elijah had or the wine his mother used to drink.

"It's a vodka martini, though this one is a vanilla vodka martini." She smiled over at Quinn, who stood up slowly to look at what she was making. Elijah frowned at him, but Quinn was too focused on what she was doing, pouring different things into a cup. He knew people mixed drinks like this, but he'd never smelled one like what she was making.

"Can I try it? None of them ever mix stuff." Quinn walked behind the bar to her side. He didn't resist the urge to get closer than necessary.

"Sure," she chuckled, handing him the glass. He took a sniff and realized maybe he shouldn't be trying to smell it. It was too strong for his sense of smell. It blocked out everything else in the room. He took a swallow and his eyes went wide. "You're supposed to sip it. Unless you want to get really fucked up. I mean, you can do that, but I don't recommend it."

"It's good," he mumbled as he handed the glass back to her. He looked at the drink, then his chair and had an idea. Elijah was probably going to be a little upset with him. "You can sit with me if you make me one as well."

"Is there room?" She chuckled, looking over at the seats. She looked a little nervous at his suggestion, but she didn't let it stop her from thinking over his request. "Oh, yeah, those things are huge. Sure, you take that one, and I'll just make a second one."

He took the drink, excited to have his own. He really liked it, and he knew it was because it was vanilla. He sat

KRISTEN BANET

down and curled into the right half of the seat. Vincent sat down with a scotch; Zander had a beer like Elijah.

"So, what are we watching tonight?" Sawyer asked as she got to the chair. Quinn helped her sit down so she didn't spill her drink.

"Some new Marvel movie," Vincent groaned. "Probably."

"Actually," Elijah laughed, "you're kind of close. We're watching Wonder Woman, from DC."

"Fuck yeah." Sawyer laughed, and Quinn's chest rumbled in pleasure for a second. He was happy she didn't notice. "I've heard this movie is fantastic."

"So have I." Elijah grinned at her. Quinn had purposefully put her between him and Elijah. Something about the seating arrangement pleased him, like it had at the swimming hole when they were on the rock. She didn't need to know that he told Shade to move.

Quinn didn't care about the movie in the beginning, but Sawyer's enthusiasm was a little infectious. She and Elijah cheering for the Amazon women made all of them start cheering. Zander made her another drink when she asked, and then another. Quinn lost count, and, by the end, he had a female curled up into him without a care in the world.

He looked over at Elijah, who was smirking at him. Quinn looked back down at her and realized that Sawyer wasn't nearly as afraid of him as she once was. That pleased him, since he didn't want her to be scared anymore. He'd done it on purpose, originally.

"Oh, hell," Sawyer giggled. "Zander, Sugar, you make drinks much stronger than I do."

"My bad," Zander chuckled, covering his mouth in an attempt to hide what Quinn had heard described before as his 'shit-eating grin'.

"Drunk Sawyer is kind of adorable," Elijah laughed, looking toward Vincent, who glowered back.

"Need help getting to your room?" Quinn asked, leaning towards her ear. His left arm had somehow gotten pinned underneath her, and he knew it had fallen asleep twenty minutes before.

"I would love that," Sawyer laughed. "I think I'm likely to kill myself on the stairs if no one is there."

He helped her to stand and blatantly checked out her ass while he was still seated. Every other guy in the room was; why couldn't he?

"Need any help, Quinn?" Jasper was standing up as well.

"No, I've got her." Quinn narrowed his eyes on the other male, but pushed back the wave of possessiveness. She wouldn't like that. She was a strong alpha female, and Quinn knew better than to try and make a scene over her. He also knew it wasn't his place. Jasper had the older claim to her, as did Zander.

"Good luck, my man." Zander laughed, jumping up and throwing an arm over Jasper. "Let's go play some COD."

"Good idea," Jasper chuckled as they left. "Good luck, Quinn."

"Good night," Vincent mumbled, and Quinn wondered why their leader practically stormed out of the room.

"Good night!" Sawyer called after him, waving. "Come on, Quinn. Let's get out of here before Elijah decides he needs to take all his clothes off, again. I'm in no place to deny him right now."

"Well..." Elijah grinned, standing up. Quinn snorted as he began to pull his shirt up like a stripper. "If that's the case..."

"Nope!" Sawyer grabbed Quinn's arm, and Quinn let her pull him out of the seat. "Good night, cowboy!"

"It's only a good night when I dream of you, darling." Elijah winked.

"Pervert," Sawyer laughed.

"Let's go," Quinn said quietly, wrapping an arm around her waist. One of hers went around his own; and they left the room together, leaving Elijah to clean up the entertainment room.

They walked up to her room in amicable silence, though it was a bit tough on the narrow stairs leading to the attic. Quinn bit back another growl when she ended up pressed against him as she tried to get the door to the attic open.

"Let me," he grumbled, reaching around her to turn the knob.

"Thank you!" She grinned, stumbling into the attic once he had the door open. He grabbed her before she went down to the floor and pulled her against him, again. While it drove him mad, it seemed to be safer.

"Let's get you to bed," Quinn murmured into her ear.

"For another night of furiously masturbating and having nightmares," Sawyer groaned. "Damn."

He didn't have a response to that, so he just got her room door open and led her inside. He took a sniff and realized how right she'd been. The room was saturated in a scent that he could only describe as heaven. She must have been doing it recently.

"What do you mean by nightmares?" he whispered, helping her sit on the edge of her bed.

"I have them," she mumbled, shaking her head.

He knew that much. His wolves would try to sleep up here with her, and he would be bombarded by the scents they picked up while she slept. They liked her room since it was always unusually colder than the rest of the house. Standing there now, he realized why.

Her magic stuck to every object. A chill. A level of emotion in that magic that rocked him to his bones for a second. Horror. Fear. Pain, both physical and emotional. *Violence.* When she'd first arrived, the room hadn't been so claimed by her yet. While many described his magic as wild, her magic was dark, deadly, and *cold*. He wondered if she knew her magic had such a distinct feeling. Every Magi's magic and Source felt different, but it took a certain something more to make it so obvious.

"You have them frequently." He met her eyes, glazed from the drink. She gave him a bitter, off-kilter smile. He needed to remember that she was incredibly drunk and that a serious topic was inappropriate.

"Every night."

"I'll leave the wolves up here for you in case you need assistance." Quinn moved on. He needed to get out of this room. He didn't want to take further advantage of her state to get questions answered that he had no right asking to begin with.

"They're cuddlers," Sawyer snorted, looking at Shade, who was already claiming an entire side of her bed. Scout was waiting for her to lay down, so he could curl up between of them. Quinn mentally touched the connection he had with his brothers and let them know to alert him to anything out of the ordinary. Scout's bouncing enthusiasm echoed back while Shade just gave a vocal huff in acknowledgement.

"They are, and they will let me know if you need to get up for anything, like the bathroom." Quinn nodded and shuffled out of the room, closing the door quietly. She could undress herself.

He hit the second floor and considered his next move. He knocked once on Elijah's door, then walked in.

"Sleeping in here tonight?" Elijah asked without looking up from what he was doing.

"Yeah, I left the boys with her in case she needs anything. I want to stay close." Quinn pulled his shirt off and began to fold it carefully.

"You don't need to do that in here," Elijah chuckled, watching him now.

"Vincent told me humans fold their clothing, so I do," Quinn huffed. "I know you think it's unnecessary."

He placed the neatly folded shirt on top of Elijah's dresser. Elijah's room was his second favorite in the house after his own room. Elijah used natural wood with minimal treatments for all his furniture, and Quinn liked the scent of them. He unbuttoned his pants and pulled them off, folding them as well.

"Vincent needs to stop telling you weird shit he does," Elijah laughed, taking Quinn's pants and tossing them on the floor. Quinn sighed, looked to where his jeans landed, and saw Elijah's pile of dirty laundry.

"Was that necessary?" Quinn met Elijah's stare and watched Elijah's large shoulder raise in a shrug.

"No, but neither is folding them." Elijah turned and claimed his bed. Quinn couldn't stop the small curl of his smile at the oaf. Oaf, such a Vincent word. "You could have stayed up there with her. No one would have tried to stop you."

"I feel you are incorrect in that assumption." Quinn narrowed his eyes. "They all would have wanted to stop me, but none of them want to get into that fight."

"I think you're right," Elijah yawned.

"And you haven't gotten couches up there, yet," Quinn mumbled under his breath.

"I heard that, and you said you didn't care." Elijah

pointed at him. "And you know what, if I'm 'required' to crash in her room for a night, I don't want a couch to be an option. Now turn off the lights and come to bed. Or brood, your choice."

"I think I'll brood," Quinn chuckled, flicking the lights off. He went to Elijah's window, which looked over the woods. He pondered for a moment before speaking again. "Her magic... it doesn't feel like just a thief."

"No, it doesn't," Elijah whispered in the dark, "and the fact that she throws that much off, even with an inhibitor, says something about how strong she really is."

"It does." Quinn nodded to himself.

"Well," Elijah groaned, "no Magi or any inhibitor can truly stop the natural flow of magic from a Magi's Source. Only death ends the flow of magic in a real way. The inhibitor just robs her of being able to use her abilities and controls that flow of magic more carefully."

"But that doesn't explain why her magic feels the way it does," Quinn mumbled. "Have you talked to Vincent about it?"

"I think he's too wrapped up in Axel, Atlanta, and Jon to worry about it right now. Zander finds it alluring in his stupid way. He likes playing dangerously, and her magic is danger. Jasper... he's been different. Something's off him with and I'm not sure what's going on." Elijah kept his voice low so that only Quinn could hear him.

"She has nightmares," Quinn whispered back.

"Well, that could definitely be a problem for Jasper," Elijah sighed. "With how strong she is, he probably can't block his mind properly while he's sleeping in order to dream his own dreams."

Quinn leaned on the window, using his arm as a rest for his forehead. He saw creatures moving, eyes reflecting light as they looked toward the house. He was in charge of everything within thirty miles of the house, so all of those animals knew who he was, but he had less of a connection to the nocturnal animals. They were elusive and independent. Like Sawyer. Creatures of the dark, owners of the shadows, all of them.

"Her magic feels like the night," Quinn whispered.

"Come to bed, Quinn," Elijah sounded muffled. "Discover the secrets of the world tomorrow."

"Fine." He pushed off the window and slid into bed next to Elijah. As Elijah drifted to sleep, an arm thrown carelessly over Quinn's abdomen, Quinn absorbed the feel of Elijah's magic. Warm, like a low-burning fire, and masculine, something to fight the chill that he'd experienced with Sawyer's.

He paid the most attention to how magic felt, out of all the members of the team. Elijah, warm and masculine. Vincent, still and calm, almost not there, even though he was strong. Vincent had the most control over the flow of his magic, so Quinn didn't pick it up very often. Jasper's magic was airy and peaceful. Zander's magic was like him, reckless. It was really the only way to describe it.

Elijah's arm tightened, and Quinn pulled him closer. Quinn ran his fingers through Elijah's light brown hair slowly.

"Go to sleep," Elijah mumbled, and Quinn stopped playing with his hair.

"You go to sleep," Quinn whispered.

Elijah growled and pushed up on the bed to stare down at Quinn.

"I'm trying, but you're thinking too loud." Elijah put his forehead to Quinn's. "My wet dreams are more important than whatever you've got on your mind right now. Go to sleep."

"I'm trying." Quinn pushed him off and bounced a little when Elijah's huge body hit the mattress.

"Liar," Elijah mumbled, his head now stuffed under a pillow. "If you are going to keep me awake, we might as well burn off whatever excess energy you seem to have."

"Not feeling it tonight," Quinn sighed. "Too much on my mind."

"Worry tomorrow," Elijah's speech was slurred, and Quinn knew he was out the moment a soft snore began.

He touched the connection to his wolves and smiled at the happiness they felt. Sawyer was sleeping just fine. With that, he rolled into Elijah's back and finally found some sleep himself.

22

SAWYER

Sawyer stared at the Range Rovers with a frown as Elijah and Zander threw in a couple of suitcases.

"Do I really need to go?" She looked to Vincent, standing next to her.

"Alas, yes," Vincent sighed. "The entire team is required to go, which means we can't leave you here alone."

"Fuck," Sawyer mumbled.

Atlanta, Georgia. It wasn't a bad city, not really. She'd grown up just outside of it with Zander and Jasper. She didn't like it, though. She loved New York more, and she wanted to keep her distance from the secrets Atlanta held.

"We're ready to roll, someone just needs to find Quinn," Elijah called. Vincent looked over at her and she rolled her eyes, walking off to find the feral man.

It didn't take her long. He was stretched out on the back porch with his wolves, both of whom were asleep.

"We're ready to go," Sawyer told him, looking down on him. He normally wore jeans, but no shirt and no shoes. Today he was in his official uniform, the simple, all black outfit every IMPO agent wore when on duty.

He looked wonderful in it. Black was definitely his color, though Sawyer thought black was everyone's color. She was a little biased.

"Fantastic," he growled, opening his ice-blue eyes. Sawyer thought they looked more vibrant when he was wearing black. Yeah, it was definitely his color. She stepped back, giving him space to stand up. "I hate the city."

"Atlanta?" She frowned. "Why?"

"All cities," he growled, snapping his fingers and making the wolves jump to attention. Sawyer was seriously impressed with his command over them. She had never had such obedience from... She stopped the thought before it continued.

"I'm sorry?" She wasn't sure what she was sorry for, but it felt like the right thing to say.

His look told her that she needed to walk away. She did just that. That movie night had been really fun, but she felt like she spoiled it with her whiny shit at the end. She normally didn't do that, talk like that while she was drunk, but she was nearing a breaking point. The secrets, the nightmares, her body's reaction to these guys. It was overloading her and getting drunk had seemed like a good way to forget it. She hadn't counted on the fact that alcohol also had the tendency to amplify emotions, and, once she'd gotten to her room, those emotions flooded her.

She didn't have any nightmares that night though, so that was a plus.

"We shouldn't be staying the night, but it's good to be prepared," Vincent was whispering to Elijah. "I don't like this. I don't like any of it."

"Me neither, boss, but the big guys say we need to sit down with Jon and review our capabilities to do the job we've been tasked," Elijah groaned.

"He's been on our ass since day one with Sawyer," Vincent snapped. Sawyer raised an eyebrow. Really? "And then there's the fact that we have evidence of Axel's people in New York, of all places. They didn't cause any trouble, but it's concerning."

Sawyer stopped, still out of sight of Vincent and Elijah. No. Axel's people couldn't be in New York. Her chest tightened.

"I know," Elijah mumbled. "Have you told her?"

"No," Vincent growled. "Are you mad? She'll make a run for it to go back and save them, even if they aren't in any danger. And they probably aren't. There's no reason for Axel to target a bunch of non-Magi children and a retired healer."

Damn right I would, she thought, feeling a bubble of anger well up in her.

"And now we need to take her Atlanta, near the fucking airport of all place," Vincent sounded frustrated.

"You shouldn't eavesdrop," a growl came from behind her. She jumped and mentally cursed herself for letting Quinn sneak up behind her. "It's rude."

"You all have been keeping secrets from me," she hissed quietly.

"Of course." Quinn made it sound like she was stupid for not figuring it out sooner. "And you have no idea how many."

He walked past her, and she followed him. Vincent's eyes went wide when she met his stare. That mother fucker knew her people in New York were in danger and didn't fucking tell her.

"Don't do anything stupid," Quinn growled back to her.

"Why would she do something stupid?" Elijah's eyes narrowed on her, and she winced at that. She didn't like that even he was suspicious. He was normally one of the guys saying she was alright.

"She overheard you both," Quinn told him mildly as he opened a door to one of the Range Rovers. Sawyer watched Shade and Scout jump in and climb to the cargo area, where they looked at everyone through the back window.

"Sawyer," Vincent whispered. "Please. We've got it covered."

"You should have fucking told me," she snapped. "I had the right to know."

"And if I could trust you not to run, I would have," Vincent snapped back. "Get in, we're heading out. You are riding with Quinn and me."

"Whatever," Sawyer mumbled, climbing into the Range Rover. She was a little mad that he didn't trust her, but he was also right. Knowing about the potential danger only made her want to find a way to escape them, damn the consequences, and go help her people.

"See you there, Elijah." Vincent nodded to the cowboy, who was wearing his cowboy hat with his uniform. Sawyer wished privately that he accidentally set it on fire or something.

The long ride was silent. Sawyer listened to the audio-book that Vincent put on, but she didn't follow the story because it was bland. It was also in Italian, which annoyed her.

"Is Italian your first language or are you one of those people who's obsessed with the language of your forefathers?"

"I was born in Rome," Vincent told her softly. Quinn had fallen asleep within the first ten minutes of the drive. "So, yes, Italian is my first language."

"I haven't been to Rome in years," she sighed. "Gorgeous place."

"It is." Vincent nodded. "When were you there?"

"I'm not telling you that," Sawyer mumbled. Axel once had his home base there, and she'd lived there with him until he decided to move them. Her heart squeezed for a moment. Midnight was buried there. Two thoughts about her in a single day. Sawyer wondered what special hell she was in.

"Of course," Vincent mumbled with disdain. "You know, life could be easier for you if you just... talked to someone."

"We have a deal, Vincent," she hissed.

"I know," Vincent sighed, turning the audiobook up. She leaned into the window and watched the trees fly past.

She didn't sleep this trip, her mind going a mile a minute about what was going on.

"What happens if they decide you aren't fit for my protection?"

"Jon will take you into his custody and back to wherever they would hide you," Vincent told her as he pulled off the freeway. "We'll go and pack all your things up and arrange a place to give them to Jon's team for you."

"Why did we come all the way to Atlanta?" She was curious. Not many people knew too much about the special IMPO teams that people like Vincent and Jon ran.

"Our homes are secure, even from each other. Only the team knows where they live. Only the top five people in the IMPO know where we live. And our handler, James. You haven't met him yet; you will today."

"Oh goodie," Sawyer sighed. "So, it's not normal for me to know where you all live."

"No, it's not normal, but we wanted you as secure as we could make you." Vincent turned them into a parking garage. "I'm going to make a simple recommendation. Do not engage with Jon or his team. If you have to, bother Special Agent Hamble. He's the nice one."

"Alright. Can I get a smoke before we go in?"

"Yeah." Vincent parked the vehicle and tapped Quinn. "We're here."

She got out and met Vincent at the back of the Range Rover. She opened the back and let the wolves out to stretch as Vincent lit two cigarettes.

"Here." He handed her one and she took a drag.

"Why did these guys come?"

"Quinn doesn't like leaving them home alone." Vincent scratched Shade behind an ear.

"I just realized something," she chuckled. "I haven't met your raven."

"Really?" Vincent raised his eyebrows. "He's always close by."

"Seriously." Sawyer flicked ash off the end of her smoke and took another pull.

Vincent whistled, and Sawyer narrowed her eyes. A huge black bird soared into the parking garage and landed on his shoulder. Its head tilted to the side as it stared at her.

"Why has it taken weeks for you to introduce yourself to her?" Vincent turned to the bird, and it bumped its head to his forehead. "You know better than to follow people around where they can't see you. I didn't want you spying on her."

The bird gave a shake, puffing up. Sawyer's heart broke a little as she heard Quinn finally get out of the Range Rover.

"Kaar." Quinn smiled, reaching out to the raven. It nipped his hand, but Quinn didn't seem to mind. "Keep an eye on everything, will you?"

"Don't tell my raven what to do." Vincent slapped

Quinn's hand away. "He's getting fat since you keep giving him food."

"I like spoiling him," Quinn chuckled.

"Spoil the wolves." Vincent glowered, stepping away from Quinn.

Sawyer watched the exchange with a raised eyebrow. Kaar was hopping around on Vincent's shoulder like he was trying to dance. Vincent looked regal though, with the large bird propped there. Vincent and Kaar were both sleek and professional while Quinn and his wolves were very much the opposite.

"I've been here for nearly an hour!" Elijah walked over to them, grinning. Sawyer sighed.

"Thanks for not making me ride with him," she whispered to Vincent, who actually laughed.

"Yes, I felt the day was too serious for you have to endure that hell," Vincent whispered back. Sawyer watched Elijah frown and grinned at him.

"What? Couldn't find something to do to pass the time?" She winked making Elijah sputter a little. She started laughing after that. She found herself too funny sometimes.

"Heartless woman." Elijah put a hand over his heart, putting on the wounded cowboy act.

"There's Zander and Jasper." Quinn jerked his chin.

Sure enough, they parked right next to Vincent and jumped out. Jasper came to her side and Zander stood next to Elijah.

"We're not going to let them drag you off," Jasper whispered to her, and she nodded silently. She hoped not. She had grown to like the unruly bunch, even if she did want to stab all of them several dozen times on occasion. Like right now.

"Don't keep secrets from me," she whispered back after a moment. "Ever again."

"We'll talk about that later," Jasper sighed. "It was Vincent's idea."

"I figured as much." Sawyer rolled her eyes.

"Let's go," Vincent said loudly, interrupting the different conversations that had started up. Zander and Elijah looked like they had been plotting something. Sawyer didn't ask. She knew it was going to be bad for her. Female intuition.

She walked in the center of the little pack. They left the parking garage and went into a boring little office building on the other side of the street. She was crammed into the elevator with all of them, her back flush to Vincent's chest.

"Did we really need to *all* take the same elevator?" She growled, trying to push Jasper away from her front.

"No," Zander laughed, grinning at her. Elijah was snickering. Were they serious about this? Sawyer realized they just liked putting everyone in uncomfortable positions. How cute.

"This is a serious meeting," Vincent snapped. "Cut the shit."

"Yes, sir," they said in unison.

They got off the elevator without incident and Sawyer was ushered into a meeting room. Vincent sat her down next to him with Elijah on her other side. Quinn took a spot at the end, where his wolves lay down on the floor, out of the way. Jasper and Zander flanked Elijah and Vincent on either side.

She met Jon's stare and shifted uncomfortably. She didn't like this. Something seemed off. She chalked it up to her lack of knowledge on the entire situation, but the moment she stepped off the elevator, a sense of foreboding hit her.

"We're here today to discuss the matter of Sawyer Matthews," said a woman at the end of the table.

"Let's cut to the chase," Jon sneered. "These kids aren't in the place to be handling such a flight risk or this dangerous of an assignment. On top of that, two of them have a previous relationship with her. They aren't going to be willing to use her for her purpose."

"And what's her purpose?" Vincent snapped. "Bait? You going to drag her through the streets until Axel shows up and tries to kill her?"

"And if that's what is necessary?" Jon growled. "Is it a bad thing to do whatever is needed to bring him to justice?"

"Axel would never fall for a ploy so childish," Vincent said with disdain. Sawyer agreed with him. Axel would see that trap coming from miles away and would just undermine it or ignore it until a more opportune moment arose for him to get what he wanted.

"Says *Vinny*," Jon hissed. "The world's 'expert' on Axel. I feel like you just say things to get your way."

"Both of you," the woman tried to cut in, "please, allow me to continue."

Sawyer looked around at Jon's team, all of whom were watching the exchange except one. He had brown hair and a reddish beard. He was moderately attractive and probably the youngest on Jon's team, appearing nearly a decade younger than the rest of them. He wore a scarf and she raised an eyebrow at it.

"Scarf in August in Georgia?" She inquired, making the table go silent.

"Ah... hickies from my girlfriend." He smiled sheepishly at her and she couldn't stop a small smile. "I'm David... Special Agent Hamble."

"Nice to meet you." She reached across the table and they shook hands. "I hear you are the nice one."

"Damn it, Sawyer," Zander coughed, hiding a laugh.

"You should sit down, thief, or I'll request that you're handcuffed to the chair," Jon growled. She raised both her hands to appear non-threatening.

"My apologies." She smiled at Jon as she sat back down. "I was just trying to be *nice*."

"I think she should go to another room," the mediator sighed. "She doesn't need to be here for this right now."

"I don't like that." Vincent shook his head. "She's required to stay under supervision at all times, and I won't have it said that I bend the rules for her."

"Well, she likes David," Jon waved a hand around. "Let him take her somewhere else."

"No." Vincent's tone was steel, and Sawyer shivered.

"You are attached," Jon chuckled. "Why's that, Vinny? Don't want big b-"

"Jon, you need to correct yourself," Vincent growled, "before I come across this table and correct you myself."

"I don't need a Castello telling me to fix myself," Jon growled. "Don't think I forget who you are."

Sawyer went still. Castello. *Castello*. Rome. Axel. *Vinny*.

"I have a younger brother, Vinny," Axel chuckled, pulling her close. "Good guy, a few years older than you, but he's a fucking stickler for the rules, the freak."

"Is that why I've never met him?" She nuzzled into Axel's chest.

"Hmmm, if you ever meet Vinny, run." Axel kissed her forehead. "He'll do his best to send you to prison. He's on their side."

She turned to Vincent, hoping her face gave away nothing. How had she lived with them for weeks and not learned his last name? She didn't know Quinn's either, now that she thought about it.

Olive-green eyes. Axel had said he got them from his father. *Vinny* must have too.

Sawyer mentally backed up on what she had just learned. The Castello crime family had imploded on itself over a decade ago. The head of the family was found murdered in his office by one of his own family members. They had destroyed themselves in the fight for power when none of Giovanni's children stepped up to take the reins. In the end, another family devoured and absorbed the Castello family, leaving it a footnote in criminal history.

Axel had told her that he was a Castello who wanted to make it big on his own. He wanted to be bigger than the family. Vincent was his younger brother.

Vincent was Axel's younger brother.

That single fact echoed in her mind for a long time, and she lost track of the conversation going on around her.

"That's rich, Jon," Elijah growled. "You're the one who harasses us every single opportunity you find."

"Look here, you fag-" Jon snarled.

"Enough!" the mediator slammed her notepad down, jumping from her seat. It startled Sawyer. "For an hour, I have only heard insults from both sides, and I am done with it. I'm requesting that you both take some time to think about what's at stake here other than your egos!"

"We haven't insulted Jon nor his team at all." Vincent was glaring at the woman.

"Your team's existence is an insult. To the IMPO and the WMC," Jon growled, and Sawyer saw all of his silent team members nodding in agreement, except David, who looked a bit guilty. No wonder Vincent told her to keep to Special Agent Hamble.

A phone went off and Sawyer saw the woman answer. She didn't say anything, only nodded and gave affirmatives.

"Both handlers are here, and they apologize for being late. We're going to take a fifteen-minute recess." The mediator left the room, and Vincent stood up.

"Let's go to another room," he told the team and they all started standing up.

Sawyer didn't know what to say. Vincent was Axel's *younger fucking brother*.

"Sawyer?" He frowned at her, and she stood up slowly. She followed him silently down the hall and into a different meeting room.

She didn't say anything as she took a seat. The team chatted quietly about how their handlers being in the room might change things.

She looked out the large window and sighed. She was Axel's ex. She couldn't be a hypocrite and hold Vincent's genetic relation to the man against him. If she were related to Axel, she wouldn't want anyone to know either.

Axel taught Vincent to play chess. She gasped, but quickly regained her composure, hoping the guys didn't know.

She used Axel's own move against Vincent. *God damn it*.

"Well, I hear you all have been having some fun." An older voice filled the room and Sawyer looked over. She hadn't heard the door open, lost in her own thoughts.

"I wouldn't call it fun, James," Vincent sighed, reaching to shake the older gentleman's hand. Sawyer looked James over for a moment as he turned to look at her. He had blonde hair that bordered on white and gray eyes. Small wrinkles stood out to her, laugh lines. He was a happy man.

"You must be Sawyer." He smiled at her and she shrugged.

"That's what I've been told."

"And you have a sense of humor." James chuckled. "It's nice to finally meet you. We'll get this sorted out, so you can get back home soon."

"That's also what I've been told," she mumbled, standing up to shake his hand. He laughed, nodding at her.

"Yes, I sure you have been. So, Jon's handler, Ken, and I were speaking on the drive over." James clapped his hands together. "He disagrees with Jon's stance on this and is going to say that it would be best for Jon to back off. But, he needs a night with Jon to make that happen. You packed to stay the night?"

"We did," Vincent told him with a sharp nod.

"Good. We're going to convince the mediator to give us a day, then head out. I've booked us rooms at the Hilton." James grinned and looked to Sawyer. "Great facilities there; you'll like it."

"Goodie. Yay." Sawyer did a fake cheer.

"Is she always like this?" James pointed at her.

In unison, all five of them said yes.

"My sympathies," James chuckled.

Sawyer snorted. These guys didn't need his sympathies. They drove her mad at every turn.

"Come on." James waved them all to follow. "Let's go get this over with."

Sawyer followed dutifully, tense and somewhat unsure. She still felt like something was about to go horrifyingly wrong. She didn't like how out in the open they were. She didn't like how many agents were around. She didn't like any of it.

It took ten minutes for the mediator to agree with the handlers. Sawyer's elbow was grabbed by Jasper and pulled slowly. She followed him back out of the room, rolling her eyes.

"Fuck, I hate those guys," he murmured. She raised an eyebrow.

"You have the capability to hate someone?" She crossed her arms, leaning against the elevator wall.

"Definitely," Jasper chuckled as Vincent and Zander joined them on the elevator.

"Do other teams treat you guys like this?" Sawyer frowned, looking to Vincent. Now everything about him reminded her of Axel, and yet, the differences were just as glaring. He wasn't beautiful like Axel. He had that permanent five o'clock shadow, whereas Axel was always clean shaven. He had the same brow line as his brother, but different eyes and a different nose.

"Eh..." Vincent looked thoughtful. "No. Lower-ranking teams don't like me, but that's because I tend to run them over. Other elite teams tend to ignore us. That's more normal. We all ignore each other and go about our business. Jon's just an ass, and he happens to be close by. It's just a pain."

They stepped out of the building together, and she saw Jon's team only ten feet in front of them. They were all stuck walking to the parking garage together.

"Until tomorrow, *Vinny*," Jon called, opening the door to his own truck. Sawyer got ballsy and flipped him off, making him glare.

Then an explosion tossed her into a pillar.

~

SAWYER GROANED, trying to stand as another explosion rocked the building. She cursed, feeling around for anything to hold onto. The concrete pillar she hit was enough to help Sawyer stand up. Smoke filled the area, and she couldn't see anything. She coughed as fire engulfed vehicles all around her. She tried to open her eyes more, to see anything, but the smoke stung, and they welled up with tears.

Another explosion had her stumbling as wreckage flew around her. She staggered towards the stairs. Well, she hoped she was going towards the stairs.

An arm grabbed her, and she couldn't see who.

"Come with me," a male voice roared. In the moment, she couldn't recognize it. "I've got you. We're going to keep you alive, Sawyer. I promise."

She followed without complaint, coughing as she was nearly dragged. She stumbled on the stairs, and the arm wrapped around her waist. She blinked and saw David, looking serious, helping her down the stairs. David was good, she thought suddenly. The guys said he was the nice one.

They broke out of the fire exit on the ground floor, coughing from the smoke. She was shoved into a car, and she realized something was off.

She turned back towards David. The scarf was gone. He was grinning, and Sawyer's eyes fell on a scar she hadn't seen inside. From the left ear, down the jaw and then the neck. David transformed into a woman in a white suit. Her blonde hair was perfect. Her eyes danced with glee and violence.

"Missy," Sawyer hissed, scrambling to get out the other side. A gun met Sawyer, pointed at her forehead through the open car window.

"Well." Colt grinned at her. "Look at this. Shadow, so good to see you again."

Sawyer grabbed the gun and pushed it away, breaking Colt's wrist in the process. He roared, and she pushed the door into him as Missy grabbed her ankle. Sawyer turned and sent her heel into Missy's nose. Missy let go and Sawyer dove out of the car and started running. She didn't know where she was going but it was going to be anywhere else.

She should have been paying more attention. She should have known that Missy was using David's form. Special Agent David Hamble was probably very much a dead man waiting to be found somewhere. Hickies. What a *stupid* fucking reason to wear a scarf in August.

"Fucking Doppler," Sawyer growled to herself as she turned to see both Missy and Colt on her tail. She picked up the speed, but without her magic, she was going to need to escape the hard way.

"Talyn, now!" Colt screamed. She powered forward, only to see Talyn drop in front of her. She glared at him, but saw the fire on his hand, ready to go.

"This time, Axel decided to share his powers." Talyn grinned. She felt the air leave her lungs as the earth grabbed her feet and pulled her down. He let her breathe again when he was positive that she wasn't getting out.

Sawyer wanted to scream in frustration and anger. In heartbreak. Her guys were probably dead in that parking garage, thanks to Missy.

Missy only had one power, the ability to change into a different human shape. Every Doppler could only do that and *only* Dopplers could do that. They were Legends for a reason though. Untrackable, incredibly strong, with above average speed, they were nightmares, and nearly all of them were criminals in some way or another. It was just too easy for them, and they weren't Registered the way other Magi were. Most Magi would never meet a Doppler and know it. They were masters at living whatever lives they wanted to.

Missy turned her lack of offensive magic into a passion for blowing everything up the conventional way, and she had a special hatred for Sawyer.

Sawyer was the one who scarred her, ruining her ability to perfectly match whoever she was copying. She wondered if that added to Missy's insanity, or if she was always just a really fucked-up freak.

Sawyer groaned as someone kicked her back. She couldn't fall forward though, with her legs pulled thigh-deep into the earth.

"You're lucky we aren't killing you right now," Missy hissed in her ear, pulling her head back by her hair. "Boss wants to see you. He's quite upset."

"Go to hell," Sawyer snarled. "And I'm amazed that Axel let you within ten feet of him, Talyn. He always found your kind disgusting."

Sawyer knew she shouldn't have said that. The earth tightened on her legs, threatening to crush them.

"You never did know how to keep your mouth shut," Colt laughed. "Please, keep pissing everyone off. We're just looking for reasons to make this even more painful."

"Like you need reasons," Sawyer scoffed.

"Drug her," Talyn snarled, "and let's get the fuck out of here."

Sawyer hissed as a sharp pain stabbed into her shoulder.

"We'll wake you up when we get to the boss," Missy giggled.

Sawyer's world went dark.

23

QUINN

Quinn pushed a piece of twisted metal off his left leg before doing anything else. The parking garage was a disaster with fire, smoke, and debris everywhere. He coughed and heard another explosion.

"ELIJAH!" He roared, hoping for any sort of answer. "VINCENT!" He spun and looked around. Where were Shade and Scout? He knew they were alive and uninjured, but they weren't in the parking garage. He could only hope they ran into the office building or found a safe place to hide while he found all the humans he was worried about. "SAWYER! ZANDER! JASPER!"

No one responded to him and he started to cough harder. He looked around again, hoping to see anything, even a body, but nothing was around him.

"QUINN!" James' voice cut through, and he spun towards it. "I have Vincent!"

He ran for it, ignoring the pain shooting up his leg. He found James pulling Vincent out from under a car door and Quinn pulled the car door off his leader.

"Fuck," Vincent snarled. "What the hell!"

"Someone blew up half the cars in the damn garage," James groaned as he helped Vincent stand. "Injuries?"

"Sore," Vincent groaned. "Nothing bleeding or broken."

"Same," Quinn growled, looking around. "We need to find everyone."

"Let's get to it." Vincent had begun to jog away when all of them jerked to a stop at Zander's touch to their minds.

"*I have Jasper. He needs to be healed now or he'll bleed out, so Elijah has to deal with the fire.*"

Quinn cursed and began running toward where he knew Elijah's truck had been parked. Vincent followed him.

"No," Quinn gave a strangled growl at the sight. Elijah's truck was a pile of burning metal. He stood there, stunned, for too long, and Vincent passed him, looking for any sign of Elijah.

"Quinn, he's over here," Vincent called.

Quinn ran to him, thirty feet from the truck on the other side of the garage. Elijah had almost been tossed out of the garage, and they were on the third floor.

Quinn could hear firetrucks as he helped Vincent pull Elijah off the car he landed on. Quinn couldn't see any injuries, and looked to Vincent whose eyes had glazed over. Quinn waited, holding Elijah's head gently.

"Zander will be on his way over once he's done with Jasper," Vincent told him, coming back to the present. "We need to find Sawyer."

Quinn nodded and searched his pockets. Vincent's eyes narrowed. Quinn knew he thought that they would actually go searching, but he had an easier way to find her.

He pulled the picture out of his back pocket and opened it. He'd folded it to bring it to Atlanta, just in case.

"What is that?" Vincent's voice was hard. Quinn showed

him as Zander walked over while supporting a limping Jasper. "Where did you get this?"

"I stole it from her," Quinn answered. It was a picture of Sawyer and a little boy as they played with a small house cat. He knew the picture meant the world to her since he could track her with it. He focused on the image and closed his eyes. His Source reached out in the direction of hers. She wasn't close by. She wasn't within five miles of the parking garage.

And she was moving further away at an alarming rate.

"Quinn?" Vincent sounded worried.

"She's running, or she's been taken," Quinn whispered. "Zander, check on Elijah."

"He's waking up now. He was just knocked out. I sent a jump start to his brain to wake him up. Like magic smelling salts." Zander told him. Quinn nodded and stood up as Elijah's eyes opened.

"Fuck me," Elijah groaned. "What the fuck happened?"

"Look around. All of our cars were blown up." Vincent reached down and helped Elijah, who swayed, to stand. "And Sawyer is on the lam."

"We don't know that," Quinn growled. "I just know that she's moving away from here."

"There's no way she orchestrated this," Jasper groaned, rubbing his leg. Quinn could see the blood stain, even on the dark pants. "We need to get out of this building before it goes down."

"We should find Jon's team," Elijah reminded them.

"I think they're all dead," Zander mumbled. "I'm not finding any living bodies in this building except us and James. I say we go and chase her. Why aren't we already?"

There was a small moment of silence before Vincent spoke up.

"Let's get James and get out of here. Firefighters are here. We'll go after Sawyer and find out what the fuck happened."

They were all limping in some way as they got out of the building. When they made it to the main street, Quinn tried again to find his wolves.

He entered Shade's mind and took a backseat ride to Shade running through the city in back alleys with Scout next to him. Where were they going? He pushed that question into Shade's mind, and Shade snarled, throwing him a memory of Sawyer being carried by two Magi that Shade didn't know. Quinn recognized one, however—Colt, known member of the Ghosts.

"Vincent." Quinn re-entered his own mind.

"Are the wolves following Sawyer like Kaar is?" Vincent must have checked in with his animal as well.

"Yes, but Shade saw who has her." Every head snapped to Quinn when he said that.

"Kaar did, too," Vincent gasped, his eyes coming back into focus.

"Go," James coughed. "Go. I'll handle things here. I see Ken and Jon. We'll take care of it."

"We might not come back, James," Vincent reminded him. Quinn didn't like the dark look in their leader's eyes.

"I know," James sighed, "but those mother fuckers need to pay for this."

"We don't have a ride," Elijah reminded them. "Jasper is recently healed, and Zander wasted a lot of energy on that. Can we do this?"

"We're going to fucking try." Zander sounded excited, and Quinn looked at him with wide eyes. "Time to steal some cars, boys."

24

SAWYER

Sawyer wasn't tied to anything. That was the first thing she noticed when she woke up. Missy was grinning down at her with a syringe in her hand, and Sawyer groaned.

Great. It hadn't been a nightmare. This was real life. Missy blew her guys to high heaven, and Sawyer was back in the tender, loving care of her least favorite people to walk the face of the earth.

"I'll make this simple." Axel's voice cut through the fog of Sawyer's mind. "If you put up a fight, this will be much more painful, and it's already going to be a long, slow death for you."

"And what did I do this time?" She groaned, pushing herself up. She met his glare. He stood nearly five feet away from her, toying with a long black dagger.

"You made me kill my brother to get to you." Axel's voice betrayed nothing except anger, and Sawyer scoffed.

"I think I care more about him than you do," she hissed. "He's a bit like you, but he's at least got a moral compass. I kind of liked him."

"You don't know fucking anything about my relationship with my brother," Axel snarled. "I let him have his fun chasing me around the world, but when I learned he had you, I was forced to make the most difficult decision of my life."

"There's nothing you can say to convince me that you gave a damn about his life," Sawyer said acidly. "Nothing. You didn't give a damn about Henry, so why should Vincent mean more? You didn't care when you murdered your s-"

"Silence!" he roared, and she slammed back to the floor and slid several feet.

She pushed herself up, glaring at the Ghosts near her. Toni and Felix were both sitting on several boxes stoically. They watched her as she stood up and swayed. She rubbed her forehead as she turned back to Axel.

"Why don't you just kill me?" she asked softly. "You have me. I have no magic. I'm completely helpless. Why am I not dead yet?"

"Because I want you to die screaming for mercy." Axel's glare would have scared her a long time ago. Back when she thought she loved him and that he loved her. When she was just his thief, looking for a good time. Young and stupid.

She had very little fear left in her, though. Acceptance was the place at which she had arrived. Today she was going to die, and she needed to be ready to meet whatever god or punishment was waiting for her. Maybe there wouldn't be an afterlife. Just a cold dark abyss, a place where she would feel at home.

Fuck that. She was going to make this a pain in Axel's ass.

"Let's go," she taunted, spreading her arms wide. She was flung across the room into a stack of boxes. It didn't hurt as much as she thought it would, and she stood back up.

Missy was waiting for her, and Sawyer grunted at the punch Missy landed to her ribs. Bones cracked.

"That's for my face," Missy snarled, grabbing Sawyer and tossing her back into the middle of the... Sawyer didn't know where she was. She regained her feet for the third time and looked around.

What stood out was the small jet and giant doors at one end of the building. They were in an airplane hangar. Not helpful, Sawyer thought, but it was something. She couldn't fly a plane, so the idea of escaping that way was dead before it even got started.

"Are you just going to toy with me, Axel?" She turned back to him. "Is this how it ends? Not with a bang, but with a whisper? You toss me around a little until I'm too broken to stand, and then you drive my own knife in me?"

"This is how it ends." She didn't like his flat voice. "To think I ever loved such a disloyal little bitch like you. You knew what would happen if I caught you with the IMPO again."

"Ha. Like you have the capability to love," she snorted. "You sure as fuck never loved me. I was your property—a tool that you could manipulate to do your bidding."

He cursed and tossed her again. She nearly landed on Felix, who kicked her while she was still in the air, so she landed away from him. That actually hurt.

"You murdered your son and then your brother. You think you have the ability to love?" she hissed to Axel in Italian as she stood up *again*. "The fucking arrogance of that astounds me."

She couldn't breathe, but she kept her glare on him. He released his hold after fifteen agonizing seconds, and she was thankful she didn't fall to her knees. Axel was never going to get her on her knees again.

"Come here," he growled. She raised her chin. She straightened her spine and met his eyes. Her body screamed in rebellion at her actions, but she didn't care.

"No." She narrowed her eyes on him. "I want a duel by the Second Law of the Old Ways."

Axel's eyes went wide for only a second, then he smiled viciously. Felix and Toni were both chuckling. Missy was laughing from behind Sawyer. Sawyer heard other Ghosts laughing around the hangar, but she wasn't embarrassed. She knew Axel would give her what she wanted. If she was going to die, she was going to take one of them down with her. The Second Law of the Old Ways meant that magic couldn't be used, so Sawyer had a fighting chance against anyone she was pitted against. It wasn't binding, but she knew that Axel had a perverse sense of humor. He would force his little posse to follow the rules for the entertainment factor alone.

"Fine." Axel threw her blade, and Sawyer saw it bury itself into the concrete two feet in front of her. "Missy, handle her. Leave her alive, though. I want to kill her. Who's ready for some entertainment?"

Sawyer jumped for the dagger as Missy jumped for her. Sawyer heard cheers come from different corners of the hangar bay, but she couldn't worry about them just yet. Missy first. Of course, he chose Missy. She didn't need magic to fuck someone up.

Sawyer got her hand on the blade and spun as Missy threw a punch. Sawyer barely ducked in time to avoid it and slashed upwards, leaving a thin red line across Missy's thigh.

"You bitch," Missy hissed.

"Let's go," Sawyer snarled, dodging Missy's grab. She could *not* let Missy get her arms around her. She was strong enough to pop Sawyer like a balloon, and Sawyer didn't want to die like *that*.

Sawyer and Missy circled in the center of the room. Missy had always been a difficult opponent for Sawyer. She was just fast enough to react to Sawyer's blinking, and she was strong enough that it only took one or two hits for Sawyer to be out of the fight. She'd already cracked several of Sawyer's ribs, and Sawyer knew she couldn't get hit a second time.

Missy darted forward, and Sawyer shot to the right, going low, and sending her blade towards Missy's ribs. She didn't get it buried in the way she wanted, scraping Missy's ribcage as Missy spun to knee Sawyer away.

Sawyer took the knee, unable to escape it. It hit the same cracked section of her own ribs and sent her flying.

"You'll pay for that." Missy stomped over to her, and Sawyer pushed herself up, knowing that one of her ribs was about to puncture a lung. Sawyer coughed and spit at Missy's feet.

"People keep telling me that," Sawyer growled. She didn't like the blood she had just spit out, but there was nothing she could do about it, either. She was going to kill Missy. It would be one less Ghost for some future IMPO agent to deal with. It would be Sawyer's last good deed, even if it killed her.

And it would.

Missy charged, and Sawyer didn't back down. She let Missy wrap her arms around her and knee Sawyer again in the same spot. Sawyer couldn't stop the scream of pain, but she had what she wanted.

She slammed the knife into Missy's gut. There wasn't a healer in the hangar bay. None of the Ghosts would be saving Missy's life today.

She staggered back, pulling the blade out as Missy began to stumble around, holding her gut.

Sawyer didn't waste another second. She grabbed Missy's hair, wrenched her head back, and shoved the dagger into her heart while she looked the Doppler in the eye.

"I'll see you in the next life," Sawyer snarled.

She wasn't playing nice anymore. Missy was the eighth person she'd killed, and Sawyer let herself fall into that dark place at the sight of Missy's blood pouring out onto the white suit she wore. She yanked the dagger back out and met Axel's shocked stare.

"How's that, Axel?" she hissed. "Thanks for that. I've been hoping to get my hands on her for years."

"You..." Axel watched Missy's body fall to Sawyer's feet.

"Yeah," she gloated. Her lung was punctured, but she wasn't done. Cold wrapped around her heart. He had made her a monster; not through training, but through pain. She could live through the pain; it only made her stronger. And she wasn't ready to die yet. Not yet. Shadow wanted to kill as many people as possible before they ended her. "Anyone else?"

"Toni," Axel snapped. "Kill her."

"Yes, sir," Toni snarled, stalking over to her. She gave Axel a disgusted look. He wouldn't fight her, even without her magic, the fucking coward.

She prepared herself, spreading her legs shoulder-width apart. She braced and brought her hands up, the dagger in her right hand, ready to go into the chest of another victim.

"SAWYER!"

She turned towards her name. Vincent was running in, the team behind him. Elijah, Jasper, Zander. No Quinn, but wolves. The wolves darted ahead, and Shade jumped on

Karen before she could even react. Scout went for her neck, and Sawyer watched the wolves tear the Magi apart while a third wolf ran for her.

They were *alive*. They looked like shit, but Sawyer didn't hold it against them. In that moment, they might as well have been fucking angels. They were alive, and she suddenly had a chance to see the next sunrise. The next sunset. Charlie and Liam.

"Kill them," Axel roared.

Sawyer didn't have much time to move as Toni clapped his hands, causing a sonic boom. It knocked things over and nearly sent her flying. She held her ribs and could barely take a breath as she ran for the guys. Goddamn sound manipulation. Her ear drums burst, and the world began to ring.

The third wolf, a gray and tan monster leapt for her. She went to dodge, but didn't have the speed. She found herself in Quinn's arms, and a wall of earth stopped a wave of fire from cascading over them.

Jasper was limping as he used his control over the air to whip the fire back around. Zander threw shields over them as he also burst water pipes under the floor and put other fires out.

In mere seconds, Sawyer realized she was in the middle of a warzone. The hangar was getting destroyed. Elijah was practically in flames, throwing out balls of fire and stopping others from hitting them.

"Sawyer," Vincent gasped, reaching her and Quinn. "You need to run. We're here but you have to get out. Save yourself."

"No." She jerked back and winced in pain.

"Yes," Vincent whispered. "Sawyer, Axel's never going to

stop. If you go now, we might defeat him, and you'll have freedom. If we don't, you'll have a head start."

"I can help," she growled.

"You're just a thief with a good right hook," Vincent growled. "I'm not letting-"

"No, Vincent," she cut him off. She grabbed his shirt and pulled him close, their chests colliding with each other. "I'm not just *some thief*. I'm not a pawn. I'm Shadow. That's why he wants me dead. I am the mess he's failed to clean up, the killer he created that broke free. I know he'll chase me to the ends of the earth. Give me this. Let me help you take him down."

She watched his eyes fall to the dagger in her right hand and then his olive-green eyes came up to her face. She'd thrown her cards on the table; now it was time to see Vincent's move. She watched confusion and knowledge dance in those eyes. She was his brother's monster.

"Shadow is dead," he whispered. She watched him figure it out. The game they had played. No one knew Axel better than them. When she had *died*, there were people all over the planet who were able to rest easy, happy someone like her, with her abilities, was gone. Vincent was clinging to a reality built on the lie.

"She's going to be if you don't give her the ability to fight back," she growled. He grabbed her left wrist and released the enchantment that wouldn't let her remove the inhibitor. He slid it off her wrist, and Sawyer gasped at the rush of getting reconnected to her magic.

"Prove it," he commanded grimly. She grinned viciously and saw him go a little pale. "But leave Axel to me."

"Don't worry, I'm going for Colt and Talyn," she snarled. "Talyn is a Vampyr. He's borrowing Axel's powers right now, so he's a major threat. Colt is an air manipulator, so Jasper's got three people against him. Those two need to go, if you want a real chance at taking down Axel."

"God damn," Vincent gasped. "You really…"

"Later," she growled. She might actually have a later now.

She blinked into the fight and grinned at Axel. He saw her and for the first time since she'd known him, she saw fear in his eyes. She didn't go for him though. She found Colt fighting directly with Jasper and blinked closer, bracing herself for the small tornados those two had started making as they fought for dominance over their element.

"Colt," she called softly. She watched him pale and turn towards her, but only for a moment. She blinked behind him. He tried to blow her back, but he didn't have the concentration for it while he was also fighting Jasper. She shoved her knife into his back and let him fall when she yanked it back out. She met Jasper's eye, then shifted into her smoke form and drifted into a dark section of the warehouse.

She had an excess of magic after not being able to use it for so long. Chaos was her enemy. It was also her best ally in this situation. It gave her plenty of cover to sneak up on Talyn, who was helping Axel, but it forced her to drain her power more quickly to avoid becoming collateral damage.

She wasn't able to get to him, though. They had shields around them, and she growled, solidifying. Talyn and Axel both gave her quick glances, and Talyn tossed her a gloating smile. She would need to find a way for someone to take the shield down.

"You," Felix hissed. She turned to him, and gave him a bored look.

"Me," she told him blandly. Felix wasn't much of a threat. He could cloak and create small illusions. She was never sure why, out of all the powerful people Axel surrounded himself with, Felix was included. "What of it?"

"This is all your fault," he murmured, looking a bit sad. Sawyer considered going after him but thought against it. He seemed... out of the fight. Lost. "Axel was going to be the ruler of this world until he got you. You couldn't just fall into line though, could you?"

"I'm not the one who started all of this." She gestured around the hangar. She could barely speak with any strength. The fighting was going to bring the building down if things kept up. It wasn't her scene. She liked the quiet, dark fights more than chaotic battles. "Axel didn't need to come after me again."

"You know, he was never able to get over you," Felix sighed. "Learning you weren't dead after it hurt him so much to have to kill you..."

"Pushed him over the edge?" Sawyer glared at him. "I've noticed, and that fucking says something."

"Yeah," Felix mumbled, and then he disappeared. She knew he'd cloaked and did the same so that he couldn't stab her while she was trying to find a way in Talyn's shields. Felix was a bit of a coward, and she figured he was running for it.

She turned back to Axel and Talyn. Toni was fighting with Vincent and losing to him, while the other team members where taking on Axel and his buddy. Axel was losing and, by the look on his face, he knew it.

She blinked over to Quinn, dropped the cloak, and stumbled behind the wall of earth he had raised in defense before a fireball took her head off. It was just some errant shot, probably from Talyn. She was almost positive it wasn't actually aimed at her. Almost.

"You need to crush their shields hard enough that I can get through," she gasped, holding her ribs. Fuck they hurt.

"Are you sure?" Quinn glanced at her.

"Crush Talyn's," she groaned. "I'll kill him, and then you only need to deal with Axel. Vincent can handle Toni."

"Knock him out," Quinn whispered. "We could use a Vampyr in custody. We don't know enough about them."

"Fine," she hissed. Of all the fucking things he could be worried about. "I'll *not* mortally wound his ass. Promise."

"Get ready," Quinn yelled, and she watched sweat break out on his forehead. This was the strongest Magi in North America, but she had no idea-

The ground rumbled like a fucking earthquake hit. She stumbled as beams fell from the ceiling and crashed down on the shields that had been raised over most of the combatants.

She knew the moment Talyn was vulnerable. A Vampyr didn't have the same type of Source as a regular Magi. They had to use their Source to steal portions of another Magi's. They could also steal directly from someone's life force, making them immortal if they chose to be. They were the only type of Magi who had to steal their abilities from others, though. This limited how much magic they could use. They could burn out the portion of Source they had stolen and be useless until they could steal from someone else. They were born with the... problem, the poor bastards.

Talyn didn't have the magic left to create another shield, and Sawyer wanted to laugh when Axel didn't shield him.

"Axel!" Talyn looked terrified, and Sawyer blinked forward, connecting her fist to his jaw. He staggered back a couple of feet and gave her a fearful look. The Ghosts didn't like her; they never had. With good reason. She had always been strong enough to kill most of them in one-on-one fights. Only Axel had outdone her in sheer magical power. Missy had always beaten her in hand-to-hand, until tonight.

"Talyn," she crooned, ice in the word. She resisted the urge to cough more. She could barely breathe, but that wasn't going to stop her from doing this.

"Shadow," he hissed. She saw a lick of fire appear in his hand. Such a waste of power. He could have grabbed any of the fire from around the hangar bay, but instead he wasted power creating it. Dumb fuck. Talyn was never that good at using others' powers. *Wasteful.*

"He's not going to save you," Sawyer scoffed. "He's not going to be able to save himself."

"You getting your magic definitely tipped the fight out of our favor, but-"

"No buts." Sawyer used her left hand and wagged a finger at him. "I'm not losing to you all a second time."

She threw her knife to the ground, letting in embed itself into the concrete. She grinned and blinked forward, giving Talyn no chance to dodge the three punches she delivered to his abdomen. She pushed the hand with fire in it away, breaking it backwards at the elbow and causing Talyn to scream as she kneed his gut. Then she backed away and delivered a strong kick to his knee, breaking it as well. She loved taking their legs out. She was beginning to notice a pattern with her behavior, but she did it for a reason.

People couldn't fight when they couldn't stand.

Talyn dropped to the floor in agony, and she spun, delivering a roundhouse kick to the side of his head. He was silenced, crumpling on the floor. She half hoped the kick had killed him.

She stopped and swayed for a moment as she saw Vincent incapacitate Toni. *Finally. Took him long enough.* She snorted. *Amateurs, all of them.*

Her mind drifted for a moment. He was pretty glorious, darker than Axel, as he had sublimated in and out of the fight. She found that impressive, even if he should have been done with Toni much faster. They were all glorious, these misfit guys and their secrets. She wasn't mad at them in that moment. Fuck it. She kept secrets, so they were allowed to, as well. Her kids in New York were safe and would remain so. Axel wasn't getting out this time. The Ghosts who could escape were just going to hide. She looked around a little.

Only Felix. Only Felix was going to get away. Poor sod.

She began walking, though it was more of a stagger, over to Vincent when a sharp pain erupted in her stomach. She saw his eyes go wide and his face pale.

"Vincent?" she mumbled, confused at Vincent's expression. She turned to Axel, whose final shield broke at that moment, and he began to laugh.

"I won't lose to you," Axel snarled with a grin as the team over-powered him, sending him into the ground. "Not to you."

She looked down.

Her own dagger was hilt-deep in her stomach. Blood gushed out of the wound, and she didn't bother worrying anymore. Her guys were alive, and he lost. That was all that mattered. She yanked it out and dropped it to the floor.

25

ZANDER

The fight was chaos. Zander whipped water to put out the fires that weren't under Elijah's control. He kept throwing shields over all of them except Quinn, who was farther from the group than Zander could manage. That didn't worry him. Quinn was more than capable of handling himself. If Zander didn't know better, he would say that Quinn was holding back so he didn't accidentally kill all of them.

Then he saw her. He'd never thought 'born to kill' was an apt description for anyone or anything, but there she was.

She shoved a knife in Colt's back, not a single bit of emotion on her face. He could feel her magic slice across the room in cold, deadly rage as Colt's body dropped. Then she was gone again, a black smoke creeping into the background of the fight. He was stunned for a moment too long, and the shield around Elijah and him shattered.

"Zander!" Elijah yelled at him. "Get your fucking head in the game!"

He threw up another shield right before a tornado of fire

ran them over. They needed to end one of those fuckers. He had no idea that there were two Magi with the Mythic control over all four elements. True elementals like them were normally born once in a century. They had known about Axel, but the other guy was an unknown.

The fight continued until Quinn nearly brought the building down on them with a surge of magic that Zander couldn't comprehend. That mother fucker *was* holding back. Dick head.

He heard Jasper scream.

"Hold on!" Zander screamed, running for him. He dove for Jasper as Quinn threw up a rock wall between him and Axel. Zander didn't have time to send a thank you as he immediately began looking over Jasper.

Fuck.

"Jasper," Zander snapped urgently. "Jasper, your leg."

"Oh, fuck," Jasper groaned, looking down.

"I..." Zander held on to what was left of Jasper's bad leg. A piece of the ceiling had shattered the shield Zander had been holding over Jasper and landed on his leg, breaking it and completely crushing everything from the knee down.

"Fuck," Jasper moaned, falling back. Zander caught him and knew his friend was going into shock.

"Jasper, look at me," Zander growled hoarsely. "Look at me!"

"The fuck do you want?" Jasper growled, glaring at him.

"For you to stay calm." Zander hoped Jasper would listen. Zander didn't have the power to save Jasper's foot or leg. It wasn't something any healer could fix, no matter how powerful they were. "We'll make it through this."

"Sawyer got the other guy out of the game!" Elijah roared. "We got this! Axel is going down!"

"See?" Zander wanted Jasper to listen, to ignore the injury for just a moment longer.

They had called for a fuck-ton of backup on their way over. Where the fuck were they?

"Go finish it," Jasper groaned, falling back again. Zander let him this time. The injury wasn't fatal, but Zander just couldn't save it. Jasper wasn't going to end the day with both of his legs. "I can still..."

Jasper passed out. Well, Zander used his magic to knock him out completely, so he wouldn't freak out later. They just needed to over-power Axel, and then everything would be over.

He rejoined the fight and began sending torrents of water into Axel's shield. It was cracking, and Axel was growing desperate, trying to fight them all off at once.

Once the shield was close to breaking, he watched Axel swing a hand out and grin at something.

He stopped, confused for a moment by what Axel was doing. He turned to Sawyer and Vincent, standing on the other side of the hangar bay. He watched in horror as Sawyer pulled the dagger out her own gut and dropped it to the floor.

He couldn't breathe as she collapsed. He couldn't hear anything as his vision tunneled in on the woman he'd loved for over a decade.

"SAWYER!" Zander roared, running for her. She was down. She couldn't be down. Not after everything. Not after all of this.

Axel had, in a last-ditch effort to take one of them out, used his telekinesis to send the knife Sawyer's way. She hadn't been paying attention, distracted and a little out of it from her injuries. Zander had known she was already injured. She'd been swaying on her feet since they'd shown up. He hadn't had the chance to help her at all.

"Sawyer," he gasped, sliding to a stop by her body. He rolled her over and touched the last bit of magic he had to try and save her.

Five broken ribs. Two had punctured her lung. She'd been slowly drowning for the entire fight. But the knife wound...

He placed a hand over it and forced his magic into her body. He forced her abdominal aortic artery to repair. It was a fatal wound. He knew that, but he was going to try anyway. He had to try. He sent a jump to her heart and forced it to beat once after the artery was repaired.

"Zander," Vincent whispered desperately. "She's gone, Zander."

"I can heal her!" he roared.

"You are out of magic, Zander!" Vincent tried to pull him away, and Zander shoved Vincent back. None of the other team members tried to stop him.

Axel was laughing.

Zander pulled magic from the last place he had—his own life force. It was a dangerous and stupid thing do, but Zander didn't care.

He had to save her.

He kept forcing her heart to beat with magic until dark spots danced in his vision. He was killing himself. His organs would start to shut down if he didn't stop soon.

He passed out as soon as her heart beat once on its own. It was all he needed. He just needed to know her heart was still beating.

26

ELIJAH

"Stop laughing," Elijah snarled, knocking Axel unconscious. Vincent was checking Sawyer's pulse, and Quinn was getting Jasper, who was out cold.

"They are alive," Vincent called over. "I'm not sure for how long. She's not bleeding out anymore so I'm not even sure what I can do at this point."

"Where the fuck is our back up?" Elijah growled. He couldn't help Vincent with them. Someone had to stick with Axel, or he could fucking disappear. Elijah was less worried about that now that Axel not only had an inhibitor on him, but was also unconscious.

"I don't know. They will probably show up any second, considering we don't fucking need them anymore," Vincent snapped.

"Sure enough," Quinn growled, laying Jasper down next to Zander and Sawyer. Elijah saw Jasper's leg and wanted to puke. "The brothers think they are a minute away."

"A full fucking minute?" Elijah groaned. "We have three down and three criminals in custody. We fucking needed them five minutes ago!"

"Elijah," Vincent pleaded, "stay calm. We can't... we can't lose focus now."

"Fuck!" Elijah ran a hand through his hair and kicked Axel when the mother fucker dared to groan in pain on the floor. "You shut the fuck up."

"Sawyer told me something important that we're going to need to deal with," Vincent whispered quietly, watching Elijah. Elijah was shocked by Vincent's lack of reaction to Axel getting kicked while he was down.

"What's that?"

"She's Shadow." Vincent's voice betrayed nothing about his own feelings.

Elijah felt a shiver of something run through. *No.*

"Shadow is dead," Elijah whispered, unwilling to believe.

"She very well could be if we don't get her to a hospital," Vincent pressed. "She told me. Did you see what she did here, today? I don't think she was lying and..."

"Axel's obsession with her," Elijah gasped. "His slip into... recklessness. His drive to see her dead. All of this. Damn it, Vincent! I told you in LA this was all because of a woman! And it's the *same woman*."

"She's an assassin," Quinn sounded thoughtful. "It all makes so much sense."

"What does?" Vincent frowned at him. He wasn't going to talk to Elijah about the other topic. He'd blatantly disregarded Elijah on it, and now that was coming back to haunt him. "And she *was* an assassin. She hasn't been active since she... died..."

"The feeling of her magic. Cold, deadly. Dark," Quinn's growly voice was soft. "I never thought it suited her, Sawyer the thief, but it makes sense with Shadow the assassin."

"Huh." Vincent looked thoughtful at that. "I... hadn't noticed..."

"Can we... worry about this later?" Elijah heard sirens. "We have a woman who looks like death, and right now, that's all that matters. We need these fuckers secured, and once all of them are in a hospital, we can debate on what to do about Sawyer's... past."

"You're right," Vincent sighed, "but we need to tell them before he does." Vincent nodded towards Axel, and Elijah agreed, nodding silently.

"Jasper's injury is my fault." Quinn knelt next to the young man's unconscious form. Elijah felt for Quinn, he really did. "A beam fell, and he couldn't get out of the way in time because of his bad leg."

"Well," Elijah gave a dark chuckle. "He won't need to worry about the bad knee anymore. There won't be anything attached to it."

"Wow, Elijah," Vincent snapped. "Funny."

"He would get a laugh out it," Elijah reminded Vincent. "You know he will, once he's awake."

"Special Agent Castello?" A voice called out, causing Vincent to turn.

"Here! Bring healers!" He yelled back.

Elijah watched people flood into the building. Healers, non-Magi medics, and IMPO agents from Atlanta. None as high ranking as himself, but at least they were IMPO. James was at the back of the pack, coming straight for them as agents secured all the unconscious Ghosts.

Healers rushed to Jasper, Zander, and Sawyer and began working. Elijah kept his eye on them, hoping they didn't lose Sawyer. He trusted Zander, but he was no healer and had no way of knowing how much healing he'd done on her. It was fucking stupid for Zander to use his life force like that.

But Elijah would never say that to him. He would have done it in a heartbeat, if he could have. Assassin or not, he didn't want her dying on him. She was Sawyer, the fierce, passionate woman who showed her middle finger to the world and told it to bite her. And she put so many others before herself. She was so layered that he hoped to never stop discovering who she really was.

She couldn't die.

"All three are stable," one healer announced. "Did your healer…"

"He used his life force to heal her," Elijah pointed at Sawyer at the female healer nodded.

"He saved her life. He just needs to rest and will be fine in no time. He nearly killed himself, though." She stood up and looked up at Elijah. "Tell him not to do something so reckless next time. He might not be so lucky."

"Will do," Elijah told her, knowing he was lying to her.

"You got him," James exclaimed to Vincent. "You fucking got him."

"What did Ken and Jon say?" Vincent asked. As the healers and medics took their injured away, Elijah joined James and Vincent. Quinn stuck to his side like glue, and Elijah threw an arm over his shoulder.

"Well…" James sighed. "Nothing that was helpful."

"What?"

"I'll explain later, but let's just say, it's bad." James shook his head as he let that trail off. "Let's get all of you to a hospital first…"

Elijah didn't like the sound of that. He didn't like it at all.

27

VINCENT

Vincent was angry: at himself, at his brother, and at the unconscious woman in the hospital bed.

"You," he whispered. "How did I not see it?"

Twenty-four hours since they captured Axel, and she hadn't moved, not even a twitch. None of the healers could figure out where she'd gone. Her body was alive, and her Source was strong. She could wake up, but nothing would rouse her.

He needed answers. He needed her story like his life depended on it. While his didn't, hers did. He always figured catching Axel would just be... the end of it. Vincent was realizing that it was nowhere close to over.

"Wake up, Sawyer," he whispered and couldn't keep the desperation out of his voice.

She was his brother's lover and killer. Ex-lover, he reminded himself. Ex-killer. In the years since she supposedly died, she'd done nothing that warranted the IMPO to even care about her existence.

Vincent didn't want her to die and didn't want her dragged off to prison. He was running out of time to stop that from happening. Axel was in solitary. No one was allowed to speak with him on Vincent's orders, but that could only last so long. Once Axel could tell someone about her, he would. He would make sure that she went down with him, a final act of revenge against the woman who betrayed him.

"Vincent," James called into the room. "Any changes?"

"No," Vincent sighed, looking at his handler. Vincent wasn't sure if James would be on his side. He'd become their handler after his last team was murdered.

By Axel. Because of her.

James had sought him out to finally let Vincent go after his brother. He had let Vincent build the team for that goal. He was on his own vengeful quest for a team he'd been with for over a decade.

"I have those files you wanted," James sighed. "Come here."

"Shadow's files," Vincent whispered.

"I don't know why you want them. It's over." James sat down at a small table and pulled the files from his briefcase.

"It's never over with Axel, and we need to nail him for the murder of those agents." Vincent kept his tone professional and gave nothing away. "Plus, I don't think you and I have ever talked about it."

"And you like to know everything about everyone," James groaned. "Sit down boy. Sometimes I wonder if it was good idea to give you the amount of power I did."

"Well, it's paid off, now, hasn't it?" Vincent gave him a wry smile and sat down. He slid the papers in front of him and began reading.

Strangely, he'd never actually read the original files on the Shadow incident.

"She cut a deal, didn't she?" Vincent asked, looking up from the files. They were all the hits she'd done for Axel.

"This file is her deal with the IMPO and the WMC," James sighed, pushing the other file to him. "What do you want to know about it?"

"Everything, obviously," Vincent answered.

"February 2013, my team received a package," James launched into a story that Vincent had never heard. James had never wanted to tell him before, and Vincent had never asked. It had never been pressing, since Vincent knew how the story ended. It hadn't been a part of his game with Axel. Vincent flicked a look to Sawyer. That had changed. Now, it was the most important thing he'd ever hear. "It contained an offer."

"Shadow wanted out and would betray Axel to do it," Vincent mumbled.

"No." James' voice went hard. Vincent looked up at him and frowned. "Shadow wanted to betray Axel. Period."

"What?" Vincent frowned.

"Let me tell you the entire story. Let me paint you the picture," James closed all the files, stopping Vincent from reading them while he spoke. "Something must have happened because the initial contact was only about Shadow wanting to change sides and betray him. Period. She didn't try to cut a deal. We offered it to her, not the other way around." James took a deep breath. "The WMC was being kept up-to-date on everything. They figured if she was willing to change sides to get back at him or something, that she could be convinced to remain on our side. So, they had the team make a deal. She would betray Axel to us. She would help the team take him down, and then get her pardon and go free. On conditions."

"What conditions?" Vincent leaned back in the uncomfortable blue chair. *Hospitals needed to invest in better furniture.*

"She would be a consultant for the IMPO and be on the WMC's call if they felt her *expertise* was needed. They wanted to use her," James was whispering. "You need to remember, Vincent, that we work for power hungry people. Someone like Shadow wasn't someone they would feel comfortable giving the death sentence or letting walk free."

"Why were they uncomfortable with catching her and giving her the death sentence?" Vincent narrowed his eyes.

"The WMC had a certain faction that believes they need more than just their army and police force. Someone like Shadow could make problems disappear for them in exchange for ongoing freedom. If she had the chance to live up to the deal, she would be *their* killer, instead."

"Did she accept?" Vincent asked softly.

"Yes," James sighed, rubbing his scruffy beard, "but I don't think she ever really knew what the implication was. I think she figured she would just continue to help them take down other criminals as a consultant and informer. Not an assassin."

"Like you were trying to have us lead Sawyer into," Vincent groaned. "Oh, James..."

"What?"

"Do you hate her? Shadow? For what happened in Charlottesville?" Vincent needed to know. Everything from here had to be done carefully and with allies he knew he could trust.

"No," James sounded mournful. "You know, I had the team ask her why. Why was someone like her doing this after everything. Her response had been a little heartbreaking."

"What did she say?"

"This was never what I wanted," James whispered. "And with Axel..."

"Yeah." Vincent swallowed and nodded. He was desperate to hear her story. From general orphan with a couple close friends to brutal assassin to the woman who saved children from their own families. "James, what would you do if she were alive?"

"Catch her?" James shrugged. "Maybe just let her hide. After all of that... The deal she made with the WMC is magically binding for the WMC. They are required to honor it, but now she can't help catch Axel. They would have no reason to keep the deal and would probably put her in a worse position. If she was still alive and not active, hiding somewhere, then she isn't harming anyone. There's no reason to drag her back in now."

"She did honor the deal," Vincent growled softly. "She did."

"She's dead, Vincent," James reminded him.

"A body was never recovered. We all took Axel's word on it because he also killed the several IMPO agents that were involved. But she might be," he mumbled, nodding towards Sawyer. James turned to her and narrowed his eyes in confusion. "No one really knows what's going on with her right now."

"Are you saying the little thief is Shadow?" James asked softly. "And *if* she is, when did *you* find out?"

"She told me in the hangar bay at Atlanta International, right after the team got there. She wanted to help with taking him down. She killed Colt and incapacitated Talyn once I took the inhibitor off her. I'm assuming she killed the woman she had been standing over, but the body wasn't recovered, so I don't know." Vincent gave a dark chuckle. "I'm mad at myself for not figuring it out

312

sooner. You should have seen it, James. She was every-thing you would think from her reputation. Cold, emotionless, and intelligent. She didn't lose her cool as she stalked the building for her targets. You know, I figured out that she and Axel had been a couple while she was in the house, but I just didn't realize she was Shadow. Like you and everyone else, I lived on the fact that Shadow was dead. That the assassin no one could catch, or defeat, was dead. Instead, my team caught her using fucking Elijah as bait. *Elijah!*" Vincent couldn't stop the dark laughter now. It was funny in a completely fucked up way.

"My God," James whispered.

"She's been a vigilante, a thief, and to some, a *hero*," Vincent gasped, wiping his eyes. "The scariest assassin to walk the earth, and she taught children to fight for free. She found them homes, pays for their college. She's decent, if a bit arrogant. She's a decent human being, and now I need to figure out what to do with her."

"She honored her deal with the WMC," James murmured. "What do you need from me?"

"Keep everyone away from Axel. This isn't over. I need to find out how he knew we were in Atlanta and how to grab her. On top of that, I want to tell the WMC about her. I don't want him to be the one who exposes her," Vincent said it quickly, laying his problems on the table for James.

"I'll keep everyone from Axel and the other Ghosts," James agreed, nodding. He was still looking towards Sawyer in her coma. "Let me approach the WMC as well. I know everything about her in terms of the situation she's in legally. Tell me one thing though."

"Anything." Vincent meant it. If James was going to help, he would tell James anything.

"Would you be comfortable if she's permanently attached to your team?"

"Why?" Vincent frowned. "She should be able to go back to New York and live her life until we need her."

"No," James sighed, shaking his head. "I have to give the WMC something, and I know what that needs to be. They won't fuck with me if I give them something more than they originally wanted."

"What are you thinking, James?"

"I'm thinking that she won't get the pardon immediately. She'll need to continue to prove herself to them, and she'll need an avenue to do that." James was speaking softly and shoving the files back in his briefcase. "I think we should make a play for her to become a probationary IMPO agent. Say a five-year enlistment into the organization. If she survives the entire five years, she walks free at the end. If she does something truly extraordinary, they can grant it earlier. That's all. Failure would be her dying or running. Obviously."

"But, she would need a team to work with," Vincent groaned, "and you want it to be us."

"It has to be you all." James' voice was firm. "No other team will give her a chance. Between you and Quinn, you all have no reason to hold her past against her. You can push her to become better and understand why she needs to."

Vincent nodded silently, looking back to her. That was the truth.

"We'll do it," he finally whispered. "We'll take her as a teammate."

"We need her agreement." James waved at her as he said it.

"She'll agree." Vincent was certain of it. "Handle it. Thank you, James."

"Not a problem." James sounded tired and stood up. He patted Vincent's shoulder as he left the room.

Vincent looked around the room, finally breaking his locked stare on Sawyer. Kaar sat outside the window, a constant presence. Kaar normally didn't stick so close to him. The raven was much more independent than Quinn's wolves and handled himself. Vincent flicked a look to said wolves. Both were curled up in a corner, watching and waiting. Vincent had a feeling they wouldn't move until she was awake, a sign that Quinn wasn't taking this well.

At least she had protectors in them. Not that she needed them, he sighed. She was more than capable of protecting herself, it seemed, as long as she had a sharp blade and her magic.

∼

"Jasper is awake," Elijah softly whispered in Vincent's ear.

"Good," Vincent sighed. Twenty-eight hours since they had captured Axel. "I made a decision on Sawyer I think everyone on the team can agree to."

"So, it's time to shatter Zander and Jasper's perception of their old friend, huh?" Elijah shuffled around, looking uncomfortable.

"Better us than Axel or the WMC," Vincent whispered. "Better us. James is with us. He's helping put my plan into action."

"That's good," Elijah nodded slowly.

They left Sawyer in the dark hospital room, Vincent throwing one more glance at her as he closed the door.

They moved, two shadows of imposing figures in black, through the pristine white hospital. The lights were too bright for Vincent after so long in the dark.

They slipped into Jasper's room silently. Zander and Quinn were already there, waiting.

Zander looked like a wreck. Dark circles under his eyes, his skin paler than normal, and his cheekbones were pronounced, causing dark shadows to fall over his face.

The repercussions of using one's life force to do magic past a Magi's Source limit. Vincent knew he would need a good chunk of time off to recover. With Jasper also out of commission until he adjusted to his new life, that wouldn't be hard to make happen.

Thinking of Jasper, Vincent turned and saw the quiet man staring down at his leg. Jasper's left leg had to be amputated from the knee down. It was a painful thing to see.

"How are you feeling?" Elijah asked quietly, moving to Jasper's bedside. Better him than Vincent. Vincent wasn't good at the touchy-feely part of being on a team, and they needed Elijah's good nature around if they were going to survive this intact.

"Well," Jasper sighed, "my knee won't hurt anymore. Maybe a prosthetic will help with my limp."

"Looking on the bright side, huh?" Elijah chuckled. "Good. I'm going to look into making you one and enchanting it. I've got a few ideas, but I need some time to research options."

"Thanks, man." Jasper gave a weak smile and looked to Vincent. "What's been going on? Zander and Quinn didn't know what you've been planning."

"I have a few things to talk about. First and foremost, Sawyer," Vincent started, keeping his voice down. He locked the door before moving closer to the bed. "Quinn and Elijah already know this, but you and Zander have to be informed, as well."

"Well," Zander growled weakly. "Get on with it."

"Sawyer is Shadow," Vincent whispered. "She admitted to it in the hangar bay at the airport when I told her to run for it."

"No," Zander snarled, standing up. Quinn grabbed him as he swayed and forced him back into his seat. "No. She's not that type of person."

"That makes so much sense," Jasper groaned, rubbing his face.

"Oh?" Vincent frowned at him.

"It's not important," Jasper said, waving a hand around in dismissal. "You have a plan. I know you do."

"I do," Vincent confirmed. "But if any of you disagree with it, I'll halt it and we'll work something else out."

"Tell us," Zander growled. "I can't fucking believe this."

Vincent let them know what he and James had decided. What he had learned from their handler about Sawyer's situation. He watched faces change. Some, like Zander, became triumphant. Jasper looked thoughtful the entire time. Quinn was the only unreadable face in the group, but Quinn was normally unreadable, and those emotions he did show were often acts to cover up his real feelings.

"Yes," Zander snapped. "Fuck yes we're doing it. Damn right, she's joining this team."

"I concur," Jasper whispered.

"Do you really need my answer?" Elijah chuckled. "Please."

Three down. Vincent looked to Quinn, who turned away and looked out a window. He wondered where Quinn's thoughts were. Vincent would probably never know, but he still wondered.

"Quinn?" Vincent asked, low and cautious.

"Yes... but I want answers, about this," Quinn's growl wasn't aggressive, but rather, a little hurt. Vincent felt a wave of confusion over it, and watched Quinn pull that picture out of his pocket. "I want to know who they are." He pointed at the cat and the little boy. "If she won't tell me, I'm changing my answer. I won't be a teammate to someone who keeps huge secrets like this. I understand why she didn't tell us who she is, but I want to know where they are. Who they are."

"She's going to be required to tell us everything if she wants to stay out of prison," Vincent informed him, reaching for his shoulder and holding it. "She'll tell us who they are."

Vincent actually didn't want the same answers as Quinn. He had a bad feeling about what might have happened to the young boy and the house cat in the picture. If he knew anything about his brother, the answers Quinn would get would be nightmare-inducing.

"Anything else?" Jasper changed the subject.

"Yes," Vincent went back to his professional, team leader voice. "We can't leave Atlanta until we figure out how Axel knew we were here and where to hit us."

"Yup," Elijah fell onto the small bed next to Jasper, making Jasper groan. Vincent nearly smiled. It was much too small for both of them, but Elijah didn't give a single fuck about that. "We need to root out what happened, and you obviously have an idea. You've been brooding for over a day on it now, haven't you?"

"I do but it's not something I think should be said out loud," Vincent said tentatively, "and Elijah, when this note makes it to you, burn it."

He pulled out his small notepad and looked at the top sheet. It was a wild guess, but he was nearly certain he was right. It was the exact type of thing that his brother would do.

Jon Aguirre

He ripped the note out and passed it to Zander, who cursed as he handed it to Quinn. Quinn's growl was something Vincent never wanted to hear again. Wild animal in a human form. Jasper and Elijah both read it at the same time. Vincent was happy to see that Jasper agreed with him, nodding once. Elijah burned the paper, and Jasper blew the ashes away.

"Fuck," Elijah mumbled. "And-"

"His team is in shambles," Vincent sighed. "Three dead, two in critical condition, one MIA. He's the only one who came out unscathed from the parking garage. I'm going after him alone. This is between him and I."

"Are you sure?" Elijah stood back up, and Vincent held up a hand.

"I'm thinking of taking Quinn as backup, but, Quinn, I expect you not to get involved unless I say." Vincent finished, turning to Quinn for confirmation.

"Of course," Quinn growled, bowing his head in Vincent's direction.

"Then we have work to do." Vincent gave him a small smile, and Quinn's responding grin was dangerous.

With that, Vincent and Quinn both walked out.

28

SAWYER

Is this what being dead feels like?

Sawyer stood in the abyss, only seeing the inky blackness of nothing in all directions. There was no sound, no light. Nothing to help her identify what her afterlife would be like.

"Maybe this is it," she whispered, her chest tightening in pain. She began walking aimlessly, trying to see anything.

A giggle caught her attention, and she spun.

Dark curly hair and olive-green eyes, but smaller than the man who had hunted and finally killed her. All of five years old, Henry was standing in a piece of light and smiling at her.

"Henry," Sawyer sobbed, covering her mouth.

"Sawyer!" He threw himself at her. She caught him and spun with him while tears fell down her cheeks. "I missed you!"

"I missed you, too!" She held him tightly and sank to her knees. "Oh, baby, I missed you too."

"Will you play a game with me?" He smiled at her, and she nodded. "Rock, paper, scissors!"

"Alright." She grinned, sitting with her legs crossed and keeping him in her lap.

They played, and Sawyer desperately wished this was her eternity. Just this.

Henry was always a light in her dark world, and if this was her afterlife, she would take it. She didn't deserve it, but she would fucking take it.

29

QUINN

Quinn followed Vincent through the hospital. Jon was somewhere inside, and they were going to find him. He didn't know how Vincent came to his suspicion about the man, but Quinn trusted Vincent's intelligence and judgement.

They found him in a dark room, smoking a cigarette as he stared at his critically injured team members. Magic could do wonderous things, Quinn knew that, but no healer could fix everything. What Zander had done for Sawyer had been miraculous and risky.

"Vincent," Jon's voice was rough. Quinn noted the smell of alcohol in the room as well as the smoke from the cigarette. "Red- Quinn."

"Yes," Vincent hissed. "Now might not be the best time for your nicknames."

"No, it's not," Jon sighed, shaking his head. "I don't need to guess why you are here. Tell me, how do you deal with being exactly like him?"

"I try my best to..." Vincent trailed off. "It doesn't matter. We have to talk."

"Ah, here he is. Vincent Castello, the *boy* responsible for the downfall of the Castello crime family," Jon sounded bitter, "telling me what I have to do. You know, it's not like you did that out of some sense of justice. You did it because your brother asked you to. You might fool our bosses, but you never fooled me."

"Thank you for the reminder." Vincent didn't sound thankful. "Tell me, did you betray our organization for a sense of justice or was it just arrogance?"

Quinn could only watch the exchange. Jon was going to call him Redskin, and normally, Quinn would have been in his face over it; but Vincent wanted to do this without Quinn's interference.

"Go to hell," Jon snarled. "I didn't betray the IMPO. I betrayed you. There's a difference."

"I don't really see the difference," Vincent stepped closer to Jon and leaned down to look him in eye. "No one else will either."

"You and your little pieces of shit will never be real IMPO agents." Jon stood up, causing Vincent to take a step back. "You have no idea how insulting it is to see you five running about with our fucking hard work and reputation at your disposal."

"I'm going to see if I have this timeline figured out." Vincent gave a dark chuckle. "We caught Sawyer. You have always been jealous of our success, and you hate our team on principle. You don't like that the spare heir for the Castello family created a rag-tag team of Magi to chase down the actual heir to the Castello family. None of us were even close to IMPO-worthy, in your opinion. Having Sawyer would bring us closer to catching Axel than anyone had ever thought possible, and that pissed you off. Once we cracked her secrets or used her for bait, we would have him. So, you hatched a plan."

"You little shit," Jon growled. Quinn looked the drunk, older man over. He didn't like that Jon was still armed, a pistol in his holster.

"I'm not done, so be quiet," Vincent snapped. "You were going to get Sawyer into your custody, and you contacted the Ghosts. You contacted him. What were you thinking? You were going to convince him you were handing her over in good faith, and then you would betray him. You probably thought he bought it and would gain allies in the IMPO that he'd never had before. Could have worked if you kept your location a secret, but you didn't. You told him you would have her in Atlanta, once you convinced the IMPO to schedule the meeting." Vincent took a deep breath.

Quinn crossed his arms and leaned against the wall. Humans. Deceiving, lying humans. He couldn't keep up with all of it, but he didn't need to. Vincent knew the human condition like Quinn knew the mind of his wolves. He could plan around it and adjust his ideas as people reacted and gave him information.

"So, you get us to the meeting," Vincent growled, clapping his hands slowly. Quinn had never seen him this angry. He was a little concerned. "And you underestimated my brother and his intelligence. You didn't realize that he's *always* several steps ahead of you. We sat in our pointless little meeting, and he had one of his flunkies set up the bombs. He'd already proven that he would kill dozens to get what he wanted, and he wanted Sawyer. He already had the deaths of one IMPO team under his belt. What was two more?"

"If you know everything, why-" Jon was beet-red with

fury, and Quinn was a little disgusted by the spittle flying out of his mouth.

"You got half your team killed! Innocent and good men!" Vincent roared. "You did this! I have a team member missing a fucking leg! You think I'm arrogant? I understand him. You didn't. You have no idea the kind of monster you were playing this game with, you piece of shit. And if those two don't make it, that's on your head, too. And you can live with that guilt in prison."

"I am not going to prison," Jon snarled. Quinn grabbed Vincent to protect him as Jon pulled the gun from his holster and fired.

Into his own temple.

Quinn was shaking a little. Vincent's eyes were wide in shock.

"Oh fuck," Vincent mumbled, staggering back into Quinn and away from the blown-out head of Jon Aguirre as the body fell to the floor. Agents rushed into the room, magic and weapons ready, only to stumble at the sight of Jon's body.

"He killed himself." Quinn was still a bit in shock.

"Why?" An agent lowered his gun and looked horrified.

"Because I figured out he betrayed us to Axel." Vincent tried to regain his composure, but Quinn could still hear the quiver in his voice. "Tell Ken and James. I'm..."

"Go," the agent mumbled. "You two go back to your team mates. We'll... figure this out. Stay close."

"Thank you," Vincent mumbled. Quinn followed him out, and, once they were down the hall, he grabbed Vincent and pulled him into a hug.

He held on as Vincent, for the first time in years, broke down.

"I just..." Vincent cried softly. "I just wanted to beat Axel. None of this was supposed to happen."

"I know," Quinn whispered. "I know."

"I wanted Jon to respect us, and look at what that led him to do." Vincent's voice was hoarse and emotional. "I wanted people to look at me and stop seeing *him*. And I drove Jon to killing himself... God, I'm exactly like him."

"You didn't do that," Quinn rubbed Vincent's back. He needed Elijah there. He wasn't sure he could even comprehend what he'd just witnessed. Suicide was such a human concept, and Quinn had never encountered even the idea of it before. He didn't know there could be such a strong emotion that would lead to such an awful end.

He pulled Vincent along, all the way back to Jasper's room, where agents were guarding the door.

"Jon killed himself," Quinn whispered. "You don't need to stand guard. Tell the hospital to get off lockdown."

"Roger that, Special Agent Judge," the low-ranking agent nodded and ran off to attend to something else.

Quinn told Elijah, Jasper, and Zander the same thing when he got Vincent sitting down. Vincent looked distraught, lost. Quinn didn't think it would last long, but he didn't know how to snap Vincent out of it.

"I think we should take the rest of the day just to relax," Elijah mumbled. "Fuck."

"Yeah," Jasper sighed.

30

SAWYER

"Henry!" Sawyer laughed and cuddled the boy to her. "I'm not sure what I can do!"

"But, Sawyer!" Henry laughed, trying to escape her. "You promised!"

"I know, but I'm not sure what to do about that now." She'd promised him that he could have his own cat, like her Midnight, a long time ago.

"Please?" Henry pouted up to her, and she put her forehead to his.

"I'll see what I can do," she whispered, a smile plastered to her face. She ruffled his dark curls and kissed his forehead.

If this was her heaven, then there had to be cat somewhere for Henry. She stood up and lifted him as well.

"I can walk!" Henry laughed, and she lowered him back to the ground. He grabbed her hand and grinned up at her. "There!"

"Good, I don't want to lose you." Sawyer blew him a kiss.

"You'll never lose me," Henry laughed. "You're stuck with me, Sawyer!"

She hoped so.

31

JASPER

"I'm not getting in the fucking wheelchair, Elijah. Find me some fucking crutches," Jasper growled, eyeing the chair with disgust. He was never getting in one of those things again.

"It's just until I make you a prosthetic. There's no reason for you to be stuck with crutches. They fucking hurt," Elijah groaned at the side of Jasper's bed. "If you want to go see Sawyer, you will get in the wheelchair."

"You will go get me crutches, or I will fucking crawl there," Jasper hissed. "Try me."

"Fine," Elijah threw his hands up and looked to Zander. "Will you fucking make him listen?"

"He's not getting in the wheelchair," Zander sighed. "Nothing will ever get him in one of those."

"Why the fuck not?" Elijah growled.

"Uh." Zander looked at Jasper, who glared at him and then back to the chair.

"I was stuck in one for six months when I first arrived at the orphanage," Jasper spat bitterly. "Torture for an eight-year-old."

"He'd just lost his family in the car accident." Zander whispered quickly to Elijah. Jasper could still hear him, and he wished he couldn't. "His leg was all mangled up; because his parents were non-Magi, they had sent him to a normal hospital. A healer volunteering there found him a couple days later, realized he was a Magi, and healed him as best she could. She got in touch with the WMC about a new Magi orphan but... the damage had been done. He was stuck in a wheelchair until he finished physical therapy and healing from the surgeries they had done on him."

"I'll get crutches," Elijah mumbled. "Why didn't I know this?"

"I don't like to talk about it," Jasper muttered darkly. He didn't. Zander and Sawyer were the only people who knew the full extent of it. He'd lost his parents and two older sisters, and then he was trapped in a hell of not being able to walk. He was teased and bullied his entire life, thanks to what happened.

"Where's Vincent?" Quinn asked softly. Jasper groaned. They hadn't seen him all day. After what happened with Jon the day before, he'd been off.

"I don't know," Zander grumbled. "No one does. James might, but I haven't tried him yet. He's busy with the WMC about Sawyer."

"We need to find him," Jasper sighed. He felt a little guilty now. Here he was, bitching about a wheelchair while their friend was dealing with a crisis. Jasper had gotten flashes of Vincent's dream the night before, but hadn't been willing to walk in and confront their leader. He'd been too scared of causing even more damage to Vincent's psyche.

Vincent was afraid of becoming his brother. They all knew it, had all seen the moments of self-doubt Vincent sometimes had when he got too far into the mental trench of trying to outdo and catch Axel, or any other criminal.

"Let's get Jasper up to Sawyer's room," Elijah growled, walking back in with crutches, "then I'll go after him."

It took nearly fifteen minutes for Jasper and Elijah to get the crutches sized correctly, and it took another five minutes for Jasper to start moving with them around the room naturally.

"This fucking sucks," Jasper mumbled, "but I'm not limping. So, there's a bright side."

"Bright side," Zander chuckled, nodding. "Yeah, keep looking on the bright side."

"I can make a dick joke about now only having two legs," Elijah chuckled. "Does that count?"

"God damn it," Jasper groaned with a small smile. Count on Elijah to bring dicks into it.

"You can still nail a chick from behind, since you have your thigh and knee," Elijah pointed out, grinning.

"Please," Jasper laughed, feeling his face heat up. "Please stop."

"Let's go," Zander chuckled, grinning at them.

They made the long walk to Sawyer's room, and Jasper sighed sadly at what he saw inside the room.

"Found Vincent," he whispered, looking through the small window at the door.

None of them opened the door yet, all taking peeks at the man lost in his nightmare.

Vincent was just staring at her, his eyes red and swollen. He sat in a chair at the end of her bed and just watched the unmoving Sawyer.

"Come on, guys," Elijah murmured, opening the door.

Jasper went in first as Elijah held the door for him. He

muttered a quick "Thanks," as he violated the deep thoughts of their leader.

"You're moving around." Vincent coughed, wiping his eyes. "Good."

"Yeah," Jasper said cautiously. "You okay?"

"I will be," Vincent sighed. "Just..."

"Why are you in here creeping on her?" Elijah said lightly.

"Because I think she's the only person who knows my brother as well as, if not better, than I do," Vincent said, taking a deep breath. "And she's in a coma, and I want her to wake up."

"Pushy," Elijah sighed. "Stop that. She'll wake up when she wants to."

Jasper eyed Sawyer's sleeping form. He frowned and crutched closer. She was dreaming, something that made her happy as hell.

"What's up, Jasper?" Zander raised an eyebrow at him, and Jasper shrugged.

"I don't know," Jasper said thoughtfully. "If she's not awake in a couple more days..."

"Why not try whatever you're thinking now?" Vincent asked, standing up. Jasper looked over his shoulder to Vin.

"Because she's dreaming... and she's happy," Jasper replied hoarsely. "Happier than she's ever been while asleep." He didn't want to take that away from her. He wanted to curl up next to her and absorb some of that beautiful, golden warmth radiating from her dreams. He closed his eyes and focused on it for just a moment. "Just... a couple of days and if she's not up by then, I have an idea."

"You do know about her nightmares," Quinn growled softly.

"I've known about them, yes," Jasper sighed. "Blood and

pain. Despair. Heartbreak. If she's dreaming something happy, I'm going to let her keep doing it for as long as I can. I can't... I can't ruin this for her. Not after everything else."

"Fine." Vincent sounded choked. "Fine. Two more days. If she's not awake on her own in two more days, you will do what you can to wake her up."

"I'll try." Jasper inclined his head to Vin and crutched towards an empty chair. He sank into it and rubbed his... leg. His knee hurt a little, and that actually annoyed the shit out of him. His knee had no right to hurt anymore. There was nothing attached to it, and it didn't have to do any work.

He looked at her, trying to ignore the mild ache. He eyed those lips of hers and remembered the kiss in town. The stupid, foolish thing he'd done. And his mind went to the same thing it did every time he thought about her since Vincent told him her... secret.

Axel had scarred that beautiful lip. Axel had scarred her toned and hard body. He'd filled her dreams with nightmares.

Axel had once kissed those lips and had that body in his hands.

Fury curled in his stomach. Not at her. Never at her, but at the entire situation. At *him*.

Axel had taken his fierce best friend, just walking into womanhood when he and Zander had left, and turned her into a cold, hard creature capable of unspeakable things. A woman who killed a man with no emotion in her eyes. A woman whose body bore the scars of a long fight against whatever the world had thrown at her.

He wouldn't wrench her from whatever happiness she had in her dreams. Not now. Not when he felt she hadn't known real happiness in so long.

Because Sawyer wasn't a killer when he'd left, and Jasper

wasn't sure he wanted to know how Axel turned her into one.

32

ZANDER

Zander and Vincent walked the halls quietly. Day three. Sawyer wasn't awake and neither of them could stand being cooped up in her room any longer.

"This sucks," Zander growled.

"Yes, it does," Vincent sighed. "We could always go to the Atlanta headquarters and see how James is fairing with the WMC. He hasn't called me yet."

"Let's go," Zander snarled, turning on his heel to head for the elevator. Vincent stumbled as he tried to keep Zander's pace.

"Calm down," Vincent hissed. "You aren't helping anyone being angry and agitated."

"Says the guy who won't stop beating himself up over Jon," Zander snapped and immediately felt guilty as he saw Vincent's eyes go hard. "Shit, Vin, I'm sorry."

"Get in the fucking elevator," Vin growled as the door opened.

They made the entire trip in silence after that. Zander

ran a hand through his hair, realizing he needed a haircut. It was falling over his eyes and ears in an annoying way.

Such a stupid thing for him to notice. Everything seemed so changed since the last time he even thought about his unruly red hair. Since his last normal thing, like a haircut. He half wondered if their house was still the same. It all seemed like so long ago and in a different reality.

"I thought catching him would fix everything," Vincent muttered bitterly. Zander raised an eyebrow.

"You knew better," Zander said softly. "You might not want to admit it, but you knew better."

"After we talk to James..." Vincent trailed off and then continued after a moment. "After we talk to James, will you accompany me to see him?"

"Of course, my brother," Zander gave him a pat on the shoulder. Vincent was pulling them into a parking spot, and once he parked the Range Rover, Zander jumped out.

He was stir-crazy. He felt like shit and looked like hell, but he still wanted to do something. Anything.

He bounced around a little as he and Vincent walked into the building. They waved to the receptionist and passed her without signing in. They weren't visitors who needed to check in with anyone. As Special Agents, they pretty much had free run wherever they were, except New York's Main Headquarters.

"Where is he?" Vincent muttered thoughtfully.

"Conference room?" Zander shrugged.

"We'll try that." Vincent turned them down a hallway that Zander never used. Well, Zander avoided this building like the plague. All the lower ranking agents tended to look at him like he was supposed to be in a cell, which was funny since he had never done something seriously criminal.

It was kind of Zander's fault. He was the one with inch-wide gauges and ink all over him. They didn't even know about the piercings underneath his clothing. They didn't need to know about those. Those wouldn't help his case.

Vincent knocked twice, then stepped into the conference room. Zander followed him, and they saw James glaring at some papers before he looked up at them.

"We were tired of the stuffy hospital," Vincent told him quickly. "We wanted to see what you were up too."

"It's not going well," James informed them, angry at something. "If it weren't for her original deal with them, they wouldn't let her out of the hospital alive. They are trying to spin in that she was knowingly leading the IMPO agents to their deaths."

Zander froze and felt his temper curl up like a pit of snakes in the bottom of his stomach.

"Fuck them," Zander snarled, causing James to startle. "You fix this, James."

"I'm not sure I can, son," James sighed. "This is a mess. This has always been a mess."

"Clean it up." Zander stepped closer, ignoring Vincent, who tried to hold him. "That's your fucking job."

"Actually, it's not my job," James snapped. "My job is to act as a go between for you and the people you answer to. This team just has a lot of fucking messes that you need some help cleaning up. Since I let Vincent make this team and convinced the WMC to allow him to do so, I am more than willing to help, but it's not my job."

"If you fail to convince them?" Vincent asked softly.

"She won't leave that hospital alive," James mumbled, looking back down at the papers on the table.

"Yes, she will," Zander growled.

"How?" James narrowed his eyes on him. "How would that happen?"

"If they don't agree to the plan, Sawyer is going to disappear," Zander told him softly. Vincent looked at him and nodded. He knew Vincent would be on his side. "If they go after her, our team will help her hide, and no one will ever see her again. We'll go rogue if we have too."

"I can't tell them that," James muttered, paling. "You can't throw that at their feet. There's a real possibility they will call your bluff, Zander."

"It's not a bluff," Zander said, smiling. "You think we can't do it? With Vincent's intelligence? With Quinn's raw power? With the entire team working together for that goal? I fucking dare them to see how far I'll go to keep her alive."

"Tell them," Vincent whispered. "Let them know this isn't a game. We're going to have her on our team, and that's the end of it. If we don't get her, they lose all of us."

"Get out of here," James sighed. "I'll call them back now. I hope you boys know what you're doing."

Zander knew exactly what he was doing. He didn't almost kill himself to keep her alive just for those high and mighty fucks to steal her away.

Vincent pulled him from the room and down the hallway.

"Zander, you just signed us up to go to war with the World Magi Council," Vincent hissed. "What the fuck?"

"You could have disagreed with me." Zander pushed him. "Why didn't you?"

"Because I agree with you, but the rest of the team might not," Vincent shoved him back.

Zander scoffed. They would all be just fine with what he'd done. Even Jasper. Especially Jasper, their little golden boy. If he was willing to work past her being Shadow, then he would help keep her alive if the WMC didn't honor their half of the agreement.

"Let's go see your brother," Zander said after a long moment of silence.

"Let's," Vincent said acidly. The poison dripping from that word sliced through Zander.

They found the elevator down to the dark cells where prisoners were kept until they could be moved. For three days, Zander knew that no one had talked to Axel. No contact whatsoever. Zander knew that also meant Axel hadn't even had something to eat. It was cruel thing, but it was their world. A Magi criminal had no rights, except the ones afforded to them by their captors—and Axel's captors afforded him none. Zander didn't feel guilty about that.

His cell was the last one and only his name, written on a notecard, gave away his location.

Zander met Vincent's eyes. Was he ready for this? Was he ready to meet his brother for one final conversation? Zander knew this was the last time Vincent would ever speak to Axel.

This was goodbye, and that's why Vincent wanted someone with him.

"Open it," Vincent whispered. "Stand at the back of the room."

"Roger that," Zander whispered back, punching the code needed into the small keypad next to the door. It beeped, and a red light flashed, alerting everyone in Prisoner Holding that a cell was being momentarily opened. It also alerted someone to wait at the door to let them out.

Vincent slid in first and Zander followed him closely. The door closed soundlessly behind them. They were now locked in with Axel.

Zander looked at the prim and proper Italian sitting silently on the tiny cot he had been issued. Tension made the air vibrate, and Zander was thankful for the collar on

Axel—the inhibitor prisoners were given. The only way to remove it was to have the key... or get beheaded, a standard method for Magi execution.

"Vinny." Axel sounded like he was happy to see his younger brother, but Zander saw something dangerous in his eyes.

"Antonio," Vincent said, straightening his spine, "I've come to say goodbye."

"Ah, yes," Axel sighed, waving a hand dismissively. "Of course you have. You always were just a bit sentimental."

"At least he had the balls to do it," Zander mumbled.

"Excuse me?" Axel snapped, and Zander nearly laughed. Vincent said it the exact same way.

"You tried to kill him without even showing up." Zander shrugged. "Vincent at least has the balls to come to his shitty brother and say goodbye."

"You'll let him talk to me like that?" Axel was insulted, that much was obvious.

"He's more of a brother to me than you are." Vincent crossed his arms as he laid out that truth for Axel. It warmed Zander's heart a little. "Moreover, he's right. You tried to blow me and my team into the stars without even a tiny warning it was going to happen."

"Missy always did have a penchant for explosions," Axel chuckled. "If it helps, it really hurt to finally have to make that decision. I just couldn't leave Sawyer in your care. She had to die, you see."

"Oh... should we tell him?" Zander raised an eyebrow at Vincent, who gave a small smile. Should they rip Axel's only perceived-victory away from him?

"She's not dead," Vincent said to his brother with that same, small smile. "She's resting at the hospital. Zander, here, was able to put her back together. And I know who she is."

"Always a surprise," Axel growled. "You always have some surprise up your sleeve. Joining the IMPO, building this team, keeping Sawyer among the living. Fine. I'll rest easy knowing she'll spend the rest of her miserable life haunted by me and, most likely, in the cell next to mine until we're both executed. I can live with that." Axel turned his head to Zander and that made Zander uncomfortable. "Tell me. What did she have to do in those three or four short weeks to gain such... devotion from you to save her life? She's not exactly the most likable person. I would know, I used to fuck her on a regular basis."

"I grew up with her," Zander growled before Vincent could gesture for him to not say anything.

"Oh?" Axel looked pleased by that. "You are one of those little boys who ran off to the IMAS? Really? And the Magi community shrinks. Were you the quiet one?" Axel looked thoughtful for a moment. "No, *you* must be the one she lost her virginity to. You'll be happy to hear that I've trained her for the bed fairly well. If you convince her to get between the sheets with you, she'll blow your fucking mind, I promise. You should do it before I tell everyone who she is though. She probably won't live very long after that."

Zander snarled and went for Axel's neck after that. No one talked about Sawyer like that. No one. Vincent grabbed him around the waist and threw him back. Zander went to charge again when he saw Vincent connect a right hook on Axel's left eye.

"You little twerp," Axel hissed, regaining his composure from the hit.

"Shut the fuck up about her, Antonio." Vincent shoved his brother to his back.

"Stop fucking calling me that." Axel sat up again, glaring at Vin. Zander was still trying to calm down from Axel's blatant disrespect for Sawyer.

"Why? It's the name our father gave you," Vincent said mildly.

"Our father was a fucking failure, we both know that. Why should I use the name a man like him gave me?"

"If there's one thing I've learned, Antonio, it's 'Once a Castello, always a Castello'. You might be known as the infamous Axel, but to me, you will always be shy Antonio, the boy who couldn't live up to our father's expectations."

Zander had always found it a little amusing in a fucked-up way, the story of Antonio and Vincent, the heirs to the Castello empire. Axel became one of the greatest criminals known in their time when he'd started out as a kid who couldn't prove himself. Only a year older than Vincent, his abilities had come in two years *after* Vincent's. Vincent had excelled in the Castello family, the rising star of the family who turned against the lifestyle at the last moment.

"Go to Hell," Axel snarled.

"I'm already there," Vincent whispered. "I've been there since the day you convinced me to kill him for you. Good bye, Antonio."

"You'll come crawling back," Axel hissed malevolently. "I'm the only family you have left."

"You're my brother but... you're not my family." Vincent sighed. "You haven't been for years. Come on, Zander."

"Vincent!" Axel stood up with a shout. Someone on the other side of the door opened it for them, and Zander let Vincent leave first. Zander slammed the door shut as Axel began to stomp over. "VINCENT!"

They walked away, letting Axel's screams become distant.

"Did you find what you were looking for in there?" Zander asked softly.

"No," Vincent sighed.

"What *were* you looking for?" Zander frowned in confusion.

"I don't know." Vincent's answer was strangled. "I don't know."

33

JASPER

"**D**o it," Vincent commanded sharply. "She's had four days. We need her up."

Jasper winced and looked to the motionless form. He hadn't told them, but he knew what was wrong with her. She was just lost in her own subconscious, probably living out something that was better than reality.

And now they were all looking at him to force her out of it. They had to wrench her away from that beautiful happiness of whatever dream she was in because things were getting time-sensitive. The WMC was demanding that she finally reveal everything she knew, and that meant the team needed to know everything. They couldn't get that information if she was asleep.

Zander and Vincent had let the rest of them know what Zander had done to James, the position the reckless redhead had put them in. Jasper had agreed immediately. He didn't need to think about it. Elijah had, after only a second of thought. Quinn's terms hadn't changed. Jasper didn't know why he was obsessed with the little-boy whose face couldn't be seen and the black runt cat, but it was obvious to all of them that he was.

"Jasper," Zander pleaded, "please."

"Fine," Jasper sighed. "It might take time, so be prepared to watch us sleep for a little while."

He leaned back in the uncomfortable hospital chair and closed his eyes. Dream-walking required an unnatural sleep, one brought on by his own magic. He was slightly lucid, but in his own mind, and he reached out towards Sawyer's, letting her dream suck him in.

THE FIRST THING he noticed was the dark. He was in a spotlight, but the rest of the world was pitch black; so dark that nothing escaped it. He stared off into the darkness and wondered how in the hell this was supposed to be a happy dream. He looked down and noticed he was whole. Well, that was nice of her. He was there in her image of him, and she still thought of him as a whole man. As far as she knew, he was.

"Jasper?" Sawyer's broken voice flooded through him, and he turned to her. Her eyes were wide, and he gave her a genuine smile. Here, she had no scars. None at all. There was no evidence on her body that she had fought the battles he knew haunted her.

"Sawyer," he started but she began shaking her head, backing away from him. "Sawyer?"

"Not you too," she sobbed, covering her mouth. "No... I was so sure you and Zander survived. So sure that all of you did."

Oh, shit. Jasper's eyes went wide. She thought she was *dead*. Oh, fuck.

"Sawyer!" A child's voice pierced the dark. That's when Jasper realized that he was spotlighted but... Sawyer wasn't. She was shadowed and dark. He watched her eyes light up just a little as she caught a jumping child, who was spotlighted like himself.

"Henry!" She laughed, swinging him around.

"Have you found me a kitten, yet?" He giggled, tugging on her hair.

"No, not yet, but maybe my friend Jasper will help?" She raised an eyebrow at him, and Jasper felt his heart fall out at the sight of the little boy. Henry.

Henry looked like Vincent. Henry looked like *Axel*. The Castello stamp was prominent on the child's features. Those dark curls, the olive skin, and the olive-green eyes.

Was he... hers?

Jasper had to end this. No wonder she had locked herself in her mind. She had no idea she could wake up. She was in her mind, living a fantasy with this little boy. And if she thought she was dead... that meant Henry was probably dead, both in her dreams and outside of them.

He shook his head, trying to clear that thought. He focused on the boy and did something that he knew would break her, but it had to be done.

He forced Henry to stop existing. The child faded away, and Jasper changed their location to the hospital room where they were both sleeping.

"What?" Sawyer gasped. "Henry? Where did he go? Where are we? Jasper, what happened?"

"Sawyer, look around you," Jasper whispered. He grabbed her shoulders and turned her slowly around the mental landscape he'd created. "This is a dream Sawyer, not the afterlife."

"No," Sawyer snapped. "I died! Bring back Henry! Bring him back!" She tried to shake him off.

"Sawyer, I'm dream-walking. I am not dead," Jasper hissed as he saw the tears form in her eyes, "and neither are you." He forced her to look at herself lying in the hospital bed. He'd spent long enough in the room to memorize every facet of it. Every little piece to an exact detail. He forced her to look at him in the chair, sleeping, trying to reach her.

"No..." Sawyer began to collapse. "Henry..."

"You have other people who need you, Sawyer," Jasper groaned desperately as he held her up. "Charlie and Liam. Jessie. Your other countless students that you saved. They need you. The team? They need you. Zander and I, we need you. You can't stay here, Sawyer. You have to wake up."

"Why?" Her voice broke. "Why can't it just be over?"

"Because I'm not ready for it to be over," he whispered into her ear. "Because I know you were once a dangerous assassin, and I'm not going to let that blind me to you. You have to wake up. It's not over yet. Not for you. Not for any of us."

She cried into his shoulder, and slammed a fist into his chest as the dream faded. He felt the tug of his own mind, calling him because he couldn't stay in hers as she woke up.

He left her mind and reentered his own, blinking into the world of those who were alive and awake.

He couldn't ignore his broken heart, though.

Who was Henry?

34

SAWYER

Sawyer gasped. Bright lights blinded her as she found herself in the very bed that Jasper had shown her. She stared at the ceiling, tears in her eyes.

Henry.

He was still dead and here she was, still alive.

"Sawyer?" Zander sounded mystified. She rolled her head towards his voice and found him at her bedside.

"Zander," she whispered, her voice hoarse.

"Why are you crying?" he asked, reaching out to wipe a tear of her cheek.

"It doesn't matter," she sighed, leaning away from his touch. "So..."

"You've been asleep for four days," Vincent told her from a seat at a small table across the room, "and we need to have a long discussion."

She knew that. Not how long she'd been asleep, but that a talk was coming once she realized she wasn't dead. She'd told him that she was Shadow the last time they spoke. Now it was time for her to deal with that decision.

"We need to know everything," Zander whispered

She forced herself to sit up and meet her new reality.

"Then, I think a little field trip is in order," she mumbled. "Where are we?"

"Atlanta," Elijah answered her, and she nodded slowly.

"We won't even have to leave the city," she tried to say, her dry throat burning from the effort of all the talking she was doing.

"Right now?" Vincent frowned at her.

"It's... important to the... information you want." She couldn't find a better way to phrase it.

"You still need time to heal," Zander growled softly. "Just..."

"I'm fine," she said, shaking her head. She turned and put her feet on the floor. She glared at the IVs she had in her arm and began pulling them out, causing several of the guys to give strangled and abrupt noises. Zander tried to stop her, but she swatted him away. "I'm not going to die with these out, am I?"

"No, but-"

"Then they are coming out," she hissed weakly, yanking the last one from her arm. She looked down and groaned. A hospital gown. "Do I have anything to wear?"

"Yeah," Elijah began shuffling around in bags near him and Vincent. When he couldn't find what he wanted, he just dropped the bags on the bed next to her. "Somewhere in there."

"Can I have the room?" she asked, standing up shakily. Four days of bedrest had made her legs stiff, but she could manage.

"Sadly, no," Vincent mumbled, shaking his head.

She sighed and looked to her left wrist. They hadn't put the bracelet back on her, so that was something.

She pushed Zander further away and pulled off the

annoying hospital gown. She had underwear on, at least. No bra, but she figured it wasn't something they would point out at that moment. Her mind was elsewhere as she searched for clothing.

She pulled on a simple pair of grey sweats, a sports bra, and a black tank top. That would have to work.

"Where are we going?" Jasper asked, still seated. She glanced at him as she found socks and tennis shoes.

Her eyes fell on his leg, and she felt her blood run a little cold. He must have noticed where she was looking because he shrugged.

"It happened during the fight," he sighed. "After all of this, I'll tell you more. It's crutches for me for a little while."

After this. She knew that after this was prison. That fact that he would visit her astounded her.

"Only because you wouldn't use a wheelchair," Elijah muttered, and Sawyer rolled her eyes.

"I could have told you he wouldn't submit to a wheel-chair," she mumbled.

"You weren't awake, little lady. Zander had to tell me." Elijah eyed her, and she narrowed her eyes on him.

Guilt was bubbling up in her. Jasper was maimed because of her, because of what she was about to tell them.

"So, what happened while I was out?" She stretched slowly. "Tell me as I take you on this little field trip."

"Will you try to run?" Vincent asked her, now waiting at the door.

"There's no reason for me to run anymore. You know I'm Shadow. Now you need to know why, and I plan on telling you that." She walked up to him and raised her chin a little to look him in the eye.

She wasn't going to be a coward. She'd thrown her cards

on the table, come what may. She was alive, and it was time to tell her story.

Her story. Midnight's story. Henry's story. They all had a little claim on it.

"Alright, where are we going?" Vincent pressed as she waited for him to let them all out of the hospital room.

"To a bank with a safety deposit box that you'll find... interesting." She lifted her shoulders in another shrug. "Georgia's Own. I'll need to have the box drilled open, though, since I purposefully lost the key a long time ago... I'm going to need to borrow some cash."

"Borrow?" Elijah chuckled. "You don't have any money, so you mean you just need some money."

"I have money at y'alls house, cash I stashed before you pulled me out of New York," she mumbled, waving her hand around to dismiss the topic.

"I'll pay," Vincent said before any of the guys could say anything. "We'll take you."

"Thank you," she sighed.

They fell in around her as they walked silently out of the hospital. She was put into a Range Rover with a guy on each side of her. Quinn took the front seat while Vincent drove. Zander and Jasper flanked her, and she leaned back to get comfortable. This was so much different than the last ride she'd taken with them.

"Jon Aguirre betrayed us, hoping to catch Axel himself, using you as bait," Vincent told her as they drove. "He killed himself when I confronted him."

She rubbed her face at that piece of news, but Vincent wasn't done with her.

"Three of his teammates were dead in the initial explosions. They had triggered the bombs and stood no chance.

Two more passed away yesterday. One is still MIA. David Hamble."

"He's dead somewhere out there," she groaned. She should have been surprised or shocked by the state of the other IMPO team, but she really wasn't. She could relate, truthfully. She'd stood on the ledge in the aftermath of Axel's cruelty and cunning more times than she could count. She just never jumped, the sole difference between her and Jon Aguirre. Not even Charlie could stop her from trying once or twice though, not until she stumbled on Liam and started that chapter of her life. "Missy was pretending to be him that day."

"Missy?" Jasper frowned at her. She nodded slowly.

"I killed her in the hangar bay before you guys showed up. She is... she was a Doppler. I'm a little irked I didn't realize it was her in the office." She rubbed her forehead.

"As a Doppler, you'd never be able to tell, so I'm not sure why you're beating yourself up over that," Jasper whispered. She saw Quinn looking at her with interest. He had some fascination with the Legends, and with a Druid for a mother, she couldn't blame him.

"Incorrect," she said to Jasper. "A Doppler can completely mimic anyone, true, but they can't remove their own disfigurements. Missy had a scar that ran from her left ear all the way down her neck. It was present in any form she took."

"How do you know that?" Quinn was now frowning at her.

"Because I gave her the scar." Sawyer chuckled bitterly. "She and I never liked each other... My relationship with Missy isn't important to any of this, though. Either way, someday, you may find David's body. If she took his place, then she definitely killed him to do so."

"So, Jon got his entire team killed," Vincent said with a bite. "After that... We have Axel, Talyn, and Toni in custody. Felix got away, and we recovered Colt's body. We haven't found Missy's body, but they are still sifting through the wreckage of the building."

"Well," she took a deep breath, "what about me?"

"That depends on what we are about to learn," Vincent said quietly.

No one said anything after that.

IT TOOK NEARLY an hour for the bank to break open her safety deposit box. She had paid for it ten years out when she bought it; and every year, she paid another ten years out so there had been no chance of them removing her things. She had a standing agreement with whoever was manager to allow her access at any time if she ever needed to get her things.

She had never expected to come back though.

They all stood in a tiny room while the manager brought in chairs for them. Vincent and Elijah set up a camera to record what she was about to tell them. They said it was so she didn't need to repeat it to the WMC, but she wasn't sure why it was important. She wasn't going to try to escape her punishment.

She was *tired*. For the first time in Sawyer's life, she was *just tired*—exhausted by carrying it around. She intended to pass these secrets and shadows, the nightmares she carried, onto the team and let them do with her what they would.

"You may begin," Vincent whispered, taking a seat. She didn't sit. She wanted to be on her feet for this.

"Don't... don't interrupt me once I get started," she told

them as she slowly opened the box. "I'm not sure... I'm not sure I'll be able to keep going if you stop me. I've never told this story when I was sober or in good physical condition."

"You've told it before?" Jasper frowned at her.

"Yes," she whispered in the lowest voice she could muster. "Just once, and over a period of months. Never all at once like this."

"Okay," Vincent agreed, just as quiet as her.

"Wait," Quinn growled, shuffling around. "I want to know something before this starts."

She watched him place a picture on the table and her heart cracked a little more. She couldn't take much more of this pain. Physical pain was easy, but the heart-wrenching emotional pain was going to slowly kill her. It festered in her soul.

"The boy's name was Henry," she choked out, "and the cat's name was Midnight. And to tell you more about them, Quinn, you'll need to hear the full story."

"Okay." Quinn nodded and leaned back, taking the picture with him. She resisted the urge to tell him to give it to Vincent. She was only able to do so because she knew Vincent would have no idea what that picture was about to mean to him.

35

SAWYER

"On June 10th, 2008," Sawyer began with a whisper, "Zander and Jasper left for the IMAS. You might think that's a weird starting point, but I see that day as the beginning of the end of my life. I was fifteen. On January 13th, 2009, my abilities manifested, and I was... the happiest person in the world. I had cool magic, and I thought I would one day rule the world in that stupid way teenagers always tend to think they will. Sixteen-year-olds tend to have a big head when they learn they can sublimate and blink and do all sorts of cool shit. On January 15th, the Reader came, did my official reading, and Registered me as a Magi. Little did I know that he was dirty."

It happened. Readers could be bribed just like any other Magi. They were just Magi, and Magi were only human.

"On January 30th, I was adopted by the fucking old man who proceeded to pull me out of school and cut me off from any form of communication. As a minor, I knew escaping would only lead to being chased and caught. I figured I could suffer through it, turn eighteen, and go find you two." She jerked her head towards Jasper and Zander. "That's why

I stopped replying to whatever letters you may have sent. I never got them."

"It was March 5th, 2009 when I met Axel. My adopted parent was throwing a party. A dress was bought for me and I wore it. And Axel proceeded to sweep me off my feet. Oh, he promised me the world, and I ate it up, already falling prey to the loneliness of being cut off from the world I had known. It had all been a set-up. I was adopted and being recruited, but I didn't know that at the time. I was sixteen, and this gorgeous man wanted me. The lanky, not-white girl who was taller than all the other boys. I ignored that he was older than me. He must have been... twenty at the time?" She considered that for a moment. He had already been a very powerful man at only twenty. She wouldn't have believed it, but then she thought of herself at twenty and it became more plausible.

"Either way, he swept me away, and I never saw the asshole who adopted me again. I don't even have a GED, can you believe that?" She gave a dark chuckle, but no one else did. They must have already known. They probably did. "He taught me how to be thief, and that was just fun. I'll be honest. I enjoyed being a thief and that worked for a while. I even had my Midnight, my wonderful little bonded animal."

"You said..." Quinn frowned at her. She would let his interruption slide. She had lied to them.

"Yes, I had a bonded animal. I lied to you all about it. She's... she's hard to talk about, hard to remember," she told him. "Midnight, the little black house cat with yellow eyes. And life was good for a time. Axel kept me away from his real empire, and I just had fun with him. We had fun, traveling the world, planning my heists. Then, on October 20th, 2010, an assassin attacked. We were in bed," she heard a strangle sound at that comment, "and he'd come to kill

Axel. He was able to get a good hit in, too. The logistics don't matter so I'll cut to the chase. I saved Axel's life, and killed the guy before he could kill Axel. None of this would have happened if I hadn't been an eighteen-year-old fool madly in love with a man that I didn't know was a monster, yet."

She spent many nights wondering what her life would be like if she had run for it like the assassin had told her—if she had let him kill Axel, who could barely do his magic when he was in pain. What-ifs were a waste of time, she knew that, but she wondered nonetheless.

"How do you remember the exact dates?" Vincent asked quietly. He was asking because this probably seemed practiced. It wasn't.

"Because I can't seem to forget them, no matter how hard I try," she sighed. "Continuing on. Axel realized I had potential to take a more... aggressive role in his empire. He trained me to fight, had the other Ghosts help. But when he told me to kill someone for him, I resisted. He took Midnight from me and held her hostage. I killed who he told me to, and he promised that if I just did as he asked, nothing had to really change. That was hit number one. January 2011. I tried to resist the second hit, but that only got me beaten. I did it swiftly, realizing he would never take no for an answer. And the pain I felt come from Midnight was a sharp reminder that someone's life was at stake if I didn't do as he asked."

"Holy shit," Elijah breathed. "He tortured your bonded animal."

"Constantly," she whispered bitterly. "Well, the ride isn't over, yet, because on October 5th, 2011, he came home with a four-year-old boy named Henry." She met Vincent's eyes and took a shuddering breath. "His son—with a prostitute."

Not a single sound. She watched Vincent process that he was, at one point, an uncle and never knew it.

"No," Jasper gasped. "No."

The second 'no' was one from a broken man. She blinked back tears, remembering what Jasper had seen in her dreams, and what she had thought. He knew.

"Shh, Jasper," she pleaded. She needed to finish this before she broke. "Let me continue."

"Please do," Vincent growled.

"Henry was given to me, and I was told to care for him. When Axel asked me to do another hit a few months later, I wouldn't do it. I wouldn't kill people and raise his child. I wasn't strong enough to cuddle a child with hands that killed people. I was a stupid nineteen-year-old who thought, maybe, Axel would care about that. He didn't. In seconds, he proved that nothing was sacred. With a single text, Midnight was killed, and Henry was on the chopping block. From that point on, for the three jobs I did in 2012, I did them without complaint. My only goal on this earth was to keep that innocent child alive."

"Why did he kill Midnight?" Quinn snarled. "Why?"

"Because Axel had no use for two pieces of collateral over me. He knew I had fallen for Henry, and Midnight was more expendable to him." Sawyer forced the words out. Anger bubbled up in her, cold rage. Dark rage. A rage that had led her to killing without mercy or guilt. "And you know what? I fucking failed. I did everything he wanted, including agreeing to marry his fucking ass. I let him violate my body, all to keep Henry safe, happy, and away from Axel's brand of *love*. He got pissy one night, and I offered myself for the beat down I knew he wanted to give. He chopped off my finger to take the stupid ring back. And Henry," her voice broke, "I think Henry wanted to help me."

"Sawyer." Zander's voice was full of emotions that Sawyer didn't want to hear.

"Henry tried to stop his daddy from hurting his Sawyer, and Axel... flung him across the room without thinking." Sawyer swayed at the memory as it flooded back to her. A dent in the wall. A pool of blood forming on the floor. She nearly dropped to the floor, but someone was holding her up. She didn't know who. "And Axel took his body from me and left. I, to this day, can't tell you where he buried him or if he even did. I wish I could, Vincent. He's was such a sweet boy. And I tried. I'm sorry. I'm so sorry."

She was pulled into a chest and sobbed, clinging to the body that pressed to her own. Finally, she pushed away and stumbled back into the table. She looked to see who had held her, and it was Vincent. Vincent. Seeing him brought another wave of tears that she could barely hold back.

"Go sit down," she growled, pointing wildly, hoping it was towards his seat. Of all of the people who could have come to comfort her, he was the one who could completely break her.

"Sawyer-" he whispered.

"Go," she snapped. "*I'm not done yet.*" She hoped those words were as forceful as she intended them to be. "After Henry... Axel didn't come back. It was the only time since I had left with him at sixteen that he and I didn't live together. He sent Colt to watch me. And after picking up the pieces of my broken heart, I started making my plans to get revenge. Yes. Revenge. And that blew up in my fucking face. You know the story from there," she hissed. "You know the story of how Shadow died."

"How many people have you killed?" Jasper asked.

"Nine," she growled. "The assassin. Hits one through five. Liam's father. Missy. Colt. Don't expect me to remember the names of those who Axel told me to kill. I didn't care then, and never committed them memory. I can remember every piece of each of those kills. I can see their eyes as they died, but fuck me, I've never been able to remember their goddamn names."

"Alright, Sawyer," Elijah stood up slowly. "Calm down."

"I am calm." She was breathing hard. Her body was overloaded with too much pain, too much regret and guilt.

"No, you aren't," he said as he leaned over the table and tapped the box. "Why don't you tell us about the stuff in the box."

"It my gear. Don't touch it. Most of it's enchanted, and some of it will kill anyone who doesn't know how to properly use it." She grabbed one side of the box and tipped it, spilling its content onto the table. Daggers, her kukri, a black, emotionless mask. Throwing daggers, and all manner of other sharp objects. "I left them here in Atlanta, thinking I could bury them with the rest of my past. Like the memory of Jasper and Zander."

She let the silence stretch out before adding one more thing.

"This is why I didn't go looking for you, Jasper," she sighed. "This is why."

"I understand," he whispered.

"Sawyer," Vincent murmured. "I have an important question for you."

"Yes?" She looked to him. He never did go back to his seat, standing much too close to her. His mere presence and those fucking eyes brought back the pain. Why hadn't she noticed before? Why hadn't she realized he was a fucking Castello, at the very least? She'd grown soft in New York. He mumbled how he could ask it later.

New York. Now, that was a distant memory. She wanted

to go back so badly, but that seemed like a far-off dream, now. A life Sawyer was never supposed to have and would never have again.

She finally collapsed into her seat, feeling drained.

She'd done it. She'd finally told her story in its entirety. She had stepped out of the dark, and now she had to deal with her new reality in the harsh light of truth.

She couldn't even begin to process her feelings about it.

I ̃T WAS the longest hour of silence she'd ever experienced. No one moved or spoke. She couldn't hear what was going on out in other areas of the bank, and she almost couldn't believe that the world was still chugging along out there.

It was, though. Out there, the world turned, and people moved on with their lives with no idea what horrors could possibly meet them in the dark.

"I should tell you what all of this is," Sawyer sighed, waving a weak hand towards the things she had dumped on the table.

"I think most of it is pretty obvious," Elijah said, and Sawyer felt a wave of guilt at the complete lack of happiness he displayed. Elijah was always happy.

But she knew how hard it was to be happy when the conversation turned to dead children, abuse, and murder.

"The daggers all have strengthening enchantments, allowing them to cut through things they shouldn't be able to," she began, steeling herself. She took on a professional tone, shoving the old memories back into their box in her mind where she wouldn't be overwhelmed by them.

"With a strong enough throw they can be embedded into things like... concrete," Elijah whispered.

"Yeah," she mumbled, picking one up and running a finger over the edge. "Not only did I cleanse them once a week to remove my own magical signature, I also had them enchanted to pick up less of my magic, so it wasn't a pain to deal with."

"And the mask?" Jasper pointed. She heard the shake in his voice and, when she looked at him, she saw how pale he was. She flicked a look at Zander. He was also pale and he held the tell-tale appearance of someone who had recently used life force to do magic. Absentmindedly, she touched her abdomen. She'd noticed the new scar. He had saved her life. She would need to... thank him for it eventually.

"The mask is special," she whispered, reaching out to touch it. And it reacted to her, sending tingles into her fingers, asking for permission to have something from her. "It's complicated."

"It's old," Elijah whispered.

"Very, and complex in its use," she sighed. "Now... isn't the time for a show and tell on how it works."

"We'll worry about it later," Vincent said calmly. She eyed him carefully and saw the red eyes he sported, as if he were about to fall apart.

"Yeah," she whispered. "What are you going to do with me?"

"Take you home," Zander croaked, standing up slowly. "You're still in our custody."

36

SAWYER

The next two days were the longest of her life. She was subjected to a thousand questions by them, and they wrote her answers word for word.

She didn't understand what was going on.

And, in spite of it all, she just didn't care.

She waited for Vincent in his office, having been told she needed to be there, but he wasn't. She heard the door knob turn and glanced over her shoulder to see him.

They had been avoiding each other. For good reason. Sawyer wasn't sure what to say to him, and she was certain he wasn't sure what to say to her. The ghost of his nephew stood between them, his name always on her tongue when she saw Vincent. Did he want to know about Henry? Would he one day visit her in prison and ask her to tell stories about the sweet child, nothing like his father or his uncle?

"How are you?" she asked softly.

"Busy," he replied, smoothly sitting down in his chair behind the ornate wooden desk. He placed a file on the desk. She nearly snorted. Him and his files. "Sawyer, you made a deal with the WMC over four years ago. If I told you that they would honor it, would you accept it? With some changes?"

"Depends on the changes," she sighed, leaning back in her seat. Jesus. Virgin Mary. Zeus. Bastet. If there were any gods listening, Sawyer didn't know whether to thank them or curse them.

"Here," Vincent whispered, pushing the file closer to her. She reached out and took it. She flipped it open without preamble. "How do you do it?"

"Do what?" she asked without looking up to him. She read over the papers inside with care.

"How do you keep moving forward? After everything is said and done, how do you keep putting one foot in front of the other?"

She closed the file and looked up at him. The pain was obvious in his eyes now, and she turned away from him and toward the only window in the room. Outside, it was bright and sunny. One day she would appreciate that again, but that day was not today.

"I remind myself that I can't change anything that's already done," she said in a hushed tone. "I can only change my future. Not my past."

"That's it?" he pressed, and she heard an edge of desperation in it.

"It will always haunt me," she sighed, placing the file back on the desk. "But that's all it can do. Haunt me. And it will do so, without mercy, for the rest of my life, but I can continue on. Memories can't kill me, and I can do whatever is in my power to never live through similar experiences. Sometimes it works, sometimes it doesn't."

"What do you think?" Vincent nodded down to the file, dropping the topic with an abruptness that didn't surprise Sawyer.

Five years completely at the World Magi Council's disposal for whatever task they put forth at any point. Probationary IMPO agent. Guarded at all times. Reports directly to the Council. Any sort of screw ups would ruin it all.

If she accepted, she would be dragged out of the darkness. The world would know that Sawyer Matthews and Shadow were the same person and that she was very much alive. Her life of shadows would become one of hard work and sweat and, she hoped, a bit of redemption.

She looked back out the window. Maybe at the end of this new chapter of her life, she would learn to truly enjoy the sun again, and not just need it to warm her weary bones.

"I, Sawyer Matthews, hereby declare that I accept the terms set forth by the World Magi Council in regard to my freedom and the conditions of my pardon."

$\sim$

ABILITIES

Note:

It's important to remember that every Magi is unique. Two Magi could have the same ability and use them in different ways due to their personal strength levels.

Example: Sawyer can walk through a thick wall with Phasing but another Magi may only be able to pass through a thin door and push an arm through a window for a short time.

Ranking Code

Common- C, Uncommon-U, Rare-R, Mythic- M

- Air Manipulation-C- The ability to manipulate the element of air or wind.
- Animal bonds-C- The ability to bond with one to five animals. A person with this ability can feel emotional currents of the animal and use the animal's senses by inserting themselves in the animal.
- Animation-C- The ability to make inanimate

objects do tasks for time periods. I.e. Dancing brooms

- Blinking-U- The ability to teleport short distances (10-20 feet) within eyesight.
- Cloaking-U- The ability to become invisible.
- Dream walking-U- The ability to walk through the dreams of others and go through the person's subconscious to reveal secrets and memories to the person.
- Earth Manipulation-C- The ability to manipulate the element of earth.
- Elemental Control-M- The ability to manipulate all elements and all combinations of them.
- Enchanting-C- The ability to enchant physical objects with specific properties, such as never losing a sharp edge for a blade.
- Fire Manipulation-C- The ability to manipulate the element of fire.
- Healing-C- The ability to heal physical wounds.
- Illusions-U- The ability to alter an individual's perception of reality.
- Magnetic Manipulation-U- The ability to control or generate magnetic fields, normally a very weak ability.
- Naturalism-C- The ability to control the growth of plant life and identify plants' properties.
- Petrification-R- The ability to freeze a person's movement without harming them by touching them.
- Phasing-C- The ability to walk through solid objects with concentration.
- Portals-U- Temporary holes through time and space to travel nearly instantly. (Not time travel)

- Reading-R- The ability to read the abilities of others, requires touching the individual.
- Shape-shifting-U- The ability to take the form of one animal, not chosen by the Magi.
- Shielding-C- The ability to create force fields that block physical interaction.
- Sound Manipulation-U- The ability to manipulate sound waves.
- Sublimation-R- The ability to transform into a gaseous form, normally looks like black smoke.
- Telekinesis-C- The ability to move objects physically with the mind.
- Telepathy-U- The ability to send thoughts to others for silent communication. Cannot invade the thoughts of others. This is a one-way ability, unless the other person also has telepathy.
- Tracking-R- The ability track a single individual by having a item that belongs to said individual.
- Water Manipulation-C- The ability to manipulate the element of water.

ABOUT THE AUTHOR

Kristen Banet has a Diet Coke problem and smokes too much. She curses like a sailor (though, she used to be one, so she uses that as an excuse) and finds that many people don't know how to handle that. She loves to read, and before finally sitting to try her hand at writing, she had your normal kind of work history. From tattoo parlors, to the U.S. Navy, and freelance illustration, she's stumbled through her adult years and somehow, is still kicking.

She loves to read books that make people cry. She likes to write books that make people cry (and she wants to hear about it). She's a firm believer that nothing and no one in this world is perfect, and she enjoys exploring those imperfections—trying to make the characters seem real on the page and not just in her head.

She *might* be crazy, though. Her characters think so, but this can't be confirmed.

 facebook.com/kristenbanetauthor

 twitter.com/KristenBanet

instagram.com/Kbanetauthor

ALSO BY KRISTEN BANET

The Kingson Pride Series

Wild Pride

Wild Fire

Wild Souls (March 2018)